She Came to Stay

Other books by Simone de Beauvoir from Norton

All Men Are Mortal
The Mandarins

She Came to Stay

a novel

by

Simone de Beauvoir

W · W · NORTON & COMPANY
New York   London

Printed in the United States of America.

Originally published as *L'Inviteé* by Simone de Beauvoir, Editions Gallimard, 1943

Library of Congress Cataloging in Publication Data
Beauvoir, Simone de, 1908–
[Inviteé. English]
She came to stay: a novel / by Simone de Beauvoir.
p.   cm.
Translation of: L'inviteé.
I. Title.
PQ2603.E362I513   1990

843'.914—dc20   89-22823

ISBN 0-393-30646-1

W. W. Norton & Company, Inc., 500 Fifth Avenue, New York, NY 10110
W. W. Norton & Company Ltd, 10 Coptic Street, London WC1A 1PU

6 7 8 9 0

TO

OLGA KOSAKIEVICZ

Each conscience seeks the death of the other.
—Hegel

Part One

1

FRANÇOISE raised her eyes. Gerbert's fingers were hopping up and down on the keyboard of his typewriter, and he was glaring at the manuscript; he looked exhausted. Françoise herself was sleepy; but there was something intimate and comfortable about her own weariness. The black rings under Gerbert's eyes worried her, his face was haggard and tense; he almost looked his twenty years.

"Don't you think we ought to stop?" she said.

"No, I'm all right," said Gerbert.

"Anyway, I've only one more scene to revise." She turned over a page. Two o'clock had already struck some time ago. Usually, at this hour, there was not a living soul left in the theater; tonight it was alive. The typewriter was clicking, the lamp cast a pink glow over the papers. . . . *And I am here, my heart is beating. Tonight the theater has a heart and it is beating.*

"I like working at night," she said.

"Yes," said Gerbert, "it's quiet."

He yawned. The ashtray was filled with cigarette butts; two glasses and an empty bottle stood on a small table. Françoise looked at the walls of her little office; the rosy atmosphere was radiant with human warmth and light. Outside was the theater, inhuman and pitch-black, with its deserted corridors encircling a great hollow shell. Françoise put down her fountain pen.

"Wouldn't you like another drink?" she asked.

"I wouldn't refuse one," he answered.

"I'll go and get another bottle from Pierre's dressing room."

She went out of the office. Not that she had any particular desire for whisky, but the dark corridors attracted her. When she was not there, the smell of dust, the half-light, the forlorn solitude, all this did not exist for anyone; it did not exist at all. Now that she was there the red of the carpet gleamed through the darkness like a timid night-light. She exercised this power: her presence revived things from their inanimateness; she gave them their color, their smell. She went down one floor and pushed open the door into the auditorium. It was as if she had been entrusted with a mission: she had to bring to life this forsaken theater filled with darkness. The safety-curtain was down; the walls smelled of fresh paint; the red-plush seats were lined up in their rows, motionless and expectant. A moment ago they had been aware of nothing. Now she was there and they held out their arms. They were watching the stage hidden behind the safety-curtain; they were calling for Pierre, for the footlights and for an enraptured audience. She would have had to remain there forever in order to perpetuate this solitude and this expectancy. But she would have had to be elsewhere as well: in the prop-room, in the dressing rooms, in the lobby; she would have had to be everywhere at the same time. She went across the proscenium and stepped onto the stage. She opened the door to the greenroom. She went on down into the yard where old stage sets lay moldering. She alone released the meaning of these abandoned places, of these slumbering things. She was there and they belonged to her. The world belonged to her.

She went out through the small iron stage-door and walked over to the little park in the middle of the square. All around her the houses were asleep, the theater was asleep; except for a pink glow from a single window. She sat down on a bench. The sky shone black above the chestnut trees; she might well have been in the heart of some small provincial town. At this moment she did not in the least miss Pierre: there were joys she could not know when he was with her; all the joys of solitude. They had been lost to her for eight years, and at times she almost felt pangs of regret.

She leaned back against the hard wood of the bench. A quick step echoed on the pavement; a truck rumbled along the avenue. There was nothing but this passing sound, the sky, the hesitant foliage of the trees, one rose-colored window in a black façade; there was no Françoise any longer; no one existed any longer, anywhere.

Françoise jumped to her feet. It was strange to become someone again, just a woman, a woman who must hurry because pressing work awaited her, and this moment was only one like so many others in her life. She put her hand on the doorknob, then turned back with a qualm of conscience. This was desertion, a loss of faith. The night would once more swallow up the small provincial square; the rose-colored window would gleam in vain; it would no longer shine for anyone. The sweetness of this hour would be lost forever. So much sweetness lost all over the earth. She crossed the yard and climbed the green wood steps. She had long since given up this kind of regret. Only her own life was real. She went into Pierre's dressing room and took the bottle of whisky from the cupboard, then ran quickly up the stairs to her office.

"Here you are, this will put new strength into us," she said. "How do you want it? Straight, or with water?"

"Straight," said Gerbert.

"D'you think you'll be able to get home?"

"Oh, I'm learning to hold my whisky," said Gerbert with dignity. "When I'm rich and have my own place, I'll always keep a bottle of Vat 69 in my cupboard."

"That will be the end of your career," she said. She looked at him with a kind of tenderness. He had pulled his pipe out of his pocket and was filling it attentively. It was his first pipe. Every evening, when they had finished their bottle of Beaujolais, he always put the pipe on the table and looked at it with childish pride; he smoked it with his glass of cognac or marc. And then they went out into the streets, a little dazed after the day's work, the wine and the brandy, and Gerbert would stride along, a shock of black hair falling over his eyes, his hands in his pockets. Now all that was over. She would still be seeing him often, but it would be with Pierre or with all the others, and once more they would be like two strangers.

"And what about you! You hold your whisky well for a woman," Gerbert said, quite impartially. He looked hard at Françoise. "But you've been overworking today, you ought to get a little sleep. I'll wake you up, if you like."

"No, I'd rather finish it," said Françoise.

"Aren't you hungry? Wouldn't you like me to get you some sandwiches?"

"No, thanks," said Françoise. She smiled at him. He had been so considerate, so attentive. Whenever she felt discouraged she only had to look into his sparkling eyes to regain her confidence. She would have liked to find words with which to thank him.

"It's almost a pity that we've finished," she said. "I've become so accustomed to working with you."

"But it will be even greater fun when we go into production," said Gerbert. His eyes glistened; the whisky had brought a flush to his cheeks. "It's so good to think that in three days everything will be starting all over again. I love the opening of the season."

"Yes, it will be fun," Françoise said. She pulled her papers toward her. He was apparently not sorry to see their ten days together coming to an end; that was only natural. She was not sorry either; surely she had no right to expect Gerbert alone to be sorry.

"Every time I walk through this dead theater I get the shivers," he said. "It's dismal. This time I really thought it was going to stay closed for the whole year."

"We've had a narrow escape."

"Let's hope it lasts."

"Oh, it will last."

She had never believed in the possibility of war. War was like tuberculosis or a railway accident—something that could never happen to her. Things like that happened only to other people.

"Are you able to imagine some really terrible misfortune happening to you personally?"

Gerbert screwed up his face: "Nothing easier," he said.

"Well, I can't," said Françoise. There was no point in even thinking about it. Dangers from which it was possible to protect oneself had to be foreseen, but war did not come within the compass of man. If one day war did break out, nothing else would matter any more, not even living or dying.

"But that won't happen," murmured Françoise. She bent over her manuscript. The typewriter began clicking, and the room smelled of tobacco, ink, and the night. On the other side of the window, the small, secluded square was asleep under the black sky; a train was moving through the empty landscape. . . . *And I am there, I am there, and for me alone this square exists and that moving train . . . all Paris, and all the world in the pink shadows of this little office . . . and in this one moment, all the long years of happiness; I am here, at the heart of my life. . . .*

"It's a pity that we have to sleep," she said.

"It's even more of a pity we can't know that we are asleep," said

Gerbert. "The moment we become aware that we're sleeping, we wake up. We gain nothing by it."

"But don't you think it's marvelous to stay awake while everyone else is asleep?" Françoise laid down her fountain pen and listened. Not a sound could be heard; the square was in darkness, the theater in darkness. "I'd like to think that the whole world is asleep, that at this moment you and I are the only living souls on earth."

"Oh no, that would give me the creeps." He tossed back the long lock of black hair that kept falling in his eyes. "It's like thinking about the moon; all those icy mountains and crevasses and nobody anywhere. The first person to go there will have to have nerve."

"I wouldn't refuse if I were asked to go." She looked at Gerbert. Usually, they sat side by side, and she was happy to feel him near her even though they did not speak. Tonight, she felt that she wanted to talk with him. "It's sort of queer to think of what things are like when you aren't there," she said.

"Yes, it does seem queer," said Gerbert.

"It's like trying to imagine you're dead; you can't quite manage it, you always feel that you're somewhere in a corner, looking on."

"It's funny to think of all the things one never will see," he said.

"It used to break my heart to think that I'd never know anything but one poor little corner of the world. Don't you feel that way?"

"Perhaps," said Gerbert.

Françoise smiled. Sometimes, talking to Gerbert, one detected hesitancy; it was difficult to extract a definite opinion from him.

"But now it doesn't bother me, because I'm convinced that wherever I go, the rest of the world will move with me. That's what keeps me from having any regrets."

"Regrets for what?" he asked.

"Having to live only in my own skin when the world is so vast."

Gerbert looked at Françoise. "Yes, especially since you rather live such a well-regulated life."

He was always so discreet; but for him this vague answer was almost audacious. Did he think her life too well regulated? Was he passing judgment on it? *I wonder what he thinks of me . . . this office, the theater, my room, books, papers, work. . . . Such a well-regulated life.*

"I came to the conclusion that I must resign myself to a choice," she said.

"I don't like having to choose," said Gerbert.

"At first it was hard for me; but now I have no regrets, because I feel that things which do not exist for me, simply do not exist at all."

"How do you mean?"

Françoise hesitated. She felt very strongly about this; the corridors, the auditorium, the stage, none of these things vanished when she closed the door on them, but they existed only behind the door, at a distance. At a distance the train was moving through the silent country-side, extending the warm life of her little office into the heart of the night.

"It's like a lunar landscape," she said. "It's unreal. It's nothing but hearsay. Don't you feel that?"

"No," said Gerbert, "I don't think I do."

"And doesn't it exasperate you never to be able to see more than one thing at a time?"

Gerbert thought for a moment. "What worries me is other people," he said. "I've a horror when someone talks to me about some fellow I don't know, especially when they speak well of him; somebody who's living his own life and who doesn't even know that I exist."

It was rare to hear him speak about himself at such length. Was he, too, aware of the touching, though transitory, intimacy of the last few hours? The two of them were enclosed in this circle of rosy light; for both of them, the same light, the same night. Françoise looked at his fine green eyes beneath their curling lashes, at his expectant mouth. *If I had wanted to. . . .* Perhaps it was still not too late. But what could she want?

"Yes, it's insulting," she said.

"As soon as I get to know the fellow, I feel better about it."

"It's almost impossible to believe that other people are conscious beings, aware of their own inward feelings, as we ourselves are aware of ours," said Françoise. "To me, it's terrifying, especially when you begin to feel that you're nothing more than a figment of someone else's mind. But that hardly ever happens, and never completely."

"That's true," said Gerbert eagerly. "Perhaps that's why I find it so unpleasant when people talk to me about myself, even in a pleasant way. I feel they're gaining some sort of advantage over me."

"Personally, I don't care what people think of me," said Françoise.

Gerbert began to laugh. "Well, it can't be said you've too much vanity."

"To me their thoughts are exactly like their words and their faces; objects in my own world. It amazes Elisabeth that I'm not ambitious; but that's precisely why. I don't want to cut out a special place for my self in the world. I feel that I'm already in it." She smiled at Gerbert. "And you're not ambitious either, are you?"

"No, why should I be?" He thought a moment. "All the same, I'd like to be a really good actor some day."

"I feel the same; some day I'd like to write a really good book. We like to do our work well; but not for any honor or glory."

"No," said Gerbert.

A milk wagon rattled by beneath the windows. Soon the night would be growing pale. The train was already beyond Châteauroux and approaching Vierzon. Gerbert yawned and his eyes became red-rimmed like a sleepy child's.

"You ought to get some sleep," Françoise said.

Gerbert rubbed his eyes. "We've got to show this to Labrousse in its final form," he said stubbornly. He took hold of the bottle of whisky and poured himself a large drink. "Besides, I'm not sleepy, I'm thirsty!" He drank and put down his glass. He thought for a moment. "Perhaps I'm sleepy after all."

"Thirsty or sleepy? Make up your mind," Françoise said gaily.

"I never really know what I want."

"Well, look," she said, "this is what you're going to do. Lie down on the couch and sleep. I'll finish looking over this last scene. Then you can type it out while I meet Pierre at the station."

"And you?"

"When I've finished I'll get some sleep too. The couch is wide, you won't be in my way. Take a cushion and pull the cover over you."

"All right," said Gerbert.

Françoise stretched and took up her fountain pen. A few minutes later she turned around in her chair. Gerbert was lying on his back, his eyes closed, his breath coming in regular intervals from between his lips. He was already asleep.

He was beautiful, and she sat there gazing at him for some time; then she turned back to her work. Out there, in the moving train, Pierre, too, was asleep, his head resting against the leather upholstery, his face innocent. . . . *He'll jump out of the train, and draw himself up to the full height of his small stature; then he'll run along the platform; he'll take my arm. . . .*

"There," said Françoise. She glanced at the manuscript with satisfaction. "Let's hope he likes this. I think it'll please him." She pushed back her chair. A pink mist suffused the sky. She took off her shoes and slipped under the cover beside Gerbert. He groaned and his head rolled over on the cushion till it rested on her shoulder.

Poor little Gerbert, he was so sleepy, she thought. She pulled up the cover and lay there motionless, her eyes open. She was sleepy, too, but she wanted to stay awake a little longer. She looked at Gerbert's smooth eyelids, at his lashes, as long as a girl's; he was asleep, relaxed and indifferent. Against her neck she felt the caress of his soft black hair.

That's all I shall ever have of him, she thought.

There must be women who have stroked his hair, hair as sleek as a Chinese maiden's; women who have pressed their lips against his childish eyelids and clasped this long, slender body in their arms. Some day he would say to one of them: "I love you."

Françoise felt her heart thumping. There was still time. She could put her cheek against his and say aloud the words that were coming to her lips.

She shut her eyes. She could not say, "I love you." She could not think it. She loved Pierre. There was no room in her life for another love.

Yet, there would be joys like these, she thought with a slight qualm. His head was heavy on her shoulder. What was precious to her was not the warm pressure of his body, but Gerbert's tenderness, his trust, his gay abandon, and the love she bestowed upon him. But Gerbert was asleep, and this love and tenderness were only parts of a dream. Perhaps, when he held her in his arms, she would still be able to cling to the dream; but how could she let herself dream of a love she did not really wish to live?

She looked at Gerbert. She was free in her words, in her acts. Pierre left her free; but acts and words could be only lies, as the weight of this head on her shoulder was already a lie. Gerbert did not love her; she could not really wish that he might.

The sky was turning to pink outside the window. In her heart rose a sadness as bitter and glowing as the dawn. And yet she had no regrets; she had not even a right to that melancholy which was beginning to numb her drowsy body. This was renunciation, final, and without recompense.

2

From the back of a Moorish café, seated on rough woollen cushions, Xavière and Françoise were watching the Arab dancing girl.

"I wish I could dance like that," said Xavière. A light tremor passed over her shoulders and ran through her body. Françoise smiled at her and was sorry that their day together was coming to an end. Xavière had been delightful.

"In the red-light district of Fez, Labrousse and I saw them dance naked," Françoise told her casually. "But that was a little too much like an anatomical demonstration."

"You've seen so many things," Xavière said with a touch of bitterness.

"So will you, one day."

"I doubt it."

"You won't remain in Rouen all your life."

"What else can I do?" the girl asked sadly. She looked at her fingers with a meditative air. They were red peasant's fingers, in strange contrast to her delicate wrists. "I could perhaps try to be a prostitute, but I'm not experienced yet."

"That's a hard profession, you know," Françoise laughed.

"I must learn not to be afraid of people," Xavière said thoughtfully. She nodded her head. "But I'm improving. When a man brushes against me in the street, I no longer let out a scream."

"And you go into cafés by yourself. That's also an advancement."

Xavière gave her a shamefaced look. "Yes, but I haven't told you everything. At that little dance hall last night, a sailor asked me to dance and I refused. I finished my calvados and rushed out of the place like a coward." She made a wry face. "Calvados is terrible stuff."

"It must have been fine rotgut," said Françoise. "I think you might have danced with your sailor. I did all sorts of things like that when I was younger, and no harm ever came of it."

"The next time I shall accept," Xavière said.

"Aren't you afraid your aunt will wake up some night? I should think that might very well happen."

"She wouldn't dare come into my room," Xavière rejoined with defiance. She smiled and began to hunt through her bag. "I've made a little sketch for you."

The sketch was of a woman, who had a slight resemblance to Françoise, standing at a bar with her elbows on the counter. Her cheeks were green and her dress was yellow. Beneath the drawing Xavière had written in large, purple letters, "The Road to Ruin."

"You must dedicate it to me," said Françoise.

Xavière looked at her, then back at the sketch, and pushed it away. "It's too difficult," she said.

The dancing girl moved toward the middle of the room; her hips began to undulate, and her stomach ripple to the rhythm of the tambourine.

"You'd think a demon were trying to tear itself from her body," said Xavière. She leaned forward, entranced. It had been an inspiration bringing her here; never before had Xavière spoken at such length about herself, and she had a charming way of telling a story. Françoise sank back against the cushions; she, too, had been affected by the shoddy glamour of the place. But what was especially wonderful was her having attached this pathetic little being to her own life. For, like Gerbert, and like Canzetti, Xavière now belonged to her. Nothing ever gave Françoise more intense joy than this kind of possession.

Xavière was absorbed in the dancing girl. She could not see her own face, its beauty heightened by emotion. Her fingers stroked the contours of the cup which she was holding lightly in her hand, but Françoise alone was aware of the contours of that hand. Xavière's gestures, her face, her very life depended on Françoise for their existence. For herself, at that moment, Xavière was no more than a flavor of coffee, a throbbing music, a dance, a vague sense of well-being; but for Françoise, Xavière's childhood, her days of stagnation, her distastes were a romantic story as real as the delicate contour of her cheeks. And it was right here in this café, among the varicolored hangings, that the story ended, this precise moment in Françoise's life when she turned to look at Xavière and study her.

"It's seven o'clock already," Françoise said. It bored her to have to spend the evening with Elisabeth, but it was unavoidable. "Are you going out with Inès tonight?"

"I suppose so," said Xavière gloomily.

"How much longer do you think you'll stay in Paris?"

"I'm leaving tomorrow." A flash of rage appeared in Xavière's eyes. "Tomorrow, all this will still be going on here and I shall be in Rouen."

"Why don't you take a secretarial course as I suggested? I could find you a job."

Xavière shrugged her shoulders despondently. "I couldn't do it," she said.

"Of course you could. It's not difficult."

"My aunt even tried to teach me how to knit," said Xavière, "but my last sock was a disaster." She turned to Françoise with a discouraged but faintly provocative look. "She's quite right. No one will ever manage to make anything of me."

"Definitely not a good housewife," said Françoise cheerfully. "But one can live without that."

"It's not because of the sock," Xavière said hopelessly. "Yet that was an indication."

"You lose heart too easily. But still, you'd like to leave Rouen, wouldn't you? You have no attachments there to anyone or anything."

"I hate the people and the place," she said. "I loathe that filthy city and the people in the streets with their leering glances."

"That can't go on."

"It will go on," Xavière said. She jumped up suddenly. "I'm going now."

"Wait, I'll go with you."

"No, don't bother. I've already taken your entire afternoon."

"You've taken nothing," said Françoise. "How strange you are!" She looked with slight bewilderment at Xavière's sullen face. What a disconcerting little person she was. With that beret hiding her fair hair, her head looked almost like a small boy's; but the face was a young girl's, the same face that had held an appeal for Françoise six months earlier. The silence was prolonged.

"I'm sorry," said Xavière, "I've a terrible headache." She pressed her temples, looking miserable. "It must be the smoke. I've a pain here, and here."

Her face was puffy under her eyes and her skin blotchy. The heavy smell of incense and tobacco made the air almost unbreathable. Françoise motioned to the waiter.

"That's too bad. If you were not so tired, I'd take you dancing tonight," she said.

"I thought you had to see a friend."

"She'd come with us. She's Labrousse's sister, the girl with the red hair and the short bob you saw at the hundredth performance of *Philoctetes*."

"I don't recall." Her face lighted up. "I only remember you. You were wearing a long, tight, black skirt, a lamé blouse, and a silver net on your hair. You were so beautiful!"

Françoise smiled. She was not beautiful, yet she was quite pleased with her face. Whenever she caught a glimpse of it in a mirror, she always felt a pleasant surprise. For most of the time, she was not even aware that she had a face.

"You were wearing a lovely blue dress with a pleated skirt," she said. "And you were tipsy."

"I brought that dress with me. I'll wear it tonight," said Xavière.

"Do you think it wise to come if you have a headache?"

"My headache's gone. It was just a dizzy spell." Her eyes were shining, and her skin had regained its beautiful pearl-like luster.

"So that settles that," said Françoise. She pushed open the door. "But won't Inès be angry, if she's counting on you?"

"Well, let her be angry," Xavière said, pouting disdainfully.

Françoise hailed a taxi.

"I'll drop you at her place, and I'll meet you at the Dôme at nine thirty. Just walk straight up the boulevard Montparnasse."

"Yes, I know."

In the taxi Françoise sat close to Xavière and slipped an arm through hers.

"I'm glad we still have a few hours ahead of us."

"I'm glad too," Xavière responded softly.

The taxi stopped at the corner of the rue de Rennes. Xavière got out, and Françoise drove on to the theater.

Pierre was in his dressing room, wearing a dressing gown and eating a ham sandwich.

"Did the rehearsal go off well?"

"We worked very hard," Pierre said. He pointed to the manuscript lying on the desk. "That's good," he said, "really good."

"Do you mean it? Oh, I'm so glad! I was a little upset at having to cut out Lucilius, but I think it was necessary."

"Yes it was," said Pierre. "Changed the whole run of the act." He took another bite of his sandwich. "Haven't you had dinner? Would you like a sandwich?"

"Of course I'd like a sandwich." She took one and looked at Pierre reproachfully. "You don't eat enough. You're looking very pale."

"I don't want to put on weight," he said.

"Caeser wasn't skinny." She smiled. "What about phoning the concierge for a bottle of Château Margaux?"

"That's not a bad idea." He picked up the receiver, while Françoise curled up on the couch. This was where Pierre slept when he did not spend the night with her. She was very fond of this small dressing room.

"There, you shall have your wine."

"I'm so happy," said Françoise. "I thought I'd never manage to lick that third act."

"You've done some excellent work." He came over to the couch, leaned over and kissed her. Françoise threw her arms around his neck. "It's you," she said. "Do you remember what you said to me in Delos? That you wanted to introduce something absolutely new to the theater? Well, this time you've done it."

"Do you really think so?"

"Don't you?"

"Well, I almost think so."

Françoise began to laugh. "You know you have done it. You look positively smug, Pierre! If only we don't have to worry too much about money, what a wonderful year it will be!"

"The minute we're in funds I shall buy you another coat."

"Oh, I'm quite used to this one."

"That's all too obvious," Pierre said. He sat down in an armchair near Françoise.

"Did you have a good time with your little friend?"

"She's very nice. It's a pity for her to rot away in Rouen."

"Did she have a lot of stories to tell you?"

"Endless stories. I'll tell them to you some day."

"Well then, you're happy; you didn't waste your day."

"I love stories," she said.

There was a knock and the door opened. With a majestic air the concierge carried in a tray with two glasses and a bottle of wine.

"Thank you very much," said Françoise. She filled the glasses.

"By the way," Pierre said to the concierge, "I'm not in to anyone."

"Of course, Monsieur Labrousse," said the woman as she closed the door.

Françoise picked up her glass and started on a second sandwich.

"I'm going to bring Xavière along with us tonight," she said. "We'll go dancing. I think that will be fun. I hope she'll neutralize Elisabeth a little."

"She must be in seventh heaven."

"Poor child, it's painful to look at her. She's so utterly miserable at having to return to Rouen."

"Is there no way out of it?"

"Hardly," said Françoise. "She's so spineless. She'd never have the grit to train for a profession. And the only future her uncle's got in store for her is a devoted husband and a lot of children."

"You ought to take her in hand," Pierre said.

"How can I? I only see her once a month."

"Why don't you have her stay in Paris? You could keep an eye on her and make her work. Let her learn to type, and we can easily find a job for her somewhere."

"Her family would never consent to that."

"Well, let her do it without their permission. Isn't she of age?"

"No," said Françoise. "That isn't the main point, and I don't think the police would be set on her trail."

Pierre smiled. "What is the main point?"

Françoise hesitated, actually she had never suspected there was a debatable point. "In other words, your idea would be for her to live in Paris at our expense until she learns to shift for herself?"

"Why not? Offer it to her as a loan."

"Oh, of course," she said. This talent he had of conjuring up a thousand unsuspected possibilities in only a few words always took her by surprise. Where others only saw an impenetrable jungle, Pierre discerned a virgin future which was his to shape as he chose. That was the secret of his strength.

"We've had so much luck in our lives," he said. "We ought to let others benefit from it whenever we can."

Françoise, perplexed, stared at the bottom of her glass.

"In a way it's very tempting," she said. "But I would really have to look after her. I hardly have the time."

"Industrious little ant," said Pierre affectionately.

Françoise colored. "You know I haven't much spare time," she said.

"Yes, I know. But it's odd, the way you draw back as soon as you're confronted by something new."

"The only something new which interests me is our future together. I can't help it. That's what makes me happy. You've no one to blame but yourself."

"Oh, I don't blame you," Pierre said. "On the contrary, I think you're far more genuine than I am. There's nothing in your life that rings false."

"That's because you attach no importance to your life as such. It's your work that counts," she reflected.

"That's true." He began to gnaw on one of his fingernails, and he looked ill at ease. "With the exception of my relationship with you, everything about me is frivolous and wasteful." He kept tormenting his finger. He would not be satisfied until he made it bleed. "But as soon as I've gotten rid of Canzetti, all that will be finished."

"That's what you say."

"I'll prove it."

"You're lucky. Your affairs are always easily terminated."

"That's because, after all, none of my women has ever been in love with me."

"I don't think Canzetti's the designing kind," said Françoise.

"No, it's not so much to get herself parts. Only she imagines I'm a great man, and she thinks that genius will rise from her sex glands to her brain."

"There's something in that," said Françoise laughing.

"I no longer enjoy these affairs," said Pierre. "It's not as if I were a great sensualist, I don't even have that excuse!" He looked at Françoise a little sheepishly. "The truth is that I get a kick out of the early stages. You don't understand that, do you?"

"Perhaps. But I wouldn't be interested in an affair which had no continuity."

"No?"

"No," she said. "I can't help myself. I'm the faithful type."

"It's impossible to talk about faithfulness and unfaithfulness where we're concerned." He drew Françoise to him. "You and I are simply one. It's true, you know. Neither of us can be defined without the other."

"That's thanks to you," Françoise said. She took his face between her hands and began to kiss his cheeks, which smelled of pipe tobacco mingled with the childish and unexpected smell of pastry. "We are simply one," she murmured.

Nothing that happened was completely real until she had told Pierre about it; it remained poised, motionless and uncertain, in a kind of limbo. Formerly, when she still felt shy with Pierre, there were many things she had let fall by the wayside: equivocal thoughts, ill-considered moves. If they were not mentioned, it was almost as if they had not existed at all, and grew instead into a shameful, subterranean vegetation under the surface of her consciousness, where she felt utterly alone and in danger of suffocation. Little by little she had surrendered everything; she no longer knew solitude, but she had rid herself of that swarming chaos. Every moment of her life that she entrusted to him, was given back to her clear, polished, completed, and they became moments of their shared life. She knew that she served the same purpose for him. He had no secret corners, no shame. Except when he needed a shave or when his shirt was dirty; then he would pretend to have a cold and stubbornly keep his muffler wrapped around his neck, so that he looked like a precocious old man.

"I must be leaving you in a moment," she said regretfully. "Are you going to sleep here or at my place?"

"I'll come over to you," said Pierre. "I want to be with you again just as soon as I can."

Elisabeth was already at the Dôme. She was smoking a cigarette and staring fixedly into space. *Something's gone wrong*, thought Françoise. She was very carefully made up, yet her face had a puffy, tired look. She caught sight of Françoise and a fleeting smile seemed to release her from her thoughts.

"Hello, I'm so glad to see you," she said effusively.

"So am I," replied Françoise. "Tell me, I hope it won't annoy you, but I've asked the Pagès girl to come along with us. She's dying to go to a dance hall. We can talk while she dances. She's no bother."

"It's ages since I've heard any jazz," said Elisabeth. "It will be fun."

"She isn't here yet. That's strange," remarked Françoise. Then she turned toward Elisabeth. "Well, what about your trip?" she asked gaily. "Are you definitely leaving tomorrow?"

"You think it's as simple as that." Elisabeth gave an unpleasant little laugh. "It seems now that it would hurt Suzanne, and Suzanne has already gone through so much because of what happened in September."

So that was it. Françoise looked at Elisabeth with indignant pity. Claude's behavior toward her was really disgusting.

"As if you hadn't suffered too."

"Yes, but I happen to be a strong, sensible person," Elisabeth said sarcastically. "I'm the woman who never makes scenes."

"Yes, but Claude is no longer in love with Suzanne," Françoise said. "She's old and ugly."

"He's no longer in love with her. But Suzanne is a superstition. Claude's convinced that, without her, he'll never succeed in anything."

Silence ensued. Elisabeth was absorbed in watching the smoke from her cigarette. She gave no outward sign, but what blackness there must have been in her heart! She had expected so much from this trip; that perhaps this long period together might finally persuade Claude to break with his wife. Françoise had grown sceptical; for two years Elisabeth had been waiting for the decisive hour. She felt Elisabeth's disappointment with a painful tightening of her own heart.

"I must say Suzanne is clever," said Elisabeth. She looked at Françoise. "She's now trying to get one of Claude's plays produced with Nanteuil. That's something else that's keeping him in Paris."

"Nanteuil!" Françoise repeated lazily. "What a strange idea!" She looked toward the door a little uneasily. *Why hasn't Xavière come?*

"It's idiotic," Elisabeth steadied her voice. "Besides it's obvious, as far as I can see, that only Pierre could put on *Partage*. He'd be magnificent as Achab."

"It's a good part."

"Do you think he might be interested?" There was an anxious appeal in her voice.

"*Partage* is a very interesting play," said Françoise. "Only it's not at all in line with what Pierre is trying to do. Listen," she added hastily, "why doesn't Claude take his script to Berger? Would you like Pierre to write Berger?"

Elisabeth swallowed painfully. "You don't know how important it would be for Claude if Pierre were to accept his play. He's got so little self-confidence. Only Pierre could get him out of that state of mind."

Françoise looked away. Battier's play was dreadful, there was no possible question of accepting it; but she knew how much Elisabeth had staked on this last chance and, confronted with Elisabeth's drawn face, she actually felt remorse. She was fully aware how much her life and her example had influenced Elisabeth.

"Frankly, that can't be done."

"But *Luce et Armanda* was quite a success," Elisabeth persisted.

"That's why, after *Julius Caesar*, Pierre wants to try to launch an unknown playwright."

Françoise stopped almost in the middle of a sentence. With relief she saw Xavière coming toward them. Her hair was carefully arranged and a light film of make-up toned down her high cheekbones and made her fleshy, sensual nose look more refined.

"I think you've already met," said Françoise. She smiled at Xavière. "You're terribly late. I feel sure you haven't had dinner. Would you like something to eat?"

"No thanks, I'm not at all hungry," Xavière said. She sat down, hanging her head; she seemed ill at ease. "I lost my way," she said.

Elisabeth looked at her searchingly. She was trying to size her up.

"You lost your way? Did you have far to come?"

Xavière turned a distressed look to Françoise.

"I don't know what happened to me. I walked straight up the boulevard, it seemed endless, and I came to an avenue that was pitch-black. I must have passed the Dôme without seeing it."

Elisabeth began to laugh. "That took some doing," she said.

Xavière gave her a black look.

"Well, anyway you're here and that's the main thing," said Françoise. "What about going to the Prairie? It's no longer what it used to be when we were young, but it's not bad."

"Just as you like," Elisabeth agreed.

They left the café. Along the boulevard Montparnasse a strong wind was sweeping up the leaves of the plane trees. It amused Françoise to crackle them as she walked. It made her think of walnuts and mulled wine.

"It's at least a year since I've been to the Prairie," she said. No one answered. Xavière, shivering, clutched her coat collar. Elisabeth was carrying her scarf in her hand; she seemed neither to feel the cold nor to see anything.

"What a crowd there is already," said Françoise when they got there. All the stools at the bar were taken. She chose one of the more secluded tables.

"I'll have a whisky," said Elisabeth.

"Two whiskies," said Françoise. "And you?"

"The same as you," said Xavière.

"Three whiskies." The smell of alcohol and smoke took Françoise back to her girlhood. She had always liked the jazz rhythms, yellow lights and swarming crowds of night clubs. How easy it was to live a full life in a world that contained both the ruins at Delphi and the bare hills of Provence, as well as all this human florescence. She smiled at Xavière.

"Look at that blonde at the bar, the one with the turned-up nose. She lives in my hotel. She wanders about the corridors for hours on end in a pale-blue nightgown. I think she's trying to hook the Negro who lives above me."

"She's not pretty," Xavière said. Her eyes widened. "But the dark-haired woman next to her is really beautiful. Oh, but she's beautiful!"

"I'd better tell you that her boy friend is a wrestler; they go around the neighborhood holding each other's little fingers."

"Oh!" said Xavière reproachfully.

"It's not my fault," Françoise laughed.

Xavière rose to her feet; two young men had come up to their table and were smiling engagingly.

"I'm sorry, I don't dance," said Françoise.

Elisabeth hesitated and she too rose.

At this moment she hates me, thought Françoise. At the next table a rather faded blonde and a very young man were tenderly holding hands. The youth was talking ardently in a low voice, as the woman smiled cautiously, not allowing a single wrinkle to furrow her once pretty face; the little professional from the hotel was dancing with a sailor, pressing against him, her eyes half closed; the attractive brunette sat on her bar stool, eating sliced bananas and looking bored. Françoise smiled inwardly with pride. Each one of these men, each one of these women here tonight was completely absorbed in living a moment of his or her little individual existence. Xavière was dancing; Elisabeth was being shaken by spasms of anger and despair. *And I—I am here in the middle of this dance hall—impersonal and free, watching all these lives and all these faces. If I turned away from them, they would disintegrate at once into a deserted landscape.*

Elisabeth came back and sat down.

"You know," said Françoise, "I'm sorry it can't be managed."

"I understand perfectly well. . . ." She lowered her face. She was incapable of being angry for any length of time, especially in the presence of others.

"Aren't things going well with you and Claude at the moment?" asked Françoise.

Elisabeth shook her head. Her face gave an ugly twitch, and Françoise thought she was going to burst into tears. But she controlled herself.

"Claude is working up for a crisis. He says he can't work as long as his play has not been accepted, that he doesn't feel really free. When he's in such a state he's terrible."

"You can hardly be held responsible."

"But everything always falls on me." Again her lips trembled. "Because I have strength of character. It just doesn't occur to him that a woman of character can suffer just as much as any other." She spoke in a tone of passionate self-pity, and then she burst into sobs.

"My poor Elisabeth!" Françoise said, taking her hand.

Through her tears Elisabeth's face regained a kind of childlike appearance.

"It's ridiculous," she said, dabbing her eyes. "It can't go on like this, with Suzanne always between us."

"What do you want him to do? Divorce her?"

"He'll never divorce her," Elisabeth began to cry again with a kind of anger. "Is he in love with me? As far as I'm concerned, I don't even know if I'm in love with him." She looked at Françoise. Her eyes were wild. "For two years I've been fighting for this love. I've been killing myself in the process. I've sacrificed everything. And now I don't even know if we love each other."

"Of course you love him," said Françoise, her courage failing. "At the moment you're angry with him, so you don't know what you feel, but that doesn't mean anything." It was absolutely essential for her to reassure Elisabeth, for if one day Elisabeth were to decide to be completely sincere with herself, she might be terrified by what she discovered. This she must have feared herself, for her flashes of lucidity always stopped in time.

"I don't know any longer," said Elisabeth.

Françoise pressed her hand. She was really moved. "Claude is weak, that's all. But he has shown you a thousand times over that he loves you." She looked up. Xavière was standing beside the table, observing the scene with a curious smile on her face.

"Sit down," said Françoise, embarrassed.

"No, I'm going to dance again," Xavière's expression was contemptuous and almost spiteful. This sudden maliciousness gave Françoise an unpleasant shock.

Elisabeth had recovered. She was powdering her face.

"I must be patient," she said. She steadied her voice. "It's a question of influence. I've always played too fair with Claude, and I don't make demands on him."

"Have you ever told him plainly that you couldn't stand the situation?"

"No," said Elisabeth. "I must wait." She had resumed her hard, sophisticated manner.

Was she really in love with Claude? She had thrown herself at him because she, too, had wanted a great love; the admiration she showered on him had been just another way of holding her own against Pierre. Yet because of him she endured suffering in which both Françoise and Pierre were powerless to help her.

What a mess, thought Françoise with a pang.

Elisabeth had left the table. She was dancing, her eyes red, her mouth set. For a moment Françoise envied her. Elisabeth's feelings might well be false, she thought, her objective false, and her whole life false, but her present suffering was violent and real. Françoise looked at Xavière who was dancing, her head thrown back, her face ecstatic. Her life had not yet begun; for her everything was possible, and this enchanted evening held the promise of a thousand unknown enchantments. For this young girl, for this heavy-hearted woman, the moment had a sharp and unforgettable taste. *And I*, thought Françoise, *just a spectator. But this jazz, and the taste of this whisky, and these orange-colored lights, these are not mere stage effects, there must be some way of finding a use for them! But what?* In Elisabeth's fierce, tense soul, the music was gently transformed into hope; Xavière transmuted it into passionate expectation; and Françoise alone found nothing in herself that harmonized with the plaintive sound of the saxophone. She searched for a desire, a regret; but behind her and before her there stretched a radiant and cloudless happiness. Pierre—that name was incapable of awakening pain. Gerbert—she was no longer concerned about Gerbert. No longer was she conscious of risk, or hope, or fear; only of this happiness over which she did not even have control. A misunderstanding with Pierre was impossible; no act would ever be irreparable. If one day she tried to inflict suffering upon herself, he would understand so well what she was doing, that happiness would once more close over her. She lit a cigarette. No, she could find nothing beyond this abstract regret of having nothing to regret. Her throat was dry; her heart beat a little faster than usual, but she could not even believe that she was honestly tired of happiness. This uneasiness brought her no moving revelation. It was only a ripple on the surface, a short and, in a way, foreseeable modulation that would resolve itself peacefully. No longer was she caught up in the violence of the passing moment: she knew that no single one of these moments was of any intrinsic value. "Imprisoned in happiness," she murmured to herself. But she was conscious of a smile somewhere deep within her.

Françoise cast a discouraged look at the empty glasses and the over-full ashtray; it was four o'clock. Elisabeth had long since left, but Xavière had never stopped dancing. Françoise had not danced, and to pass the time she had drunk and smoked too much. Her head was heavy and she was beginning to ache all over from want of sleep.

"I think it's time to go," she said.

"Already!" cried Xavière. She looked at Françoise with disappointment. "Are you tired?"

"A little," Françoise admitted. She hesitated. "You can stay on without me," she said. "You've been to a dance hall alone before."

"If you leave, I'll go with you," said Xavière.

"I don't want to oblige you to go home."

Xavière shrugged her shoulders with an air that accepted the inevitable. "Oh, I may just as well go home."

"No, that would be a pity," said Françoise. She smiled. "Let's stay a bit longer."

Xavière's face brightened. "This place is so nice, isn't it?" She smiled at a young man who was bowing to her and followed him onto the dance floor.

Françoise lit another cigarette. After all, nothing obliged her to resume her work the very next day. It was slightly absurd to spend hour after hour here without dancing, without speaking to a soul, but if one wanted to one could find deep fascination in this kind of self-absorption. Years had passed since she had last sat this way, lost in alcohol fumes and to-bacco smoke, pursuing little dreams and thoughts that led nowhere.

Xavière came back and sat down beside her.

"Why don't you dance?"

"I dance very badly," said Françoise.

"But aren't you bored?" Xavière asked in a plaintive tone.

"Not at all. I love to look on. I'm fascinated by just listening to the music and watching the people."

She smiled. It was to Xavière she owed this hour and this night. Why reject this offer of refreshing richness, a young, completely new companion, with her unreasonable demands, her reticent smiles and unexpected reactions?

"I can see that it can't be very amusing for you," Xavière said, her face looking quite dejected; she, too, now seemed a little tired.

"But I assure you that I am quite happy," said Françoise. She lightly touched Xavière's wrist. "I enjoy being with you."

Xavière smiled without conviction. Françoise looked at her affectionately. She no longer understood too clearly why she had resisted Pierre's suggestion. This faint sense of risk and mystery in what she was about to do intrigued her.

"Do you know what I was thinking last night?" she asked abruptly. "That as long as you stay in Rouen you will never do anything. There's only one way out of it and that's to come and live in Paris."

"Live in Paris?" Xavière cried in astonishment. "I'd love to."

"I'm serious," said Françoise. But she hesitated; she was afraid Xavière might think her tactless. "I'll tell you what you could do. You could stay in Paris, at my hotel, if you'd like. I would lend you whatever money you need and you could train for a career, stenography perhaps. Or, better still, I have a friend who runs a beauty salon and she'd employ you as soon as you have your certificate."

Xavière's face darkened. "My uncle would never consent to that," she said.

"You can do without his consent. You aren't afraid of him, are you?"

"No," said Xavière, staring at her sharply pointed nails. Her pale complexion, her long light hair slightly disordered from dancing, gave her the woebegone look of a jellyfish washed up on dry sand.

"Well?"

"Excuse me," said Xavière, and she rose to rejoin one of her partners who was making signs to her, her face suddenly radiant again. Françoise's glance followed her in utter amazement. Xavière had strange abrupt changes of mood, and Françoise was a little disconcerted that Xavière had not even taken the trouble to consider her suggestion. And yet, this plan was eminently sensible. With some impatience she waited for Xavière to come back.

"Well, what do you think of my plan?"

"What plan?" asked Xavière. She seemed honestly at a loss.

"To come and live in Paris."

"Oh, to live in Paris."

"But this is serious," said Françoise. "You seem to think that I'm romancing."

Xavière shrugged her shoulders. "But it can't be done," she said.

"It can—if you want to do it," said Françoise. "What's standing in your way?"

"It's impossible," Xavière said with annoyance. She looked around. "This place is getting weird, don't you think? All these people seem to have eyes in the middle of their faces. They're planted here because they haven't even the strength to drag themselves elsewhere."

"Well, let's go," said Françoise. She crossed the room and opened the door. A faint gray dawn was visible in the sky. "We could walk a little," she suggested.

"We could," said Xavière. She pulled her coat snugly around her neck and began walking quickly. Why had she refused to take the offer seriously? Françoise was irritated to feel this small, hostile, stubborn mind beside her.

I must convince her, she thought. Until this moment, the discussion with Pierre, the vague fantasies of the evening, even the beginning of this conversation, had been only a game. Suddenly, everything had become earnest. Xavière's resistance was real, and Françoise now wanted to break it down. It was outrageous; she had felt so completely that she had dominated Xavière, possessing her even in her past and in the still unknown meanderings of her future. And yet there was still this obstinate will, against which her own will was foundering.

Xavière walked faster and faster, scowling and looking wretched. It was impossible to talk. Françoise followed her silently for a while, then lost her patience.

"You're sure you don't mind walking?" she asked.

"Not at all," said Xavière, a painful expression on her face. "I hate the cold."

"You should have said so. We'll go into the first bistro we find open."

"No, let's walk if you feel like it," said Xavière, ignoring her discomfort.

"I'm not particularly keen on walking any further, and I'd very much like a cup of hot coffee."

They slackened their pace a little. Near the Gare Montparnasse, at the corner of the rue d'Odessa, people were crowded around the counter of the Biard café. They went in and sat down in a corner at the far end of the room.

"Two coffees," she ordered.

At one of the tables a woman was asleep, her body slumped forward. There were suitcases and bundles on the floor around her. At another table three Breton peasants were drinking calvados.

Françoise looked at Xavière. "I don't understand you," she said.

Xavière gave her an uneasy glance. "Do I aggravate you?"

"I'm disappointed," said Françoise. "I thought you would be brave enough to accept my offer."

Xavière hesitated. She looked around her with an agonized expression. "I don't want to do facial massage," she said plaintively.

Françoise laughed. "There's nothing to force you to do that. I might well be able to get you a job as a mannequin, for instance. Or you could certainly learn to type."

"I don't want to be a typist or a mannequin," Xavière said vehemently. Françoise was taken aback.

"My idea was that it would be only a beginning. Once you were trained for some kind of a job you'd have time to look about you. What exactly interests you? Studying, drawing, acting?"

"I don't know," Xavière said. "Nothing in particular. Is it absolutely necessary for me to do something?" she asked a little haughtily.

"A few hours of boring work doesn't seem to me too much to pay for your independence."

Xavière wrinkled her face in disgust. "I hate these compromises. If you can't have the sort of life you want, you might as well be dead."

"The fact is that you'll never commit suicide," said Françoise a little sharply. "So it would be just as well to try to live a suitable life."

She swallowed a little coffee. This was early-morning coffee, bitter and sweet like the coffee you drink on a station platform after an all-night journey, or in country inns, waiting for the first bus. Its rank flavor softened Françoise's heart.

"What do you think life should be like?" she asked amiably.

"Like it was when I was a child," Xavière said.

"Having things come to you without your having to look for them?

Like the time when your father took you for a ride on his big horse?"

"There were lots of other times," said Xavière. "When he took me hunting at six o'clock in the morning and the grass was all covered with cobwebs. Everything seemed important."

"But you'll find similar happiness in Paris," Françoise insisted. "Just think, music, the theater, dance halls."

"And I'd have to be like your friend, counting how many drinks I'd had and looking at my watch all the time, so I could get to work in the morning."

Françoise felt hurt, for she too had looked at the time.

She almost seems annoyed with me. But why? she wondered. This moody and unpredictable Xavière interested her.

"Yet you're prepared to accept a far drearier life than hers," she said, "and one ten times less free. As a matter of fact, it's obvious—you're afraid. Perhaps not afraid of your family, but afraid of breaking with your own little ways, afraid of freedom."

Xavière lowered her head without replying.

"What is it?" Françoise asked gently. "You're so obstinate. You don't seem to have any confidence in me."

"But I have," said Xavière coldly.

"What is it then?"

"It drives me mad when I think of my life," said Xavière.

"But that's not all," Françoise said. "You've been queer the whole evening." She smiled. "Were you annoyed at having Elisabeth with us? You don't seem to care very much for her."

"Why?" asked Xavière, then adding stiffly, "She must surely be a very interesting person."

"You were shocked to see her crying in public, weren't you?" Françoise said. "Admit it. I shocked you, too. You thought me disgracefully sentimental."

Xavière stared, wide-eyed. She had the frank blue eyes of a child.

"It gave me a queer feeling," she said ingenuously.

She remained on the defensive, and it was useless to press the matter. Françoise stifled a little yawn. "I'm going home," she said. "Do you want to go back to Inès's place?"

"Yes, I'll try to pick up my things and get out without waking her," said Xavière. "Otherwise she'll jump on me."

"I thought you were fond of Inès?"

"Yes, I am fond of her," said Xavière. "But I can't even drink a glass of milk in front of her without having a guilty conscience. She's that sort of person."

Was the bitterness of her voice aimed at Inès or at her? In any case it was wise not to insist.

"Well, let's go," said Françoise, placing her hand on Xavière's shoulder. "I'm sorry you didn't have a pleasant evening."

Xavière's face suddenly fell limp and all the hardness disappeared. She looked at Françoise with despair.

"But I've had a lovely time," she said, looking down, and she quickly added, "But you couldn't have had a very good time dragging me around like a poodle."

Françoise smiled. *So that's it,* she thought. *She really thinks I took her out simply out of pity.* She looked affectionately at this touchy little person.

"On the contrary, I was very happy to have you with me, otherwise I wouldn't have asked you. But why did you think that?"

Xavière looked at her warmly and trustfully.

"Your life is so full," she said. "So many friends, so much to do. I felt about as small as an atom."

"That's foolish," said Françoise. It was astonishing to think that Xavière could have been jealous of Elisabeth. "Then when I spoke to you about coming to Paris, you thought I was offering you charity?"

"I did—a bit," said Xavière humbly.

"And you hated me for it."

"I didn't hate you for it. I hated myself."

"That's the same thing," said Françoise. Her hand moved from Xavière's shoulder and slipped down her arm. "But I'm fond of you," she said. "I would be extremely happy to have you near me."

Xavière turned overjoyed and incredulous eyes toward her.

"Didn't we have a good time together this afternoon?" Françoise asked.

"Yes," said Xavière, embarrassed.

"We could have lots of times like that! Doesn't that tempt you?"

Xavière squeezed Françoise's hand.

"Oh, how I'd like to," she said eagerly.

"If you agree, it's as good as done. I'll get Inès to send you a letter saying that she's found you a job. And the day you make up your mind, all you'll have to do is write and say, 'I'm coming,' and you will come." She patted the warm hand that lay trustingly in hers. "You'll see, you'll have a beautiful, rich, little life."

"Oh, I do want to come," said Xavière. She pressed with all her weight against Françoise's shoulder; for some time they remained motionless, leaning against one another. Xavière's hair brushed against Françoise's cheek, and their fingers remained intertwined.

"It makes me sad to leave you," Françoise said.

"Me too," Xavière rejoined softly.

"My dear little Xavière," murmured Françoise. Xavière looked at her, her eyes shining, her lips parted, soft, yielding; she had surrendered herself completely. Henceforth Françoise would lead her through life.

I shall make her happy, she decided with conviction.

3

A RAY OF light shone from under Xavière's door. Françoise heard a faint jingling and a rustle of garments. She knocked. There was a prolonged silence.

"Who is it?"

"It's I, Françoise. It's almost time to leave."

Ever since Xavière had arrived at the Hotel Bayard, Françoise had learned never to knock at her door unexpected, and never to arrive early for an appointment. All the same, her arrival always created mysterious agitation on the other side of the door.

"Would you mind waiting for me a minute? I'll come up to your room right away."

"All right. I'll wait for you," said Françoise.

She went upstairs. Xavière liked formality. She never opened her door to Françoise until she had made elaborate preparations to receive her. To be taken by surprise in her everyday privacy would have seemed obscene to her.

I only hope everything goes well tonight, thought Françoise. *We'll never be ready in three days.* She sat down on the sofa and picked up one of the manuscripts piled on the night table. Pierre had asked her to read the plays sent in to him and it was work she usually found entertaining. *Marsyas, or The Doubtful Metamorphosis.* Françoise looked despondently at the titles. Things had not gone at all well that afternoon; everyone was worn out. Pierre's nerves had been on edge, he hadn't slept for a week. With anything less than a hundred performances to full houses, expenses would not be covered.

She threw down the manuscript and rose to her feet. She had plenty of time to make up her face again, but she was too nervous. She lit a cigarette, and a smile came to her lips. Actually she was enjoying this last-minute excitement, knowing perfectly well that everything would be ready when the time came. Pierre could do wonders in three days. That question of mercury lights would be settled. And if only Tedesco would make up his mind to fall into line with the rest of the company. . . .

"May I come in?" asked a timid voice.

"Come in," said Françoise.

Xavière was wearing a heavy coat and her ugly little beret. On her childlike face was a faint, contrite smile.

"Have I kept you waiting?"

"No, it's all right. We're not late," said Françoise hastily. She had to avoid letting Xavière think she might have been in the wrong; otherwise, she would become spiteful and sullen. "I'm not even ready myself."

She dabbed some powder on her nose just on principle and turned quickly away from the mirror. Whatever face she wore that night did not really matter. It did not exist for her and she had a vague hope that it would be invisible to everyone else. She picked up her key and gloves and closed the door.

"Did you go to the concert?" she asked. "How was it?"

"No, I haven't been out," said Xavière. "It was too cold and I didn't feel like going."

Françoise took her arm.

"What have you done all day? Tell me about it."

"There's nothing to tell," Xavière said plaintively.

"That's the answer you always give me," Françoise objected. "But I've told you, all the same, that it gives me pleasure to imagine your life in detail." Smiling, she looked at her closely. "You've washed your hair."

"Yes," said Xavière.

"You've set it beautifully. One of these days I'll ask you to do mine. And what else? Did you read? Did you sleep? What sort of lunch did you have?"

"I didn't do anything at all."

Françoise insisted no further. There was a kind of intimacy that one could never achieve with Xavière. The trifling occupations of a day seemed to her as indecent a subject of conversation as her bodily functions, and since she hardly ever left her room she rarely had anything to relate. Françoise had been disappointed by her lack of curiosity. Tempting movies, concerts, outings had been suggested to her to no avail; she remained obstinately in her room. That first morning in the Montparnasse café, Françoise had known a passing exaltation when she thought she had found a rare treasure. But Xavière's presence had brought her nothing new.

"Well I've had a very busy day," she said gaily. "This morning I gave the wig-maker a piece of my mind; he'd only delivered half the wigs. And then I went hunting for props. It's difficult to find just what you want; it's a real treasure hunt. But you can't imagine what fun it is rummaging among curious old theater props. I must take you with me some day."

"I would like to go along very much," said Xavière.

"There was a long rehearsal this afternoon and I spent a lot of time putting the finishing touches on the costumes." She laughed. "One of the actors, who's quite stout, padded his buttocks instead of his stomach. You should have seen him!"

Xavière gently squeezed Françoise's hand. "You mustn't tire yourself out," she said. "You'll make yourself ill!"

Françoise looked at the anxious face with sudden affection. At times Xavière's reserve melted; she was just a fond, ingenuous little girl, and you wanted to cover her pearly cheeks with kisses.

"It won't last much longer," said Françoise. "You know, I wouldn't lead this sort of life forever; but as it lasts only a few days and we're looking forward to success, it's worth giving everything in one's power."

"You're so energetic," Xavière said.

Françoise smiled at her.

"I think it will be interesting tonight. Labrousse always gets his finest inspirations at the last minute."

Xavière said nothing. She always appeared embarrassed when Françoise spoke of Pierre, although she made a show of admiring him greatly.

"It doesn't bore you, I hope, to go to this rehearsal?"

"It amuses me very much." Xavière hesitated. "But obviously I'd prefer to see you under different circumstances."

"So would I," Françoise said without warmth. She hated these occasional veiled reproaches from Xavière. Unquestionably she had not given her much of her time, but surely she could not be expected to sacrifice to Xavière the few hours she had for her own work!

When they reached the theater, Françoise affectionately looked up at the old building ornamented with rococo festoons. It had a friendly sedate look that warmed the heart. In a few days, at the gala opening, it would be ablaze with all its lights. But at the moment, it was plunged in darkness. Françoise walked towards the stage-door.

"It's strange to think that you come here every day, much as you might go to an office," Xavière said. "The inside of a theater has always seemed so mysterious to me."

"I remember before I knew Labrousse," said Françoise, "how Elisabeth used to put on the solemn air of an initiate whenever she took me backstage. I felt all puffed up with pride myself." She smiled; the mystery had faded. But this yard, cluttered with old stage sets, had lost none of its poetry in becoming an everyday sight. The little wooden staircase, the same color as a garden bench, led up to the greenroom. Françoise paused for a moment to listen to the murmur coming from the stage. As always, when she was about to see Pierre, her heart began to beat faster.

"Don't make any noise. We're going to cross the stage," she said.

She took Xavière by the hand and they tiptoed across behind the scenery. In a garden of green and purple shrubs, Tedesco was pacing up and down like a soul in torment. Tonight, his voice sounded curiously husky.

"Sit down here. I'll be back in a moment," said Françoise.

There were a great many people in the theater. As usual, the actors and the small-bit players were grouped together in the back seats, while Pierre was alone in the front row. Françoise shook hands with Elisabeth, who was seated beside a young actor from whom she had scarcely been separated during the last few days.

"I'll see you in just a moment," she said. She smiled at Pierre without speaking. He was seated all hunched up, his head muffled in a big red scarf. He looked anything but satisfied.

Those clumps of shrubbery are a failure! thought Françoise. They will have to be changed. She looked uneasily at Pierre and he made a gesture of utter helplessness. Tedesco had never been so bad. Was it possible they had been completely mistaken about him up till now?

Tedesco's voice broke completely. He put his hand up to his forehead. "I'm sorry. I don't know what's the matter with me. I think I'd better rest a while. Fifteen minutes and I'll be all right."

There was a deathly silence.

"Okay," said Pierre. "Meanwhile, we'll adjust the lighting. And will somebody get Vuillemin and Gerbert. I want this set changed." He lowered his voice. "How are you? You don't look well."

"I'm all right," said Françoise. "You don't look too chipper yourself. Stop rehearsal at midnight tonight. We're all worn out; you can't keep up this pace until Friday."

"I know," Pierre said. He looked around. "Did you bring Xavière with you?"

"Yes, I'll have to spend a little time with her," Françoise hesitated. "Do you know what I've been thinking? All three of us could go and have a drink together when we leave. Would you mind that?"

Pierre laughed. "I haven't told you yet. This morning when I was coming up the stairs I met her on her way down. She scurried off like a scared rabbit and locked herself in the lavatory."

"I know," said Françoise. "You terrify her. That's why I'm asking you to see her for once. If you're really friendly toward her, it will simplify matters."

"I'd be only too glad to," said Pierre. "I find her rather amusing." At that moment Vuillemin came into the theater. "Oh, there you are. Where's Gerbert?"

"I've looked everywhere for him," said Vuillemin, coming up almost out of breath. "I've no idea where he's gone."

"I said good-bye to him at seven thirty in the prop-room," said Françoise. "He told me he was going to try to get some sleep." She raised her voice: "Régis, would you please go and look backstage and see if you can find Gerbert?"

"It's appalling, that barricade you've landed me with over there," said Pierre. "I've told you a thousand times I don't want any painted scenery. I want a built-up set."

"And another thing, the color won't do," Françoise put in. "Those bushes could be very pretty, except for that dirty red."

"We can easily fix that," said Vuillemin.

Gerbert ran across the stage and jumped down into the auditorium. His suède jacket was open over a checkered shirt. He was covered with dust.

"I'm sorry," he said. "I fell sound asleep." He ran his hand through his tousled hair. His face was livid and there were deep circles under his eyes. While Pierre talked to him, Françoise scanned his tired face with tender commiseration. He looked like a poor sick monkey.

"You make him do too much," said Françoise, when Vuillemin and Gerbert had gone off.

"He's the only one I can rely on," answered Pierre. "Vuillemin will make another mess of things if he isn't watched."

"I know, but Gerbert isn't as strong as we are," she said rising. "I'll see you later."

"We're going to try out the lighting," shouted Pierre. "Give me night; only blue backstage floods."

Françoise went over and sat down beside Xavière.

Still, I'm not quite old enough, she thought, for there was no denying it, she had a maternal feeling toward Gerbert—and feelings she considered slightly incestuous. She would have liked to put his weary head against her shoulder.

"Do you find it interesting?" she asked Xavière.

"I don't understand what's supposed to be happening," said Xavière.

"It's night. Brutus has gone down into his garden to meditate. He has received messages asking him to revolt against Caesar. He hates tyranny, but he loves Caesar. He's perplexed."

"Then that fellow in the brown jacket is Brutus?" Xavière asked.

"When he wears his beautiful white toga and make-up he looks much more like Brutus."

"I never imagined him like that," Xavière said sadly. Her eyes shone. "Oh, how beautiful the lighting is!"

"Do you think so? That makes me very happy," said Françoise. "We worked like slaves to get just that impression of early morning."

"Early morning?" Xavière said. "It's so chilly. This light makes me think of . . ." she hesitated, then added in one breath, "of a light like the beginning of the world, before the sun and the moon and the stars were created."

"Good evening, Mademoiselle," said a throaty voice. Canzetti was smiling with timid coquetry. Two thick black curls framed her charming gypsy face. Her lips and cheeks were very heavily made up.

"Does my hair look all right now?"

"I think it's very becoming," Françoise said.

"I took your advice," said Canzetti with a friendly smile.

There was a short blast of a whistle and Pierre's voice shouted, "We'll take the scene again from the beginning, with the lighting, and we'll go right through. Is everyone here?"

"Everyone's here," said Gerbert.

"Good-bye, Mademoiselle, and thank you," said Canzetti.

"She's nice, isn't she?" Françoise said.

"Yes," said Xavière, then adding petulantly, "I loathe that type of face and I think she looks dirty."

Françoise laughed. "Then you don't think she's nice at all.

Xavière scowled and made a wry face. "I'd tear my nails out, one by one, rather than speak to anyone the way she spoke to you. A worm couldn't be as low."

"She used to teach at a school near Bourges," said Françoise. "She gave up everything to try her luck in the theater. She's starving to death here in Paris." Françoise looked with amusement at Xavière's inscrutable face. Xavière hated anyone who was at all close to Françoise. Her timidity toward Pierre was mingled with hatred.

For some time Tedesco had been pacing the stage once more. Out of religiouslike silence, he began to speak. He seemed to have recovered himself.

That still isn't it, thought Françoise in distress. In three days there would be the same darkness in the theater, the same lighting on the stage, and the same words moving through space. But instead of this silence they would come into contact with a world of sounds: creaking seats, the rustling of programs, old men coughing persistently. Through layer upon layer of indifference, the subtle phrases would have to blaze a trail to a blasé and intractable audience; all these people, preoccupied with their digestion, their throats, their fine clothes, their household squabbles—bored critics, malicious friends—it was a challenge to try to interest them in Brutus's dilemma. They had to be taken by surprise, taken out of themselves. Tedesco's restrained, lifeless acting was inadequate.

Pierre's head was bowed, and Françoise regretted that she had not gone back and sat down beside him. What was he thinking? This was the first time he had put his esthetic principles so strictly into effect, and on so large a scale. He himself had trained all these actors. Françoise had adapted the play according to his instructions. Even the stage designer had followed his orders. If he succeeded it would mean the acceptance of his conceptions of art and the theater. Françoise's clenched hands became moist.

There's been no stint either in work or money, she thought, with a lump in her throat. If we fail, it will be a long, long time before we're in a position to start over again.

"Wait," said Pierre suddenly. Tedesco stopped abruptly, and Pierre went up onto the stage.

"What you're doing is all very well," he said. "It's quite correct. But, don't you see, you're acting the words, you're not acting the situation enough. I want you to keep the same nuances—but at a different level."

Pierre leaned against the wall and bowed his head. Françoise relaxed. Pierre did not know how to talk to actors very well. It embarrassed him to have to bring himself down to their level. Yet when he demonstrated a part he was prodigious.

"I know no personal cause, to spurn at him, But for the general."

Françoise watched the miracle with never failing wonder. Physically, Pierre in no way looked the part. He was stocky and his features were irregular, and yet, when he raised his head, it was Brutus himself who turned a tortured face to the heavens.

Gerbert leaned forward toward Françoise. He had sat down behind her without her having noticed him.

"The angrier he gets the more amazing he is," he said. "He's in a blind rage at this moment."

"With good reason," said Françoise. "Do you think Tedesco will ever make anything of his part?"

"He's close to it," said Gerbert. "He only has to make a start, and the rest will follow."

"You see," Pierre was saying, "that's the pitch you must give me, and then you can be as restrained as you like. I will feel the emotion. If the emotion isn't there, it's no damn good."

Tedesco leaned against the wall, and bowed his head.

"It must be by his death: and for my part, I know no personal cause, to spurn at him, But for the general."

Françoise gave Gerbert a triumphant smile. It seemed so simple, and yet she knew that nothing was more difficult than to awaken in an actor this sudden enlightenment. She looked at the back of Pierre's head. She would never grow tired of watching him work. Of all her lucky breaks, the one she valued most was the one which gave her the opportunity to work with Pierre. The great efforts they exerted and the weariness they shared united them more securely than an embrace. There was not a moment in all the harassing rehearsals that was not an act of love.

After the conspirators' scene had gone off without a hitch, Françoise stood up. "I'm just going to say hello to Elisabeth," she said to Gerbert. "If I'm needed I'll be in my office. I don't feel up to staying any longer. Pierre isn't through with Portia." She hesitated. It was not very nice to leave Xavière, but she had not seen Elisabeth for ages, and her neglect was verging on rudeness.

"Gerbert, I'm leaving my friend Xavière in your hands. You might take her backstage while the scenery's being changed. She doesn't know what a theater is like."

Xavière said nothing. Since the beginning of the rehearsal there had been a look of resentment in her eyes.

Françoise put her hand on Elisabeth's shoulder.

"Come and smoke a cigarette," she said.

"I'd love to. It's tyrannical not to allow people to smoke. I'll have to speak to Pierre about it," Elisabeth said with mock indignation.

Françoise stopped in the doorway. A few days earlier, the auditorium had been repainted a light yellow which gave it a rustic, friendly look. A faint smell of turpentine still hung in the air.

"I hope we never leave this old theater," Françoise said, as they climbed the stairs.

"I wonder if there's anything left to drink," she said, when they reached her office. She opened a cupboard half filled with books and looked at the bottles lined up on the top shelf. "There's a little whisky here. Would you like that?"

"Splendid," said Elisabeth.

Françoise handed her a glass. There was such warmth in her heart that she felt a burst of affection for Elisabeth. She felt that same youthful comradeship she used to feel when they came from a difficult and interesting lesson and strolled arm in arm in the lycée yard.

Elisabeth lit a cigarette and crossed her legs. "What was the matter with Tedesco? Guimiot insists that he's taking drugs. Do you think that's true?"

"I've no idea," Françoise said, blissfully taking a long drink of whisky.

"That little Xavière isn't very pretty," said Elisabeth. "What are you doing about her? Was everything put right with her family?"

"I know nothing about that," said Françoise. "Her uncle may show up any day and kick up a row."

"Do be careful," Elisabeth said, with an air of importance. "You may run into trouble."

"Careful of what?" Françoise asked.

"Have you found her any work?"

"No. She's got to get used to things first."

"What's her particular bent?"

"I don't think she'll ever be capable of much work."

Elisabeth thoughtfully exhaled a puff of smoke. "What does Pierre say about it?"

"They haven't seen much of each other. He rather likes her."

This cross-examination was beginning to irritate her. It almost seemed as if Elisabeth were calling her to account. She cut her short.

"By the way, what about your latest?" she asked.

Elisabeth gave a little laugh. "Guimiot? He came over to talk to me during the rehearsal last Tuesday. Don't you think he's handsome?"

"Very handsome. That's exactly why we took him on. I don't know him at all. Is he nice?"

"He certainly knows how to make love," Elisabeth replied in a detached tone.

"You didn't lose much time," said Françoise a little taken aback. Whenever Elisabeth took a liking to a man she began to talk about sleeping with him. But actually, she had remained faithful to Claude for the last two years.

"You know my principles," said Elisabeth gaily. "I'm not the sort of woman who is taken. I'm a woman who does the taking. That very first evening, I asked him to spend the night with me. He was flabbergasted."

"Does Claude know?"

Elisabeth very deliberately tapped the ash from her cigarette. Whenever she was embarrassed, her movements and her voice became hard and emphatic. "Not yet, I'm waiting for just the right moment." She hesitated. "It's all very complicated."

"Your relations with Claude? It's a long time since you've spoken to me about him."

"Nothing's changed," said Elisabeth. The corners of her mouth drooped. "Only I've changed."

"I thought you had it out with him a month ago?"

"He keeps on telling me the same old thing: I'm the one who has the better part of the bargain. I'm fed up with that old story. I almost said to him, 'Thanks, but it's much too good for me, I'd be satisfied with the other.'"

"You must have been too conciliatory again," said Françoise.

"Yes, I think so," she said, staring into space; an unpleasant thought was passing through her mind. "He thinks he can make me swallow anything," she said. "He'll get a big surprise."

Françoise studied her with interest. At this moment she was not consciously striking a pose.

"Do you want to break off with him?" Françoise asked.

At that Elisabeth's face relaxed. She became reasonable. "Claude is far too attractive a person for me ever to let him go out of my life," she said. "But I would like to be less dependent on him."

Her eyes crinkled and she smiled at Françoise with a sort of complicity that was rarely revived between them nowadays.

"We've poked enough fun at women who let themselves be victimized. And say what you like, it's not in my line to be a victim."

Françoise returned her smile. She would have liked to advise her, but it was difficult. What was essential, was for Elisabeth not to be in love with Claude.

"Merely putting an end to it in your own mind won't get you very far," she said. "I wonder if you ought not to frankly compel him to make a choice."

"This isn't the moment," said Elisabeth sharply. "No, I think that when I've won back my inner independence, I'll have made great progress. But to do that, I must succeed in dissociating the man from the lover in Claude."

"Will you stop sleeping with him?"

"I don't know. But what I do know is that I shall sleep with other men." Then she added with a shade of defiance, "Sexual faithfulness is perfectly ridiculous. It leads to pure slavery. I don't understand how you can tolerate it."

"I assure you I don't feel that I'm a slave," Françoise replied.

Elisabeth could not help confiding in someone, but immediately afterward she invariably became aggressive.

"It's odd," said Elisabeth slowly, and as if she'd been thinking about it with sincere astonishment. "The way you were at twenty, I would never have thought you'd be a one-man woman. Especially, considering that Pierre has affairs."

"You've said that before, but I really refuse to put myself out."

"Nonsense. You're not going to tell me that you've never felt the desire for a man," Elisabeth said. "You're talking like all those who won't admit they have prejudices. They pretend it's only a matter of personal choice. But that's just so much nonsense."

"Pure sensuality does not interest me," said Françoise. "And besides, does it mean anything: pure sensuality?"

"Why not? It's very pleasant," said Elisabeth with a sneering little laugh.

Françoise rose.

"I think we might go down. The sets must have been changed by now."

"You know, that young Guimiot is really charming," said Elisabeth as she walked out of the room. "He deserves more than a small part. He could be a worth-while recruit for you. I'll have to speak to Pierre about it."

"Do speak to him," said Françoise. She gave Elisabeth a quick smile. "I'll see you later."

The curtain was still down. Someone on stage was hammering. Heavy footsteps shook the flooring. Françoise walked to Xavière who was talking to Inès. Inès blushed furiously and got up.

"Don't let me disturb you," Françoise said.

"I was just going," said Inès. She shook hands with Xavière. "When am I going to see you?"

Xavière made a vague gesture.

"I don't know. I'll ring you up."

"We might have dinner together tomorrow, between rehearsals."

Inès remained standing in front of Xavière looking unhappy. Françoise had often wondered how the notion of becoming an actress could have ever entered that thick Norman skull. Inès had slaved for four years without making any appreciable progress; out of pity, Pierre had given her one line to speak.

"Tomorrow . . ." said Xavière. "I'd rather ring you up."

"You'll come through all right, you know," said Françoise encouragingly. "When you're not excited your diction is good."

Inès smiled faintly and walked away.

"Will you ever ring her up?" Françoise asked.

"Never," said Xavière irritably. "Just because I slept at her place three times, there's no reason why I should have to see her all my life."

"Didn't Gerbert show you round?"

"He suggested it."

"It didn't interest you?"

"He seemed so embarrassed," said Xavière. "It was painful." She looked at Françoise with unveiled bitterness. "I loathe foisting myself on people," she said vehemently.

Françoise felt herself in the wrong. She had been tactless in leaving Xavière in Gerbert's hands, but Xavière's tone surprised her. Could Gerbert really have been offhand with Xavière? That certainly wasn't his way.

She takes everything so seriously, Françoise thought with annoyance. She decided once and for all not to let Xavière's childish fits of sulkiness poison her life.

"How was Portia?" Françoise asked.

"The big dark girl? Monsieur Labrousse made her repeat the same sentence twenty times. She kept getting it all wrong." Xavière's face glowed with scorn. "Is it really possible for anyone as stupid as that to be an actress?"

"There are all kinds," Françoise said.

Xavière was bursting with rage. Françoise was aware of it and felt that she had not paid enough attention to her. But Xavière would get over it. Françoise looked at the curtain impatiently. The change of scenery was taking far too long. At least five minutes would have to be saved.

The curtain went up. Pierre was reclining on Caesar's couch and Françoise's heart began to beat faster. She knew Pierre's every intonation, his every gesture. She anticipated them so exactly that she felt as if they sprang from her own will. And yet, it was outside her, on the stage, that they materialized. It was agonizing. She felt herself responsible for the slightest failure and she could not raise a finger to prevent it.

It's true that we are really one, she thought with a burst of love. It was Pierre who was speaking and his hand that was raised, yet his gestures, his tones, were as much a part of Françoise's life as they were of his. Or rather, there was but one life between them and at its core one entity, which could be termed neither he nor she but they.

Pierre was on the stage, Françoise was in the audience, and yet for both of them it was the same play being performed in the same theater. Their life was like that. They did not always see it from the same angle, for through their individual desires, moods, or pleasures, each discovered a different aspect. But it was, for all that, the same life. Neither time nor distance could divide them. There were, of course, streets, ideas, faces, that came into existence first for Pierre, and others first for

Françoise; but they would faithfully embody these scattered moments into a single whole, in which "yours" and "mine" became indistinguishable. Neither one nor the other ever withheld the slightest fragment. That would have been the worst, the only possible betrayal.

"Tomorrow afternoon at two o'clock, we'll rehearse the third act without costumes," said Pierre. "And tomorrow night we'll go through the whole thing, from beginning to end and in costume."

"I'm going to scram," said Gerbert. "Will you need me tomorrow morning?"

Françoise hesitated. With Gerbert the worst drudgery became almost fun; the morning without him would be arid, but his pathetic tired face was heartbreaking.

"No, there isn't much left to do," she said.

"Is that really true?" he asked.

"Absolutely true. You can go and sleep like a log."

Elisabeth walked up to Pierre.

"You know, this Julius Caesar of yours is really extraordinary," she said. Her face carried an intent expression. "It's so different and at the same time so realistic. That silence when you raise your hand—the feeling of that silence—it's magnificent."

"That's sweet of you," said Pierre.

"I assure you it will be a success," she said emphatically. She looked Xavière up and down with amusement.

"This young lady doesn't seem to care very much for the theater. So blasé already."

"I had no idea the theater was like this," Xavière said in a disdainful tone.

"What did you think it was like?" Pierre asked.

"They all look like store clerks. They seem to be working so hard."

"But how wonderful it is," said Elisabeth. "All this groping, all this seemingly confused effort which finally takes form as a thing of beauty."

"Personally, I find it disgusting," Xavière said. Anger was getting the better of her timidity. She gave Elisabeth a black look. "Effort isn't ever attractive. But when an effort doesn't even succeed," she sneered, "it's ludicrous."

"It's the same in every art," Elisabeth replied curtly. "Beautiful things are not easily created. The more precious they are, the more work they require. You'll find out."

"The things I call precious," said Xavière, "are those that fall like manna from heaven," she pouted. "If they have to be bought, they're merchandise just like anything else. That doesn't interest me."

"What a little romantic!" said Elisabeth with a chilly laugh.

"I know what she means," Pierre said. "There's nothing very inviting about our sweatshop."

Elisabeth turned an almost belligerent face toward him. "Well! That's news! Do you now believe in inspiration?"

"No, but it's true that our work isn't beautiful. On the whole, it's a disgusting mess."

"I didn't say this work was beautiful," said Elisabeth hastily. "I know that beauty lies only in the completed work, but I find it thrilling to watch the transition from the formless to the pure and completed state."

Françoise looked at Pierre imploringly. It was painful to argue with Elisabeth. If she didn't have the last word, she felt she had lost prestige. To compel others to esteem her, to win their love, she'd fight them with vicious dishonesty. This could go on for hours.

"Yes," said Pierre looking vague, "but you have to be a specialist to appreciate all that."

There was silence.

"I think we'd better go," said Françoise.

Elisabeth looked at her watch.

"Heavens! I'll miss the last métro," she said with dismay. "I'm off. See you tomorrow."

"We'll take you home," Françoise offered halfheartedly.

"No, no, you'll only delay me," said Elisabeth. She seized her gloves and bag, cast a wavering smile into space and disappeared.

"We could go somewhere and have a drink," suggested Françoise.

"If you two aren't too tired," Pierre agreed.

"I don't feel the least bit sleepy," said Xavière.

Françoise locked the door and they left the theater. Pierre hailed a taxi.

"Where shall we go?"

"To the Pôle Nord. It's quiet there," said Françoise.

Pierre gave the driver the address. Françoise turned on the light and powdered her nose. She wondered if it had been wise to suggest that they go out together. Xavière was sullen and the silence was already becoming uncomfortable.

"Go in. Don't wait for me," Pierre said, looking for change to pay the driver.

Françoise pushed open the leather door of the café.

"Is that table in the corner all right?" she asked.

"Yes. This place looks very nice," Xavière remarked. She took off her coat. "Will you excuse me for a moment. I feel a little untidy and I don't like making up my face in public."

"What shall I order for you?" Françoise asked.

"Something strong."

Françoise's eyes followed her as she made her way to the powder room. *She said that deliberately because I powdered my face in the taxi,* she thought. When Xavière adopted this attitude of discreet superiority, it was because she was frothing with rage.

"Where has your little friend gone?" said Pierre, taking his place at the table.

"She's primping. She's in a queer mood tonight."

"She really is rather charming," he said. "What are you having?"

"An aquavit," said Françoise. "Order two."

"Two aquavits," Pierre told the waiter. "But give us the real aquavit. And one whisky."

"How sweet of you," said Françoise. The last time there she had been served some cheap ersatz. That had been two months before but Pierre had not forgotten. He never forgot anything concerning her.

"Why is she in a bad mood?" Pierre asked.

"She thinks I don't see enough of her. It's annoying, all the time I waste with her and she still isn't satisfied."

"You've got to be fair," he said. "You don't see much of her."

"If I were to give her any more time, I wouldn't have a minute to my-self," Françoise vehemently rejoined.

"I understand," said Pierre. "But you can't expect her to be particu-larly pleased. She has only you and she's very fond of you. Not very gay for her, is it?"

"I don't say it is," she admitted, thinking that perhaps she had been a little too offhand with Xavière. She found the idea unpleasant, as she disliked finding the slightest reason for blaming herself. "Here she is," she said.

Françoise looked at Xavière slightly surprised. The blue dress perfectly fitted the slender, rounded body, and it was the delicate face of a young girl that was now framed by the carefully brushed hair. This supple, feminine Xavière, Françoise had not seen since their first meeting.

"I ordered an aquavit for you," said Françoise.

"What is it?" Xavière asked.

"Taste it," said Pierre, pushing a glass toward her.

Xavière cautiously put her lips to the transparent liquid. "It's terrible," she said smiling.

"Would you like something else?"

"No, alcohol is always terrible," she said soberly, "but you have to drink it." She leaned her head back, half closed her eyes and lifted the glass to her mouth. "It burned all the way down my throat," she said, running her fingers along her lovely slender neck. Then her hand slipped slowly down the length of her body. "And it burns here. And here. It's odd. I feel as if I were being lighted up inside."

"Was that the first time you've been to a rehearsal?" asked Pierre.

"Yes," said Xavière.

"And you were disappointed?"

"A little."

"Do you really believe what you said to Elisabeth?" Françoise asked Pierre, "Or did you say it because she annoyed you?"

"She did annoy me," Pierre said. He pulled out a tobacco-pouch and began filling his pipe. "In fact, to a pure and uninitiated soul, the solemn way we keep trying to find the exact nuance for something that doesn't even exist must seem positively wanton."

"There's no choice, since we really do want to make it exist," Françoise said.

"If at least we succeeded the first time, and enjoyed it! But no, we just go on groaning and sweating. All that drudgery to produce a ghost. . . ." He smiled at Xavière. "You think it's ridiculous obstinacy?"

"I never like to take trouble over anything," said Xavière demurely.

Françoise was a little surprised that Pierre took these childish whims so seriously. "You're questioning the validity of art as a whole, if you take that line," she said.

"Yes, why not?" Pierre returned. "Don't you realize? The world is ready to explode. We may have war within the next six months. And here I am trying to reproduce the color of dawn."

"What do you want to do?" said Françoise. She was completely taken aback. It was Pierre who had convinced her that the greatest thing in the world was the creation of beauty. Their whole life together had been built on this belief. He had no right to change his opinion without warning her.

"Why, I want *Julius Caesar* to be a success," he replied. "But I feel about as big as an insect."

When had he begun to think that? Did it really worry him or was it one of those brief flashes which gave him a moment's pleasure and then disappeared without leaving a trace? Françoise was afraid to continue the conversation. Xavière did not seem bored, but her expression was noncommittal.

"If Elisabeth could hear you!" Françoise cried.

"Yes, art is like Claude. Is mustn't be touched, otherwise . . ."

". . . Otherwise it will collapse immediately," said Françoise. "Elisabeth seems to have almost had a premonition." She turned to Xavière. "Claude, you know, is the one she was with at the Flore the other evening."

"That horrible dark fellow!" said Xavière.

"He's not that ugly," Françoise said.

"He's what you'd call pseudo-handsome," said Pierre.

"And a pseudo-genius," Françoise added.

Xavière brightened suddenly. "What would she do if you were to tell her that he is stupid and ugly?"

"She wouldn't believe it," Françoise said. Then she thought a moment. "I think she would break with us and she would hate Battier."

"You haven't a very high opinion of Elisabeth," said Pierre cheerfully.

"Not very," said Xavière, a little embarrassed. She seemed determined to be pleasant to Pierre. Perhaps in order to show Françoise that her ill-humor was directed at her alone. Perhaps, too, because she was flattered that he took her side.

"What exactly do you dislike about her?" Pierre asked.

Xavière hesitated. "She's so artificial. Her scarf, her voice, the way she taps her cigarette on the table, it's all done deliberately." She shrugged her shoulders. "And it's done badly. I'm sure she doesn't like tobacco. She doesn't even know how to smoke."

"She's been practicing since the age of eighteen," said Pierre.

Xavière smiled furtively, in a way that intimated a secret understanding of things.

"I don't particularly dislike people who act a part in front of others," she said. "The ridiculous thing about her is that, even when she's alone, she has to walk with a firm step and make deliberate movements with her mouth."

There was so much hardness in her voice that Françoise felt wounded by it.

"But I imagine you too like to disguise yourself," said Pierre. "I wonder what your face is really like without the bangs and those rolls that hide half of it. And your handwriting is disguised, too, isn't it?"

"I've always disguised my handwriting," said Xavière proudly. "For a long time I wrote in a round hand, like this." She traced letters in the air with the point of her finger. "Now I use a pointed hand. It's more refined."

"The worst thing about Elisabeth," he continued, "is that even her feelings are false. Fundamentally, she doesn't give a damn about painting. She's also a communist and yet admits she doesn't give a damn about the proletariat!"

"Lying doesn't bother me," Xavière said. "What to me is monstrous is this method of making up one's mind by decree. Imagine her painting every day at a set hour without having any desire to paint. She goes to meet her man whether she has any desire to see him or not. . . ." Her upper lip curled in a contemptuous sneer. "How can anyone endure living according to a plan, with timetables and homework, as if she were still at a boarding school? I'd rather be a failure!"

Xavière had achieved her aim, and Françoise had been struck by the indictment. Usually, Xavière's insinuations left her cold; but tonight, it was a different matter. The attention Pierre was giving to the girl's opinions lent them weight.

"You make appointments and then don't keep them," said Françoise. "It's all very well when you do that to Inès, but you might also ruin some real friendships by going through life that way."

"If I like the person, I'll always want to keep the appointment," Xavière rejoined.

"Not necessarily," Françoise said.

"Well, that's just too bad," said Xavière. She pouted disdainfully. "I've always ended up by quarreling with everyone."

"How could anyone quarrel with Inès?" asked Pierre. "She's like a lamb."

"Oh, don't be so sure of that!" Xavière said.

"Really?" said Pierre, his eyes crinkling with amusement. He was curious. "With that big, innocent face, do you mean to tell me she's capable of biting? What has she done to you?"

"She hasn't done anything," said Xavière reticently.

"Oh, please tell me," Pierre begged in his most cajoling voice. "I'd be delighted to know what's hidden in the depths of those still waters."

"Nothing at all. Inès is a dunce. The point is, I don't like anyone to feel they hold any proprietary rights over me." She smiled and Françoise's uneasiness crystallized. When alone with Françoise, Xavière let feelings of disgust, pleasure, or tenderness rise uncontrollably in her face, a child's face. Now she felt herself a woman sitting before a man, and her features displayed precisely the shade of confidence or reserve she wanted to express.

"Her affection must be a burden on you," Pierre conceded, and Xavière was taken in by his look of complicity and innocence.

"That's right," said Xavière brightening. "Once I put off an appointment at the last minute—the evening we went to the Prairie. She pulled a face a yard long. . . ."

Françoise laughed.

"Yes," Xavière went on vehemently. "I was rude, but she dared to make some uncalled-for remarks," she blushed and added, "about something that was none of her business."

So that was it. Inès must have questioned Xavière about her relations with Françoise, and perhaps, with her calm Norman heavy-handedness, joked about it. In back of all of Xavière's vagaries was without question a whole world of obstinate and secret thoughts. To Françoise it was a somewhat disquieting idea.

Pierre laughed. "I know someone, our little Eloy, who always answers when a friend breaks a date: 'It so happens that I'm no longer free!' But not everyone is as tactful."

Xavière frowned. "In any case, not Inès," she said, aware of the sarcasm in her voice.

"It's very complicated, you know," Pierre said seriously. "I can readily understand that you find it distasteful to follow the rules, but it's also impossible to live only for the moment."

"Why?" cried Xavière. "Why do people always have to drag so much dead weight about with them?"

"Look," Pierre said, "time isn't a heap of little separate fragments you can wrap yourself up in one after the other. When you think you're living in the present, you're involving your future whether you like it or not."

"I don't understand," said Xavière. Her tone was not friendly.

"I'll try to explain." When Pierre became interested in a person he was capable of carrying on a discussion for hours with angelic sincerity and patience. It was one form of his generosity. Françoise, on the other hand, rarely took the trouble to explain what she thought.

"Let's assume you've decided to go to a concert," Pierre continued. "Just as you're about to set out, the idea of walking or taking the métro strikes you as unbearable. So you convince yourself that you are now free of your previous decision, and you stay at home. That's all very well, but ten minutes later when you find yourself sitting in an armchair, bored stiff, you are no longer in the least free. You're simply suffering the consequences of your own act."

Xavière laughed dryly. "Concerts! That's another of your beautiful inventions. As if anyone could want to hear music at fixed hours! It's utterly ridiculous," she said, adding in a tone of almost bitter hatred: "Has Françoise told you that I was supposed to go to a concert this afternoon?"

"No, but I do know that as a rule you can never bring yourself to leave your room. It's a shame to live like a hermit in Paris."

"Well, this evening isn't going to make me want to change my mind," she said scornfully.

Pierre's face darkened.

"You'll miss scores of precious opportunities if you carry on that way," he said.

"Always being afraid of losing something! To me there's nothing more sordid. If it's lost, it's lost, that's all there is to it!"

"Is your life really a series of heroic renunciations?" Pierre asked with a sarcastic smile.

"Do you mean I'm a coward? If you know how little I care!" said Xavière smugly, with a slight curl of her upper lip.

There was a silence. Pierre and Xavière both assumed poker faces.

We'd do better to go home to bed, thought Françoise. What aggravated her most was that she no longer accepted Xavière's ill-humor as lightly as she had during the rehearsal. Xavière had suddenly begun to count, although it was impossible to say why.

"Have you noticed that woman facing us?" Françoise asked. "Just listen for a second. She's been telling her boy friend at great length all the secrets of her peculiar soul."

The woman was young, with heavy-lidded eyes hypnotically trained on her companion. "I've never been able to follow the rules of flirting," she was saying. "I have a morbid horror of being touched."

In another corner, a young woman with green and blue feathers in her hair was looking uncertainly at a man's huge hand that had just pounced on hers.

"There are always a lot of couples here," Pierre said.

Once more a long silence ensued. Xavière was engaged in gently blowing the fine down on her arm which she was holding up to her mouth. Françoise felt the need to say something, but everything sounded false even as she spoke. "Have I ever told you anything about Gerbert?" she asked Xavière.

"A little," said Xavière. "You've told me he's very nice."

"He's had a queer childhood. He comes from a completely poverty-stricken, working-class family. His mother went mad when he was a baby, his father was usually out of work, and the boy earned a few sous a day selling newspapers. One fine day a pal of his took him along to a film studio to look for jobs as extras, and as it happened both of them were taken on. He couldn't have been more than ten years old at the time. He was extremely likable and attracted attention. He was given minor parts and, later on, more important ones. He began to make good money, which his father squandered royally." Françoise gazed apathetically at a tremendous white cake, decorated with fruit and arabesques of icing, which reposed upon a nearby tray; just looking at it was enough to make anyone feel sick. No one was listening to her story.

"People began to take an interest in him. Péclard more or less adopted him; he's still living with him. He's had as many as six adoptive fathers at one time. They dragged him to cafés and night clubs; the women would stroke his hair. Pierre was one of these fathers; he helped him with his work and his reading." She smiled and her smile was lost in space. Pierre, huddled into himself, was smoking his pipe. Xavière looked barely polite. Françoise felt ridiculous, but she kept on talking with stubborn animation.

"It was a funny education they gave the boy. He was an expert on surrealism without ever having read a line of Racine. It was touching, because to fill in the gaps, he used to go to the public libraries and pore over atlases and books on mathematics, but he kept it all a secret. And then he had a very hard time of it. He was growing up; people could no longer treat him like a performing monkey for their own amusement. About the same time that he lost his job in the movies, his adoptive fathers dropped him, one by one. Péclard dressed and fed him when he thought of it, but that was all. It was then that Pierre took him in hand

and persuaded him to take up the theater. Now he's made a good start. He still lacks experience, but he's talented and has a great stage-sense. He'll get somewhere."

"How old is he?" Xavière asked.

"He looks sixteen, but he's twenty."

Pierre smiled faintly.

"I must say, you do know how to make conversation," he said.

"I'm very glad you've told me his story," Xavière said eagerly. "It's terribly amusing to picture all those self-important characters patting that boy condescendingly on the back, feeling so strong and generous and patronizing."

"And you see me perfectly cast for the part, don't you?" said Pierre, pulling a wry face.

"You? Why? No more than the others," Xavière innocently rejoined. She looked at Françoise with marked affection. "I always love the way you tell things."

She was offering Françoise a transference of her allegiance. They could hear the woman with the green and blue feathers talking in a flat voice, ". . . I only rushed through it, but for a small town it's very picturesque." She had decided to leave her bare arm on the table and it lay there, forgotten, ignored; the man's hand was stroking a piece of flesh that no longer belonged to anyone.

"It's funny the feeling it gives you when you touch your eyelashes," Xavière remarked. "You touch yourself without touching yourself. It's as if you touched yourself from a distance."

She spoke to herself and no one answered her.

"Have you noticed how pretty those green and golden-yellow windows are?" observed Françoise.

"In the dining room at Lubersac," said Xavière, "there were stained-glass windows, too. But they weren't wishy-washy like these, they had beautiful rich colors. When you saw the park through the yellow panes it was the way it looked before a thunderstorm; through the green and blue ones it was like paradise, with trees of precious stones and lawns of brocade; and when the park got all red I thought I was in the bowels of the earth."

Pierre made a perceptible effort to be amiable. "Which did you prefer?" he asked.

"The yellow, of course," said Xavière. She stared dubiously into space, "It's terrible the way one loses things as one grows older."

"But you can't remember everything?" he said.

"Why not? I never forget anything," she replied scornfully. "For instance, I remember very clearly how beautiful colors used to move me in the past; now . . ." she gave a disillusioned smile, "I only find them pleasing."

"It's sad, but that always happens when you grow older," Pierre agreed. "But there are other things. You now understand books and pictures which were meaningless to you in your childhood."

"But I don't give a damn about understanding with my mind alone," Xavière cried with unexpected violence. And with a kind of sneer, she added. "I'm not an intellectual."

"Why do you have to be so disagreeable?" Pierre said abruptly.

Xavière's eyes opened in surprise.

"I'm not being disagreeable."

"You know very well that you are. You dislike me on the slightest pretext, and I think I can guess why."

"All right then. Tell me," said Xavière. Anger had brought a flush to her cheeks. Her face was extremely attractive, with such subtle and variable shades of expression that it did not seem to be made of flesh; it was made of ecstasies, resentments, sadness which by some alchemy, were rendered visible to the eye. Yet, in spite of this ethereal transparency, her nose and mouth were extremely sensual.

"You thought I wanted to criticize your way of life," Pierre said, "that's not so. I was arguing with you as I would argue with Françoise, or with myself, and for the simple reason that your point of view interested me."

"Of course you chose the most malicious interpretation at once," said Xavière. "I'm not a sensitive child. If you think I'm weak and capricious and I don't know what else, you might just as well say so."

"Not at all, I'm very envious of your capacity to feel things so strongly," Pierre said. "I understand your putting a higher value on that than on anything else." If he had decided to win his way back into Xavière's good graces, this was only the beginning.

"Yes," said Xavière with a certain gloom; her eyes flashed. "I'm horrified that you should think that of me. It's not true. I didn't get angry like a child."

"Still, don't you see," said Pierre, in a conciliatory tone, "you put an end to the conversation, and from that moment on you were no longer in the least friendly."

"I didn't realize it," said Xavière.

"Try to remember; you're sure to realize it now."

Xavière hesitated. "It wasn't for the reason you thought."

"Then what was the reason?"

Xavière made a brusque gesture. "No, it's stupid, it's of no importance. What good does it do always to hark back to the past? It's over and done with now."

Pierre sat up and faced Xavière squarely, determined to spend the whole night there rather than give in. To Françoise, such persistence sometimes seemed tactless, but Pierre was not afraid of being tactless. He had consideration for other people's feelings only in small things. But what exactly was it he wanted from Xavière. Polite banter on the hotel stairs? An affair? Love? Friendship?

"It's of no importance if we're never to see one another again," said Pierre. "But that would be a pity. Don't you think we could establish pleasant relations?" He had infused a kind of wheedling timidity into his voice. He had such absolute control over his face and his slightest inflections, that it slightly disturbed Françoise.

Xavière threw him a defiant glance that was now, at the same time, almost affectionate. "Yes, I think so," she said.

"Then let's get this straight," said Pierre. "What did you hold against me?" His smile already implied some secret understanding.

Xavière was playing with a strand of hair. Watching the slow, regular movement of her fingers, she said:

"It suddenly occurred to me that you were trying to be nice to me because of Françoise, and I disliked that." She flung back the golden strand. "I have never asked anyone to be nice to me."

"Why did you think that?" Pierre asked, champing on the stem of his pipe.

"I don't know," said Xavière.

"You thought that I'd been too hasty in putting myself on intimate terms with you. And that made you angry with me and with yourself. Isn't that so? Therefore, out of some sort of cantankerousness, you decided that my cordiality was only a pretense."

Xavière said nothing.

"Was that it?" Pierre asked warmly.

"Yes, in a way," Xavière replied with a flattered and embarrassed smile. Again she took hold of a few hairs and began to run her fingers up and down, squinting at them with an idiotic expression. Had she given it so much thought? Certainly Françoise, out of laziness, had oversimplified Xavière. She even wondered, a little uneasily, how she could have treated her as insignificantly as she did for the last few weeks; but wasn't Pierre wantonly complicating her? In any case, they did not both view Xavière in the same light. Slight as it was, Françoise was conscious of the difference.

"If I hadn't wanted to see you, I would have simply gone back to the hotel," said Pierre.

"You might have wanted to see me out of curiosity," Xavière replied. "That would be natural; you and Françoise have a way of pooling everything."

A whole world of secret resentment was discernible in this offhand little sentence.

"You thought we had mutually agreed to lecture you?" Pierre asked. "But that was not the case."

"You were like two grown-ups giving a child a good talking-to," she said, now seeming to sulk only on principle.

"But I didn't say anything," Françoise said.

Xavière assumed a knowing air. Pierre looked at her intently, smiling but serious. "You'll understand, after you've seen us together often enough, that you need have no scruples about considering us as two distinct individuals. I could no more prevent Françoise from being friendly toward you than she could me if I didn't feel so inclined." He turned to Françoise. "Isn't that so?"

"Certainly," Françoise replied with a warmth that did not seem to ring false. She felt a little sick at heart. It was all very nice to say they were one, all very nice, but Pierre was demanding his independence. Of course, in a sense, they were two, that she knew very well.

"You both have so many ideas in common," said Xavière. "I'm never sure which of you is speaking or to whom to reply."

"Does it seem preposterous that I, personally, should have a feeling of affection for you?" Pierre asked.

Xavière looked at him with some hesitation. "There's no reason why you should. I've nothing interesting to say, and you . . . you have so many ideas about everything."

"You mean that I'm so old," said Pierre. "You're the one who's being malicious now. You think I feel self-important."

"How could you think that!" said Xavière.

Pierre's voice became grave, smacking a little of the actor. "If I'd considered you just a charming, inconsequential, little person, I'd have been more polite. But as it is, I wish for something more than mere politeness between us, because it so happens I think very highly of you."

"You are wrong," Xavière said without conviction.

"And it's on purely personal grounds that I hope to win your friendship. Would you like to make a pact of personal friendship with me?"

"Yes, I would," said Xavière. She opened her innocent eyes wide. She smiled a charming smile of assent, an almost amorous smile. Françoise looked at a face unknown to her, filled with reticence and promise, and she saw again the other face, innocent and childish, that had leaned on her shoulder one gray dawn. She had been unable to hold it; it had been destroyed; it was lost, perhaps forever. And suddenly, with regret, with resentment, she felt how much she might have loved her.

"Your hand on it," said Pierre. He put his open hand on the table. His hands were dry and delicate. Xavière did not hold out her hand.

"I don't like that gesture," she said coldly. "It seems adolescent to me."

Pierre withdrew his hand. When he was thwarted, his upper lip jutted forward, making him look stiff and a little priggish. Silence ensued.

"Are you coming to the dress rehearsal?" Pierre asked.

"Of course, I'm looking forward to seeing you as a ghost," Xavière replied eagerly.

The room was almost empty. Only a few half-drunk Scandinavians were left at the bar. The men were flushed, the women bedraggled, and they were kissing with alcoholic shamelessness.

"I think we ought to go," Françoise said.

Pierre turned to her anxiously. "That's right, you've got to get up early tomorrow. You're not too tired?"

"No more than expected."

"We'll take a taxi."

"Another taxi?" said Françoise.

"Well, that can't be helped. You must get some sleep."

They went out and Pierre stopped a cab. He sat on the folding seat opposite Françoise and Xavière.

"You look sleepy, too," he said amiably.

"Yes, I am sleepy," Xavière said. "I'm going to make myself some tea."

"Tea!" cried Françoise. "You'd much better go to bed. It's three o'clock."

"I detest going to bed when I'm dead tired," said Xavière by way of an excuse.

"You prefer to wait until you're wide awake?" Pierre laughed.

"The very thought of being subject to natural needs disgusts me," Xavière rejoined haughtily.

They got out of the taxi and went upstairs.

"Good night," said Xavière. She opened her door without holding out her hand.

Pierre and Françoise continued up another flight. Pierre's dressing room at the theater was upside down these days and he had been sleeping in Françoise's room every night.

"I thought you were going to get angry again when she refused your hand," Françoise said.

Pierre sat down on the edge of the bed. "I thought she was going to put on her shy act again and it irritated me," he said. "But on second thought, I decided it sprang from a good motive. She didn't want an agreement, which she took seriously, to be treated like a game."

"That's so much like her, of course," said Françoise. There was a strange, unpleasant taste in her mouth that she could not get rid of.

"What a proud little devil she is!" Pierre said. "She was well disposed toward me at first, but as soon as I dared to express a shadow of criticism, she despised me."

"You explained things to her charmingly," said Françoise. "Were you merely being polite?"

"Oh, there was a lot on her mind tonight," said Pierre. He did not go on, he appeared absorbed in his thoughts. She wondered what exactly was going on in his mind? She looked at his face questioningly. It was a face that had become too familiar and no longer told her anything. She had only to reach out her hand to touch him, but this very proximity made him invisible. It was impossible to think about him. There was not even a name with which to describe him. Françoise called him Pierre or Labrousse only when she was speaking to others about him; when she was with him, or even when she was alone, she never used his name. He was as intimate and as unknowable to her as she was to herself. Had he been a stranger, she would at least have been able to form some opinion of him.

"What do you want of her, when all's said and done?" she asked.

"To tell you the truth, I'm beginning to wonder. She's no Canzetti, I can't expect just to have an affair with her. If I wanted a satisfactory relationship with her, I would have to commit myself up to the hilt. And I've neither the time nor the inclination for that."

"Why not the inclination?" asked Françoise. This fleeting uneasiness that had just come over her was absurd; they told each other everything, they had no reservations.

"It's complicated," said Pierre, "the very thought of it tires me. Besides, there's something childish about her that I find a little nauseating. She still smells of mother's milk. All I want is for her not to hate me, to be able to talk to her once in a while."

"I think you can count on that," Françoise said.

Pierre looked at her hesitatingly. "You weren't offended when I suggested to her that she and I should have a more personal relationship?"

"Of course not," said Françoise. "Why should I be?"

"I don't know, you seemed to be a little put out. You're fond of her, you might want to be the only one in her life."

"You know perfectly well that she's rather a burden."

"I know that you're never jealous of me," said Pierre, smiling. "All the same, if you ever do feel like that, you ought to tell me. This damned mania of mine for making a conquest . . . it makes me feel like a worm; and it means so little to me."

"Of course I would tell you," Françoise said. She hesitated, perhaps that night's uneasiness should really be called jealousy; she had not liked Pierre's taking Xavière too seriously, and she had been worried by the way Xavière smiled at Pierre. It was a passing depression, caused largely by fatigue. If she spoke of it to Pierre, it would become a disquieting and gripping reality instead of merely a fleeting mood, and from then on he would be aware of it even when she herself attached no importance to it. No, there was nothing to it, she was not jealous.

"You may even fall in love with her, if you wish," she said.

"There's no question of that," Pierre shrugged. "I'm not even sure that she doesn't hate me now even more than before."

He slipped into bed. Françoise kissed him as she lay down beside him. "Sleep tight," she said fondly.

"Sleep tight," said Pierre, kissing her.

Françoise turned toward the wall. In the room below, Xavière was drinking tea. She had lit a cigarette. She was free to go to sleep when she chose, all alone in her bed, far removed from any alien presence; she was mentally and emotionally free. And without doubt, at this moment, she was revelling in this freedom, was using it to condemn

Françoise. She was imagining Françoise, lying beside Pierre, spent with fatigue, and she was delighting in her proud contempt.

Françoise stiffened, but she could no longer simply close her eyes and blot out Xavière. Xavière had been growing steadily all through the evening, she had been weighing on her mind as heavily as the huge cake at the Pôle Nord. Her demands, her jealousies, her scorn, these could no longer be ignored, for Pierre had mentioned them and that was enough to lend them importance. Françoise tried with all her strength to thrust into the background this precious and encumbering Xavière who was gradually taking shape; she felt something close to hostility. But there was nothing to be done, no way of going back. Xavière was a reality.

4

ELISABETH opened the door of her wardrobe with a sigh of despair. Of course, she could keep on her gray suit; it was not out of place anywhere and that was just why she had bought it. But for once she was going out in the evening, and she would have liked to wear something else; a different dress to be a different woman. That evening, Elisabeth was in a languorous mood, with a feeling of voluptuous expectancy. "A blouse for every occasion! They make me sick with their millionaire's conception of economy."

At the back of the wardrobe was an old black satin dress that Françoise had admired two years before; it was not really out of date. Elisabeth made up her face again and slipped on the dress. She looked at herself in the mirror a little dubiously. She was not sure; in any case, her hair was all wrong now. She brushed it vigorously. "Your hair of burnished gold," she whispered to herself. She might have had a different life; but she regretted nothing, she had chosen freely to sacrifice her life to art. Her nails were ugly, an artist's nails. No matter how short she cut them, they were always tinged with a little cobalt or indigo; fortunately they made nail polish very thick nowadays.

Elisabeth sat down at her dressing table and began to cover them with a creamy red lacquer.

I would have been really elegant, she thought, *more elegant than Françoise. She always looks unfinished.*

The telephone rang. Elisabeth carefully put the tiny wet brush back into its bottle and got up.

"Is that you, Elisabeth?" the voice asked.

"Yes."

69

"This is Claude. How are you? Well, everything is all right for tonight. Can I come back with you afterward?"

"Not here," she said quickly. She gave a little laugh. "I'd like a change of atmosphere." This time she would really have it out with him, to the finish—not here, or it would only start all over again, as it had the month before.

"As you wish. But where then? At the Topsy, or the Maisonette?"

"No, just let's go to the Pôle Nord, it's the best place for talking."

"Okay. Half past twelve at the Pôle Nord. See you then."

"Good-bye."

Claude was looking forward to an idyllic evening. But Françoise had been right. To break with him in her own mind would be meaningless unless he was made aware of it. Elisabeth sat down and resumed her painstaking labor. The Pôle Nord was perfect. The leather upholstery would deaden a voice raised in anger, and the subdued lighting would be merciful to a ravaged countenance. All those promises Claude had made to her! And everything remained obstinately the same; one moment of her weakness had been enough for him to feel reassured. The blood rushed to her face. What a disgrace! For an instant he had hesitated, his hand on the doorknob; she had driven him away with unforgivable words. All he had to do was to go; but without a word, he had come toward her. The memory stung her so that she closed her eyes. Again her mouth felt his mouth on hers, so warm that her lips parted in spite of herself; she felt the gentle, urgent hands on her breasts. Her breasts swelled and she sighed as she had sighed in the intoxication of defeat. If only the door were to open now, and he were to come in. . . . She suddenly raised her hand to her mouth and bit her wrist.

"I'm not to be had like that," she said aloud. "I'm not a bitch." She had not hurt herself, but she noticed with satisfaction the small white marks her teeth had made on her skin. She also noticed that the wet polish had smeared on three of her nails; there was a bloodlike deposit under them.

"What an ass!" she murmured. Eight thirty. Pierre would already be dressed. Suzanne would be putting on her mink cape over an impeccable dress, her nails would be glistening. With a sudden movement, Elisabeth reached out for the polish remover. There was a crystalline tinkle, and on the floor lay small pieces of glass sprinkled over a yellow puddle that smelled like candy fruit drops.

Tears rose to her eyes; not for anything in the world would she go to the dress rehearsal with these butcher's fingers; it would be better to go straight to bed. Without money it was a gamble trying to be well dressed. She slipped on her coat and ran down the stairs.

"Hôtel Bayard, rue Cels," she told the cab driver.

When she got to Françoise's she would repair the damage. She took out her compact—too much rouge on her cheeks, and her lipstick too thick and badly applied. No, not in the taxi—you'll spoil everything in taxis—taxis give you a chance to relax; taxis and elevators, brief respite for women who exhaust themselves; other women are lying on couches with fine linen tied around their heads, as in the Elizabeth Arden advertisements, with gentle hands massaging their faces—white hands, white linen in white rooms—they will have smooth, relaxed faces, and Claude will say with his masculine naïveté, "Jeanne Harbley is really extraordinary." Elisabeth and Pierre had called them tissue-paper women —competition on that basis was impossible.

She got out of the taxi. For an instant she stood motionless in front of the hotel. It was most aggravating: she could never approach without strong feelings any place where Françoise had lived. The wall of the hotel was gray and peeling a little. It was shabby like so many other hotels; yet Françoise certainly could afford a smart apartment. She opened the door.

"May I go up to Mademoiselle Miquel's room?"

The porter handed her the key. She climbed the stairway where there lingered a faint smell of cabbage. She was in the very heart of Françoise's life; but, for Françoise the smell of cabbage and the creaking of the stairs held no mystery. Françoise passed through this setting without noticing what Elisabeth's feverish curiosity distorted.

I must try to imagine that I'm coming home, like any other day, Elisabeth said to herself as she turned the key in the lock. She remained standing in the doorway. It was an ugly room, the gray wallpaper was covered with huge flowers. Clothes were strewn over all the chairs, piles of books and papers on the desk. Elisabeth closed her eyes: she was Françoise, she was returning from the theater, she was thinking about tomorrow's rehearsal. She opened her eyes. Above the washbasin was a notice:

> *Guests are kindly requested:*
> *Not to make any noise after ten p.m.*
> *Not to wash any clothes in the basin.*

Elisabeth looked at the couch, the mirror-wardrobe, the bust of Napoleon on the mantelpiece beside a bottle of eau de Cologne, hair brushes, stockings. She closed her eyes once more, and then opened them. It was impossible to make this room her own: it was only too unalterably evident that it remained an alien room.

Elisabeth went over to the looking glass in which the face of Françoise had so often been reflected and she saw her own face. Her cheeks were fiery. She should at least have kept on her gray suit; it had been agreed that it was becoming. Now she could do nothing about this unusual reflection, yet it was the final image people would take away with them that night. She snatched up a bottle of nail-polish remover and a bottle of lacquer, and sat down at the desk.

A volume of Shakespeare's plays lay open at the page Françoise had been reading when she had suddenly pushed back her chair. She had thrown her dressing gown on the bed and it still bore, in its disordered folds, the impress of her careless gesture; the sleeves were puffed out as if they still enclosed phantom arms. These tossed-about objects evoked an image of Françoise more intolerable than Françoise herself. When Françoise was near her, Elisabeth felt a kind of peace. Françoise never betrayed her true face, but at least, when her smile was friendly, her true face did not exist at all. Here, in this room, Françoise's true face had left its mark, and this mark was inscrutable. When Françoise sat down at this desk, alone with herself, what remained of the woman Pierre loved? What became of that happiness of hers, her quiet pride, her austerity?

Elisabeth pulled toward her some sheets of paper which were covered with notes, rough drafts, ink-stained sketches. Scratched out and badly written, Françoise's thoughts lost their definiteness; but the writing itself and the erasures made by Françoise's hand still bore witness to her indestructible existence. Elisabeth pushed away the papers in sudden fury. This was ridiculous. She could neither become Françoise, nor could she destroy her.

Time, just give me time, she thought passionately. *I, too, will become someone.*

A great many cars were parked in the little square. With an artist's trained eye, Elisabeth looked at the yellow façade of the theater gleaming through the bare branches. Those ink-black lines standing out against the luminous background were beautiful. It was a real theater, like the Châtelet and the Gaieté Lyrique which at one time had seemed so marvelous to them! All the same, it was tremendous to think that the great actor, the great producer all Paris was talking about was none other than Pierre. It was to see him that this surging perfumed crowd was thronging into the foyer. *We weren't ordinary children—we swore that we'd be famous—I always had faith in him.* But this was it, she thought, dazzled. This was it, really it; the dress rehearsal at the Tréteaux, Pierre Labrousse in *Julius Caesar.*

Elisabeth tried to say it as if she were just any Parisian and then quickly to herself, "He is my brother," but it didn't come off. It was maddening. All around her there were hundreds of such potential pleasures, pleasures she could never quite grasp.

"What's happened to you?" said Luvinsky. "You're never around these days."

"I'm working," Elisabeth said. "You must come and see my canvases."

She loved dress rehearsals. Perhaps it was childish, but she derived tremendous pleasure from shaking hands with all the writers and actors; she had always needed a congenial environment in which to find and be herself. "When I'm painting," she had said, "I don't feel that I'm a painter; it's thankless and discouraging." Here, she was a young artist on the threshold of success, Pierre's own sister. She smiled at Moreau who looked at her admiringly, he had always been a little in love with her. In the days when she used to spend a lot of time at the Dôme with Françoise, in the company of beginners with no future and old failures, she would have looked with wide-eyed envy at this vigorous, gracious young woman who was talking casually to a lot of famous people.

"How are you?" asked Battier. He looked very handsome in his dark suit. "The doors here are well guarded at least," he added peevishly.

"How are you?" Elisabeth asked, shaking hands with Suzanne. "Did you have trouble getting in?"

"That doorman scrutinized all the guests as if they were criminals," said Suzanne. "He kept turning over our card for at least five minutes." She looked well, all in black, exactly right; but she also looked distinctly old, one could hardly suppose that Claude still had physical relations with her.

"They have to be careful," Elisabeth said. "Look at that fellow with his nose glued to the window, there are dozens like him in the square, trying to palm off fake invitations. We call them 'swallows,' or gate-crashers."

"What a picturesque name," said Suzanne. She smiled politely and turned to Battier. "We ought to go in now, don't you think?"

Elisabeth followed them in; for a moment or so, she stood motion-less at the back of the auditorium. Claude was helping Suzanne off with her mink cape; then he sat down beside her; Suzanne leaned toward him and laid her hand on his arm. A sharp stabbing pain suddenly went through Elisabeth. She recalled that December evening when she had walked through the streets drunk with triumph and joy because Claude had said to her, "You're the one I really love." On her way home to bed she had bought a huge bunch of roses. He loved her, but that had changed nothing. His love was hidden; but that hand on his sleeve could be seen by every eye in the theater, and everyone would take it for granted that this was its natural place. A formal bond, a real bond, perhaps the only reality one could be certain of; but this love of Claude's for her, for whom did it exist? At this moment, even she did not be-lieve in it, nothing remained of it anywhere in the whole of existence.

I've had enough, she thought; once more she was going to suffer through an entire evening, and she foresaw the whole gamut: trembling, fever, moist hands, throbbing head. The very thought of it made her feel sick.

"Good evening," she said to Françoise. "How beautiful you look."

She was really beautiful that evening. She wore a large comb in her hair and her dress was ablaze with vivid embroidery; she attracted a great many glances without seeming to be aware of them. It was a joy to feel that this brilliant and calm young woman was her friend.

"You look lovely, too," Françoise said. "That dress is so becoming."

"It's old," said Elisabeth.

She sat down to the right of Françoise. On her left sat Xavière, in-significant in her little blue dress. Elisabeth fingered the material of her skirt. It had always been her principle to own few things but things of good quality. If she had money she would certainly be able to dress well, she thought. She looked with a little less distress at Suzanne's impeccable back. Suzanne belonged to the tribe of victims. She accepted anything from Claude—but she, Elisabeth, belonged to a different species, strong and free, women who lived their own lives. It was out of pure generosity that Elisabeth did not reject the tortures of love, and not because she needed Claude; she was not an old woman, *I shall say* to him gently but firmly, "You see, Claude, I have thought it over. I believe that we should change the basis of our relationship."

"Have you seen Marchand and Saltrel," asked Françoise, "in the third row on the left. Saltrel has already begun coughing; he's getting ready to pounce. Castier is waiting for the curtain to go up before taking out his spittoon. You know he always carries it with him; it's an exquisite little box."

Elisabeth glanced at the critics, but she was in no mood to be amused by them. Françoise was obviously preoccupied with the success of the play; that was to be expected, and Elisabeth could look for no help from her.

The lights dimmed and three metallic raps rang out across the silence. Elisabeth felt herself grow completely limp. *If only I could be carried away by the acting, she thought, but I know the play by heart—the scenery is charming and so are the costumes—I'm sure though I could have done at least as well, but Pierre is like all relatives—no one ever takes members of their own family seriously—he ought to see my paintings without knowing they're mine. I have no social front—it's screaming the way you have to bluff all the time. If Pierre didn't always treat me as a negligible little sister, Claude might have looked upon me as an important, dangerous person.*

The familiar voice startled Elisabeth.

Stand you directly in Antonius' way . . . Calpurnia!

Pierre was really astounding as Julius Caesar. There were a thousand things you could say about his acting. "He's the greatest actor of the day," Elisabeth said to herself.

Guimiot rushed onto the stage and Elisabeth looked at him apprehensively. Twice during rehearsals he had knocked over the bust of Caesar. He dashed across the open space and ran round the bust without touching it; he help a whip in his hand; he was almost naked, with only a strip of silk around his loins.

He has a stunning body, she thought, without feeling the slightest thrill. He was charming to sleep with, but when it was over you didn't give it another thought—it was about as substantial as the white meat of chicken—Claude. . . .

I'm too nervous, I can't concentrate. She forced herself to look at the stage. *Canzetti looks pretty with that heavy bang on her forehead— Guimiot says that Pierre doesn't have much to do with her any longer, and that she's now after Tedesco—I don't really know—they never tell me anything.* She studied Françoise. Her face had not changed since the curtain had risen; her eyes were riveted on Pierre. How severe her profile was! One would have to see her in a moment of affection or of love, but even then she would be capable of preserving that Olympian air. *She's lucky to be able to lose herself in the immediate present,* Elisabeth thought, *all these people are lucky.* Elisabeth felt lost in the midst of this docile audience that was letting itself be carried away by images and words. Nothing held her attention, the play did not exist; there were only minutes that were slowly ebbing away. The day had been spent in the expectation of these hours, and now they were emptily flowing by, filled in their turn with nothing but waiting. And Elisabeth knew that when Claude stood before her she would still be waiting; she would await the promise, the threat, that would tinge the next day's waiting with hope or horror. It was a journey without end, leading to an indefinite future, eternally shifting just as she reached the present. As long as Suzanne was Claude's wife the present would be intolerable.

There was a burst of applause. Françoise stood up, her cheeks were slightly flushed.

"Tedesco never fumbled a line, everything went off perfectly," she said excitedly. "I'm going to see Pierre. If you won't mind, it might be better for you to go round during the next intermission. The crush is terrible at the moment."

Elisabeth stood up as well. "We could go into the foyer," she said to Xavière. "We can listen to people's comments. It's always amusing."

Xavière followed her obediently. *What on earth can I say to her?* Elisabeth wondered. She didn't really like her.

"Cigarette?"

"Thank you," said Xavière.

Elisabeth held up a match.

"Do you like the play?"

"Yes, I do," said Xavière.

How vigorously Pierre had defended her the other day! He was always inclined to be generous when it came to strangers; but this time he hadn't shown very good taste.

"Would you like to go on the stage yourself?" Elisabeth asked.

She was trying to discover the crucial question, the question that would draw the reply by which Xavière could once and for all be classified.

"I've never thought about it," Xavière said.

Surely she spoke to Françoise in a different tone and with a different look! But Françoise's friends never showed their true selves to Elisabeth.

"What interests you in life?" Elisabeth asked abruptly.

"Everything interests me," Xavière replied politely

Elisabeth wondered if Françoise had talked to Xavière about her. How did people talk about her behind her back?

"You have no preferences?"

"I don't think so."

Xavière seemed absorbed by her cigarette. She had kept her secret well; all Françoise's secrets were well kept. At the other end of the foyer, Claude was smiling at Suzanne. His features reflected his servile affection.

The same smile he gives me, thought Elisabeth, and a savage hatred filled her. She would speak to him without a trace of gentleness. She would lean her head back against the cushions and break into ruthless laughter.

The bell sounded for the end of the intermission. Elisabeth caught a glimpse of herself as she passed a mirror: there was something bitter and smoldering about her red hair and the expression on her face. She had made up her mind. Tonight would be decisive. At times Suzanne drove Claude mad and at others she filled him with maudlin pity, and he never could quite decide to detach himself from her. The auditorium grew dark. A picture flashed through Elisabeth's mind—a revolver—a dagger—a phial labeled poison—to kill someone. . . . Claude? Suzanne? Herself? It didn't matter. This dark murderous desire violently took possession of her. She sighed—she was no longer young enough for insane violence—that was too easy. No, what she had to do was to keep him at a distance for a time; yes, to keep his lips at a distance, his breath, his hands. She desired them so intensely—she was suffocating with desire. There, in front of her, on the stage, Caesar was being assassinated. *Pierre is staggering across the Senate, and it is I, I who am really being assassinated*, she thought in despair. It was insulting, all this vain agitation in the midst of their cardboard scenery, while she was sweating her agony in flesh and blood, and with no possibility of resurrection.

Although Elisabeth had sauntered slowly up the boulevard Montparnasse, it was only twenty-five minutes past twelve when she walked into the Pôle Nord. She could never succeed in being deliberately late, and yet she felt certain that Claude would not be punctual, for Suzanne would purposely keep him with her, counting each minute as a tiny victory. Elisabeth lit a cigarette. She was not specially anxious for Claude to be there, but the thought that he was elsewhere was intolerable.

She felt her heart contract. It was the same each time: as soon as she saw him before her, she was seized with anguish. He was there, he held her happiness in the palm of his hand and he was coming toward her casually, with no suspicion that she considered each one of his gestures a threat.

"I'm so glad to see you," said Claude. "At last, a whole evening to ourselves!" He smiled eagerly. "What are you drinking? Aquavit? I know that stuff; it's filthy. Give me a gin fizz."

"You may be glad, but aren't you rather sparing of your pleasures?" said Elisabeth. "It's one o'clock already."

"Seven minutes to one, darling."

"Seven minutes to one, if you prefer," she gave a slight shrug.

"You know very well it's not my fault," he said.

"Of course."

Claude's face darkened. "Please, my darling, don't look so cross. Suzanne left me with a face like a thundercloud. If you start sulking too, that will be the last straw. I was so looking forward to seeing that radiant smile of yours again."

"I don't smile all the time," said Elisabeth, hurt by Claude's complete lack of understanding.

"That's a pity. It's so becoming to you." He lit a cigarette and looked about him affably. "This place isn't bad. It's a bit gloomy though, don't you think?"

"So you said the other day. On one of the rare occasions when I do see you, I'm not anxious to have a crowd around us."

"Don't be cross," he said. He put his hand on hers, but he looked annoyed. A second later she drew her hand away. *This is a bad start*, she thought. *An important heart-to-heart explanation ought not to begin with petty squabbling.*

"On the whole, it was a success," Claude remarked. "But I wasn't really carried away for an instant. I don't think Labrousse knows precisely what he's after. He's wavering between complete stylization and pure and simple realism."

"It's just that subtle transposition he's after," Elisabeth insisted.

"But there isn't any special subtlety about it," he said in cutting tones. "It's a series of contradictions. Caesar's assassination looked like a funereal ballet, and as for Brutus's vigil in his tent—well, it was like going back to the days of the *Théâtre libre*."

Claude was being too clever. Elisabeth did not let him settle questions as arbitrarily as that. She was pleased because a reply came readily to her lips.

"That depends on the situation," she said quickly. "An assassination has got to be stylized, or else it degenerates into melodrama, and by contrast a supernatural scene has to be played as realistically as possible. That's only too obvious."

"That's just what I'm saying. There's no unity. Labrousse's esthetic theory is simply a kind of opportunism."

"Not at all," said Elisabeth. "Of course, he takes the text into account. You're amazing; you used to accuse him of making the setting an end in itself. Do make up your mind."

"But it is he who can't make up his mind. I'd very much like to see him carry out his famous plan of writing a play himself. Then we might know where we stand."

"He'll certainly do that," said Elisabeth. "Probably next year."

"I'll be curious to see it. You know I have great admiration for Labrousse, but I don't quite understand him."

"But it's so easy," Elisabeth said.

"I'd be very grateful if you'd explain."

Elisabeth was silent for a while, tapping her cigarette on the table. Pierre's esthetic theory was no mystery to her. From it she had taken the inspiration for her painting, but she found it hard to put into words. She saw once again the Tintoretto that Pierre loved so much; he had explained things to her about the attitudes of the figures, just what, she could not remember. She thought of Dürer's woodcuts, of a marionette show, of the Russian ballet, of the old silent movies; the idea was there, familiar and obvious. It was terribly annoying.

"Obviously, it's not so simple that you can pin a label on it—realism, impressionism, naturalism—if that's what you want," she said.

"Why are you being so gratuitously disagreeable?" Claude rejoined. "I'm not used to technical terms."

"I'm sorry, but it was you who started talking about stylization and opportunism. But don't make excuses; your fear of being mistaken for a professor is really too ludicrous."

Claude dreaded nothing so much as sounding in the least academic, and, in all fairness, no one could have looked less like a professor than he.

"I can assure you I have nothing to fear on that account," he said dryly. "It's you who always introduces a kind of Teutonic ponderousness into our discussions."

"Ponderousness. . . ." Elisabeth said. "Yes, I know, every time I disagree with you, you accuse me of being pedantic. You're amazing. You can't bear to be contradicted. What you mean by intellectual companionship is the devout acceptance of all your opinions. Ask Suzanne for that, not me! Unfortunately I have a brain and occasionally like to use it."

"There you go! You get so violent right away!" he said.

Elisabeth controlled herself. He was detestable; he always found a way of putting her in the wrong.

"I may be violent," she said with crushing calm, "but you can't even hear yourself talk. You sound as if you were delivering a lecture."

"Let's not squabble again," said Claude in a conciliatory tone.

She looked at him resentfully. He had clearly made up his mind to be nice to her tonight; he felt affectionate, charming and generous, but she would show him. She coughed a little to clear her throat.

"Frankly, Claude, have you found this month's experiment a happy one?" she asked.

"What experiment?"

The blood rushed to Elisabeth's face and her voice trembled a little. "If we've kept on seeing one another after our heart-to-heart talk a month ago, it was only by way of an experiment. Have you forgotten?"

"Oh, of course . . ."

He had not taken the idea of a complete break seriously; she had ruined everything, of course, by sleeping with him that same night. For a moment she was put out of countenance.

"Well, I think I've reached the conclusion that the present situation is impossible," she said.

"Impossible? Why so suddenly impossible? What's happened now?"

"That's just it, nothing," said Elisabeth.

"Well, then what do you mean. I don't understand."

She hesitated. Of course, he had never said that he would one day leave his wife; he had never made any promises; in a sense, he was unassailable.

"Are you really happy this way?" she asked. "I put our love on a higher plane. What intimacy have we? We see one another in restaurants, in bars, and in bed. Those are nothing but dates. I want to share your life."

"Darling, you're raving," said Claude. "No intimacy between us? Why, I haven't a single thought I don't share with you. You understand me so perfectly."

"Oh, yes, I have the best part of you," Elisabeth said savagely. "Actually, you see, we should have kept to what, two years ago, you called an ideological friendship. My mistake was in loving you."

"But since I love you . . ."

"Yes," she said. It was maddening; she was unable to pin down any definite grounds for complaint against him without making them seem only petty grievances.

"Well?" he asked.

"Well, nothing." She had summed up a world of misery in those words, but Claude did not choose to take notice. He looked around the room with a beaming smile; he felt relieved and was already preparing to change the subject when she hurriedly added, "Fundamentally you're a very simple soul. You were never really aware that I wasn't happy."

"You take pleasure in tormenting yourself," Claude rejoined.

"Perhaps that's because I'm too much in love with you," she said dreamily. "I wanted to give you more than you were prepared to accept. And, if one is sincere, giving is a way of insisting on some return. I suppose it's all my fault."

"We aren't going to question our love every time we meet," Claude said. "This sort of conversation seems absolutely pointless to me."

Elisabeth looked at him angrily. He could not even see the emotional impact his last sentence had on her. What was the good of it all? Suddenly, she felt herself growing cynical and hard.

"Never fear. We shall never question our love again," she said. "That's just what I wanted to tell you. From now on, our relations will be on an entirely different basis."

"What basis? What basis are they now on?" Claude looked very annoyed.

"From now on all I want is a peaceful friendship with you," she said.

"I'm also tired of all these complications. Only, I never thought I could stop loving you."

"You've stopped loving me?" Claude sounded incredulous.

"Does that really seem so extraordinary to you?" she asked. "Please understand me. I'll always be very fond of you, but I shan't expect anything from you, and as far as I'm concerned, I shall take back my freedom. Isn't it better that way?"

"You're out of your mind," said Claude.

Elisabeth turned scarlet with anger. "You're unbelievable! I'm telling you that I no longer love you! A feeling can change. And you—you weren't even conscious of the fact that I had changed."

Claude gave her a puzzled look. "Since when have you stopped loving me? A few minutes ago, you said that you loved me too much."

"I used to love you too much." She hesitated. "I'm not sure just how it all happened, but it's true, things are not as they used to be. For instance . . ." she added quickly in a slightly choked voice, "before, I could never have slept with anyone but you."

"You've been sleeping with someone?"

"Does that upset you?"

"Who is it?" he asked inquisitively.

"It doesn't matter. You don't believe me."

"If it's true, you might have been loyal enough to tell me," he said.

"That's exactly what I'm doing," said Elisabeth. "I am informing you. Surely you don't expect me to consult you beforehand?"

"Who is it?" Claude repeated. His expression had changed, and Elisabeth was suddenly frightened. If he was suffering, she would suffer too.

"Guimiot," she said in a wavering voice. "You know, the naked messenger in the first act." It was done; it was irreparable; it would be useless to deny it; Claude would not believe her denials—she didn't even have time to think—she must go blindly ahead. In the shadows, something horrible was threatening her.

"Your taste isn't bad," he said. "When did you meet him?"

"About ten days ago. He fell madly in love with me."

Claude's face became inscrutable. He had often showed suspicion and jealousy, but he had never admitted to it. He would far rather have been hacked to pieces than utter a word of censure, but that was of no reassurance to her.

"After all, that's one solution," he said. "I've always thought it a pity that an artist should limit himself to one woman."

"You'll soon make up for lost time," Elisabeth retorted. "Why, that Chanaux girl is just waiting to fall into your arms."

"The Chanaux girl . . ." Claude grinned. "I prefer Jeanne Harbley."

"There's something to be said for that," said Elisabeth.

She clutched her handkerchief in her moist hands; now she could see the danger and it was too late. There was no way of retreating. She had thought only of Suzanne. There were all the other women, young and beautiful women, who would love Claude and who would know how to make him love them.

"You don't think I stand a chance?" said Claude.

"She certainly doesn't dislike you."

This was insane. Here she was trying to brazen it out, and with each word she became more inextricably involved. If only they could get away from this bantering tone. She swallowed, and with great difficulty said, "I don't want you to think, Claude, that I wasn't open with you."

He stared at her. She blushed. She did not know exactly how to go on.

"It was really a surprise. I had always meant to speak to you about it."

If he kept looking at her in that way she would start crying. Whatever happened she must not cry; it would be cowardly, she refused to fight with that woman's weapon. Yet it would simplify everything. He would put his arm round her shoulders, she would snuggle against him and the nightmare would be ended.

"You have lied to me for ten days," Claude said. "I could never have brought myself to lie to you for one hour. I put our relationship on such a high level." He had spoken with the dismal dignity of a judge, and Elisabeth rebelled.

"But you haven't been loyal to me," she said. "You promised me the best part of your life and never once have I had you to myself. You have never stopped belonging to Suzanne."

"You aren't going to blame me for behaving correctly to Suzanne," Claude protested. "Pity and gratitude alone dictated my behavior toward her, as you know very well."

"I don't know anything of the kind. I know that you'll never leave her for me."

"There was never any question of that."

"But if I were to raise the question?"

"You'd be choosing a very strange moment," he said coldly.

Elisabeth remained silent. She should never have mentioned Suzanne.

She could no longer control herself, and he was taking advantage of this. She saw him exactly as he was, weak, selfish, self-seeking and corroded with petty conceit. He knew his faults, but with ruthless dishonesty he gave a faultless picture of himself. He was incapable of the slightest impulse of generosity or sincerity. She loathed him.

"Suzanne is useful to your career," she said. "Your work, your ideas, your career. You have never given me a thought."

"How contemptible!" he said. "So I'm a careerist, am I? If that's what you think, how could you ever have been fond of me?"

There was a sudden burst of laughter and footsteps echoed on the black-tiled floor. Françoise and Pierre were arm in arm with Xavière, and all three seemed hilariously happy.

"Look who's here!" Françoise cried.

"I'm very fond of this place," said Elisabeth. She wished she could hide her face, she felt as if her skin were stretched to the point of cracking; it was drawn tight under her eyes, and around her mouth and beneath it the flesh was swollen. "So you've got rid of the bigwigs?"

"Yes," Françoise said. "We just about managed it."

Why wasn't Gerbert with them? Elisabeth wondered. Was Pierre afraid of his charm? Or was it Françoise who feared Xavière's charm? With an angelic and obstinate expression, Xavière smiled without uttering a word.

"It was an undoubted success," said Claude. "The critics will probably be severe, but the audience was enthusiastic."

"On the whole, it went off very well," Pierre said. He smiled warmly. "We must get together one of these days. We'll have more time now."

"Yes, there are a number of things I'd like to talk to you about," said Claude.

Elisabeth felt suddenly faint with despair. She saw her empty studio where she would no longer wait for the ring of the telephone, the empty letter rack in the concierge's office, empty restaurants, empty streets. It was impossible, but she did not want to lose him. Weak, selfish, hateful, it didn't matter. She needed him in order to live. She would accept anything at all if she could keep him.

"No, don't do anything about Berger until after you've had your answer from Nanteuil," Pierre was saying. "That would be unwise. But I'm sure he'll be very much interested."

"Phone me some afternoon," said Françoise. "We'll make a date."

They went toward the back of the room.

"Let's sit here. It's just like a little chapel," said Xavière. The excessive sweetness of her voice grated on one's nerves like a fingernail scraping over silk.

"The youngster is very sweet," Claude remarked. "Is that Labrousse's new love?"

"I suppose so. For someone who dislikes attracting attention as much as Pierre, their entry was a bit noisy."

There was a silence.

"Don't let's stay here," said Elisabeth nervously. "It's horrible to feel them staring at our backs."

"They're not paying any attention to us."

"I hate them . . . all these people." Her voice broke. Tears rose to her eyes. She would not be able to hold them back much longer. "Let's go to my studio," she said.

"As you like." He called the waiter and Elisabeth put on her coat in front of the mirror. Her face was distraught. In the glass she caught sight of the others. Xavière was talking. She was gesticulating, and Françoise and Pierre were looking at her as if fascinated. It was more than she could bear. They wasted their time on any idiot, but they were blind and deaf to Elisabeth. If only they had been willing to admit her and Claude into their intimate life, if only they had accepted *Partage* . . . It was their fault. Anger shook Elisabeth from head to foot; and she felt as if she were choking. They were happy, they were laughing. Would they be everlastingly happy, with such overwhelming perfection? Would not they, too, some day fall into the depths of their own sordid hell? They, too, wait in fear and trembling, calling in vain for help, imploring, remaining alone in the midst of regrets, anguish and endless disgust of oneself. They were so sure of themselves, so proud, so invulnerable. By watching them carefully could not some way be found to hurt them?

Silently Elisabeth stepped into Claude's car. They did not exchange a word until they reached her door.

"I don't think we have anything left to say to each other," Claude observed when he had stopped the car.

"We can't part like this," said Elisabeth. "Come up for a minute."

"What for?"

"Come up. We haven't really thrashed it out," Elisabeth insisted.

"You don't love me any more, you have insulting opinions of me. There's nothing to discuss."

This was blackmail, pure and simple, but it was impossible to let him go—when would he come back?

"You mean a great deal to me, Claude," said Elisabeth. These words brought tears to her eyes.

He followed her. She climbed the stairs crying spasmodically, with no effort at self-control; she staggered a little, but he did not take her arm. When they had entered the studio, Claude began to pace up and down frowning.

"You're quite free not to love me any more," he said, "but there was something else besides love between us, and that, you should try to salvage." He glanced at the couch. "Did you sleep here, with that fellow?"

Elisabeth had let herself drop into an armchair.

"I didn't think you'd be angry with me for it, Claude," she said. "I don't want to lose you over a thing like that."

"I'm not jealous of a second-rate little actor," said Claude. "I'm angry with you for not having told me anything. You should have spoken to me sooner. And, besides, tonight you said things to me that even make friendship between us impossible."

Jealous, he was just plain jealous. She had wounded his male pride and he wanted to make her pay for it. She was well aware of that, but it didn't help, his cold, cutting voice was torture to her.

"I don't want to lose you," she repeated. She began to sob undisguisedly.

It was stupid to abide by the rules, to play the game loyally; there were no thanks for that. She had thought that when one day all her pent up sufferings were revealed to him, together with all her sensitivities and inner struggles, he would be overwhelmed with admiration and remorse. But no, this had been just so much wasted effort.

"You know that I'm at the end of my tether," said Claude. "I'm going through a spiritual and intellectual crisis that's exhausting me. You were all I had to lean on, and this is the moment you've chosen!"

"Claude, you're unfair," she said weakly. Her sobs increased; her emotions carried her away with so much violence, that dignity and shame became mere futile words, and she no longer cared what she said. "I was too much in love with you, Claude. It's because I was too much in love with you that I wanted to free myself from you." She hid her face in her hands. This passionate confession should bring Claude to her side. Let him take her in his arms; let everything be blotted out! Never again would she utter a complaint.

She looked up, he was leaning against the wall, the corners of his mouth were trembling nervously.

"Say something to me," she said. He was looking viciously at the couch, it was easy to guess what he saw there; she should never have brought him here, the picture was too vivid.

"Will you stop crying?" he said. "If you treated yourself to that little pansy, it was because you wanted to. You no doubt got what you wanted."

Elisabeth stopped, almost choking in the effort; she felt as if she had received a direct blow on her chest. She could not bear coarseness, it was purely physical.

"I forbid you to speak to me that way," she said furiously.

"I'll speak to you in whatever way I choose," he said raising his voice. "I find it amazing that you now take the line that you're the victim."

"Don't shout," she cried. She was trembling all over, she seemed to be listening to her grandfather when the veins on his forehead became swollen and purple. "I won't allow you to shout."

Claude directed a kick at the chimney piece.

"Do you want me to hold your hand?" he asked.

"Don't shout," Elisabeth repeated more dully. Her teeth were beginning to chatter, she was on the verge of hysteria.

"I'm not shouting. I'm going." Before she could move, he was out of the door. She dashed to the landing.

"Claude," she called. "Claude."

He did not look back. She saw him disappear, and the street door slammed. She went back into the studio and began to undress; she was no longer trembling. Her head felt as if it were swollen with water and darkness, it became enormous and so heavy that it pulled her toward the abyss—sleep, or death, or madness—a bottomless abyss into which she would disappear forever. She threw herself on her bed.

When Elisabeth opened her eyes, the room was flooded with light; she had a taste of brine in her mouth, but she did not move. Pain, still somewhat deadened by fever and sleep, throbbed in her burning eyelids and her pulsing temples. If only she could fall asleep again until the next day—not to have to make any decisions—not to have to think. How long could she remain in this merciful torpor? She pretended to be dead—pretended to be floating—but already it was an effort to keep her eyes closed and see nothing at all. She rolled herself up tighter in the warm sheets. Once again, she was slipping toward oblivion when the bell rang.

She jumped out of bed, her heart beginning to race. Was it Claude already? What would she say? She glanced in the mirror. She did not look too haggard, but there was no time to choose her expression. For one second she was tempted not to open the door—he would think she was dead or had disappeared—he would be frightened. She listened intently. She could hear nothing on the other side of the door. Perhaps he had already turned away, slowly; perhaps he was going down the stairs—she would be left alone—awake and alone. She rushed to the door and opened it. It was Guimiot.

"Am I disturbing you?" he asked, smiling.

"No, come in." She looked at him with a kind of horror.

"What time is it?"

"It's noon, I think. Were you asleep?"

"Yes," Elisabeth said. She pulled up the covers and smoothed the bed; in spite of everything, she felt better with someone there. "Give me a cigarette," she said, "and sit down."

He irritated her, walking around the furniture like a cat. He liked to show off his body; his movements were supple and smooth, his gestures graceful and overdone.

"I was only passing by. I don't want to disturb you," he said. He also overdid his smile, a thin smile that lifted the corners of his eyes. "It's a pity that you couldn't come last night. We drank champagne until five this morning. My friends told me that I was a sensation. What did Monsieur Labrousse think?"

"It was very good," said Elisabeth.

"It seems that Roseland wants to meet me. He thinks I have a very interesting head. He expects to put on a new play soon."

"Do you think it's your head he's after?" Roseland made no secret of his tastes.

Guimiot gently pressed one moist lip against the other. His lips, his liquid blue eyes, his whole face made her think of a wet spring day.

"Isn't my head interesting?" he said coquettishly. A pansy grafted onto a gigolo, that was Guimiot, she thought.

"Isn't there a scrap to eat here?"

"Go and look in the kitchen," said Elisabeth. Bed, breakfast and what have you, she thought harshly. He always managed to cadge something, a meal, a tie, a little money borrowed but never returned. Today she did not find him amusing.

"Do you want some boiled eggs?" he shouted.

"No, I don't want anything." The sound of running water, and the clatter of pots and dishes came from the kitchen—she didn't even have the strength to throw him out—but when he left she would have to think.

"I've found a little wine," he announced. He put a plate, a glass and a napkin on one corner of the table. "There's no bread, but I'll make the eggs soft-boiled. Soft-boiled eggs can be eaten without bread, can't they?" He sat himself on the table and began to swing his legs.

"My friends told me that it's a pity I have such a small part. Do you think Monsieur Labrousse might at least let me be an understudy?"

"I mentioned it to Françoise Miquel," Elisabeth said. Her cigarette tasted acrid and her head ached. It was just like a hangover.

"What did Mademoiselle Miquel say?"

"That she would have to see."

"People always say they'll have to see," Guimiot said. "Life is very difficult." He leapt toward the kitchen door. "I think I hear the kettle singing."

He ran after me because I was Labrousse's sister, thought Elisabeth. It was not a new discovery—she had known it for ten days. But now she put her thoughts into words. She added, *I don't care.* With unfriendly eyes she watched him put the pot on the table and open an egg with finicky gestures.

"There was a stout lady, rather old and very smart, who wanted to drive me home last night."

"Fair, with a pile of little curls?"

"Yes. I refused to go because of my friends. She seemed to know Monsieur Labrousse."

"That's our aunt," said Elisabeth. "Where did you and your friends have supper?"

"At the Topsy, and then we wandered round Montparnasse. At the bar of the Dôme we met the young stage manager who was tight as a coot."

"Gerbert? Whom was he with?"

"There were Tedesco and the Canzetti girl and Sazelat and somebody else. I think Canzetti went home with Tedesco." He opened a second egg.

"Is the young stage manager interested in men?"

"Not that I know of," Elisabeth said. "If he made any advances to you it was because he was plastered."

"He didn't make any advances toward me," Guimiot looked shocked. "It was my friends who thought he was so handsome." He smiled at Elisabeth with sudden intimacy. "Why don't you eat?"

"I'm not hungry," she said. This couldn't last much longer, she thought, soon she would begin to suffer; she could feel it beginning.

"That's pretty, that thing you're wearing," Guimiot said, his feminine hands running lightly over her silk pajamas. The hand became gently insistent.

"No, leave me alone," said Elisabeth wearily.

"Why? Don't you love me any more?" His tone suggested lewd complicity, but Elisabeth had ceased to offer any resistance. He kissed the nape of her neck, he kissed her behind the ear; funny nibbling little kisses as if he were grazing. It would at least put off the moment when she would have to think.

"How cold you are!" he said almost accusingly. His hand had slipped beneath the silk, and he was watching her through half-closed eyes. Elisabeth surrendered her mouth and closed her eyes; she could no longer bear that look, that professional look. She felt suddenly that these deft fingers which were scattering a shower of downy caresses over her body were the fingers of an expert, endowed with a skill as precise as that of a masseur, a hairdresser, or a dentist. Guimiot was conscientiously doing his job as a male. How could she tolerate these services rendered, ironic as they were?

She made a movement to free herself. But she was so heavy, so weak, that before she could pull herself together she felt Guimiot's naked body against hers. The ease with which he had stripped, this too, was one of the tricks of the trade. His was a sinuous and gentle body that too easily embraced hers. Claude's clumsy kisses, his crushing embrace. . . . She half opened her eyes. Guimiot's mouth wore a grimace of pleasure and his eyes were drawn up at the corners. At this moment, he was thinking only of his own pleasures, with the avidity of an animal. She closed her eyes once more, and a scorching humiliation swept over her. She was anxious for it to end.

With a caressing movement Guimiot snuggled against Elisabeth's shoulder. She let her head sink into the pillow. But she knew that she would not be able to sleep. Now things must take their course, there was no help for it. That was that: suffering could no longer be put off.

5

"THREE COFFEES, and bring them in cups," Pierre ordered.

"You're pigheaded," said Gerbert. "The other day, with Vuillemin, we measured; the glasses hold exactly the same amount."

"After a meal, coffee should be drunk from a cup," Pierre said with finality.

"He maintains that the taste is different," said Françoise.

"He's a dangerous dreamer!" Gerbert said. He thought for a minute. "Strictly speaking, we might agree that it cools less rapidly in cups."

"Why does it cool less rapidly?" Françoise asked.

"Surface of evaporation is reduced," Pierre explained sententiously.

"Now you're all off," said Gerbert. "What happens is that china retains the heat better."

They were always amusing when they debated a physical phenomenon, usually without any regard for facts.

"It cools all the same," Françoise said.

"Just listen to her!" cried Pierre.

Gerbert put a finger to his lips with mock discretion, and Pierre nodded his head knowingly, which was the usual way they expressed their impertinent complicity. But today, there was no conviction in this ritual. The luncheon had dragged out cheerlessly, and Gerbert seemed spiritless. They had discussed the Italian demands at great length; it was unusual for their conversation to be swamped with such generalities.

"Did you read Soudet's criticism this morning?" asked Françoise.

"He's got nerve. He asserts that translating a text word for word is falsifying it."

"Those old drivellers!" Gerbert said. "They won't dare admit Shakespeare bores them stiff."

"That's nothing to worry about, we've got vocal criticism on our side," Françoise said. "That's the most important thing."

"Five curtain calls last night, I counted them," said Gerbert.

"I'm delighted," Françoise said. "I felt sure we could put it across without making the slightest compromise." She turned gaily to Pierre. "It's quite obvious now that you're not merely a theorist, an ivory-tower experimenter, a coterie esthete. The porter at the hotel told me he cried when you were assassinated."

"I always knew the man was a poet," Pierre smiled, but with constraint, and Françoise's enthusiasm subsided. Four days earlier, when they had left the theater at the close of the dress rehearsal, Pierre had been feverishly happy and they had spent an intoxicating night with Xavière! But the very next day, this feeling of triumph had left him. That was just like him. He would have been devastated by a failure, but success never seemed to be any more to him than an insignificant step forward, toward still more difficult tasks to which he immediately set himself. He never succumbed to the weakness of vanity, but neither did he experience the serene joy of work well done. He looked at Gerbert questioningly. "What is the Péclard clique saying?"

"That you're completely off the track," Gerbert replied. "You know they're all for the return to the natural and all that tripe. All the same, they would like to know just what you've got up your sleeve."

Françoise was quite sure she was not mistaken, there was a certain restraint in Gerbert's cordiality.

"They'll be on the lookout next year when you produce your own play," said Françoise. She added gaily, "Now, after the success of *Julius Caesar*, we can count on the support of the public. It's grand to think about."

"It would be a good thing if you were to publish your book at the same time," Gerbert said.

"You'll no longer be just a sensation, you'll be really famous."

A little smile played on Pierre's lips. "If the swine don't gobble us up."

The words fell on Françoise like a cold shower. "Do you think we'll fight for Djibouti?"

Pierre shrugged his shoulders. "I think we were a little hasty in our rejoicings at the time of the Munich deal. A great many things can happen between now and next year."

There was a short silence.

"Put your play on in March," Gerbert suggested.

"That's a bad time," Françoise objected, "and besides, it won't be ready."

"It's not a question of producing my play at all costs," said Pierre. "It's rather one of finding out just how much sense there is in producing plays at all."

Françoise looked at him uneasily. A week earlier when they were at the Pôle Nord with Xavière, and he had referred to himself as a persistent insect, she had chosen to interpret *it* as a momentary whim; but it seemed that the seed of real anxiety had taken root. "You told me in September that, even if war came, we should have to go on living."

"Certainly, but how?" Pierre vaguely contemplated his fingers. "Writing, producing . . . that's not after all an end in itself."

He was really perplexed and Françoise felt something like resentment against him. For her, it was necessary to be able to believe in him serenely. "If that's the way you look at it, what is an end in itself?"

"That's exactly why nothing is simple," Pierre rejoined. His face had clouded and his expression was almost as stupid as the way he looked mornings when, with his eyes still red with sleep, he began desperately searching for his socks all over the room.

"It's half-past two. I'll beat it," said Gerbert. As a rule he was never the first to leave; he liked nothing so much as the moments he spent with Pierre.

"Xavière is going to be late again," Françoise said. "It's most aggravating. Your aunt is so particular about our being there for the first glass of port at three o'clock sharp."

"She's going to be bored stiff there. We should have arranged to meet her afterward."

"She wants to see what a first showing is like," said Françoise. "I don't know what her idea of it can be."

"You'll have a good laugh!" Gerbert put in.

"It's one of aunt's protégés," said Françoise. "We simply can't get out of it. As it is, I cut the last cocktail party, and that didn't go down too well."

Gerbert got up and nodded to Pierre. "Until tonight."

"See you soon," said Françoise warmly. She watched him walk off in his big overcoat which flapped over his ankles; it was one of Péclard's old castoffs. "That was all rather forced," she said.

"He's charming, but we don't have a great deal to say to one another," Pierre said.

"He's never been like that before; I thought he seemed depressed. Do you think it's because we let him down on Friday night? But it was perfectly reasonable that we should have wanted to go home to bed right away when we were that exhausted."

"So long as nobody ran into us," said Pierre.

"Let's say that we buried ourselves at the Pôle Nord, and then jumped straight into a taxi. There's only Elisabeth, but I've warned her." Françoise ran her hand across the back of her head and smoothed her hair. "It would be too bad," she said. "Not so much the fact itself, but the lie would hurt him terribly."

Gerbert had retained from his adolescence a rather timid sensitivity, and, above all, he dreaded feeling that he was in the way. Pierre was the only person in the world who really counted in his life; he was quite willing to be under an obligation to him, but only if he felt that it was not merely out of a sense of duty that Pierre took an interest in him.

"No, that's not the reason," Pierre said. "Besides, yesterday evening he was still in good humor and friendly."

"Perhaps he's worried." It saddened her that Gerbert should be sad, and that she could do nothing for him. She liked to know that he was happy; his pleasant, regular life delighted her. He worked with taste and with good results. He had a few friends whose varied talents fascinated him: Mollier, who played the banjo so well; Barbisson, who spoke flawless slang; Castrel, who had no trouble holding six Pernods. Often at night in Montparnasse cafés Gerbert would test his own capacity for Pernods, but he had more success with the banjo. The rest of the time he deliberately shunned company. He went to the movies, he read; he wandered about Paris, cherishing modest and persistent little dreams.

"Why doesn't that girl come?" fumed Pierre.

"Perhaps she's still asleep."

"Of course not, yesterday evening when she dropped into my dressing room she told me explicitly that she'd have herself called. Perhaps she's ill, but then she would have telephoned."

"Not she, she's got a holy fear of the telephone, she thinks it's an instrument of evil," Françoise laughed. "But I think it's likely she's forgotten the time."

"She never forgets the time except out of spite," said Pierre, "and I don't see why she should have a sudden change of mood."

"She does occasionally, for no known reason."

"There's always a reason," said Pierre, irritably. "Only you don't try to understand them."

Françoise found his tone unpleasant; the situation was in no way her fault.

"Let's go and fetch her."

"She'll think we're indiscreet," protested Françoise. Perhaps she did treat Xavière rather like a piece of machinery, but at least she handled the delicate mechanism with the greatest of care. It was very annoying to have to offend Aunt Christine, but, on the other hand, Xavière would take it greatly amiss if they went to her room after her.

"But it's she who's in the wrong," he said. Françoise rose. After all, Xavière might very well be ill. Since that discussion with Pierre a week earlier, she had not had the slightest change of mood: that evening the three of them had spent together, the Friday after the dress rehearsal, had passed in cloudless merriment.

The hotel was quite near and it took them only a moment to get there. Three o'clock. There was not a minute more to lose. As Françoise started up the stairs the proprietress called her.

"Mademoiselle Miquel, are you going up to see Mademoiselle Pagès?"

"Yes, why?" asked Françoise a little arrogantly. This querulous old woman was fairly accommodating, but her inquisitiveness was sometimes misplaced.

"I would like to have a word with you about her." The old woman stood hesitatingly on the threshold of the little sitting-room, but Françoise did not follow her in. "Mademoiselle Pagès complained a little while ago that the basin in her room was stopped up. I pointed out to her that she had been throwing tea leaves, wads of cotton-wool and garbage into it." She continued, "Her room is in such a mess! There are cigarette ends and fruit-rinds in every corner, and the bedspread is singed all over."

"If you have any complaints to make about Mademoiselle Pagès, please address them to her," said Françoise.

"That's just what I've done and she told me she wouldn't stay here another day. I think she's packing her bags now. I have no trouble letting my rooms you know. I have enquiries every day, and I'd be only too happy to see a tenant like that go. The way she keeps the lights burning all night, you have no idea how much it costs me." She added ingratiatingly, "But because she's a friend of yours, I wouldn't want to inconvenience her. I wanted to tell you, so that if she changes her mind I won't raise any objections."

Ever since Françoise had lived there, she had been treated with unusual consideration. She showered the good woman with complimentary tickets which flattered her no end, but still more important, Françoise paid her rent regularly.

"I'll tell her," said Françoise. "Thank you," and with decisive steps, she went up the stairs.

"We can't let that old crow become a damned nuisance," growled Pierre, following her. "There are other hotels in Montparnasse."

"But I'm very comfortable in this one," Françoise said. It was well heated and well located, and Françoise liked its mixed clientele and her ugly-flowered wallpaper.

"Shall we knock?" asked Françoise hesitantly. Pierre knocked. The door was opened with unexpected promptness, and Xavière stood there, her hair disheveled and an unaccustomed color in her cheeks; she had rolled up her sleeves and her skirt was covered with dust.

"Oh, it's you!" she said with a look of complete surprise.

It was useless to try to anticipate Xavière's greeting, one was always wrong. Françoise and Pierre stood rooted to the spot.

"What are you doing here?" he asked.

Xavière's chest rose. "I'm moving," she said in a tragic tone of voice. The sight in the room was stupefying. Françoise thought vaguely of Aunt Christine whose lips were no doubt beginning to tighten, but everything seemed trivial in comparison with the cataclysm that had ravaged the room before them as well as Xavière's face. Three suitcases lay wide open in the middle of the room; the closets had disgorged onto the floor piles of crumpled clothing, papers, and toilet articles.

"And do you expect to be finished soon?" inquired Pierre, looking sternly at this devastated sanctuary.

"I'll never be finished!" cried Xavière, sinking into an armchair and pressing her fingers against her forehead. "That old hag . . ."

"She spoke to me just now," said Françoise. "She told me you could stay on for tonight, if you like."

"Oh!" A look of hope flashed in Xavière's eyes but then died immediately. "No, I have to leave at once."

Françoise felt sorry for her. "But you can't find a room this very evening."

"I know," said Xavière. She bowed her head and sat prostrated for some time, while Françoise and Pierre, as if spellbound, stood there staring at her golden head.

"Well, leave all this now," said Françoise, suddenly recovering herself. "Tomorrow we'll go and look together."

"Leave it?" said Xavière. "But I couldn't live in this rubbish heap for even an hour."

"I'll help you clear it up tonight," Françoise added. Xavière gave her a look of doleful gratitude. "Listen to me," Françoise continued, "you are going to get dressed and wait for us at the Dôme. We'll dash off to the private showing and be back in an hour and a half."

Xavière jumped to her feet and clutched her hair. "Oh, I would so like to go! I'll be ready in ten minutes."

"Aunt must be fuming already," Françoise demurred.

Pierre shrugged his shoulders. "In any case, we've missed the port," he said angrily. "Now there's no point in getting there before five o'clock."

"As you wish," said Françoise. "But the blame will fall on me again."

"Well, after all, you don't give a damn."

"And you'll give her your prettiest smile," said Xavière.

"All right," agreed Françoise. "But you'll have to think up a good excuse."

"Okay," Pierre growled.

"Then we'll wait for you in my room," Françoise said, and they went upstairs.

"It's an afternoon wasted," Pierre grumbled. "There won't be enough time left to go anywhere after we leave the exhibition."

"I told you she didn't know how to live." She walked over to the mirror: with this upsweep it was impossible to keep the back of her neck looking neat. "If only she doesn't insist on moving."

"You don't have to move with her." Pierre seemed furious. He was always in such good humor with Françoise that she had almost forgotten his impossible disposition; yet at the theater his temper was legendary. If he took this affair as a personal affront, the afternoon was going to be grim.

"But I do; you know that. She won't insist, but she'll sink into utter despair."

Françoise glanced over the room. "My nice little hotel. Fortunately, I can rely on her inertia."

Pierre went over to the pile of manuscripts stacked on the table. "You know," he said, "I think I'll hang on to *Monsieur le Vent*. This fellow interests me, he ought to be encouraged. I'll ask him to have dinner with us one of these evenings so that you can form some opinion of him."

"I also want you to look at *Hyacinthe*," said Françoise. "I think it's promising."

"Let me see it." He began looking through the manuscript and Françoise leaned over his shoulder to read with him. She was not in a good mood. Alone with Pierre, she would have disposed of the preview quickly enough, but with Xavière everything seemed suddenly to weigh on her; she felt as if she had tons of clay sticking to the soles of her shoes. Pierre should never have decided to wait. He too looked as if he had got out of bed on the wrong side. Nearly half an hour passed before Xavière knocked. Then they hurried downstairs.

"Where do you want to go?" Françoise asked.

"I don't care," said Xavière.

"Since we've only an hour," Pierre suggested, "let's go to the Dôme."

"How cold it is," Xavière said, pulling her scarf up around her face.

"It's only a few steps away," said Françoise.

"We haven't the same idea of distances," Xavière replied, her face distorted.

"Or of time," Pierre curtly added.

Françoise was beginning to see through Xavière. Xavière knew that she was in the wrong. She thought they were angry with her and she wanted to forestall them by seizing the initiative. Besides, her attempts at moving had worn her out. Françoise started to take her arm: Friday night, wherever they had gone, they had always walked arm in arm, keeping step.

"No," said Xavière, "it's much faster walking separately."

Pierre's face darkened again. Françoise was afraid he was going to lose his temper. When they arrived at the café, they took a table in the rear against the wall.

"You know," said Françoise, "this first showing won't be at all interesting. Aunt's protégés never have an ounce of talent; her instinct is infallible."

"I don't care a hang about that," said Xavière. "It's the reception I'm interested in. Paintings always bore me stiff."

"That's because you've never seen any," Françoise protested. "If you were to go to a few exhibitions with me, or even to the Louvre . . ."

"That wouldn't make any difference." She made a wry face. "Paintings are so austere and flat."

"If you learned a little about painting, I'm sure you'd enjoy it."

"You mean I'd understand why I ought to enjoy it," Xavière said. "I'd never be satisfied with that. The day I no longer feel anything, I'm not going to look for reasons for feeling."

"What you call feeling is really a way of understanding," Françoise said. "You like music, well then . . !"

Xavière stopped her short. "You know, when people speak about good and bad music, it goes right over my head," she said with aggressive modesty. "I don't understand the first thing about it. I like the notes for themselves; the sound alone is enough for me." She looked straight at Françoise. "The pleasures of the mind are repulsive to me."

When Xavière was being obstinate it was useless to argue. Françoise looked reproachfully at Pierre; after all, it was he who had wanted to wait for Xavière, he could at least have joined in the conversation, instead of entrenching himself behind a sardonic smile.

"I warn you that the reception, as you call it, will not be a bit amusing," Françoise repeated. "Just a lot of people exchanging polite remarks."

"But there'll be a crowd, and excitement," Xavière said with a tone of passionate insistence.

"Do you feel a need for excitement now?"

"And how!" cried Xavière, and suddenly there was a wild glint in her eyes. "Shut up in that room from morning till night, why, I'll go mad! I can't stand it there any more, you can't imagine how happy I'll be to leave that place."

"Who stops you from going out?" Pierre asked.

"You complain it isn't any fun to go out dancing with women. But Begramian or Gerbert would be only too glad to take you, and they dance very well," said Françoise.

Xavière shook her head. "When you make a planned effort to have a good time, it's always pitiful."

"You want everything to fall into your lap like manna from heaven," said Françoise. "But you won't deign to lift your little finger, and then you proceed to blame the whole world. Obviously . . ."

"There must be countries in the world," Xavière said dreamily, "warm countries—like Greece or Sicily—where you don't have to lift a finger." She scowled, "Here you have to grab with both hands—and to get what?"

"You have to do the same there too."

Xavière's eyes began to sparkle. "Where is that red island that's completely surrounded by boiling water?" she asked eagerly.

"Santorin, one of the Greek Islands. But that isn't exactly what I told you. Only the cliffs are red, and the sea boils only between two small, black islets thrown up by volcanic eruptions. Oh," she went on, warming to her subject, "I remember a lake of sulphurous water in the midst of the lava. It was all yellow and bordered by a tongue of land as black as anthracite, and on the other side of this black strip the sea was a dazzling blue."

Xavière looked at her with rapt attention.

"When I think of all you've seen!" she said in a voice filled with resentment.

"You consider it quite undeserved," observed Pierre.

Xavière looked him up and down. Then she pointed to the dirty leather chairs and the old tables. "To think, after seeing all that, you can still come and sit here."

"What good would it do to pine away with regrets?" Françoise said.

"Of course, you don't want to have regrets," Xavière said. "You're so anxious to be happy." She looked off into space. "But I wasn't born resigned."

Françoise was cut to the quick. Was it possible that her bias in favor of happiness, which seemed to her so obviously compelling, was being rejected with scorn? Right or wrong, she no longer considered Xavière's words as mere outbursts: they contained a complete set of values that ran counter to hers. She might refuse to recognize them, but their existence was none the less invidious.

"It isn't resignation," she said sharply. "We love Paris, and these streets, and these cafés."

"How can anyone love sordid places and hideous things, and all these wretched people." Xavière's contemptuous tone emphasized each of her epithets.

"The point is that the whole world interests us," said Françoise.

"You happen to be a little esthete. You want unadulterated beauty; but that's a very narrow point of view."

"Am I supposed to be interested in this saucer merely because it exists?" asked Xavière, and she looked at the saucer with annoyance. "It's quite enough that it's there." Then with intentional naïveté she added, "I should have thought that, being an artist, one naturally liked beautiful things."

"That depends on what you call beautiful things," Pierre said.

Xavière stared at him. "Heavens! You're listening," she said, with gentle surprise. "I thought you were lost in deep thought."

"I'm listening all right."

"You're not in a very good mood," Xavière remarked sweetly.

"I'm in an excellent mood," he retorted. "I think we're spending a most delightful afternoon. We're about to start off for the preview, and when we're through with that, we'll have just enough time for a sandwich. An ingenious arrangement."

"You think it's all my fault," said Xavière, showing her teeth in a sarcastic grin.

"I certainly don't think it's mine."

It had been merely for the purpose of behaving disagreeably toward Xavière that he had insisted on meeting her again as soon as possible. *He might have considered me,* Françoise reflected with bitterness. She was beginning to find the situation intolerable.

"That's true. When for once you've got some free time," Xavière said, still with her fixed smile, "what a tragedy it is, if a little of it is wasted!"

This reproach surprised Françoise. Had she once more misunderstood Xavière? Only four days had passed since Friday and at the theater, the evening before, Pierre had greeted Xavière most amiably. She no doubt already felt very strongly about him to consider herself now neglected.

Xavière turned to Françoise.

"I imagined the life of writers and artists to be something quite different," she said in a sophisticated tone. "I had no idea it was regulated this way—by the ring of a bell."

"You'd prefer them wandering about in the storm with their hair streaming in the wind?" Françoise said, feeling utterly fatuous under Pierre's mocking eye.

"No, Baudelaire didn't let his hair stream in the wind," Xavière said, then adding seriously, "What it amounts to is that, except for him and Rimbaud, artists are just like civil-service employees."

"Because we work regularly every day?" Françoise asked.

Xavière made a charming little face. "And then you count the number of hours you sleep, you eat two meals a day, you pay visits, and neither of you ever goes for a walk without the other. I suppose that's the way it has to be. . . ."

"But do you consider that so terrible?" asked Françoise with a forced smile. Xavière's picture of them had been by no means flattering.

"It seems queer to sit down at one's desk every day and write line after line of sentences," Xavière said. "Of course," she added quickly, "I can see why people write. There's something voluptuous about words. But only when the spirit moves you."

"It's possible to be interested in a piece of work as a whole," said Françoise, feeling the need to justify herself in Xavière's eyes.

"I admire the exalted level of your conversation," broke in Pierre. His malicious smile was aimed at Françoise as well as at Xavière, and Françoise was disturbed by it; was he able to judge her impersonally, like a stranger, she who could never keep the slightest thing from him? This was disloyalty.

Xavière never batted an eyelash. "It becomes drudgery," she said and she laughed indulgently. "But then that's the way you always do things, you turn everything into a duty."

"What do you mean?" asked Françoise. "I can assure you I don't feel my shackles." She would have to have it out with Xavière, and would in turn tell her just what she thought of her; it was all very well to let her assume all these little superiorities, but Xavière was overdoing it.

"Your relations with people, for example," Xavière counted on her fingers. "Elisabeth, your aunt, Gerbert, and so many others. I'd rather live alone in the world and keep my freedom."

"You don't understand; to follow a more or less consistent line of conduct does not constitute slavery," Françoise said with growing irritation. "It's quite of our own free will, for example, that we try not to hurt Elisabeth."

"You give them rights over you," Xavière said scornfully.

"Absolutely none," Françoise retorted. "With Aunt, it's a kind of cynical bargain, because she gives us money. Elisabeth takes what she's given, and we see Gerbert because we like to."

"Oh, but he certainly feels he has rights over you," Xavière replied with assurance.

"No one could be less conscious of having any rights than Gerbert," said Pierre calmly.

"You think so? But I happen to know otherwise."

"What can you possibly know?" asked Françoise, intrigued. "You haven't exchanged three words with him."

Xavière hesitated.

"It's one of those intuitions," Pierre observed, "which are only granted to superior persons."

"Well, since you want to know," Xavière burst out with sudden anger, "he looked like offended royalty when I told him last night that I went out with you on Friday."

"You told him?" cried Pierre.

"We warned you to say nothing," Françoise said.

"Oh, it slipped out," Xavière returned nonchalantly. "I'm not used to all this diplomacy."

Françoise exchanged a look of consternation with Pierre. Xavière had clearly done it deliberately, out of mean jealousy. She was not in the least absent-minded and she had stayed in the foyer for only a moment.

"There you are, we should never have lied to him."

"But, who would have dreamed . . ." said Pierre. He began biting one of his nails, he seemed deeply concerned. This was a blow to Gerbert's blind faith in Pierre from which he might never recover. Françoise felt a lump in her throat when she thought of Gerbert wandering alone about Paris at that moment.

"We've got to do something," she said nervously.

"I'll have a talk with him this evening. But what is there to explain? Having chucked him isn't so bad, but the lie seems so gratuitous."

"A lie always seems gratuitous when it's discovered," sighed Françoise.

Pierre looked severely at Xavière. "What exactly did you say to him?"

"He was telling me how they all got drunk on Friday, with Tedesco and Canzetti, and what fun it was. I said that I regretted very much not having met them, but that we had been cooped up in the Pôle Nord and hadn't seen anything."

She's all the more inexcusable, thought Françoise, since it was she who had insisted on staying at the Pôle Nord all that night.

"Are you sure that's all you said?" Pierre asked.

"Of course, that's all," Xavière said ungraciously.

"Well, perhaps it can still be straightened out." He looked at Françoise. "I'll tell him that it had been our firm intention to go home, but that at the last minute Xavière appeared to be so upset that we resigned ourselves to staying up."

Xavière pursed her lips.

"Either he'll believe you or he won't," Françoise said.

"I'll see to it that he believes me. At least, we have the advantage of never having lied to him before."

"That's true. You ought to try to see him right away."

"And Aunt? Well, to hell with her."

"No, we'll call on her at six o'clock," Françoise said nervously. "We must drop in, without fail, or she'll never forgive us."

Pierre got up. "I'll ring him up," he said, and went off.

Françoise lit a cigarette to keep her composure. Inside, she was trembling with rage; it was awful to think of Gerbert being unhappy, and unhappy through their fault.

Xavière tugged at her hair in silence. "After all, it won't kill him," she said with barely restrained insolence.

"I'd like to see you in his shoes," Françoise observed bitterly.

Xavière was taken aback. "I didn't know it was so serious," she said.

"You were warned."

There was a prolonged silence. Françoise felt a little frightened as she contemplated this catastrophe in human form that had surreptitiously invaded her life. It was Pierre who, by his deference toward her, his esteem, had broken down the walls within which Françoise had confined Xavière. Now that she was let loose, where would it all end? The day's balance sheet was already considerable: the landlady's anger, the preview by then more than half missed, Pierre's uneasy irritability, the quarrel with Gerbert. Françoise, too, felt an uneasiness, had felt it already for the past week; perhaps that was what frightened her most of all.

"Are you angry?" Xavière murmured. The dismay on her face did not soften Françoise.

"Why did you do it?"

"I don't know," she said dropping her voice and looking down. "It's just as well, at least now you'll know what I'm worth, you'll be disgusted with me. It's just as well."

"That I should be disgusted with you?"

"Yes. I'm not worth having anyone take an interest in me," she said with desperate vehemence. "Now you know me. I told you, I'm worthless. You should have left me in Rouen."

All the reproaches Françoise had on the tip of her tongue were suddenly futile in the face of these impassioned self-accusations. Françoise was silent. The café was now filled with people and smoke. At one table a group of German refugees were attentively watching a game of chess; at a neighboring table, alone with a glass of coffee, a pitiful creature who evidently thought she was a whore was preening herself for an imaginary customer.

"He wasn't there," Pierre announced.

"What kept you so long?"

"I took the opportunity to go for a little walk. I wanted some air." He sat down and lit his pipe; he seemed relaxed.

"I'm going," said Xavière.

"Yes, it's time to go," Françoise agreed.

No one moved.

"What I would like to know," Pierre asked, "is why you told him that?" He stared at Xavière with an interest so keen that it seemed to sweep away his anger.

"I don't know," Xavière said once more. But Pierre did not give up so easily.

"Of course you know," he said gently.

Xavière shrugged her shoulders despondently. "I couldn't help myself."

"You had something in mind," Pierre said. "What was it?" He smiled. "Did you want to be unkind to us?"

"Oh, how could you think that?"

"You thought this little mystery gave Gerbert a slight advantage over you, didn't you?"

Xavière's eyes flashed with resentment. "I can't stand always being so secretive," she said.

"Is that the reason?"

"No, of course not. I told you it just happened, that's all," she said with a tortured look.

"You said yourself that this secret annoyed you."

"But that's beside the point," said Xavière.

Françoise looked at the clock impatiently; what difference did it make what her reasons were, her behavior was inexcusable.

"You didn't like the idea that we had to account to anyone for what we did. I understand. It's unpleasant to feel that you're with people who aren't free."

"Yes, in a way," said Xavière. "And besides . . ."

"And besides what?" Pierre's tone was friendly. He looked as if he were quite ready to agree with her.

"No, it's contemptible," Xavière said, and she hid her face in her hands. "I'm contemptible. Leave me alone."

"But there's nothing contemptible about it," he said. "I would like to understand you." He hesitated. "Was it a kind of revenge because Gerbert hadn't been nice to you the other evening?"

Xavière uncovered her face; she seemed completely astonished. "But he was nice, at least as nice as I was."

"Then it wasn't in order to hurt him?"

"Of course not." She hesitated, then took the plunge: "I wanted to see what would happen."

Françoise looked at her with increasing uneasiness. Pierre's face showed a curiosity so eager that it almost looked like affection. Was he excusing the jealousy, the perversity, the selfishness to which Xavière had all but confessed? If Françoise had uncovered the beginnings of such feelings in herself, she would have immediately combatted them. And Pierre was smiling.

Suddenly Xavière blurted out, "Why do you make me say all this? To despise me even more? But you can't despise me more than I despise myself!"

"How can you think that I despise you?" he asked.

"Yes, you do despise me, and you're right. I don't know how to behave! I make trouble everywhere. I feel as if there were a curse on me," she wailed passionately.

She leaned her head against the leather upholstery of the wall and turned her face toward the ceiling trying to keep back her tears. Her throat swelled convulsively.

"I'm certain this whole incident will be straightened out," Pierre said in an urgent tone. "Don't get so upset."

"It's not only that," Xavière said. "It's . . . everything." She looked fiercely into space and said quietly, "I'm disgusted with myself. I loathe myself."

Whether she wanted to or not, Françoise was touched by her tone. She could feel that these words had not just come to her lips; they had been torn from the very depths of her being. How many hours, during long sleepless nights, she must have brooded over them, Françoise thought.

"You shouldn't," said Pierre. "We think so highly of you. . . ."

"Not now," Xavière returned weakly.

"But we do," Pierre assured her. "And I can well understand that momentary aberration."

Françoise had a sudden feeling of revolt. She didn't think as highly of Xavière as all that; she did not excuse this aberration, and Pierre had no right to speak for her. He went his own way without even looking back at her and then insisted that she had followed him; this was really too presumptuous. From head to foot she felt turned into a solid block of lead; separation was agony, but nothing could induce her to follow this mirage which led, heaven only knew, to what unknown depths.

"Brainstorms and lethargy," said Xavière, "that's all I'm capable of."

Her face was colorless and there were purple rings under her eyes. She was extraordinarily ugly with her red nose and her sorrowful looking hair that suddenly seemed to have lost its sheen. There could be no doubt that she was genuinely upset. But it would be too convenient, thought Françoise, if remorse could obliterate everything.

Xavière continued, her voice dismally plaintive. "When I was in Rouen, people could still find excuses for me, but what have I done since I've been in Paris?" She began to cry again. "I no longer feel anything, I no longer am anything."

She looked as if she were in the throes of some physical pain of which she was the helpless victim.

"All that will change," said Pierre. "Trust us and we'll help you."

"No one can help me," Xavière cried in a burst of childlike despair. "I'm ruined!" Sobs choked her; and she sat bolt upright, her face distorted in agony, allowing her tears to flow freely. At the sight of them —disarming and ingenuous—Françoise felt her heart melt. She groped for a gesture, a word, but it was not easy, she had come back from being too far away. A long, heavy silence followed. In the café, between the tarnished mirrors, a weary day still hesitated before dying. The chess players had not budged. A man had come to sit down beside the lunatic woman, and she seemed much less crazy, now that her companion had found a body.

"I'm such a coward," Xavière said, "I ought to kill myself, I ought to have done it a long time ago." Her face was contorted. "I will do it," she said, suddenly defiant.

Pierre looked at her, perplexed and wretched, and turned sharply to Françoise. "Well! Don't you see what a state she's in? Try to calm her," he said indignantly.

"What do you want me to do?" she asked, her pity instantly chilled.

"You ought to have put your arm round her long ago and said— said something to her," he added lamely.

Mentally, Pierre had taken her in his arms and was gently rocking her, but a sense of conformity and decency paralyzed his action, his warm compassion being only embodied in Françoise. Inert, frozen, Françoise didn't move. Pierre's imperious voice had drained her of her own will, but with all the strength of her stiffened muscles she shut herself off from any outside intrusion. Pierre, too, remained motionless, immobilized by useless tenderness. For a moment Xavière's agony continued in silence.

"Calm yourself," he repeated gently. "You must trust us. Up until now you've lived haphazardly, but life, you know, is a real enterprise. We'll talk it over together and make plans."

"There's no plan to make," Xavière said gloomily. "No, all I can do is go back to Rouen. That's the best thing."

"Go back to Rouen! That would really be smart!" said Pierre. "But we aren't angry with you." He cast an impatient look at Françoise. "Tell her at least that you're not angry with her."

"Of course I'm not angry with you," Françoise said in a toneless voice. With whom was she angry? She had the painful impression of being divided against herself. It was already six o'clock, but there was no question of leaving.

"Stop being so tragic," said Pierre. "Let's talk sensibly." There was something so reassuring, so steadying about him that Xavière became calmer; she looked at him almost submissively.

"What you need more than anything else," he said, "is something to do." Xavière made a derisive gesture. "Not a job just to kill time. I appreciate the fact that you are too exacting to be willing to camouflage a void, you can't be satisfied merely with distractions. You want something that will give your days real meaning."

Françoise listened with annoyance to Pierre's analysis. She had never suggested anything but distractions to Xavière. Once again she was being made aware that she had not taken her seriously enough. And now Pierre was trying to reach an understanding with Xavière without her.

"But I tell you I'm not good at anything," Xavière insisted.

"How can you know until you've tried?" Pierre smiled. "I've got a good idea."

"What is it?" she asked.

"Why not go on the stage?"

Xavière's eyes opened wide. "On the stage?"

"Why not? You have a very good figure, a keen natural sense of bodily attitudes and facial expressions. That doesn't necessarily mean that you have talent, but it's a good reason for hoping so."

"I could never do it."

"But wouldn't you like to?"

"Of course, but that doesn't get me anywhere."

"You're sensitive and intelligent—gifts that are not given to everyone," said Pierre. "They're trump cards." He looked at her seriously. "Damn it all, you've got to work. You'll come to the school. I'm taking two courses myself, and Bahin and Rambert are as nice as can be."

A flash of hope flickered in Xavière's eyes. "I'll never manage it," she said.

"I'll give you lessons myself to get you started. I promise you, that if you have the faintest shadow of talent I'll bring it out."

Xavière shook her head. "It's a beautiful dream," she said.

Françoise made an effort to be co-operative. It was possible that Xavière might be talented; in any case it would be all to the good if they could succeed in getting her interested in something.

"You said the same thing about coming to Paris," she said. "And yet here you are."

"That's true," Xavière conceded.

Françoise smiled. "You're so wrapped up in the present, that any future at all seems to you like a dream. It's time itself that you distrust."

Xavière smiled faintly. "It's so uncertain," she said.

"Are you in Paris or not?" Françoise insisted.

"Yes, but that's not the same thing."

"To come to Paris, you only had to do it once," said Pierre cheerfully. "In the theater, you'll have to begin all over again each time. But you can rely on us. We have enough will power for all three."

"And how!" Xavière said, smiling. "You're bursting with it."

Pierre pressed home his advantage. "From Monday on, you'll attend the pantomime classes. It's just like the games you used to play when you were a little girl. You'll be asked to imagine, for instance, that you're lunching with a friend, that you're caught shoplifting. You'll have to improvise the scene as well as act it."

"That should be fun."

"And then you'll choose a part to work on immediately; that is, selections from it." Pierre looked at Françoise questioningly. "What do you think we ought to suggest?"

Françoise thought it over. "Something that doesn't call for too much experience, but that doesn't let her simply act with her natural charm. Mérimée's *l'Occasion*, for example." The notion amused her, that Xavière might become an actress; at any rate, it would be quite interesting to try.

"That wouldn't be bad at all," Pierre said.

Xavière looked happily at them. "I would so love to be an actress! Could I act on a real stage like you?"

"Of course, and perhaps by next year you'll be ready for a small part."

"Oh!" Xavière cried ecstatically. "Oh! I'll work hard. You'll see."

Everything about her was so completely unpredictable, and perhaps, after all, she would really work; Françoise once more began to be fascinated by the future she imagined for Xavière.

"Tomorrow is Sunday, so that's no good," Pierre said, "but on Thursday I can give you your first lesson in diction. Would you like to meet me in my dressing room on Mondays and Thursdays from three to four?"

"But that will put you out," said Xavière.

"On the contrary, it will interest me enormously."

Xavière's calm was completely restored, and Pierre was beaming. It had to be admitted that he had accomplished an almost impossible feat in pulling Xavière from the depths of despair to her present state of confidence and joy. He had completely forgotten about Gerbert and the preview as well.

"You ought to ring up Gerbert again," said Françoise. "It would be better if you saw him before the show."

"Do you think so?"

"Don't you?" she rejoined a little dryly.

"Yes," he agreed reluctantly. "I'll go."

Xavière looked at the clock. "Oh! Now I've made you miss the preview," she said penitently.

"It doesn't matter," said Françoise. But on the contrary, it did matter a good deal. She would have to go the very next day to apologize to her aunt, and the apologies, of course, would not be accepted.

"I'm ashamed," Xavière said softly.

"But you mustn't be." Xavière's remorse and her resolutions had really touched Françoise; the girl could not be judged by any rule of thumb. She placed her hand on Xavière's. "You'll see, everything will be all right."

For a moment Xavière looked at her with devotion. "When I look at myself and when I look at you," she said fervently, "I'm ashamed!"

"That's absurd."

"You're so perfect," she cried passionately.

"Oh, that's certainly not true," said Françoise. At one time these words would have only made her smile, now they made her feel uncomfortable.

"Sometimes, at night, when I think about you," Xavière said, "it dazzles me so, I can't believe you really exist." She smiled. "And you do exist," she said with charming tenderness.

Françoise had always known that only at night, in the secrecy of her room, did Xavière surrender herself to her love for Françoise; for it was only then that no one existed to dispute her exclusive possession of the image in her heart, and sitting comfortably in her armchair, staring into space, she could lose herself in ecstatic contemplation of that image. The flesh-and-blood woman who belonged to Pierre, to everyone, and to herself, caught only faintest echoes of this jealous cult.

"I don't deserve to be thought of in that way," said Françoise with a feeling of remorse.

Pierre came back looking happy. "He was there. I asked him to be at the theater at eight o'clock and told him I wanted to speak to him."

"What did he answer?"

"He said 'okay.' "

"Then go ahead, and don't be afraid of sophistries."

"Just leave it to me," Pierre said. He smiled at Xavière, "Let's go to the Pôle Nord for a drink before saying good-bye."

"Oh, yes, let's go to the Pôle Nord," said Xavière tenderly.

That was where they had sealed their friendship and the place had already become symbolic for them. When they left the Dôme, Xavière, of her own accord, took Pierre's arm and Françoise's arm, and, all three walking in step, they set out on their pilgrimage to the Pôle Nord.

Out of squeamishness and probably because she objected to having any strange hand, even that of a divinity, touch her possessions, Xavière would not let Françoise help her with her room. So Françoise went straight upstairs, put on a dressing gown, and spread out her papers on her table. It was usually at this time of day, while Pierre was acting, that she worked on her novel; she began to read over the pages she had written the night before, but she had difficulty in concentrating. In the next room the Negro was giving the blonde a lesson in tap-dancing; with them was a little Spanish girl, who was a barmaid at the Topsy; Françoise recognized their voices. She took a nail file out of her bag, and began filing her nails. Even if Pierre succeeded in convincing Gerbert, would there not always be a shadow between them? How angry would her Aunt Christine be tomorrow? She couldn't get these irritating thoughts out of her head. But above all, she could not forget that she and Pierre had spent the afternoon in disunion. No doubt, after she talked it over with him, this unpleasant impression would dissipate; but, in the meantime, it weighed heavily on her heart. She looked at her nails. Her anxiety was stupid. She ought not to attach so much importance to a slight disagreement. She ought not to have felt herself so lost the moment Pierre's s... failed her.

Her nails were not right, she could not get them to match. Françoise picked up her file again. It was wrong to depend so entirely on Pierre, that was a real mistake. She ought not to thrust responsibility for herself upon someone else. With impatience, she brushed off the white nail dust clinging to her dressing gown. If she were to take full responsibility for herself, she would first have to want to; but she didn't want to. Even her self criticism was subject to Pierre's approval; her every thought was with him and for him. An act that bespoke of genuine independence, an act that was self-initiated and had no connection with him, was beyond her imagination. This, however, did not worry her; she would never find it necessary to call upon her own resources against Pierre.

Françoise tossed aside her nail file. It was absurd to waste three precious working hours. This was not the first time Pierre had been interested in another woman. Why, then, did she feel injured? What disturbed her was this feeling of obdurate hostility she had discovered in herself, and which had not yet completely dissipated. She hesitated, and, for a moment, she was tempted to try to analyze her uneasiness; but she did not feel like making the effort. She bent over her papers.

It was barely midnight when Pierre returned from the theater. His face was red from the cold.

"Did you see Gerbert?" Françoise inquired anxiously.

"Yes, everything's all right." Pierre was in high spirits. He took off his muffler and overcoat. "He began by telling me that it didn't matter and that he didn't want any explanation; but I insisted. I argued that we never stood on ceremony with him and that if we'd wanted to chuck him we'd have said so roundly. He was a little distrustful, but that was just to keep up appearances."

"You really are wonderful," Françoise said. There was a tinge of bitterness blended with her relief. It annoyed her to feel that she was conspiring with Xavière against Gerbert, and she would have liked Pierre to feel the same way about it, instead of happily rubbing his hands as he was doing. A slight tampering with truth was nothing, but to lie deliberately in a heart-to-heart talk spoiled something between people.

"Still, it was pretty rotten of Xavière," she said.

"I thought you were a bit hard on her," Pierre smiled. "You'll be terribly severe when you get old!"

"You were severe enough yourself at the beginning," Françoise said. "In fact you were insufferable." With a feeling of distress she realized that it would not be so easy to blot out the day's misunderstandings with a friendly conversation; whenever she thought of them she was overwhelmed with a hostile bitterness.

Pierre began to undo the tie he had put on in honor of the preview. "I thought it showed unspeakable thoughtlessness that she should have forgotten her appointment with us," he said in an offended tone, but with a smile that mocked the severity of his words. "And besides, when I went to take a little walk to calm down, I saw things in another light." His careless good humor only served to increase Françoise's irritability.

"So I perceived," she said. "Her behavior with Gerbert suddenly made you indulgent; you almost congratulated her."

"It was becoming too serious to be mere thoughtlessness," Pierre said. "It occurred to me that everything—her nervousness, her need for entertainment, the forgotten appointment, her telling Gerbert—was part of the same thing and that there must have been some reason for it."

"She told us the reason."

"You mustn't believe all she says."

"Well, then, it was hardly worth wasting so much time," Françoise said, thinking resentfully of his interminable questions.

"She isn't really lying either. You have to interpret her words." It seemed almost as if they were talking about a Pythian oracle.

"Just what is your point?" asked Françoise impatiently.

Pierre gave a crooked smile. "Didn't it strike you that fundamentally she resented my not seeing her since Friday?"

"Yes, that proves that she's beginning to grow very fond of you."

"For that girl, beginning and continuing to the end are one and the same thing."

"What do you mean?"

"I think the girl likes me!" Pierre said with a facetious complacency that nevertheless revealed his inner satisfaction. Françoise was shocked; usually, when Pierre was deliberately coarse it amused her; but he respected Xavière, and the tenderness of his smiles at the Pôle Nord had not been faked. It made his cynicism all the more distasteful.

"I'm wondering in what way Xavière's liking for you excuses her?" she said.

"You must put yourself in her place. She's a proud, emotional creature. I solemnly offered her my friendship, and the very first time it was a question of seeing her again, it seemed as if I had to move mountains to devote a few hours to her. That hurt her."

"Not at the time, at any rate," Françoise said.

"I dare say. But she thought it over, and since she didn't see me when she wanted to during the following days, it developed into a terrible grievance. Add to this that on Friday it was you who raised the objections about Gerbert. She may be devoted to you, but nevertheless in her possessive little soul you are still the biggest obstacle between her and me. Behind that secret we insisted she keep, she suddenly perceived many other things. And she behaved like a child who mixes up the cards when she sees that she is losing the game."

"You give her credit for a lot," said Françoise.

"You don't give her credit for enough," Pierre impatiently retorted, and this was not the first time that day that he had used this biting tone with her when they were on the subject of Xavière. "I don't say that she could have put it in so many words, but that was the meaning of what she did."

"Maybe," said Françoise.

So, according to Pierre's interpretation, she was someone in the way, and an object of jealousy. Françoise remembered with displeasure how moved she had been by Xavière's worshipping face; she saw it now as an expert piece of play acting.

"That's an ingenious explanation," she said, "but I don't think there can ever be any final explanation where Xavière is concerned; she lives far too much according to her moods."

"Well, that's just it, her moods have a twofold basis," Pierre said. "Do you think she would have flown into a rage over a washbasin if she hadn't been already upset? This idea of moving was a form of escape; and I'm certain that she was escaping from me, because she was angry with herself for being fond of me."

"In short, you think there's a key to her strange conduct and that the key is a sudden passion for you?"

Pierre's lip jutted out slightly. "I didn't say that it was a passion."

Françoise's phrase had irritated him. In fact, it was the kind of stark conclusion for which they so often criticized Elisabeth.

"A truly deep love!" said Françoise. "I don't think Xavière is capable of that." She thought a moment. "Ecstasy, desire, resentment, unreasonable demands, certainly; but the sort of acquiescence necessary to form something lasting out of all those emotions, that I don't think you can expect of her."

"That's what the future will show," said Pierre, whose profile became still sharper. He took off his jacket and disappeared behind the screen. Françoise began to undress. She had spoken openly; she never tried to spare Pierre's feelings; he had no self-pity and he was not secretive, so she did not have to handle him with kid gloves; and she had been in the wrong. This evening she had to think twice before speaking.

"Certainly, she's never looked at you in the way she did tonight at the Pôle Nord," Françoise conceded.

"Did you notice that, too?" said Pierre.

Françoise felt a lump in her throat. That sentence had been meant for a stranger, and it had struck its mark in Françoise. The man now brushing his teeth behind the screen was a stranger. An idea flashed into her mind. Had Xavière refused her help because she couldn't wait to be alone so that she could think of Pierre? It was possible that he had guessed the truth; it had been nothing but a dialogue between the two of them all afternoon; it was in Pierre that Xavière confided most readily, and between them there existed an understanding. Well, so much the better. It relieved her of the whole responsibility, which was beginning to be a burden. Pierre had already adopted Xavière to a far greater extent than Françoise had ever been willing to; she was handing her over to him. From then on, Xavière belonged to Pierre.

6

"YOU CAN'T find coffee like this anywhere else," Françoise said as she put her cup down on the saucer.

Madame Miquel smiled. "Well, of course, this isn't what they give you in your cheap restaurants."

She was looking through a fashion magazine and Françoise came over and sat down on the arm of her chair. Her father was reading *Le Temps*, sitting beside the fireplace in which crackled a wood fire. Practically nothing had changed during the past twenty years; it was suffocating. Whenever Françoise came back to the apartment, she felt as if all those years had led absolutely nowhere; time was spread out all around her in a quiet, stagnant pool. To live was to grow old, nothing more.

"Daladier really spoke well," Monsieur Miquel observed. "With great firmness, with great dignity; he won't give an inch."

"It's rumored that Bonnet, personally, would be willing to make concessions," said Françoise. "It's even said that he has engaged in secret negotiations over Djibouti."

"You know, as such, the Italian demands aren't so outrageous," Monsieur Miquel continued, "but it's their tone that's insufferable. After such an ultimatum, a compromise is quite out of the question."

"All the same, you wouldn't start a war over a matter of prestige?" Françoise asked.

"We can hardly resign ourselves to becoming a second-rate nation, huddled behind our Maginot Line."

"No," admitted Françoise. "It's very difficult." By always avoiding questions of principle, she was able to maintain friendly relations with her parents.

"Do you think I'd look well in this sort of dress?" her mother asked.

118

"Of course you would, Mother, you're so slim."

She glanced at the clock. It was almost two. Pierre would be already sitting at a table with a cup of that bad coffee in front of him. Xavière had arrived so late for her first two lessons, that they decided to meet an hour earlier at the Dôme for the next one, and then they could be sure of beginning their work at the proper time. Perhaps she was already there—she was unpredictable.

"I must have a new evening gown for the hundredth performance of *Julius Caesar*," Françoise said. "I don't really know what to choose."

"There's plenty of time for that," Madame Miquel replied.

Monsieur Miquel put down his newspaper. "Are you really counting on a hundred performances?"

"At least that. We have a full house every night." She roused herself and walked over to the mirror; the atmosphere was depressing.

"I'll have to be going," she said. "I have an appointment."

"I don't like this fashion of going out without a hat," said Madame Miquel, as she fingered Françoise's coat. "Why didn't you buy a fur coat as I told you? There's no warmth in this."

"Don't you like this three-quarter style? I think it's charming."

"It's a between-season coat." Her mother shrugged her shoulders. "I can't imagine what you do with your money."

"When are you coming again?" her father asked. "Wednesday evening Maurice and his wife will be here."

"Then I'll come on Thursday evening. I'd rather see you alone."

She walked slowly downstairs and out into the rue de Médicis. The air was clammy, but she felt better outside than upstairs in the warm library. Slowly, time had begun to move again. She was going to meet Gerbert; that at least gave some meaning to these moments.

Xavière must have arrived by now, Françoise thought with a slight tightening of her heart. She pictured her wearing either her blue dress or her beautiful red-and-white striped blouse, with her hair in smooth rolls framing her face, and she would be smiling. What was this unknown smile? How was Pierre looking at her? Françoise stopped short on the edge of the pavement; she had the painful impression of being in exile. Ordinarily, the center of Paris was wherever she happened to be. Today, everything had changed. The center of Paris was the café where Pierre and Xavière were sitting, and Françoise felt as if she were wandering about in some vague suburb.

She sat down near a brazier on the sidewalk terrace of the Deux

Magots. Pierre would tell her the whole story that night, but for some time now she had less and less confidence in words.

"Black coffee," she said to the waiter. She felt a sudden anguish; it was not a definite pain, but she began to delve deep into the past to unearth a similar pain. Then she remembered. The house was empty, the blinds had been drawn to shut out the sun, and it was dark; on the first-floor landing a little girl was standing flat against the wall, holding her breath. It was funny to be there all alone when everyone else was in the garden, it was funny and frightening; the furniture looked just as it always did, but at the same time it was completely changed: thick and heavy and secret; under the bookcase and under the marble console there lurked an ominous shadow. She did not want to run away but her heart seemed to turn over.

Her old jacket was hanging over the back of a chair. Anna had probably cleaned it with benzine, or else she had just taken it out of moth balls and put it there to air; it was very old and it looked very worn. It was old and worn but it could not complain as Françoise complained when she was hurt; it could not say to itself, "I'm an old worn jacket." It was strange; Françoise tried to imagine what it might be like if she were unable to say, "I'm Françoise, I'm six years old, and I'm in Grandma's house." Supposing she could say absolutely nothing: she closed her eyes. It was as if she did not exist at all; and yet other people would be coming here and see her, and would talk about her. She opened her eyes again; she could see the jacket, it existed, yet it was not aware of itself. There was something disturbing, a little frightening, in all of this. What was the use of its existing, if it couldn't be aware of its existence? She thought it over; perhaps there was a way. "Since I can say, 'I,' what would happen if I said it for the jacket?" It was very disappointing; she could look at the jacket, see absolutely nothing but the jacket, and say very quickly, "I'm old, I'm worn;" but nothing happened. The jacket stayed there, indifferent, a complete stranger, and she was still Françoise. Besides, if she became the jacket, then she, Françoise, would never know it. Everything began spinning in her head and she ran downstairs and out into the garden.

Françoise emptied her coffee cup in one gulp, it was almost stone cold; the incident was irrelevant, but why had she remembered it? She looked at the clouded sky. She felt the world around her suddenly out of reach. Not only was she exiled from Paris, she was exiled from the whole world. The people who were sitting on the sidewalk terrace, the people who were walking in the street, they were insubstantial, they were shadows; the houses were nothing but painted backdrops with no depth. And Gerbert, who was coming toward her with a smile, was nothing but a light and a charming shadow.

"Greetings," he said.

He was wearing his big beige overcoat, a shirt with small brown and yellow checks, and a yellow tie that set off his mat complexion. He always dressed with taste. Françoise was happy to see him, but she knew immediately that he could not help her recover her place in the world; he would be just a pleasant companion in exile.

"Shall we still go to the flea-market in spite of the horrible weather?" Françoise asked.

"It's only a thin drizzle," he said, "it's not really raining."

They crossed the square and went down the steps to the subway.

What can I talk to him about all day? thought Françoise. It had been a long time since she had gone out alone with him like this and she wanted to be particularly nice to him, to dispel any last trace of doubt which might have remained even after Pierre's explanation. But after all! She worked, and Pierre worked too. The life of civil-service employees—as Xavière had put it.

"I thought I'd never be able to get away," Gerbert said. "There was a crowd at lunch: Michel, and Lermière, and the Abelsons, all top-notch, as you can see. And what talk! Real fireworks—it was awful. Péclard has written a new anti-war song for Dominique Oryol. It wasn't bad, I must admit. Only their songs don't get them very far."

"Songs, speeches—" said Françoise, "never has there been such a flood of words."

"Oh! the newspapers nowadays are terrific," Gerbert said, and his face broke into a broad grin. Indignation always took a jocular form with him. "What a song and dance they're making about how France is standing firm! And all because Italy doesn't scare them out of their wits like Germany."

"Well, they certainly won't go to war for Djibouti," said Françoise.

"That may be," Gerbert admitted, "but whether it's in two years or six months, it's not very encouraging to know that we're in for it sooner or later."

"That's putting it mildly," said Françoise.

With Pierre she was far more casual: "We'll see what we'll see." But Gerbert made her feel uncomfortable; it wasn't amusing to be young these days. She looked at him a little anxiously. What was he really thinking? About himself, about his life, about the world? He never spoke of personal things. She would try to talk seriously with him in a little while; for the time being the noise of the subway made conversation difficult. She looked at a shred of yellow poster on the black wall of the tunnel. Even her curiosity lacked conviction today. It was a blank day, a good-for-nothing day.

"Did you know that there's a slight chance of my acting in the film *Déluges?*" Gerbert told her. "Nothing but a stand-in, but it would be good pay." He frowned. "As soon as I've saved up a little cash, I'm going to buy an old car; I'd be able to get one secondhand for next to nothing."

"That's a great idea," said Françoise. "You're sure to kill me, but I'll go out with you anyway."

They emerged from the subway.

"Or else," he said, "I might start a marionette theater with Mollier. Begramian is still supposed to put us in touch with the *Images* crowd, but you can't count on him."

"Marionettes are great fun," said Françoise.

"Only it cost a fortune to get a hall and your own equipment."

"Well, you may be able to one of these days."

That day, Gerbert's plans did not amuse her; she even wondered why, ordinarily, his life seemed to her to have such quiet charm. He was there, he had come from a boring meal at Péclard's, that evening he would play the part of young Cato for the twentieth time; there was nothing especially exciting in that. Françoise looked about her; she wished she could find something that would arouse her interest, but this long straight avenue had nothing to say to her. Only boring things were being sold in the little carts lined up along the edge of the pavement: cotton frocks, socks, or soap.

"Let's take one of these little streets," she suggested.

Here laid out on the muddy ground were old shoes, phonograph records, silks that were falling to pieces, enamel bowls, chipped crockery. Dark-skinned women dressed in brightly colored shawls were sitting on newspapers or old rugs, leaning against the wooden barrier. All that meant nothing to her either.

"Look," said Gerbert. "We're sure to find some props among all that junk."

Françoise glanced listlessly at the bric-à-brac displayed at her feet; all these filthy old objects could no doubt tell many a strange story, but to the casual onlooker they were only bracelets, broken dolls, faded stuffs, devoid of any personal history. Gerbert picked up and ran his hand over a glass ball with multicolored confetti floating in it.

"It looks like a fortuneteller's crystal," he said.

"It's a paperweight," said Françoise.

The vendor was watching them out of the corner of her eye. She was a fat, heavily-painted woman, with wavy hair, her body enveloped in woollen shawls and her legs wrapped in old newspapers. She, too, had no history, no future, she was nothing but a mass of shivering flesh. And these wooden barriers, these corrugated-iron huts, these wretched gardens with their dumps of old rusting metal, failed to create for Françoise, as they usually did, the strange world of squalid and fascinating objects; they were there, massed together, inert and formless.

"What's this story about our going on tour?" Gerbert asked. "Bernheim talks as if it were settled for next year."

"It's Bernheim's idea, naturally," said Françoise. "He's only interested in money; but Pierre won't hear of it. Next year there'll be other things to do."

She stepped over a puddle. It had been the same years before, when she had closed the door of her grandmother's house on the softness of the evening and the scents of the open fields: she had the sublime feeling of forever being deprived of the world outside. Somewhere else something was in the process of existing without her being there, and it was that thing only which really mattered. This time, she couldn't say, "It doesn't know it exists, it doesn't exist." For it did know. Pierre did not miss one of Xavière's smiles and Xavière, with rapt attention, was devouring every word Pierre uttered. Together, their eyes reflected Pierre's dressing room with its portrait of Shakespeare hanging on the wall. Were they working? Or were they resting and talking about Xavière's father, about the aviary full of birds, about the smell of the stables?

"Did Xavière do anything yesterday in the diction class?" Françoise asked.

Gerbert laughed. "Rambert asked her to repeat, 'Round the rugged rock the ragged rascal ran!' She blushed furiously and looked down at her feet without uttering a sound."

"Do you think she has any talent?"

"She's got a good figure," Gerbert seized Françoise's arm. "Come and look," he said suddenly, and pushed through the crowd. People were gathering around a large piece of black silk, once the cover of an umbrella, now spread out on the muddy ground; on it a man was spreading out cards.

"Two hundred francs," said an old gray-haired woman, looking wildly about her, "two hundred francs!" Her lips were trembling; someone roughly pushed her away.

"They're thieves," said Françoise.

"Everyone knows that," Gerbert agreed.

Françoise looked with curiosity at the cardsharp, whose deceptive hands were nimbly sliding about three bits of grimy cardboard on the black cover of the umbrella.

"Two hundred on this one," said a man, placing two hundred-franc notes on one of the cards. He winked slyly; one of the corners of the card was slightly bent and the king of hearts could be seen.

"And he wins," said the cardsharp turning up the king. The cards slipped through his fingers again.

"Here it is—watch the cards—keep your eyes peeled—here it is, here it is, here it is: two hundred francs on the king of hearts."

"That's the one. Who'll go a hundred with me?" said the man.

"A hundred francs! Here's a hundred francs," someone shouted.

"And he wins," said the sharp, throwing four crumpled notes down in front of him. He was letting them win to encourage the crowd. This would have been the time to bet, it was easy. Françoise guessed the whereabouts of the king at each deal. It made you dizzy to watch the quick shuffling of the cards; they slipped and flipped to right, to left, to center, to left.

"It's foolish," said Françoise. "You can see it every time."

"Here it is," said a man.

"Four hundred francs," said the sharp.

The man turned to Françoise. "I've only two hundred francs, here it is—put down two hundred francs with me," he said breathlessly.

Left, center, left, that was certainly the one. Françoise put down her two notes on the card.

"Seven of clubs," said the sharp, and he snatched up the notes.

"How stupid!" Françoise said. She stood there dumbfounded, like the old woman a few moments before; a quick little gesture—it couldn't be possible that the money was really lost—surely she could win it back. If she really paid attention to the next deal. . . .

"Come on," said Gerbert, "they're all stooges. Come on, or you'll lose your last sou."

Françoise followed him. "And when I know perfectly well that you can never win," she said angrily. This was just the sort of day for doing such stupid things. Everything was absurd—places, people, the things people said. How cold it was! Her mother had been right, this coat was much too light.

"Suppose we go and have a drink," she suggested.

"I'm all for it," said Gerbert. "Let's go to the big *café chantant*."

It was now almost dark. . . . *The lesson was over by this time, but no doubt they had not yet said good-bye. Where were they? Perhaps they have gone back to the Pôle Nord; when Xavière likes a place she immediately makes it her nest.* Françoise saw the leather-covered banquettes with their big copper nail-heads, and the windows, and the red and white checkered lamp shades, but it was all useless; the faces and the voices and the honey-flavored cocktails—they had all been clothed with a mysterious meaning which would vanish the moment Françoise opened the door. They would both smile affectionately, Pierre would continue their conversation and she would sit drinking something through a straw; but never would the secret of their tête-à-tête be revealed, not even by themselves.

"This is the café," said Gerbert. It was a kind of shed heated by enormous braziers and very crowded; an orchestra was blaringly accompanying a man dressed as a soldier.

"I'll have a marc," Françoise said, "that will warm me up." The clammy persistent drizzle had permeated her very being, she shivered; she did not know what to do with her body or her thoughts. She looked at the women wearing clogs and wrapped in big shawls drinking coffee and brandy at the bar. Why were the shawls always mauve? she wondered. The soldier had his face daubed with rouge; he was clapping his hands and leering obscenely, though he had not yet come to the smutty couplet.

"Would you mind paying now?" the waiter asked. Françoise took a sip from her glass; a violent flavor of gasoline and mildew filled her mouth. Suddenly, Gerbert burst out laughing.

"What is it?" Françoise asked; at that moment he didn't look a day over twelve.

"Smut always makes me laugh," he said, embarrassed.

"What was the word that made you laugh all of a sudden?"

"Squirt," said Gerbert.

"Squirt!"

"Oh, but I have to see it written!" Gerbert said.

The orchestra broke into a paso doble. On stage, next to the accordion player, stood a big doll in a sombrero, and it looked almost alive.

There was a long silence. *He'll be thinking again that he bores us,* Françoise thought regretfully. Pierre had not exerted himself very much to retain Gerbert's confidence; even in the most sincere of friendships he gave so little of himself! Françoise tried to shake herself out of this torpor; she had to explain a little to Gerbert why Xavière had taken such an important place in their lives.

"Pierre thinks that Xavière could become an actress."

"Yes, I know, he seems to think a lot of her," Gerbert said a little stiffly.

"She's a funny person," Françoise continued. "It isn't easy to be friends with her."

"She's a bit of an iceberg," said Gerbert. "I never know what to say to her."

"She will have nothing to do with the amenities," Françoise explained. "It may be noble, but it's also somewhat inconvenient."

"At the school she never says a word to anyone. She stays in a corner with her hair half covering her face."

"What exasperates her more than anything else," she continued, "is that Pierre and I are always on such good terms."

Gerbert looked astonished. "Yet, she knows how things are between you, doesn't she?"

"Yes, but she thinks people should be untrammelled where their emotions are concerned. She seems to think that constancy can only be achieved by continual compromise and lies."

"That's a laugh! She ought to see that you and Pierre have no need of that."

"Of course." She looked at Gerbert with some annoyance; love was, after all, less simple than he thought. It was stronger than time, but it existed in time, and there were continual misgivings, sacrifices and sometimes sadness. Naturally all that didn't really count, but only because she refused to let it count. A little effort was called for occasionally.

"Let me have a cigarette," she said, "it will give me the illusion of warmth."

Gerbert held out his packet with a smile; his smile was charming and nothing more, yet one might have found its appeal overwhelming; Françoise realized how enchanting those green eyes would have seemed to her if she had loved them. She had renounced all these treasures without even having known them; she would never know them. She did not regret their loss to her, although really they deserved regretting.

"It's a scream to watch Labrousse with little Pagès," said Gerbert. "He acts as if he's walking on eggs."

"Yes, for someone who's usually so interested in what he finds in people of ambition, taste, and courage, it's quite a change," Françoise said. "No one could care less about her future than Xavière. Quite a change, indeed."

"Is he really so fond of her?" Gerbert asked.

"It's not so easy to say just what being fond of someone means to Pierre," said Françoise. She stared in uncertainty at the tip of her cigarette. In the past, when she had spoken about Pierre, she had looked into herself; now, she had to stand off from him when she tried to discern his features. It was almost impossible to answer Gerbert. Pierre rejected the idea of consistency. He demanded continual progress and with the fury of a renegade offered up his past in sacrifice to his present. She thought she had held him enclosed in an enduring passion, made up of affection, sincerity and suffering, but he was already floating off like a sprite at the other end of time. He left behind in her hands a ghost whom he now sternly condemned from the higher plane of his newly attained virtues. The worst of it was that he begrudged his dupes for being able to content themselves with an image, and an out-of-date image at that. She crushed out her cigarette in the ashtray. In the past, she found it amusing that Pierre could never be bound to any moment. But she wondered to just what extent she herself was protected from those two who were now alone. Of course, Pierre would never admit to any complicity against her with anyone. But what about with himself? It was understood that he had no secret life; all the same, it required a positive will to believe to give this idea full meaning. Françoise was aware that Gerbert was observing her surreptitiously, and she pulled herself together.

"The point is she disturbs him," she said.

"Really!" Gerbert was very surprised; Pierre had always seemed so self-sufficient to him, so impervious, so perfectly shut up in himself; it was impossible to imagine any fissure through which misgivings could infiltrate. And yet, Xavière had breached this serenity. Or had she only revealed an imperceptible crack?

"I've often told you, that if Pierre stakes so much on the theater, on art in general, it's because of some sort of decision he's made," said Françoise. "And when you begin to question a decision, it's always disturbing." She smiled. "Xavière is a living question mark."

"Still, he's strangely stubborn on the subject," Gerbert objected.

"All the more reason. It stimulates him when someone insists in his face that drinking a cup of coffee is just as significant as writing *Julius Caesar*." Françoise's heart contracted. Could she really believe that in all these years Pierre had never had any doubts? Or was it simply that she had refused to worry about it?

"What do you think?" Gerbert asked.

"About what?"

"About the significance of a cup of coffee?"

"Oh, I!" Françoise said. She recalled a particular smile of Xavière's. "I want to be happy," she said with a curl of her lip.

"I don't see the connection."

"Introspection is tiring," she said. "It's dangerous." She was really like Elisabeth. Once and for all she had performed an act of faith, and she was now peacefully relying on evidence that did not exist. She would have had to re-examine everything from the beginning; but that required superhuman strength.

"And you? What do you think about it?"

"Oh, it all depends," said Gerbert with a smile, "on whether you feel like drinking or writing."

Françoise looked at him. "I've often wondered just what you expect to get out of your life," she said.

"First of all, I'd like to be sure they'll let me keep it for a while longer," he said.

Françoise smiled. "That's fair enough. But let's suppose that you have that much luck."

"Then I don't know." He thought for a moment. "Perhaps, in other times, I might have known better."

Françoise assumed an air of detachment. Perhaps if Gerbert failed to see the importance of the question he might answer.

"But are you satisfied with your life or not?"

"There are some good moments and others not so good," he said.

"Yes," said Françoise, a little disappointed. She hesitated a moment. "If you limit yourself to that, it's a little depressing."

"It depends on the day," Gerbert said. Then he made an effort. "Whatever they may say about life, it always seems to me to be just so many words."

"To be happy or unhappy—are they simply words to you?"

"Yes, I don't really understand what they mean."

"But you're rather gay by nature."

"I'm often bored."

He had said it calmly. Long periods of boredom, punctuated by short bursts of pleasure, seemed completely natural to him. "Good moments and others not so good." Wasn't he right, after all? she thought. Wasn't the remainder of time just illusion and literature? There they were sitting on a hard wooden bench; it was cold, and there were soldiers and family parties all round them. Pierre was sitting at another table with Xavière; they had smoked cigarettes and had had a few drinks, and had spoken words; and those sounds and the smoke had not been condensed into mysterious hours of forbidden intimacy that Françoise might envy; they were about to leave one another, and no bond would remain anywhere to bind them together. There was nothing anywhere to envy, or to regret, or to fear. The past, the future, love, unhappiness, were no more than sounds made with the mouth. Nothing existed except the musicians in their crimson blouses and the black-robed doll with a red scarf around its neck, its skirts, raised above a wide, embroidered petticoat, revealing a pair of thin legs. It was there; it was enough to fill one's eyes as they rested on it for an eternal present.

"Give me your hand, my beauty, and I'll tell your fortune." Françoise shuddered and automatically held out her hand to a handsome gypsy dressed in yellow and purple.

"Things aren't going as well for you as you'd really like, but have patience, you'll soon receive some news that will bring you happiness," recited the woman in one breath. "You have money, my beauty, but not as much as people think. You're proud and that's why you have enemies, but you'll triumph over all your enemies. If you come with me, my beauty, I'll tell you a little secret."

"Go ahead," Gerbert urged her.

Françoise followed the gypsy who produced a little piece of light-colored wood from her pocket.

"I'll tell you a secret. There's a dark young man in your life, you're very much in love with him, but you're not happy with him because of a blonde girl. This is a charm. You must put it into a small handkerchief and keep it on you for three days and then you'll be happy with the young man. I wouldn't give it to everybody, for this is a very precious charm; but I'll give it to you for a hundred francs."

"No thank you," said Françoise. "I don't want the charm. Here's something for the fortune."

The woman seized the coin. "A hundred francs for happiness is nothing. How much do you want to pay for your happiness, twenty francs?"

"Nothing at all," Françoise said. She went back and sat down beside Gerbert.

"What did she tell you?"

"Just a lot of twaddle," Françoise smiled. "She offered me happiness for twenty francs, but I found that too dear, if, as you say, it's nothing but a word."

"I didn't say that!" Gerbert said, startled to have involved himself to such an extent.

"Perhaps it's true," said Françoise. "With Pierre one uses so many words, but what exactly lies behind them?"

She was seized by a sudden anguish, so violent that she wanted to scream. It was as if the world had suddenly become a void; there was nothing more to fear, but nothing to love either. There was absolutely nothing. She was going to meet Pierre, they would exchange meaningless phrases, and then they would part. If Pierre's and Xavière's friendship was no more than a mirage, then neither did her love for Pierre and Pierre's love for her exist. There was nothing but an infinite accumulation of meaningless moments, nothing but a chaotic seething of flesh and thought, with death looming at the end.

"Let's go," she said abruptly.

Pierre was never late for an appointment, and when Françoise walked into the restaurant, he was already sitting at their usual table. A wave of joy swept over her when she caught sight of him. But immediately she thought, We have only two hours ahead of us, and her pleasure vanished.

"Have you had a pleasant afternoon?" Pierre asked affectionately. A broad smile expanded across his face and imparted a kind of innocence to his features.

"We went to the flea-market. Gerbert was charming, but the weather was so wretched. I lost two hundred francs betting on the three-card trick."

"What on earth made you do that? You are an idiot!" He smiled as he handed her the menu. "What will you have?"

"A Welsh rarebit," said Françoise.

Pierre studied the menu carefully. "There's no egg mayonnaise," he said. His look of perplexity and disappointment did not soften Françoise; she noted coldly that it was a touching face.

"Well, two Welsh rarebits, then."

"Would you like to know what we talked about?" Françoise asked.

"Of course I would," Pierre replied warmly.

She looked at him warily. In the past, she would have simply thought that he wanted to hear about it, and she would have told him at once; when he spoke to her or when he smiled at her, his words and his smiles were Pierre. Suddenly, they had become ambiguous symbols, deliberately created by him, and behind which his true feelings were hiding. All she could say was that he said he wanted to hear about it, and nothing more.

She put her hand on his arm. "You tell me first," she said. "What did you do with Xavière? Did you manage to get some work done?"

Pierre looked at her a little sheepishly. "Not much," he said.

"Well, really!" Françoise did not conceal her annoyance. Xavière had to work for her own sake and for theirs; she could not go on living for years as a parasite.

"We spent three quarters of the afternoon squabbling."

Françoise felt that she was controlling her expression, without really knowing what she was afraid of revealing.

"About what?" she asked.

"About her work," said Pierre smiling into space. "This morning in the pantomime class, Bahin asked her to walk in the woods and gather flowers; she told him with horror that she loathed flowers and she wouldn't budge. She told me about it with great pride and it made me furious." Quite calmly Pierre was drowning his steaming Welsh rarebit with Worcestershire sauce.

"And then?" Françoise asked with impatience. Pierre certainly was taking his time; he had no suspicion how important it was for her to know.

"Oh! That's simple," he went on, "she got furious. She had arrived, all sweetness and smiles, certain that I was going to pat her on the back, but I—well I practically wiped up the floor with her. She began to explain, but with that perfidious politeness of hers, that you and I were worse than any bourgeois couple because what we craved was moral comfort. She wasn't that far from wrong, but it put me in a hell of a temper. For over an hour we sat there at the Dôme facing each other without saying a word."

All those theories of Xavière's on the hopelessness of life, the futility of making any effort, became extremely irritating in the long run. Françoise held her peace, however; she did not want to keep criticizing Xavière.

"It must have been gay!" she said. This constraint, which caused a lump to rise in her throat, was stupid. Surely she had not reached the stage where she had to keep up appearances in front of Pierre!

"It's not an unpleasant sensation to feel yourself simmering with rage," he said. "I don't think she dislikes it either; but she has less resistance than I, and in the end she broke down. Then I made an attempt at reconciliation. That was difficult because she had immured herself in her hatred, but I won in the end." He added complacently, "We signed a solemn peace, and to seal the reconciliation she invited me to her room for tea."

. "To her room?" Françoise exclaimed. It was a long time since Xavière had invited her to her room, she felt a slight stab of resentment.

"Did you finally manage to drag some good resolutions out of her?"

"We talked about other things," Pierre said. "I told her all about our travels, and we pretended that we were on a trip together." He smiled. "We made up a number of little scenes. An encounter, in the heart of a desert, between an English woman on her travels and a famous adventurer—you know the sort of thing. She has imagination, if only she could make use of it."

"She has to be handled firmly," Françoise said a little reproachfully.

"Yes, I know," said Pierre. "Don't scold me." He had a queer smile, humble and seraphic. "All of a sudden she burst out, 'I'm having a wonderful time with you!'"

"Well, that's a triumph," Françoise said. *'I'm having a wonderful time with you . . .'* Had she been standing with a vague look in her eyes, or had she been sitting on the edge of the couch, looking straight at Pierre? There was no use in asking him. How could the exact tone of her voice or the scent of her room at that moment be described? Words

brought you nearer to the mystery, but without making it less impenetrable; it only spread a colder shadow over the heart.

"I can't quite make out her feelings toward me," Pierre went on
with a preoccupied air. "I think I'm gaining some ground, but the
ground is constantly shifting."

"You're progressing every day," Françoise assured him.

"When I left her, the signs were ominous again," he said. "She was
angry with herself for not having had her lesson, and she had a fit of
self-disgust." He looked gravely at Françoise. "Be very nice to her when
you see her later."

"I'm always nice to her," replied Françoise a little stiffly. Whenever
Pierre tried to tell her how she ought to behave to Xavière, she bristled;
she had no desire to go and see Xavière and be nice, now that it was
expected of her as a duty.

"That vanity of hers is terrible," she said. "She has to be certain of
an immediate and striking success before committing herself."

"It's not only vanity," he said.

"Then what is it?"

"She's told me a hundred times that she loathes the idea of stooping
to all this scheming and opportunism."

"And do you consider it 'stooping'?"

"I haven't any morals," Pierre said.

"Do you honestly think that her behavior is due to her moral sense?"

"In a way it is," Pierre replied with some annoyance. "She has a very
definite outlook on life, and she doesn't choose to compromise. That's
what I call morals. She's looking for completeness; and that's the kind
of exacting attitude we've always admired."

"There's a good deal of apathy in her case," said Françoise.

"Apathy, what is apathy?" exclaimed Pierre. "A way of shutting yourself up in the present; it's the only way in which she can find completeness. If the present has nothing to offer, she buries herself in her lair
like a sick animal. But you know, when you carry inertia to the point
she carries it, the word apathy no longer pertains; it assumes a kind of
power. Neither you nor I would have the moral strength to stay in a
room for forty-eight hours without seeing a soul or doing a thing."

"I don't deny it," said Françoise. She felt a sudden, painful need to
see Xavière; there was unusual warmth in Pierre's voice. Yet, admiration, he always insisted, was a feeling he had never known.

"On the other hand," Pierre said, "when something does appeal to her, it's quite amazing how she enjoys it; I feel very anemic by comparison; I almost feel humiliated."

"It must certainly be the first time in your life that you've experienced that sensation," Françoise said, with an attempt to laugh.

"When I left her, I told her she was like a little black pearl," Pierre said seriously. "She shrugged her shoulders, but I really meant what I said. Everything about her is so pure—and so violent."

"Why black?" said Françoise.

"Because of that kind of perversity of hers. It almost seems at times that she has a need to harm people, to harm herself, to make herself hated." He let his thoughts wander for a moment. "You know, it's curious. Often, if you tell her that you think highly of her, she shies off as if she were afraid; she feels herself fettered by our esteem."

"She's been quick enough about shaking off the fetters." Françoise hesitated; she almost wanted to believe in this seductive figure. If she often felt herself separated from Pierre, these days, it was because she had allowed him to progress alone down these paths of admiration and affection. Their eyes no longer saw the same things. Where she beheld only a capricious child, Pierre saw a wild and exacting soul. If she were willing to stand by his side once more, if she were to give up this obstinate resistance. . . .

"There's some truth in all that," she said. "I very often feel something pathetic about her." Again, she felt herself stiffen from head to foot; that alluring mask was a delusion, she would not yield to such witchcraft. She had not the faintest idea of what might happen to her if she were to yield. All she knew was that some danger was threatening her.

"But with her, a real friendship is impossible," she said bitterly. "Her selfishness is something monstrous. It isn't only that she considers herself superior to other people, she is utterly unaware of their existence."

"Still, she loves you very much," Pierre returned a little reproachfully. "And you're pretty severe with her, you know."

"It isn't a pleasant love," Françoise said. "She treats me as an idol and at the same time as a doormat. It's possible that somewhere in the depths of her secret self she contemplates my essence with adoration, but she treats this poor flesh-and-blood creature with a nonchalance that's sometimes embarrassing. It's quite understandable; an idol doesn't get hungry, or sleepy, or suffer from headaches; it is adored without being asked its opinion on the form of adoration it receives."

Pierre began to laugh. "There's some truth in that. You'll think I'm biased, but her inability to have warm relations with people makes me feel sorry for her."

Françoise, too, smiled. "I think you are slightly biased," she said.

They left the restaurant. Again they had talked about nothing but Xavière. When she was not with them, they spent the entire time talking about her; it was becoming an obsession. Françoise glanced sadly at Pierre. He had not asked her a single question, he was completely uninterested in the thoughts that had passed through her mind during the day; and when he seemed to be listening to her with interest, was it not only out of politeness? She pressed her arm against his, so that she might at least feel some contact with him. Pierre gently squeezed her hand.

"You know, I'm a little sorry I'm not sleeping at your hotel any more," he said.

"Still," said Françoise, "your dressing room does look very handsome now that it's been repainted."

It was a little frightening—the caressing phrase, the affectionate gesture. She saw them only as the results of his kindness; they weren't real, they didn't touch her. She shivered. Something had snapped in her. And now that doubt was growing, could it ever be stopped?

"Have a pleasant evening," Pierre said tenderly.

"Thanks, see you in the morning."

She watched him disappear through the small side door of the theater, and an agony of doubt assailed her. What was there beneath the phrases and gestures? We are one. This convenient fallacy had always served her as an excuse for not worrying about Pierre—but they were only words: they were two separate entities. She had felt it that evening at the Pôle Nord. That was what she had held as a grievance against him several days later. She had not wanted to face her misgivings, she had taken refuge in anger, so as not to see the truth; yet Pierre was not at fault, he had not changed. It was she, who for years had made the mistake of looking upon him only as a justification of herself. Today she realized that he lived his own life, and that the result of her blind trust was that suddenly she found herself facing a stranger. She quickened her pace. The only way she could bring herself nearer to Pierre was by being with Xavière and trying to see her through his eyes. How long ago the time when Françoise thought of Xavière simply as a part of her own life! Now it was toward a world that would never be quite open to her that she was hurrying with breathless and hopeless anxiety.

For a moment, Françoise stood motionless before the door. This room made her feel timid: it was really a holy place. Here more than one worship took place, but the supreme deity for whom there rose the smoke of cigarettes and the scent of tea and lavender was Xavière herself, as she saw herself with her own eyes.

Françoise knocked softly.

"Come in," a voice called gaily.

A little surprised, Françoise opened the door. Standing in her long green and white housecoat, Xavière was smiling, enjoying the astonishment she had clearly intended to arouse. A shaded lamp threw a deep red glow over the room.

"Would you like to spend the evening in my room?" she asked. "I've prepared a little supper." Beside the washstand, the kettle was purring on an alcohol stove, and in the dim half-light Françoise could make out two plates of multicolored sandwiches; she could not refuse, for despite her surface timidity, Xavière's invitations were always imperious orders.

"How sweet of you," she said. "If I'd known this was going to be a gala evening, I would have dressed for it."

"You look very beautiful as you are," said Xavière affectionately. "Make yourself comfortable. Look, I've bought some green tea. The tiny leaves look as if they're still alive, and you'll see in a moment how pungent it is."

She puffed out her cheeks and blew hard at the flame of the stove. Françoise was ashamed of her ill will. *It's true, I'm hard,* she thought, *I'm growing sour.* How bitter her voice had been just then, when she was talking to Pierre!

The rapt attention with which Xavière was bending over the teapot was certainly very disarming.

"Do you like red caviar?" Xavière asked.

"Oh, very much."

"I'm glad. I was afraid you might not like it."

Françoise looked at the sandwiches a little apprehensively. Slices of rye bread, cut in rounds, squares and diamonds were covered with some kind of colorful spread, with here and there an anchovy, an olive, or a slice of beet.

"No two are alike," Xavière announced proudly. She poured the steaming tea into a cup. "I had to put a drop of tomato sauce on a few of them," she added quickly, "it made them so much prettier, but you won't even taste it."

"They look delicious," Françoise said with resignation; she loathed tomatoes. She chose the sandwich that looked the least red. It had a queer taste, but was not too bad.

"Did you notice that I have some new photographs?" Xavière asked. On the green-and-red flowered wallpaper she had pinned a set of artistic nudes. Françoise carefully studied the long curved backs, the proffered breasts.

"I don't think Monsieur Labrousse thought them very pretty," Xavière said with a little pout.

"The blonde is perhaps a bit too fat," said Françoise, "but that little brunette is charming."

"She has a beautiful long neck like yours," said Xavière in a caressing voice.

Françoise smiled at her. She suddenly felt relieved, and all the melodramatics of the day vanished. She looked at the couch, at the armchairs covered with yellow, green, and red lozenges like a Harlequin costume. She liked the play of bold and faded colors in the dim light, and the scent of dead flowers and warm living flesh that always floated around Xavière. Pierre had not known more than this, and the face Xavière had turned toward him was no more moving than the one she now raised to Françoise. These charming features went to make up the honest face of a child, and not the disquieting mask of a witch.

"Do have some sandwiches," Xavière urged.

"I've really had enough."

"Oh!" said Xavière, looking downcast, "you don't like them!"

"Of course I like them," said Françoise reaching toward the plate. She was only too familiar with this gentle tyranny. Xavière did not try to make others happy; she selfishly delighted in the pleasure of giving pleasure. But should she be blamed for that? Wasn't she lovable this way? Her eyes shining with satisfaction, she watched Françoise swallow the thick tomato paste; one would have had to be made of stone not to be moved by her joy.

"I had a real thrill a little while ago," Xavière said, in a confidential tone.

"What was that?" asked Françoise.

"You know that handsome Negro dancer! He spoke to me."

"Look out that the blonde doesn't scratch your eyes out!" Françoise smiled.

"I met him on the stairs as I was coming back with my tea and all my little parcels." Xavière's eyes sparkled. "He was so nice! He had on a light-colored overcoat and a pale gray hat—it went so well with his dark skin. My parcels fell out of my hands. He picked them up for me and with a big smile said, 'Good evening, Mademoiselle, enjoy your dinner.'"

"And what did you answer?"

"Nothing!" said Xavière in a shocked tone. "I ran." She smiled. "He's as graceful as a cat, and he looks just as ruthless and treacherous."

Françoise had never really taken a good look at this Negro; beside Xavière, she felt prosaic. What reminiscences Xavière would have brought back with her from the flea-market! And all she had been able to see were filthy rags and tumble-down hovels.

Xavière refilled Françoise's cup.

"Did you work much this morning?" she asked with a fond look.

Françoise smiled. Xavière was obviously making advances; usually, she loathed the work Françoise devoted most of her time to.

"Quite a lot," Françoise said. "But I had to leave at noon and lunch with my mother."

"May I read your book some day?" Xavière asked with a coquettish little pout.

"Of course," said Françoise. "I'll show you the first chapters whenever you like."

"What's it about?" She sat down on a cushion, tucked her legs up under her, and blew lightly on her scalding tea. Françoise looked at her with a little remorse; she was touched by Xavière's interest; she really should have tried to carry on serious talks with her more often.

"It's about my youth," said Françoise. "I want to explain in my story why young people so often have a sense of inadequacy."

"Do you think we're inadequate?"

"Not you," said Françoise. "You were born immune." She thought a moment. "You see, when you're a child, you very easily resign yourself to being regarded as of little account, but at seventeen things change. You begin wanting to have a definite adult existence, but since you still *feel* the same inside, you foolishly look for external guarantees."

"How do you mean?" Xavière asked.

"You seek the approbation of others, you write down your thoughts, you compare yourself with accepted models. Take Elisabeth, for instance, in a sense, she has never passed that stage. She's a perennial adolescent."

Xavière laughed. "You're certainly not like Elisabeth," she said.

"I am, in a way. Elisabeth annoys us because she listens slavishly to Pierre and me, because she keeps remodeling herself. But if you study her sympathetically, you'll perceive in all that a clumsy attempt to give a definite value to her life and to herself as a person. Even her respect for the social formulas—marriage, fame—is still a form of this anxiety."

Xavière's face clouded slightly. "Elisabeth is a vain, pathetic jellyfish," she said. "That's all."

"No, that isn't precisely all," said Françoise. "You still have to understand the cause of it."

Xavière shrugged her shoulders. "What's the good of trying to understand people who aren't worth it?"

Françoise suppressed a movement of impatience. Xavière always felt injured as soon as anyone but herself was spoken of indulgently or even impartially.

"In a way, every one is worth it," she said to Xavière, who was listening with sulky attention. "Elisabeth is completely bewildered when she looks into herself, because all she finds is a void. She doesn't realize that it's the common fate. On the other hand, she sees other people from without, in the fullness of their words, gestures, and faces. It creates a kind of mirage."

"It's funny," said Xavière. "Usually, you don't make so many excuses for her."

"But it's not a question of excusing or condemning."

"I've already noticed that," Xavière said. "You and Monsieur Labrousse always make people out to be far too mysterious. But they're a lot simpler than that."

Françoise smiled. That was the reproach she had once made to Pierre—of taking pleasure in complicating Xavière. "They're simple if you look only at the surface!" she said.

"Perhaps," said Xavière, and her polite, indifferent tone definitely closed the discussion. She pushed away her cup and gave Françoise a winning smile.

"Do you know what the chambermaid told me?" she said. "There's someone in Room Nine who's both a man and a woman."

"Room Nine. That accounts for the rouged features and the booming voice," said Françoise. "The person you mean is dressed as a woman?"

"Yes, but he has a man's name. He's an Austrian. It seems that when he was born they couldn't make up their minds. Finally, they decided that he was a boy and when he was fifteen something happened to him that was decidedly feminine, but his parents didn't change his birth certificate." Xavière lowered her voice and added, "Besides, he has hair on his chest and other male characteristics. He was famous in his own country. They made a film about him and he made a lot of money."

"I should imagine that in the heydey of psychoanalysis and sexology, it must have been a godsend to be a hermaphrodite in Vienna," Françoise observed.

"Yes, but when there were all those political goings-on, you know," said Xavière vaguely, "he was driven out. Then she took refuge here. She's penniless and it seems that she's very unhappy because she likes men, but men won't have anything to do with her."

"Naturally, the poor thing! And with homosexuals she'd hardly fill the bill either."

"She cries all the time," said Xavière, looking wretched. She glanced at Françoise. "And it isn't her fault. Why should you be driven out of a country because you're made one way or another? People have no right to do that."

"Governments have the rights they take."

"I don't understand that," Xavière said disapprovingly. "Isn't there any country where people can do as they like?"

"No."

"Then I'll have to go to a desert island," said Xavière.

"Even desert islands belong to people now. So you're cooked."

Xavière shook her head. "Oh, I'll find a way," she said.

"I don't think so," said Françoise. "You'll have to learn to accept a number of things you don't like, just like everyone else." She smiled. "Does that idea disgust you?"

"Yes," said Xavière. She looked sideways at Françoise. "Did Monsieur Labrousse tell you that he was not pleased with my work?"

"He told me that you had a long talk about it," Françoise replied, adding gaily, "He was extremely flattered at having been invited to your room."

"Oh, it just happened," Xavière said abruptly.

She turned away to fill the kettle with water, and there was a brief silence. Pierre was wrong if he thought she had forgiven him; with Xavière, the last impression was no sure indication of her true feelings. She must have angrily thought over the events of the afternoon and been particularly infuriated by the final reconciliation.

Françoise looked at her thoughtfully. Wasn't this charming welcome just another form of exorcism? Had she not been taken in again? Surely the tea, the sandwiches, the beautiful green gown were not intended to honor her, but rather to deprive Pierre of a privilege foolishly granted. Françoise felt a lump in her throat. No, it was impossible to give herself up unreservedly to this friendship; she had a peculiar taste in her mouth, the taste of metal shavings.

7

"Won't you have some fruit salad?" Françoise said. She elbowed a
path to the buffet for Jeanne Harbley. Aunt Christine had never left
the table for an instant; she was now smiling adoringly at Guimiot,
who was eating a coffee ice with an air of condescension. Françoise
ran her eyes over the plates of sandwiches and petits fours to make
certain they still looked presentable. There were twice as many people
as had been at the previous New Year's Eve party.

"The decorations are lovely," said Jeanne Harbley.

For the tenth time Françoise answered, "Begramian is responsible
for them. He has excellent taste."

He did deserve some credit for his rapid transformation of a Roman
battlefield into a ballroom, but Françoise didn't really like all this pro-
fusion of holly, mistletoe and pine branches. She glanced around the
stage, looking for new faces.

"It was so nice of you to come! Labrousse will be so happy to see
you!"

"Where is the dear master?"

"Over there, with Berger, do go and rescue him."

Blanche Bouguet was hardly any more amusing than Berger, but
she would at least be a change. Pierre looked anything but festive.
From time to time his eyes roved apprehensively; he was worried about
Xavière, afraid that she would get drunk or suddenly leave. At that
moment she was sitting beside Gerbert on the proscenium, their legs
dangling over the edge, and they seemed horribly bored with each
other. The phonograph was playing a rumba, but the stage was too
crowded for anyone to dance on.

Well, it's just too bad about Xavière! thought Françoise. The eve-

142

ning was trying enough as it was; it would become intolerable if her criticisms and her moods had to be taken into account. *Just too bad!* Françoise repeated to herself, a little uncertainly.

"Are you leaving so soon? Oh, what a pity!" She followed Abelson's retreating figure with some satisfaction; when all the important guests were gone, she could afford to relax a little. Françoise made her way toward Elisabeth who, for the past half-hour, had been leaning against an upright, smoking and staring at nothing, and not speaking to a soul. But to cross the stage was like going on a perilous voyage.

"It was so nice of you to come! Labrousse will be so happy! He's in Blanche Bouguet's clutches, do try to rescue him." Françoise gained a few inches. "You look simply stunning, Marie-Ange. That blue with the purple is really lovely."

"It's a little ensemble I picked up at Lanvin's; it *is* pretty, isn't it?"

Several more handshakes, and several more smiles, and Françoise found herself at Elisabeth's side. "That was tough going," she said brightly. She suddenly felt very tired; she was often tired these days.

"It's a real fashion show tonight!" Elisabeth said. "Do you notice what ugly complexions all those actresses have?"

Elisabeth's own skin, puffy and rather yellowish, was not very beautiful either. *She's letting herself go,* thought Françoise. It was hard to believe that six weeks earlier, at the dress rehearsal, she had been almost dazzling.

"It's the grease paint," said Françoise.

"But their figures are wonderful," Elisabeth commented impartially. "When you think that Blanche Bouguet is over forty!" The bodies were young and so was the too exact coloring of the hair, and even the firm outline of the faces, but this youth had none of the freshness of living things, it was an embalmed youth; not a wrinkle, not a crow's-foot marred this carefully massaged flesh; but that worn look around the eyes was only the more disturbing. They were aging underneath, and they would go on aging for a long time before the glaze cracked; and then one day, suddenly, this flawless shell, grown thin as tissue paper, would crumble into dust, an old woman would emerge, complete in every detail, with wrinkles, large brown moles, swollen veins, and knotted fingers.

"Well-preserved women," said Françoise. "What a dreadful expression. It always makes me think of tinned lobster and of the waiter saying, 'It's every bit as good as the fresh.' "

"I don't think so much of the young, either," Elisabeth said. "Those young things are so badly turned out that they look like nothing on earth."

"Don't you think Canzetti is charming in the wide gypsy skirt? And look at the Éloy girl, and Chanaud! Obviously, the cut has much to be desired. . . ."

These dresses, many of them a little clumsy, had all the charm of the tentative lives of their wearers, reflecting their ambitious dreams, difficulties and resourceful ideas: Canzetti's wide yellow belt, the embroidery Éloy had plastered over the bodice of her dress were as intimate a part of them as their smiles. That was just the way Elisabeth used to dress.

"Believe me, these young hopefuls would give anything to look like Harbley or Bouguet," Elisabeth said bitterly.

"They certainly would, and if they make good, they'll be exactly like the others."

Françoise absorbed the scene at a glance: beautiful successful actresses, beginners, respectable failures, a whole host of separate faces went to make up this seething throng; it really made her a little dizzy. At certain moments, it seemed to Françoise that the orbits of these lives had intersected expressly for her at that particular point in time and space where she happened to be: at other moments it was quite the contrary; people seemed to be scattered about everywhere, everyone on his own.

"In any case, Xavière seems positively dowdy tonight," said Elisabeth. "Those flowers she's stuck in her hair—what atrocious taste!"

Françoise had spent some little time with Xavière arranging that modest spray, but she did not want to contradict Elisabeth; there was hostility enough in her expression even when she agreed with her.

"They're a riot, the two of them," Françoise said.

Gerbert was about to light a cigarette for Xavière, but he carefully avoided catching her eye in the process; he looked very prim and proper in an expensive dark suit that he probably had borrowed from Péclard. Xavière was obstinately staring at the tips of her little shoes.

"The whole time I've watched them, they haven't exchanged a word," said Elisabeth. "They're as shy as two lovers."

"They're frightened to death of each other," Françoise laughed. "It's a pity. They might have been good friends."

Elisabeth's malice did not affect her; her affection for Gerbert was completely devoid of jealousy, but it was not pleasant to feel herself so violently hated. It was almost an avowed hostility; Elisabeth had ceased to confide in her, and her every word, her every silence was a living reproach.

"Bernheim told me that you were definitely going on tour next year," Elisabeth said. "Is it true?"

"Of course it isn't true," Françoise said. "He's got it in his head that Pierre will end up by giving in, but he's wrong. Next winter Pierre's putting on his own play."

"Are you going to open the season with that?" Elisabeth asked.

"I don't know yet."

"It would be a pity to leave Paris," Elisabeth said, looking preoccupied.

"That's just what I think," Françoise agreed. She wondered with some surprise whether Elisabeth still hoped to get something out of Pierre; perhaps she was making up her mind to approach him again on the question of opening with Battier's play in October.

"The place is beginning to empty a little."

"I must see Lise Malan," said Elisabeth. "I hear that she has something important to tell me."

"And I'll go and rescue Pierre."

Pierre was shaking hands effusively, but try as he might, he could not put any warmth into his smiles. This was an art Madame Miquel had taken great pains to inculcate in her daughter.

I wonder where she stands with Battier, thought Françoise while showering good-byes and regrets. Elisabeth had got rid of Guimiot on the pretext that he had stolen some cigarettes from her, and she had patched it up with Claude, but it could not be going too well; she had never looked more dismal.

"Well, where's Gerbert gone to?" Pierre asked.

Xavière, with her arms hanging loosely at her sides, was standing alone in the middle of the stage.

"Why doesn't anyone dance?" he added. "There's plenty of room." There was irritation in his voice. With her heart a little heavy, Françoise scanned the face she had loved for so long in blind serenity; she had learned to read it; it was not reassuring that night; tense and set as it was, it seemed more fragile.

"Ten past two," she said. "Nobody else will come now."

Pierre was so constituted that he got little pleasure out of the moments when Xavière was pleasant to him; on the other hand, her slightest frown drove him wild with rage or remorse. To be at peace with himself, he had to feel that she was in his power. When people came between them, he was always disturbed and irritable.

"You're not too bored?" Françoise asked her.

"No," Xavière replied. "Only it's terrible to listen to good jazz and not be able to dance."

"But you can surely dance now," Pierre said. There was a moment's silence, during which all three smiled, but they found nothing to say.

"Later, I'll teach you the rumba," Xavière said to Françoise with a shade too much animation.

"I'd rather stick to the slow steps. I'm too old to rumba."

"How can you say that?" cried Xavière. She looked dolefully at Pierre. "She could dance very well if she wanted to."

"It's nonsense to say you're old!" Pierre said.

When he had come up to Xavière, he had deliberately allowed his face and voice to brighten. He could regulate every shade of expression with disturbing precision; he must have been extra touchy, for he actually felt none of the lighthearted, tender gaiety that was sparkling in his eyes.

"Exactly the same age as Elisabeth," said Françoise. "I've just seen her. It's not very consoling."

"Why talk about Elisabeth?" Pierre said. "Just look at yourself."

"She never looks at herself," Xavière said sorrowfully. "Someone ought to take moving pictures of her one day without her knowing it, and then show them to her as a surprise. Then she'd have to look at herself, and she'd be astounded!"

"She likes to think she's a stout, middle-aged woman," Pierre said. "If you only knew how young you look!"

"But I have no desire to dance," she said; this chorus of affection was making her feel ill at ease.

"Well, do you mind if we two dance?" Pierre asked.

Françoise watched them; they were a pleasure to look at. Xavière was as light as a puff of smoke, her feet scarcely touched the floor. Pierre's body, though heavy, gave the impression of being released from the laws of gravity and being controlled by invisible threads. He danced with the miraculous ease of a marionette.

I wish I knew how to dance, thought Françoise.

She had given it up ten years before. Now, it was too late to start over again. She drew aside a curtain and, in the darkness of the wings, lighted a cigarette. Here, at least, she would have a little respite. Too late. She would never be a woman who had absolute mastery over her body. Whatever she might acquire today was not important; all the embellishments would remain external to her. That was what it really meant to be thirty; a mature woman! She was forever a woman who did not know how to dance, a woman who had had only one love in her life, a woman who had not shot the Colorado River Canyon in a canoe, who had never crossed the Tibetan plateaus. These thirty years were not only a past that she dragged along behind her; they had settled all about her and within her. They were her present, her future. They were the very substance of which she was made. No heroism, no absurdity could change anything. Naturally, there was still time enough before her death to learn Russian, read Dante, see Bruges and Constantinople; she could still sprinkle her life from time to time with unexpected incidents, new talents; but none the less it would still remain, to the very end, this same life and none other; and her life could not be seen apart from herself. Françoise closed her eyes, suddenly dazzled by a painful white light that illuminated all her secret corners and left her without hope. She stood motionless for a moment watching the red tip of her cigarette glowing in the dark. A little laugh, hushed whisperings, roused her from her daydreaming; these dark corridors were always popular with couples. Silently, she moved away and went back to the stage. Everybody seemed to be thoroughly enjoying themselves.

"Where have you been?" Pierre asked. "We've just been talking to Paula Berger. Xavière thinks she's very beautiful."

"I've seen her," Françoise said. "I even invited her to stay on until morning." She was fond of Paula, but it was difficult to think of her apart from her husband and without the rest of their group.

"She's amazingly beautiful," said Xavière. "Not a bit like all these mannequins."

"She looks a little too much like a nun or a missionary," Pierre objected.

Paula was talking to Inès; she was wearing a long, high-necked, black velvet dress. Her red-gold hair was parted in the middle, framing a face that had a broad, smooth forehead and deep-set eyes.

"Her cheeks are a little ascetic," Xavière agreed, "but she has such a large generous mouth and such expressive eyes."

"Transparent eyes," Pierre said. He looked at Xavière and smiled. "Personally I prefer sultry eyes."

It was rather dishonest of Pierre to speak of Paula in that way, for he really admired her; he was taking a perverse pleasure in gratuitously sacrificing her to Xavière.

"She's really marvellous when she dances," said Françoise, "but it's miming rather than dancing. Her technique isn't very elaborate, but she can express almost anything."

"I'd love to see her dance!" said Xavière.

Pierre looked at Françoise. "Why don't you ask her," he said.

"I think that might be tactless."

"She doesn't usually need much persuasion."

"She intimidates me." Paula Berger was delightfully affable with everyone, but you never knew what she was thinking.

"Did you ever hear of Françoise being intimidated by anyone?" Pierre said, laughing. "It's the first time!"

"It would be so lovely!" Xavière begged.

"All right, I'll do it." Smiling, she walked towards Paula Berger. Inès looked depressed. She was wearing a striking red moiré dress and a gold net over her light hair. Paula's eyes were gazing into hers, and she was speaking in an encouraging and slightly motherly tone. She turned to Françoise vivaciously. "Isn't it true that on the stage all the talent in the world amounts to nothing if you don't have courage and faith?"

"Of course," Françoise agreed. That was not the question and Inès knew it only too well, but still she looked rather pleased.

"I've come to make a request," Françoise said. She felt herself blushing and was aware of a sudden fury against Pierre and Xavière. "If you'd rather not, please be perfectly frank, but we would be so happy if you would dance for us."

"I'd like to," said Paula, "but I have neither my music nor my props." She smiled her apologies. "I dance with a mask now, and a long dress."

"That must be beautiful," said Françoise.

Paula looked at Inès hesitantly. "Inès could play the accompaniment for the dance of the machines," she said, "and then I'll do the charwoman without music. But you know that one."

"That doesn't matter. I'd love to see it again," said Françoise. "It's so good of you. I'll go and turn off the phonograph."

Xavière and Pierre were watching her with an air of conspiracy and amusement.

"She'll do it," Françoise announced.

"You are a good ambassador," Pierre said. He looked so childishly happy that it astonished Françoise. Her eyes were fixed on Paula Berger and Xavière stood waiting, entranced. There was this childlike joy reflected in Pierre's face.

Paula moved to the middle of the stage. She was not yet very well known to the general public, but here everyone admired her art. Canzetti was sitting on her heels, her wide mauve skirt spread out all round her. Éloy had assumed a seductive pose on the floor a few feet from Tedesco. Aunt Christine had disappeared, and Guimiot, standing beside Mark Antony, smiled coyly. Everyone seemed interested. Inès struck the first chords on the piano. Slowly, Paula's arm came to life, the slumbering machine was beginning to operate. Little by little the rhythm accelerated, but Françoise saw neither the driving rod, nor the rotating wheels, nor any of the motions of steel. She saw only Paula. A woman of her own age, a woman who also had her history, her work, and a life of her own; a woman who was dancing without giving Françoise a thought; and when, a little later, she would smile at her, it would only be to one among many other spectators. To her, Françoise was no more than a piece of scenery.

If only it were possible to calmly prefer oneself to all others, thought Françoise with anguish.

At that moment, there were thousands of women all over the world listening breathlessly to the beating of their own hearts; each woman to her own heart, each woman for herself. How could she believe that she was the center of the world? There were Paula, and Xavière, and so many others. She could not even compare herself with them.

Françoise's hands slowly fell to her side.

Just what am I? she wondered. She looked at Paula. She looked at Xavière whose face radiated shameless admiration. She knew what these women were. They had their own special memories, tastes, and ideas which distinguished them, personalities that were expressed in their features. But in herself Françoise could not see any clear-cut shape. The light that had flashed through her a short while before had revealed nothing but emptiness. "She never looks at herself," Xavière had said. It was true. She never gave her face a thought except to take care of it as something impersonal. She searched her past for landscapes and people, but not for herself; and it was not her ideas and her tastes that made her face what it was. That face only reflected the truths that had revealed themselves to her, and they no more belonged to her than the bunches of mistletoe and holly that hung from the flies.

I am no one, she thought. Often she had taken pride in not being circumscribed like other people in narrow individual boundaries, as on that night, not so very long ago, at the Prairie, with Elisabeth and Xavière. She thought of herself as a consciousness naked before the world. She touched her face: to her it was no more than a white mask. And yet all these people saw it; and, whether she liked it or not, she too was in the world, a part of this world. She was a woman among other women, and she had permitted this woman to grow at random without shaping her. She was utterly incapable of passing any judgment on this unknown entity. And yet Xavière had judged her, had compared her with Paula. Which of them did she prefer? And Pierre? When he looked at her what did he see? She turned her eyes toward Pierre, but Pierre was not looking at her.

He was looking at Xavière. With parted lips and eyes filled with tears, Xavière scarcely breathed. She no longer knew where she was; physically she didn't exist. Françoise looked away, embarrassed. Pierre's insistence was indiscreet and almost obscene; that rapt face was not for public view. Françoise could at least be certain of one thing—she would never have been capable of going into such passionate trances. She did know with reasonable certainty what she was not; it was agonizing to know herself only in a series of negatives.

"Have you seen Xavière's face?" Pierre asked.

"Yes," said Françoise.

He had spoken without taking his eyes off Xavière.

That's the way it is, thought Françoise. Her features were no more distinct to him than they were to herself; amorphous, invisible, she was vaguely a part of him. He spoke to her as to himself, but his eyes remained fixed on Xavière. At this moment, with distended lips, and two tears trickling down her pale cheeks, Xavière was beautiful.

Applause broke out.

"I must thank Paula," said Françoise, thinking, *And for me, I don't feel a thing.* She had hardly watched the dance; she had been gloating over her own thoughts like an old woman with her obsessions.

Paula accepted her congratulations gracefully; Françoise admired her for knowing so perfectly how to behave.

"I feel like sending home for my dress and my records and masks," she said. She turned her large candid eyes to Pierre. "I'd like so much to know what you think."

"I am very curious to see along what lines you are working at present," Pierre said. "There are so many possibilities in what you've just shown us."

The phonograph was playing a paso doble and couples were beginning to dance again.

"Dance this with me," Paula said authoritatively to Françoise. Françoise followed her docilely. She heard Xavière say sulkily to Pierre, "No, I don't want to dance."

It made her suddenly furious. Again she was in the wrong. Xavière was fuming and Pierre was going to reproach her because of Xavière's rage. Paula led so well that it was a pleasure dancing with her; Xavière had no conception of how to lead.

There were some fifteen couples on the stage; others were scattered in the wings and in the boxes; one group was sitting in the balcony. Suddenly, Gerbert leapt up from the proscenium like a bounding elf; Mark Antony was in pursuit, miming a dance of seduction, and, in spite of his somewhat massive body, with great vivacity and grace. Gerbert seemed a little drunk and his long black hair kept falling over his eyes. He would stop with hesitant, mock modesty, then dash away again, coyly hiding his face against his shoulder; he would dart away and return again, faunlike and provocative.

"They're charming," Paula smiled.

"The joke is," Françoise said, "that Ramblin really is like that. What's more, he makes no bones about it."

"I have always wondered whether that feminine quality he gives Mark Antony was due to art or nature."

Françoise glanced at Pierre. He was talking animatedly to Xavière who hardly seemed to be listening to him; she was watching Gerbert with a strangely eager and fascinated look. Françoise was hurt by this look; it was like a secret and imperious possessiveness.

The music stopped and Françoise left Paula.

"I can make you dance, too," Xavière cried as she seized Françoise. She put her arm around her, her muscles taut, and Françoise wanted to smile as she felt the small hand tighten against her waist; with a feeling of tenderness, she inhaled that odor of tea, honey and skin—Xavière's odor.

If I could have her to myself, I would love her, she thought. This domineering little girl, too, was nothing more than a tiny fragment of the warm, defenseless world.

But Xavière did not persevere in her efforts: she soon began, as usual, to dance for herself, without a thought for Françoise, and Françoise could not follow her.

"It's not going so well," Xavière said with a look of discouragement. "I'm dying of thirst," she added. "Aren't you?"

"Elisabeth is at the buffet," Françoise remarked.

"What does that matter?" said Xavière. "I want something to drink."

Elisabeth was talking to Pierre. She had danced several times and seemed a little less gloomy; she had been gossiping and now gave a little giggle. "I was telling Pierre that Eloy has spent the entire evening hanging around Tedesco," she said. "Canzetti is simply furious."

"Éloy looks very well tonight," Pierre said. "Her hair like that changes her. She's more attractive than I thought."

"Guimiot says she throws herself at the head of every man she meets."

"At the head. That's one way of putting it," Françoise smiled. The words had slipped out. Xavière did not bat an eyelash, perhaps she had not understood. When conversation with Elisabeth was not strained, it was apt to become bawdy. It was annoying to feel this virtuous little person at her side.

"They all treat her like the lowest of door mats," Françoise went on. "And what's so funny is that she's a virgin, and determined to remain one."

"Is it a complex?"

"It's for the sake of her complexion," Françoise rejoined with a laugh. She stopped. Pierre seemed not to be enjoying this.

"Aren't you dancing any more?" he hurriedly asked Xavière.

"I'm tired."

"Are you interested in the stage?" Elisabeth asked in her most engaging manner. "Do you really feel it to be your vocation?"

"You know, when you first start, it's rather thankless," Francoise put in.

There was a silence; Xavière was a mass of resentment from head to foot. Whenever she was there, everything assumed such tremendous importance that it became oppressive.

"What about you, are you working now?" Pierre asked.

"Oh, yes. I've nothing to complain about," Elisabeth said, adding casually, "Lise Malan has been throwing out hints that Dominique would like me to decorate her night club. I might accept."

Françoise had the impression that Elisabeth would have preferred to keep the secret, but that she could not resist her desire to impress them.

"Accept it!" said Pierre. "That's a job with a future. Dominique will make a fortune with that joint."

"Little Dominique," said Elisabeth laughing. "It's funny!" Elisabeth always classified people once and for all. All possibility of change was excluded from this rigid universe where she sought so stubbornly to find landmarks.

"She has a lot of talent," Pierre said.

"With me she was charming. She's always had a tremendous admiration for me." Elisabeth's voice was perfectly matter-of-fact.

Françoise felt Pierre's foot kicking her under the table as he said, "You simply must keep your promise. You're far too lazy. Xavière is going to make you dance this rumba."

"All right!" said Françoise in a tone of resignation. She rose and went off with Xavière.

"It's just so that we can get away from Elisabeth," she said. "We'll only dance a minute."

Pierre crossed the stage. "I'll wait for both of you in your office," he said. "We'll have a quiet drink up there."

"We might ask Paula and Gerbert?" Françoise suggested.

"No. Let's just the three of us go," Pierre's tone was a little curt.

He disappeared. Françoise and Xavière followed shortly afterward. On the stairway, they passed Begramian ardently kissing the Chanaud girl. A chain of dancers swept across the first-floor landing.

"At last we'll have a little peace," Pierre said.

Françoise took a bottle of champagne from her cupboard; it was good champagne, kept for special guests. There were also some sandwiches and petit fours which would be served at dawn before the party finally broke up.

"Here, uncork this for us," she said handing the bottle to Pierre. "The dust you swallow on that stage is amazing, it makes your throat so dry."

Pierre skillfully popped the cork and filled the glasses.

"Are you having a good time?" he asked Xavière.

"Heavenly!" she said. She drained her glass and began to laugh. "Goodness, you looked so important when you were talking to that stout fellow. I thought I was looking at my uncle!"

"And now?" asked Pierre. The tenderness that flitted across his face was still restrained and almost veiled; a slight change of expression would have been enough to restore a mask of smooth indifference.

"Now, it's you again," said Xavière, pouting.

The restraint vanished from Pierre's face, and Françoise eyed him with uneasy concern. In the past, whenever she looked at Pierre, she had seen the whole world through him, but now she saw only him. Pierre was precisely where his body was, a body that could be focused in a single glance.

"That stout fellow?" Pierre asked. "Do you know who that was? Berger—Paula's husband."

"Her husband?" For a second, Xavière seemed disconcerted; then she said sharply, "She does not love him."

"She's strangely attached to him," Pierre said. "She was married before, had a child, and she got a divorce so that she could marry him; all of which caused a great to-do because she comes from a very devout Catholic family. Have you ever read any of Masson's novels? He's her father. She's very much the great man's daughter."

"She's not in love with him, not really," Xavière insisted with a little blasé air. "People get into such muddles!"

"I like your gems of worldly wisdom," Pierre said gaily. He smiled at Françoise. "If you'd only heard her a little while ago! Young Gerbert is the sort of chap who is so in love with himself, he doesn't even bother to make himself agreeable! . . ." He had imitated Xavière's voice to perfection and she looked at him half in amusement and half in anger.

"The worst of it is that she's often right," smiled Françoise.

"She's a witch," Pierre said tenderly.

Xavière laughed foolishly, as she did when she was very happy.

"What I think can be said about Paula Berger is that she's frigidly passionate," said Françoise.

"She can't possibly be frigid," Xavière said. "I adore her second dance. At the end, when she falters with fatigue, she gives the impression of such utter exhaustion that it's almost voluptuous." Her fresh lips had slowly picked off each syllable of the word vo . . lup . . tu . . ous.

"She knows how to evoke sensuality," Pierre said, "but I don't think she herself is sensual."

"She's a woman who is aware of her body," Xavière said with a smile of hidden connivance.

I am not aware of my body, thought Françoise. That was another lesson learned, but what was the use of adding to the sum total of negatives.

"In that long black dress," Xavière said, "when she stands motionless, she makes me think of those stiff, medieval virgins; but when she moves, she's like a bamboo in the wind."

Françoise refilled her glass. She was not in the conversation. She, too, might have commented on Paula's hair, her lithe figure, the curves of her arms, yet she had stayed out of it because Pierre and Xavière were so deeply engrossed in what they were saying. There was a long empty silence. Françoise had ceased to follow the ingenious arabesques the voices were weaving in the air. Then she heard Pierre saying, "Paula Berger is pathos, and pathos is yielding. Pure tragedy for me was in your face while you were watching her."

Xavière blushed. "I made a spectacle of myself," she said.

"No one noticed it," Pierre reassured her. "I envy you for feeling things so intensely."

Xavière stared at the bottom of her glass. "People are so funny," she said, ingenuously. "They all applauded, but no one seemed really moved. Perhaps it's because you know so many things, but even you do not seem to see the difference." She shook her head and added sternly, "It's very strange. You spoke to me about Paula Berger in an offhand way, much as you speak about someone like Harbley, and you dragged yourself to this party tonight just as if you were going to work. I've never had such a wonderful time."

"That's true," Pierre said. "I don't discriminate enough." He stopped. There was a knock at the door.

"Excuse me," said Inès entering. "I came up to tell you that Lise Malan is going to sing her latest numbers, and then Paula will dance. I went to fetch her music and her masks."

"We'll come down in a moment," said Françoise.

Inès closed the door.

"We were so comfortable here," Xavière pouted.

"I don't give a damn for Lise's songs," said Pierre. "We'll go down in a quarter of an hour." As a rule, he never made a final decision without consulting Françoise; she felt the blood mounting to her cheeks.

"That's not very kind," she said. Her voice sounded more abrupt than she would have wished, but she had drunk too much to be able to control it perfectly. It was gross discourtesy not to go down; surely they were not going to start following Xavière in all her whims.

"They won't even notice our absence," said Pierre with finality.

Xavière smiled at him. Each time something, or more especially someone, was sacrificed for her, a look of angelic sweetness spread over her face.

"We ought never, never to leave this room," she said, and laughed. "We'll lock the door, and we can have our meals sent up from outside on a rope."

"And you'll teach me to discriminate," said Pierre.

He smiled affectionately at Françoise. "She's a little witch," he said. "She looks at things with virgin eyes, and lo and behold, the things begin to exist for us exactly as she sees them. In the old days we would go around shaking hands, and it was nothing but an endless series of little worries. Thanks to her, this is a real New Year's Eve tonight!"

"Yes," said Françoise.

Pierre's words were not intended for her, nor for Xavière; Pierre had spoken for himself. That was the greatest change of all: formerly, he had lived for the stage, for Françoise, for ideas; one could always work with him; but there was absolutely no way of participating in his relations with himself. Françoise drained her glass. She would have to make up her mind once and for all to face all the changes that had taken place; for days and days now her thoughts had carried a tinge of bitterness, the kind she felt Elisabeth must feel in her heart of hearts. But she must not be like Elisabeth.

I want to see clearly, Françoise said to herself. But her head was only a whirling fiery turmoil. "We must go down," she said brusquely.

"Yes, now we really must," Pierre conceded.

Xavière's face tightened. "But I want to finish my champagne," she said.

"Drink it down," said Françoise.

"But I don't want to pour it down, I want to sip it while I finish my cigarette." She threw herself back in her chair. "I don't want to go down."

"You were so anxious to see Paula dance," said Pierre. "Come along, we simply must go down."

"Then go without me." She settled herself more comfortably in her armchair and repeated stubbornly, "I want to finish my champagne."

"All right, we'll see you presently," Françoise said, opening the door.

"She'll finish all the bottles," Pierre said uneasily.

"She's intolerable with all her caprices!"

"This wasn't a caprice," rejoined Pierre acidly. "She was happy to have us to herself for a while."

Naturally, the moment Xavière seemed fond of him, he found nothing to criticize; Françoise almost told him so, but she held her tongue. There were so many thoughts that she now kept to herself.

Am I the one who has changed? she wondered. She was suddenly appalled to feel how much hostility she had put into her thought.

Paula was wearing a kind of gandoura of white wool; in her hand she held a mask of closely woven mesh. "I'm nervous, you know," she said, smiling.

Very few people were left. Paula's face disappeared behind the mask; wild music burst from the wings and she leapt onto the stage. She was miming a storm. She was a hurricane personified. Sharp, pulsating rhythms, inspired by Hindu music, controlled her movements. Suddenly the fog in Françoise's head lifted, and she saw clearly what lay between herself and Pierre. They had built beautiful, faultless structures in the shadows of which they had taken shelter, and they had not given any further thought to what these structures contained. Pierre still repeated, "We are one," but now she had discovered that he lived only for himself. Without losing its perfect form, their love, their life, was slowly losing its substance, like those huge, apparently invulnerable cocoons, the soft integument of which conceals microscopic worms that painstakingly consume them.

I'll speak to him, Françoise thought, and she felt relieved; there was a danger ahead, but they would face it together; they must above all be more watchful of each passing moment. She turned toward Paula and concentrated on watching her beautiful gestures, without allowing her mind to wander.

"You ought to give a recital as soon as possible," Pierre said warmly.

"Ah, I wonder," Paula replied with a note of uncertainty. "Berger says that it is not an art which can stand by itself."

"You must be tired," Françoise said. "I have some fairly good champagne upstairs, we'll drink it in the foyer; we'll be much more comfortable there than here."

The stage floor was far too vast for the few people who were left, and it was strewn with cigarette ends, fruit pips, and scraps of paper.

"Would you collect the records and glasses," Françoise said, turning to Canzetti and Inès. She drew Pierre towards the switch box and pulled down the levers.

"I want to break it up quickly, and then I'd like the two of us to go for a walk together," she said.

"Gladly," said Pierre. He looked at her questioningly. "Don't you feel well?"

"Of course I feel well," she said, with a shade of annoyance. Pierre did not seem to think that she could be hurt in any way but physically. "But I want to see you. This sort of party wears one out."

They began to climb the stairs and Pierre took her by the arm. "I thought you looked a little low," he said.

She shrugged her shoulders; her voice trembled slightly. "When you look at people's lives—Paula, Elisabeth, Inès—it gives you such a peculiar impression. You begin wondering how yours would look if you could see it from the outside."

"You're not satisfied with your life?" Pierre said anxiously.

Françoise smiled. It was not so very serious. After all, as soon as she had explained things to Pierre, it would all be forgotten.

"The trouble is when you can't have proofs," she began, "everything requires an act of faith." She stopped. With a tense and almost agonized expression, Pierre was staring at the door at the head of the stairs, behind which they had left Xavière.

"She must be dead drunk," he said.

He dropped Françoise's arm and rushed up the last steps. "There's not a sound."

For a moment he stood motionless. The anxiety which now strained his face was not the same kind of anxiety Françoise had stirred in him, and to which he had calmly responded; this time he was shaken in spite of himself.

Françoise felt the blood ebbing from her cheeks. Had he suddenly struck her, the shock could not have been more violent. She would never forget how his friendly arm had unhesitatingly withdrawn from her own.

Pierre pushed open the door. On the floor, in front of the window,

Xavière lay sound asleep, curled up into a ball. Pierre bent over her. Françoise took a carton of food and a butler's basket filled with bottles from the cupboard and left without a word. She wanted to get away, anywhere, to try to think, and to be able to cry. So it had come to this. A pout from Xavière was more important than all her own distress; and yet Pierre kept on telling her that he loved her.

The phonograph was grinding out some old melancholy refrain. Canzetti took the basket from Françoise's hands and went behind the bar. She passed the bottles to Ramblin and Gerbert who, along with Tedesco, were perched on stools. Paula, Berger, Inès, Éloy and Chanaud were seated near the big bay windows.

"I'd like a little champagne," said Françoise.

Her head was throbbing. She felt as if something inside her—an artery, or her ribs, or her heart—were going to burst; she was not accustomed to suffering; it was, literally, unbearable. Canzetti was walking toward her, with precaution, carrying a brimming glass; her long skirt gave her the dignity of a young priestess. Suddenly Éloy stepped between them, also holding forth a glass of champagne. For a second, Françoise hesitated and then she took the glass from Éloy.

"Thank you," she said, and she smiled at Canzetti with a look of apology. Canzetti threw Éloy a mocking glance.

"One gets even when one can," she murmured between her teeth; and also between her teeth, Éloy answered something that Françoise did not catch.

"How dare you! And in front of Mademoiselle Miquel!" cried Canzetti.

Her hand struck Éloy's pink cheek. Éloy looked at her for a moment, too surprised to move, then she hurled herself upon Canzetti. They grabbed each other by the hair and began struggling, their faces set. Paula Berger jumped up.

"What's come over you?" she said, laying her beautiful hands on Éloy's shoulders.

A shrill laugh rang out. Xavière was coming toward them, with glazed eyes, and looking as white as chalk. Pierre was directly behind her. Every face turned toward them. Xavière's laugh stopped short.

"That music is horrible," she said. With a look of sullen determination, she walked toward the phonograph.

"Wait, I'll put on another record," Pierre said.

Françoise looked at him in pained bewilderment. Up to then, when she thought: "We are separate," that separation was a misfortune that struck the both of them, one that together they could remedy. Now she understood that to be separate meant to live out the separation alone.

Her forehead pressed against a windowpane, Éloy was quietly weeping. Françoise put her arm around her shoulder. She felt a slight repulsion for this plump little body, so often pawed, yet so immaculate, but it was a convenient excuse.

"You mustn't cry," Françoise said, her mind a blank; there was something soothing about these tears and this warm flesh. Xavière was dancing with Paula, Gerbert with Canzetti. Their faces were expressionless, their movements feverish. For every one of them, this night was already an old story which was turning into weariness, deception, regret, and making them sick at heart. One felt that they found no pleasure in being there, but yet dreaded going home. All of them would have liked to curl up on the floor and fall asleep, as Xavière had done. Françoise herself had no other desire. Outside, one could distinguish the black outlines of the trees against the pale dawn sky.

Françoise shivered. Pierre was at her side. "I ought to take a look around before leaving," he said. "Are you coming with me?"

"Yes," said Françoise.

"We'll see Xavière home and then we'll go to the Dôme, just the two of us. It's nice there in the early morning."

"Yes," said Françoise.

There was no need for him to be so kind to her; what she wanted was to have him turn to her, just for once, that artless face he had bent over the sleeping Xavière.

"What's the matter?" he said. The theater was plunged in darkness and he could not see that Françoise's lips were trembling. She pulled herself together.

"Nothing, what should be the matter? I'm not ill, the evening went off well. Everything's fine."

Pierre seized her wrist. Abruptly she freed herself.

"Perhaps I've drunk too much," she said with an attempt to laugh.

"Sit down here," Pierre said, and he sat beside her in the first row of seats. "And tell me what's come over you. You act as if you were angry with me. What have I done?"

"You haven't done anything," she said softly. She took his hand. It was unfair to be angry with him, he was so perfect with her. "Of course you've done nothing," she repeated in a choked voice. She dropped his hand.

"It isn't because of Xavière, is it? She can't change anything between us, you know that. But you also know that if this affair is in the very least distasteful to you, you need only say the word."

"That's not the question," she said quickly. It was not by sacrifices that he could bring joy back to her; certainly in all their joint activities, he always put Françoise above everything. But today she was not looking to this man encased in ethical scruples and deliberate tenderness for help; she longed to reach him, in his nakedness, beyond esteem and hierarchies and self-approbation. She forced back her tears.

"It's just that I feel our love is growing old," she said. And suddenly she began to cry.

"Old?" Pierre said, shocked. "But my love for you has never been stronger. What makes you think that?" It was only natural for him to try at once to reassure her—and to reassure himself.

"You don't realize it," she said, "and that's not surprising. You've so set your mind on this love of ours, that you've put it in safekeeping, beyond time, beyond life, beyond reach. From time to time, you think about it with satisfaction, but what has actually become of it, you never look to see." She burst into sobs. "But I—I want to look," she said, swallowing her tears.

"Calm yourself," Pierre said, pressing her to him. "I think you're talking nonsense."

She pushed him away; he was wrong, she was not talking just for the sake of being calmed. It was much too simple to dismiss her thoughts in this way.

"I'm not talking nonsense. Perhaps it's because I'm drunk that I'm talking tonight, but I've been thinking about it for days."

"You might have told me sooner," he said in an irritated tone. "I don't understand. What are you reproaching me with?" He was on the defensive; he had a horror of being in the wrong.

"I'm not reproaching you with anything," said Françoise. "You can have a perfectly clear conscience. But is that the only thing that counts?" she cried fiercely.

"I can't make head or tail of this scene. I love you. You ought to know that, but if it pleases you not to believe it, I have no way of proving it to you."

"Faith, always faith," said Françoise. "That's how Elisabeth succeeds in believing that Battier loves her and perhaps in believing that she still loves him. Evidently, that makes everything secure. Your feelings must always wear the same faces, all neatly arranged around you, immutable. And even if there's nothing inside it's all the same to you. They're like the white sepulchers of the Holy Bible—they sparkle on the outside. They're firm, they're faithful, they can even be white-washed periodically with beautiful words." She was again overcome by a flood of tears. "Only, they must never be opened, because you'll find only dust and ashes inside." She repeated, "Dust and ashes." It was blinding evidence. "Oh," she said, hiding her face in the crook of her arm.

Pierre pulled her arm away. "Stop crying," he said. "I'd like to talk reasonably."

Presently he would find a whole slue of lovely arguments, and it would be so easy to give in to them. Françoise did not want to lie to herself, like Elisabeth; she saw things too clearly. She kept on sobbing.

"But it's not as serious as all that," he said gently. He gave her hair a light caress.

"It *is* serious. I know what I'm saying. Your feelings are unchangeable. They can endure for centuries because they're embalmed. It's like all these women." She thought with horror of Blanche Bouguet's face, "It doesn't move; it's like a mummy's."

"You're being impossible," Pierre said. "Either cry or talk, but not both at once." He pulled himself together. "It's true I'm not much given to lovelorn agonies. But are they proof of love? Why does it suddenly shock you today? You've always known I was like that."

"And take your friendship for Gerbert," Françoise went on. "It's the same thing. You hardly see him nowadays, but you shout to high heaven if I say that you've grown less fond of him."

"I don't have much need to see people, that's quite true."

"You don't need anything," said Françoise, "it's all the same to you." She was crying desperately. She loathed the thought of that moment when she would cease crying and return to the world of merciful deception. If she could only find some spell that would arrest the present moment forever.

"Are you there?" asked a voice.

Françoise sat up; it was astonishing how quickly those relentless tears could stop. Ramblin's outline emerged from the shadow of the doorway, and he came forward laughing.

"I'm being trailed. That Éloy girl dragged me into a dark corner, telling me how wicked the world was, and there she attempted to deliver a frontal attack upon my person." He assumed the modest attitude of the Venus de Medicis. "I had the greatest difficulty defending my virtue."

"She's out of luck tonight," said Pierre. "She tried in vain to seduce Tedesco."

"If Canzetti hadn't been there, I don't know what would have happened," Françoise said.

"Please note that I have no prejudices," Ramblin continued, "but I find such behavior unhealthy."

He perked up his ears attentively. "Do you hear?"

"No," said Françoise. "What is it?"

"I can hear someone breathing."

A faint noise was coming from the stage. It did, indeed, sound like breathing.

"I wonder who it is?" Ramblin said.

They climbed onto the stage. It was pitch black.

"To the right," said Pierre.

A body was lying behind the velvet curtain; they bent over it.

"Guimiot! It would have surprised me if he'd gone home before the last bottle had been emptied."

Guimiot had a beatific smile, his head resting on his crooked arm. He was really very charming, Françoise thought.

"I'll wake him, and bring him upstairs for you," Ramblin said.

"We'll finish our rounds," said Pierre.

The greenroom was now empty. Pierre shut the door.

"I'd like to talk things over," he said. "I find it very distressing that you should doubt our love." His face showed honest concern, and Françoise, looking at him, was moved.

"I don't think you've stopped loving me," she murmured.

"But you said that we're dragging an old corpse at our heels. That's so unfair! First of all, it's not true that I don't need to see you. The minute you're not with me I'm bored, and when you're there I'm never bored; whenever anything happens to me, I at once think of telling you, for it happens to you as well as to me. You're my life, you know that. Perhaps I don't often get upset about you, but that's because we're happy. If you were ill, or if you were set against me, I'd be at my wit's end."

He spoke these words in a calm, earnest manner that forced a tender smile from Françoise. She took his arm and together they went up to the dressing rooms.

"I am your life," Françoise said, "but don't you see what I feel so strongly tonight—that our lives are here around us, almost in spite of ourselves, without our even choosing it to be so. We no longer have to choose one another, and you're no longer free not to love me."

"The fact remains that I do love you," Pierre insisted. "Do you really think that freedom consists of questioning things at every turn? We've often said, apropos of Xavière, that that was the way to become slaves of our slightest moods."

"Yes," said Françoise. She was too tired to find her way in her own thoughts, but she saw once again Pierre's face when he had dropped her arm; the evidence of that was irrefutable.

"And yet life is made up of moments," she said vehemently. "If every one of them is empty, you won't convince me that they add up to something that is whole."

"But I have hundreds of full moments with you," Pierre protested. "Isn't that obvious? You talk as if I were a big callous brute."

Françoise touched his arm. "You're so sweet," she said. "Only, you see, full moments cannot be distinguished from the empty ones, because you're always perfect."

"From which you conclude that they're all empty! How perfectly logical! Okay! I presume that from now on, I'm allowed to be as temperamental as I like?" He looked reproachfully at Françoise. "Why are you in such a state when I love you so much?"

Françoise looked away. "I don't know; I feel bewildered." She hesitated. "For instance, you always listen to me very politely when I talk to you about myself, whether it interests you or not. Then, I ask myself, if you weren't quite so polite would you listen to me?"

"It always interests me," Pierre said with astonishment.

"But you never ask me questions spontaneously."

"I feel that as soon as you have something to say, you'll say it." He stared at her a little uneasily. "When did it happen?"

"What?" Françoise asked.

"That I didn't ask questions?"

"Several times recently," Françoise gave a little laugh. "You looked as if you were thinking of something else." She hesitated, doubtful. Confronted by Pierre's trust, she was ashamed. Every willful silence of hers had been an ambush into which he had quietly fallen. He did not suspect that she had been laying traps for him. Wasn't she the one who had changed? Wasn't it she who was lying when she spoke of blissful love, of happiness, of jealousy overcome? Her words, her behavior no longer responded fully to her deeper feelings. And he continued to believe her. Was that faith or indifference?

The dressing rooms and corridors were empty and everything seemed in order. In silence, they went back to the greenroom and onto the stage. Pierre sat down on the edge of the proscenium.

"I think I've neglected you lately," he said. "I think that had I really been perfect with you, you wouldn't have worried about this perfection."

"Perhaps," said Françoise. "It's not just a question of negligence." She took a little time to steady her voice. "It seemed to me that whenever you let yourself go unrestrained, I didn't mean very much to you."

"In other words, I'm sincere only when I'm in the wrong, and if I behave properly to you it's only through conscious effort? Does that make sense to you?"

"It's valid," she said.

"Certainly, because my attentions condemn me as much as my blunders. If you start from that basis you'll always be right, whatever I do."

Pierre seized Françoise by the shoulder.

"It's wrong, ridiculously wrong. I'm not hiding an indifference that occasionally comes out when I'm not looking. You mean everything to me, and when by chance, because of some worry or other, I'm less aware of it for five minutes or so, even you say that anyone can notice it." He looked at her. "You don't believe me?"

"I believe you," said Françoise. She believed him; but that was not precisely the point. She did not really know any longer just what the point was.

"That's sensible," said Pierre, "but never start that again." He squeezed her hand. "I think I understand, all right, the effect it has on you. We've tried to build our love beyond each individual moment, yet we can only be certain of the moments. For the rest, there has to be faith. And is faith courage or laziness?"

"That's what I was wondering a little while ago," Françoise said.

"Sometimes I wonder about it when it comes to my work. I get annoyed when Xavière tells me that I cling to it out of a desire for moral security—and yet?"

Françoise felt her heart contract. The one thing she could least bear was for Pierre to question the value of his work.

"In my case there's a certain blind obstinacy." Pierre smiled. "You know, when you make a big hole in the back of a honeycomb, the bees continue spitting honey into it with the same cheerfulness. That's somewhat the impression I have of myself."

"You don't really think that?" Françoise said.

"At other times I see myself as a little hero resolutely following his way through the darkness," Pierre said, frowning and looking resolute and foolish.

"Yes, you're a little hero," said Françoise, laughing.

"I'd like to believe it." He had risen, but stood motionless, with his back against a piece of scenery. Above them the phonograph was playing a tango and people were still dancing; they would have to go up and join them.

"It's too ridiculous," he said, "she really makes me uncomfortable, that little devil, with her philosophy that makes less of us than dust. It seems to me that if I could get her to love me, I'd be as sure of myself as I was before. I would feel that I'd compelled her approval."

"You're amazing," Françoise said. "She can love you and disapprove of you at the same time."

"But then it would be no more than an abstract kind of disapproval. To make her love me would be to dominate her, to enter her world and conquer in accordance with her own values." He smiled. "You know the need for this kind of victory is a mania with me!"

"I know," Françoise said.

Pierre looked at her gravely. "Only, I don't want this inexcusable obsession to betray me into spoiling anything between us."

"It can't spoil anything, you said so yourself."

"It can't spoil anything vital," said Pierre, "but the fact is that when I'm worried because of her, I neglect you. When I look at her I don't look at you." His voice grew urgent. "I wonder if it wouldn't be better to call a halt to this affair. It's not love I feel for her: it smacks more of superstition. If she resists, I become obstinate, but as soon as I think I'm sure of her, I become indifferent about her. And if I decide not to see her any more, I know very well that from one minute to the next I'll stop thinking about her."

"But there's no reason for that," said Françoise quickly.

Surely, if he took the initiative and broke with her, he would not regret it; life would go on again where it had left off before the advent of Xavière. With some astonishment, Françoise realized that this assurance awakened in her only some kind of disappointment.

"You know," Pierre said smiling, "I can't accept anything from anyone. Xavière brings me absolutely nothing. You need have no qualms." He again became solemn. "Think it over carefully; it's serious. If you think it threatens our love in any way, you must say so. I don't want to run that risk at any price."

There was a silence. Françoise's head felt heavy; she was conscious only of her head, she no longer felt a body. And her heart too was quiet. It was as if layers of fatigue and indifference had separated her from herself. Without jealousy, without love, ageless, nameless, confronted with her own life, she was no longer anything but a calm, detached spectator.

"I've thought it all over," she said. "There's no doubt about it."

Tenderly Pierre put his arm around Françoise's shoulders, and they went to join the others. It was now daylight, and everyone's face showed haggard lines. Françoise opened the bay window and stepped out onto the flat roof. The cold gripped her. A new day was beginning.

And now what is going to happen? she thought.

But whatever happened, she could not have decided in any other way than she had. She had always refused to live in dreams, and she was not likely now to imprison herself in a mutilated world. Xavière existed and could not be ignored; and Françoise would have to accept the risks inherent with that existence.

"Come inside," Pierre said. "It's too cold."

She shut the window. Tomorrow perhaps might bring suffering and tears, but she felt no compassion for that tormented woman she would become again so soon. She looked at Paula, Gerbert, Pierre, Xavière. She felt nothing but an impersonal curiosity, a curiosity so violent that it had the warmth of joy.

8

"Naturally," Françoise said, "the character is not brought out clearly enough, your acting is much too subjective; but you do feel the character, and you get the right nuances." She sat down on the edge of the couch beside Xavière and took hold of her shoulders. "I solemnly swear to you that you can do that scene for Labrousse. You're good, you know, you're really good."

It was a triumph even to have persuaded Xavière to recite the monologue for her; she had had to be coaxed for an hour, and Françoise felt completely exhausted; but it would all be useless if she could not now persuade her to work with Pierre.

"I don't dare," said Xavière in despair.

"Labrousse is not so frightening," Françoise assured her with a smile.

"But he is!" cried Xavière. "As a teacher, he frightens me."

"Never mind," said Françoise. "You've been working on this scene for over a month now. You're turning into a neurotic, and you've got to stop it."

"But I'd like to," said Xavière.

"Listen, you can trust me," Françoise insisted, with great warmth. "I wouldn't tell you to risk Labrousse's opinion if I didn't think you were ready. I'll take the responsibility." She looked Xavière in the eyes. "Don't you believe me?"

"I believe you, but it's perfectly horrible to feel that you are being judged."

"If you want to work, you must get rid of all false pride," Françoise said. "Be brave, do it at the very beginning of your lesson."

Xavière thought it over. "I'll do it," she said with a look of conviction. Her eyelids fluttered. "I do so want you to be a little satisfied with me."

"I'm sure you will become a real actress," said Françoise tenderly.

"That was a good idea of yours," Xavière said, her face brightening. "The end is much more effective if I'm standing up."

She rose and recited with vivacity, "*If this twig has an even number of leaves, I shall give him the letter. . . . Eleven, twelve, thirteen, fourteen . . . even.*"

"You've got it perfectly," cried Françoise gaily.

The inflections of Xavière's voice, her facial expressions were still only hints, but natural and charming. *If only it were possible to instill a little determination in her,* thought Françoise. *It will be so wearing if she has to be spoon-fed to success.*

"There's Labrousse," Françoise said, "he's scrupulously punctual as usual." She opened the door, she had recognized his step. Pierre smiled cheerfully.

"Greetings!" he said. He was weighed down by a heavy camel-hair overcoat that made him look like a teddy bear.

"Oh, what a boring time I've had! All day long I've been going through accounts with Bernheim."

"Well, we haven't wasted our time," said Françoise. "Xavière has gone over her scene from *l'Occasion* for me. You'll see how well she's worked."

Pierre looked encouragingly at Xavière. "I'm at your disposal," he said.

Xavière was so afraid to venture out of doors that she had finally consented to take her lessons in her room; but she did not budge.

"Not now," she implored. "Can't we wait awhile?"

Pierre glanced questioningly at Françoise.

"Would you mind if we stayed here a little?" he asked.

"You may stay until six thirty," Françoise agreed.

"Yes, no more than a half-hour," said Xavière, turning from one to the other.

"You seem a little tired," said Pierre, looking at Françoise.

"I think I've caught a chill," she said. "It's the weather." It was the weather, but it was also lack of sleep. Pierre was blessed with an iron constitution, and Xavière was able to catch up on her sleep during the day; and both of them gently teased Françoise if she wanted to go to bed before six in the morning.

"What did Bernheim have to say?" she asked.

"He spoke to me again about that plan for a tour." Pierre hesitated a moment. "Of course the figures are very tempting."

"But we aren't in such need of money," Françoise rejoined quickly.

"A tour? Where?" Xavière asked.

"Greece, Egypt, Morocco." He smiled. "Wherever it happens to be, we'll take you with us."

Françoise was startled. They were only idle words, but she was annoyed that Pierre had said them; he was impulsively generous. If ever this tour were to take place she was fiercely determined to go alone with him. Naturally they would have to drag the company along, but that didn't count.

"It won't be for a long time," she said.

"Do you think it would be so terrible if we gave ourselves a little vacation?" Pierre asked coaxingly.

This time Françoise was shaken by rage from head to foot; Pierre had never even envisaged this idea. He was working now in full swing. Next winter his plays would be produced, his book published, and he had a whole heap of plans for the development of the dramatic school. Françoise was desperately anxious for him to reach the peak of his career, and to finally give his work its definitive form. She had difficulty in controlling the trembling in her voice.

"This is not the right moment," she said. "You know perfectly well that in the theater so much depends on the right psychological moment. After *Julius Ceasar*, people will be waiting impatiently to see what you're going to do next season. If you let a year go by, they'll begin thinking about something else."

"Your words are golden, as always," said Pierre with a shade of disappointment.

"How sensible you are!" Xavière's face expressed genuine but shocked admiration.

"Oh, but we'll surely do it some day," Pierre gaily assured her. "It'll be great fun playing in those moth-eaten little theaters in Athens or Algiers. At the end of the show, instead of going to the Dôme, we'll go and recline on mats in a Moorish café and smoke kief."

"Kief?" questioned Xavière, fascinated.

"It's an opiate plant they grow there; it seems that it induces enchanting visions. But," he added with a disappointed air, "I've never tried it."

"In you, that doesn't surprise me," Xavière said with affectionate indulgence.

"It's smoked in nice little pipes the shopkeepers make to order for you. Wouldn't you be proud to have a little pipe of your own."

"I would certainly have visions!"

"Do you remember Moulay Idriss," Pierre turned to Françoise with a smile, "when we smoked the pipe those Arabs—who were probably riddled with syphilis—were passing around from mouth to mouth?"

"I certainly do remember," Françoise said.

"You were scared to death."

"You weren't too happy about it yourself." She had difficulty in getting the words out, she was so tense with emotions. Still, these were far-off plans and she knew that Pierre would decide nothing without her consent. She would say no; that was simple, there was nothing to worry about. No. No, they would not leave next winter; no, they would not take Xavière with them. No. She shivered; she must be feverish, her hands were moist and her whole body was on fire.

"We'll go and work now," Pierre finally decided.

"I'll do some work, too."

She forced herself to smile. They must have sensed that something unusual was going on inside her; there had been a hint of embarrassment. Usually, she had better control over herself.

"We still have five minutes," said Xavière with a sullen smile. "Only five minutes," she sighed. Her eyes again turned to Françoise's face, then dropped to her hands with their tapering fingernails. In the past, Françoise would have been moved by this furtive and fervent glance, but Pierre had pointed out to her how Xavière had often used this little trick when she was overwhelmed by her feeling for him.

"Three minutes," said Xavière; she was now staring at the alarm clock, and reproach was barely disguised beneath regret.

I don't think I'm as miserly with my time, thought Françoise; but evidently by comparison with Pierre, she seemed greedy. Of late, he hadn't been writing at all, he was wasting himself unconcernedly. She could not compete with him; she had no desire to. Another burning shiver ran through her.

Pierre stood up. "Shall I come back at midnight and pick you up?"

"Yes, I shan't move," said Françoise. "I'll wait for you to have supper." She smiled at Xavière. "Be brave. It will soon be over." Xavière sighed. "I'll see you tomorrow," she said.

"Till tomorrow, then."

Françoise sat down at her table and joylessly looked at the blank sheets. Her head was heavy and she ached all down her neck and back. She knew that she would work badly. Xavière had again nibbled off a half-hour. It was terrible, the amount of time she devoured. There was no longer any leisure or solitude, or even simple rest; one reached a state of inhuman tension. No! She would say no! With all the strength at her command she would say no! And Pierre would listen to her.

Françoise felt herself grow weak, something seemed to snap inside her. Pierre would readily give up this trip, he wasn't so terribly keen on it; and then what? What good would it do? What was agonizing was that he hadn't, of his own accord, immediately turned down the proposal. Did he value his work so little? Had his perplexity already given way to complete indifference? It was senseless to lend him the semblance of a faith he no longer possessed. What use was her desiring something for him, if it was without him and even against him. The decisions Françoise expected of him had to come from his own will; all her happiness rested on his free will, and over that she had no hold.

She gave a start. There was the noise of running feet on the stairs, and the next moment knocks shook the door.

"Come in!" she called.

Their two faces appeared together in the doorway, both smiling. Xavière had tucked her hair under a big plaid hood; Pierre had his pipe in his hand.

"Would you be cross with us if we went for a walk in the snow instead of doing the lesson?"

Françoise felt her heart skip a beat. She had taken such pleasure in imagining Pierre's surprise and Xavière's glowing satisfaction when he would shower praises on her. She had put her whole heart into making Xavière work; she was really a fool, they never took the lessons seriously, and now in addition wanted to shift the responsibility for their laziness onto her.

"That's your concern," she said. "I have nothing to do with it."

Their smiles vanished; they had not expected this serious voice.

"Are you really cross with us?" asked Pierre, disconcerted. He glanced at Xavière, who glanced back uncertainly; they looked guilty. For the first time, because of the complicity that joined them in Françoise's own mind, they stood there before her as a pair of lovers. They felt it themselves, and they were ill at ease.

"No, no," said Françoise, "have a nice walk."

She shut the door a little too quickly and stood leaning against the wall, while, without speaking, they went downstairs. She could see their guilty faces. They were certainly not going to work, and she had only ruined their walk. A kind of sob shook her. What good was it? She had only succeeded in poisoning their pleasures and making herself hateful in her own eyes; she could not will their actions—that was a dead certainty. Suddenly she threw herself face down on the bed and burst into tears. There was too much pain in this rigid will of hers she persisted in preserving. She had only to let things take their own course, and she would see what happened.

"We'll see what will happen," Françoise said aloud; she felt utterly at the end of her strength, longing for that blissful peace that falls in white flakes on the exhausted traveler. She had only to give up everything—Xavière's future, Pierre's work, her own happiness—and she would know true peace; she would be protected from these palpitations, these spasmodic contractions of her throat, and this terrible dry burning at the back of her eyeballs.

All she had to do was to make the simplest of gestures—to open her hands, to let go. She lifted one hand and moved her fingers; they responded, in surprise and obedience, and this obedience of a thousand little unsuspected muscles was in itself a miracle. Why ask for more? She couldn't make up her mind to let go. She had no fears for tomorrow, there was no tomorrow; but she saw herself surrounded by a present so naked, so glacial, that her heart failed her. It was like the time at the café near the flea-market with Gerbert—a scattering of instants, a confusion of endless gestures and incoherent images. Françoise jumped up, it was unbearable; any suffering, no matter what, was better than this surrender in the midst of emptiness and chaos.

She put on her coat and pulled her fur toque down over her ears. She had to get hold of herself. She had to talk secretly and truthfully with herself, something she should have done a long time before, instead of submerging herself in work whenever she had a spare moment. Tears had spoiled her eyelashes and darkened the rings under her eyes. It would be easy to repair the damage, but it wasn't worth the effort; between now and midnight she would not see a soul, she wanted to satiate herself with solitude during all these hours. For a moment she stood before the glass, staring at her face. It was a face which conveyed nothing; it was stuck on her head like a label: Françoise Miquel.

Xavière's face, in contrast, was the source of inexhaustible conjecture. That was unquestionably why she smiled at herself so mysteriously in mirrors. Françoise left her room and went downstairs. The pavements were covered with snow; the cold was biting. She boarded a bus. To recapture her solitude, her freedom, she had to escape from this neighborhood.

With the palm of her hand, Françoise wiped off the film that covered the window. Brightly lit shop windows, street lamps, passers-by, sprang out from the night; but she had no sensation of motion, these apparitions followed one another without her altering her own position; it was a voyage in time, outside space; she closed her eyes. She had to somehow pull herself together. Pierre and Xavière had stood up to her; she in turn wanted to stand up to them. Pull herself together! But pull on what? Her ideas melted away. She found absolutely nothing to think about.

The bus stopped at the corner of the rue Damrémont, and Françoise got off; the Montmartre streets were stark in whiteness and silence; Françoise hesitated, completely encumbered by her freedom. She could go anywhere she liked, but she had no desire to go anywhere. Mechanically, she began to climb up toward the Butte. At first the snow was slightly resilient to her tread, but then subsided with an unctuous crunch; it was disappointing and tiresome to feel its resistance melt away before bearing the full pressure of one's step. *Snow—cafés—steps —houses . . . what have they to do with me?* Françoise thought in a kind of daze; she felt a despair so deadly seeping into her that her legs seemed on the point of giving way. What could all these unfamiliar things mean to her? They were set at a distance; they had no contact with the whirling emptiness, the maelstrom which was sucking her under; she was being sucked down spirally, deeper and deeper. It seemed that in the end she must touch something: peace of mind or despair, something definite; but always she remained at the same level, on the brink of emptiness. Françoise looked round her in distress. No, nothing could help her; she would have to eradicate pride, self-pity, and tenderness from within herself. Her back and her temples ached, and even this pain was impersonal. Someone should have been there to say, "I'm tired. I'm unhappy." Then this vague and aching moment would have had meaning in her life. But there was no one.

It's my fault, Françoise thought, as she slowly climbed the steps. It was her fault, Elisabeth was right, for many years now she had ceased to be an individual; she no longer even possessed a face. The most destitute of women could at least lovingly touch her own hand, and she looked at both of hers with surprise. Our past, our future, our ideas, our love . . . never did she say: "I." And yet, Pierre determined his own future and his own heart; he disengaged himself, he retreated to the boundaries of his own life. She remained behind, separated from him, separated from everyone and without a link with herself; neglected, and finding in this abandonment no true solitude.

She leaned against the railing and looked down at the big, cold, blue puff of smoke that was Paris; it lay sprawled before her with insulting unconcern. Françoise sprang back. What was she doing here, in the cold, with these white domes above her head, and, at her feet, this pit that lay gaping to the stars? She ran down the stairs. She must go to a cinema or telephone somebody.

"It's pitiful," she murmured to herself.

Solitude was not a friable morsel that could be consumed piecemeal. It had been childish of her to think that she could take refuge in solitude for just one evening. She had to reject it totally until she had totally regained it.

A piercing pain cut short her breath; she stopped and put her hands to her sides. *What's the matter with me?* A violent shiver went through her from head to foot. She was perspiring and her head was throbbing.

I'm ill, she thought with a kind of relief. She beckoned a taxi. All she could do was return home, go to bed and try to sleep.

A door slammed on the landing and someone shuffled across the passage; it must be the blonde tart getting up. In the room above, the Negro's phonograph was softly playing *Solitude*. Françoise opened her eyes, it was almost dark; she had probably been lying there in the warmth of the sheets for almost forty-eight hours. That gentle breathing at her side came from Xavière, who had not moved from the big armchair since Pierre had left. Françoise took a deep breath—the stabbing pain was still there. She was almost glad, because then she could be sure she was really ill, it was so restful. There was nothing in the world to worry about, she was not even expected to talk. If only her pajamas had not been drenched with sweat, she would have felt perfectly content; they were glued to her body. On her right side, too, she felt the burning sensation of a large mustard plaster. The doctor had been indignant about the way it had been applied; but that was his fault, as he should have explained things better.

Someone was tapping lightly at the door.

"Come in," Xavière called.

The hall-porter appeared in the doorway.

"Does Mademoiselle need anything?" He timidly approached the bed. He came every hour to offer his services, with a look of mournful solicitude.

"No, thank you very much," Françoise answered.

She was so short of breath, she could say nothing more.

"The doctor says that tomorrow, Mademoiselle must go to the hospital. Doesn't Mademoiselle wish me to make any telephone calls?"

Françoise shook her head. "I don't intend to go," she said.

There was a sudden rush of blood to her face and her heart began to pound violently. Why had this doctor stirred up everyone in the hotel? They would now surely tell Pierre, and Xavière, too, would tell him. Françoise herself knew she could not lie to him, and that Pierre would force her to go. But she did not want to go. They would not, after all, take her away against her will. She watched the door close behind the hall porter, and her eyes wandered over the room. It smelled like a sickroom. For two days, the room had not been cleaned, nor the bed made; the window had not even been opened. On the mantelpiece, Pierre, Xavière, Elisabeth, had stacked appetizing foods in vain. The ham had begun to shrivel, the apricots had candied in their own juice, the custard had collapsed into a sea of caramel sauce. The room was beginning to look like a leper's den; but it was her room and Françoise did not want to leave it. She loved the peeling chrysanthemums of the wallpaper, and the threadbare carpet, and all the confused sounds of hotel life. Her room, her life. She was quite willing to stay there, prone and passive, but not to go into exile surrounded by white, anonymous walls.

"I don't want to be taken away from here," she said in a choking voice; again, scorching waves ran through her and nervous tears started to her eyes.

"Don't lose heart," said Xavière looking terribly unhappy. "You're going to get well quickly." She suddenly threw herself on the bed and, pressing her own cool cheek against Françoise's feverish face, she clung to her.

"My darling Xavière," whispered Françoise with emotion. She put her arms round the warm, supple body. Xavière pressed against her with all her weight, so that Françoise could hardly breathe, but she was unwilling to let her go; one morning she had pressed her to her heart like this. Why had she been unable to keep her? How she loved this worried face, now filled with tenderness.

"My darling Xavière," she repeated. A sob rose in her throat. No, she would not leave. There had been a mistake, she wanted to start all over again. In her morbid state she had made herself believe that Xavière had broken away from her, but there could be no doubt about the sincerity of the emotion that had made Xavière fling herself on Françoise's bed. Françoise would never forget those eyes with their dark rings of anxiety, the attentive, feverish love that Xavière had lavished on her without reserve during those last two days.

Xavière drew gently away from Françoise and stood up.

"I'll go now," she said. "I hear Labrousse's step on the stairs."

"I'm certain he'll want to send me to a hospital," Françoise said nervously.

Pierre knocked and came into the room. He looked worried.

"How do you feel?" he asked, taking Françoise's hand in his. He smiled at Xavière. "Has she been good?"

"I'm all right," Françoise whispered. "It's a little difficult to breathe." She wanted to sit up, but a sharp pain stabbed her chest.

"Will you knock on my door when you leave," said Xavière, giving Pierre a friendly look. "And I'll come back."

"It's not necessary," Françoise said. "You ought to go out for a while."

"Am I not a good nurse?" Xavière reproached her.

"The best possible nurse," Françoise said affectionately.

Xavière noiselessly closed the door behind her and Pierre sat down at the side of the bed.

"Now, then, have you seen the doctor?"

"Yes," said Françoise suspiciously, and her face puckered; she did not want to start to cry but she felt completely helpless.

"Send for a nurse, but let me stay here," she said.

"Listen," said Pierre putting his hand on her forehead. "They told me downstairs that you have to be watched very closely. It's not critical, but when lungs are affected, it is serious all the same. You need injections, a lot of care, and a doctor within reach. A good doctor. That old man is an ass."

"Find another doctor and a nurse," she said. The tears welled up; she continued to resist with what little strength remained in her; she did not give in; she would not let herself be torn from her room, from her past, from her life. But she no longer had any means of defending herself, even her voice was no more than a whisper.

"I want to stay with you," she said. She began to cry with her whole self. She was so completely at the mercy of others, a body trembling with fever, without strength, without speech, even without thought.

"I'll be there all day," said Pierre. "It will be exactly the same." He looked at her pleadingly and in great distress.

"No, it will not be the same thing," she was choking with sobs. "Everything's finished.

She was too weak to decide what exactly it was that was dying in the yellow light of the room, but she would never, never get over it. She had struggled so hard; she had felt threatened for so long; she saw, in a confused jumble, tables at the Pôle Nord, banquettes at the Dôme, Xavière's room, her own room, and she saw herself tense and clutching at something she could no longer discern. Now the moment had come; it was useless to keep her hands clenched, clinging to all this in a last effort, they would take it away from her in spite of herself; nothing depended on her will any longer, and her only means of defense was tears.

Françoise was very feverish all through the following night, and she fell asleep only toward dawn. When she again opened her eyes a pale winter sun shone in the room, and Pierre was leaning over the bed.

"The ambulance is here," he said.

"Ah!"

She remembered that she had cried the previous evening, but she could not remember why. Her mind was empty, she was completely calm.

"I'll have to take some things with me," she said.

Xavière smiled. "We packed your bag while you were asleep. Pajamas, handkerchiefs, eau de Cologne—I don't think we've forgotten anything."

"Don't worry," Pierre laughed. "She managed to fill the big suitcase."

"You would have let her go away like an orphan, with nothing but a toothbrush tied up in a handkerchief," Xavière said indignantly.

She came up to Françoise and looked at her anxiously. "How do you feel? It won't tire you too much?"

"I feel all right."

Something had happened while she was asleep; not for weeks and weeks had she known such peace. Xavière's features looked tortured. She took Françoise's hand and squeezed it.

"I hear them coming up," she said.

"Will you come and see me every day?"

"Oh yes, every day!" She bent over Françoise and kissed her; her eyes were filled with tears. Françoise smiled at her. She still knew how to smile, but not how to be moved by tears, nor how to be moved by anything. She watched dispassionately as the two ambulance attendants entered, lifted her, and laid her on the stretcher. One last time she smiled at Xavière, who stood paralyzed beside the empty bed. And then the door closed on Xavière, on her room, on the past. Françoise was hardly more than an inert mass, she was not even an organic body. She was carried down the stairs, head first, nothing more than a heavy piece of luggage that the stretcher-bearers handled in accordance with the laws of gravity and their own personal convenience.

"Good-bye, Mademoiselle Miquel. Get well quickly." The proprietress, the hall porter and his wife were lined up in the hall.

"I'll be back soon," Françoise said.

A cold gust of fresh air woke her to full consciousness. A number of people were assembled in front of the door. An invalid being carried away in an ambulance; many times, Françoise had witnessed the same scene in the streets of Paris.

But this time I am the one on the stretcher, she thought with astonishment; she did not quite believe it. Sickness, accidents, all those stories printed in newspapers by the thousand, she had never imagined herself figuring in one of them; she had told herself the same thing about war; these impersonal, anonymous misfortunes could not happen to her. *How can I be just anyone?* And yet there she was stretched out in an ambulance that was starting without the least jolt; Pierre was seated beside her. She was the person on the stretcher. It had happened after all. Had she really become just anyone? Was that why she felt so light, released from herself, from her whole escort of suffocating joys and worries? She closed her eyes. Smoothly, the car drove on, and time slipped by

The ambulance drew up outside a big garden. Pierre wrapped the blanket tightly around her and she was carried along icy paths, along linoleum-covered corridors. She was laid on a big bed, and she felt with delight under her cheek and around her body the freshness of clean linen. Everything here was so clean, so restful. A little nurse with olive skin came and smoothed her pillows and spoke to Pierre in a low voice.

"I'll leave you," Pierre said. "The doctor will be coming to see you. I'll be back later."

"Until later."

She let him go without regret; she no longer needed him—she needed only the doctor and the nurse. She was just a patient, number 31, just another pneumonia case. The sheets were fresh, the walls white, and she was overcome with a tremendous sense of well-being. That was that! All she had to do now was to let herself go, to give in—it was so simple, why had she hesitated? Now, instead of the endless babbling of the streets, of faces, of her own head, she was surrounded by silence and she wanted nothing more. Outside, a branch snapped in the wind. In this perfect void, the slightest sound radiated in broad waves which could almost be seen and touched: it reverberated to the ends of eternity in thousands of vibrations which remained suspended in the ether, beyond time, entrancing the heart more magically than music. On the night table, the nurse had set a pitcher of orange juice; it seemed to Françoise that she would never tire of looking at its gay transparency; there it was; the miracle consisted in something being there, without any effort, this delicate coolness or anything else at all. It had come there without any fuss or bother, and there it was going to remain. Why then should her eyes cease to be enchanted by it? Yes, this was precisely what Francoise had not dared to hope for three days earlier: released, satisfied, she was lying in the lap of peaceful moments turned in upon themselves, smooth and round as pebbles on a beach.

"Can you raise yourself a little?" the doctor asked. He helped her sit up. "Are you all right like that? It won't take long."

He looked friendly and efficient; he took an instrument from his case and put it against Françoise's chest.

"Take a deep breath," he said.

Françoise inhaled. Her breathing was so labored that the effort exhausted her. When she tried to breathe deeply, she felt a stab of pain.

"Count, one, two, three."

He was listening to her back. He sounded the thoracic cavity, with a series of short taps, like a detective in the films tapping a suspicious wall. Obediently, Françoise counted, coughed, inhaled.

"There, that's over," said the doctor. He arranged the pillow under Françoise's head and surveyed her with a kindly look.

"It's a slight inflammation of the lungs. We'll start injections immediately to sustain the heart."

"Will it be long?" Françoise asked.

"Normally, it takes about nine days, but you'll need a long convalescence. Have you ever had trouble with your lungs?"

"No. Why? Do you think there's something wrong?"

"One can never be sure," the doctor said vaguely. He patted Françoise's hand. "As soon as you feel better we'll X-ray you, and see what has to be done."

"Are you going to send me to a sanatorium?"

"We'll cross that bridge later," said the doctor, smiling. "In any case a few months' rest won't hurt you. But above all, don't worry."

"I'm not worrying," Françoise assured him.

Tuberculosis! Months in a sanatorium! Years, perhaps. How strange it was. All these things could really happen. How far away that Christmas Eve party seemed when she believed herself enclosed in an unchangeable life. Now the future spread itself out in the distance, smooth and white like the sheets; the walls were a long soft expanse of peaceful snow. Françoise was just anyone, and just anything had suddenly become possible.

Françoise opened her eyes. She loved these awakenings that no longer tore her away from her repose, but only made her more blissfully aware of it; she did not even have to change her position, she was already sitting up. She had grown quite accustomed to sleeping in this way, for her sleep was no longer a fierce, sensuous retreat, it was one of many activities, carried out in the same position as the others. Her eyes slowly absorbed the oranges and the books that Pierre had piled on the night table; a peaceful day lay lazily ahead of her.

Presently they'll X-ray me, she thought.

That was the principal event around which all other events revolved. She felt indifferent about the results of the examination. What interested her was the thought of crossing the threshold of this room in which she had been immured for three weeks. Today, she felt that she was completely recovered; surely she would have no difficulty in standing up or even walking.

The morning went by very quickly. While helping her with her toilet, the thin dark nurse, who looked after Françoise, delivered a lecture on the modern woman and her destiny and the beauty of education. Then the doctor came in. Madame Miquel arrived at about ten o'clock; she brought with her two pairs of freshly ironed pajamas, a pink angora bedjacket, some tangerines, and a bottle of eau de Cologne; she stayed on to lunch and was profuse in her gratitude to the nurse. When she left, Françoise stretched out her legs and, lying almost on her back, she let the world slip away into darkness; it slipped away, then returned toward the light; it slipped away again; it was swinging gently back and forth. Suddenly, the swinging ceased. Xavière was leaning over the bed.

"Did you have a good night?" she asked.

"I always sleep well when I take those drops," Françoise replied.

With her head thrown back and a faint smile on her lips, Xavière was undoing the scarf tied over her hair; when she was thinking about herself, there was always something mysterious and ritualistic in her gestures. The scarf slipped off, and she came back to earth. Cautiously, she picked up the bottle.

"You mustn't get into the habit," she said, "for then you won't be able to do without it. Your eyes will become glassy and your nostrils pinched. You'll frighten people."

"And you'll conspire with Labrousse to hide all my little bottles," said Françoise, "but I'll outwit you." She began to cough, it tired her to talk.

"I didn't go to bed at all last night," Xavière said proudly.

"You'll have to tell me all about it."

Xavière's statement affected her no more than a dentist's drill in a dead tooth; she felt nothing but the empty cavity where there was no longer any pain. Pierre is tiring himself out, and Xavière will never accomplish a thing: these thoughts were still there, but ineffective and insensitive.

"I have something for you," said Xavière.

She took off her raincoat and drew from the pocket a small cardboard box tied with a green ribbon. Françoise untied the knot and lifted the lid; it was stuffed with cotton wool and tissue paper. Under the thin paper lay a bunch of snowdrops.

"How pretty they are!" said Françoise. "They look both real and artificial at the same time."

Xavière blew gently on the white corollas. "They were up all night too, but this morning I put them on a special diet. They're in good health."

She got up and filled a glass with water and arranged the flowers in it. Her black velvet suit made her lithe body look even more slender; no longer had she anything of the little peasant girl about her. She was a perfect young lady and certain of her charm. She drew an armchair up to the bed.

"We really spent an amazing night," she said.

Almost every evening Xavière met Pierre at the close of the performance, and there was now not a shadow between them; but never before had Françoise seen this rapt, excited expression on her face; her lips were parted slightly as if they were about to offer themselves and her eyes were smiling. Under the tissue paper, under the cotton wool, carefully enclosed in a well-sealed box, lay the memory of Pierre, and it was that which Xavière was caressing with her lips and her eyes.

"You know, I've wanted for a long time to see all the sights of Montmartre," Xavière said, "but somehow it could never be arranged."

Françoise smiled; there was a magic circle bounding Montparnasse that Xavière could never bring herself to cross; almost at once cold and fatigue deterred her, and she would timorously take refuge at the Dôme or the Pôle Nord.

"Labrousse really took things in hand yesterday evening," Xavière went on. "He carried me off in a taxi and landed me at Place Pigalle. We didn't really know where we wanted to go, we were on an exploration." She smiled. "There must have been tongues of flame over our heads, because in five minutes we were in front of a little red house with clusters of tiny panes and red curtains in the windows; it looked very intimate but a little dubious. I was afraid to go in, but Labrousse bravely opened the door. It was as warm as toast and full of people, but we even managed to find a table in a corner. It had a pink tablecloth and charming little pink napkins that looked like the silk handkerchiefs frivolous young men wear sticking out of their breast pockets. So we sat down." Xavière paused for her final effect. "And we ate sauerkraut."

"You ate sauerkraut!" Françoise exclaimed.

"Yes, we did," said Xavière, in seventh heaven at having created her effect. "And I thought it was delicious."

Françoise could see Xavière's intrepid, radiant look. "Sauerkraut for me too," she had said. It was a mystical communion that she had offered Pierre. They were seated side by side, a little apart; they looked at the people and then they looked at one another with mutual and happy affection. There was nothing disquieting in these images: Françoise thought of them with perfect calm. All this happened outside these bare walls, outside the garden of this hospital, in a world as chimerical as the black-and-white world of the films.

"There was a queer bunch of people there," said Xavière, with mock prudishness. "Dope-peddlers, I should say, and habitual criminals. The proprietor is a tall, very pale man with dark hair and thick pink lips; he looks like a gangster. Not a brute, but the subtle, cruel type gangster." She added, as if to herself only, "I'd like to make a man like that fall for me."

"What would you do with him?" said Françoise.

Xavière's lips curled back over her white teeth.

"I'd make him suffer," she said voluptuously.

Françoise looked at her with a touch of uneasiness; it seemed sacrilegious to think of this priggish child as a woman, with the desires of a woman. But how did she think of herself? What dreams of sensuality and amorous desires made her nose and mouth quiver? What picture of herself, concealed from the eyes of the world, was she smiling at with mysterious connivance? Xavière, at this moment, was aware of her body, she knew herself to be a woman, and Françoise felt that she was now being duped by a stranger ironically hiding behind familiar features.

The mysterious smile left Xavière's face, and she added in a childish tone: "And then he'd take me to opium dens and he'd introduce me to criminals." She daydreamed for a moment. "Perhaps if you went there every evening, they'd finally accept you as one of them. We got to know plenty of the people—two women at the bar, completely drunk." She added confidentially, "Pansies."

"You mean Lesbians?" Françoise asked.

"Isn't it the same thing?"

"Pansy is used only for men," Françoise explained.

"Anyway, they live together," Xavière said with a shade of impatience. Her face brightened. "One had her hair cut very short and looked just like a young man, a charming young man doing his best to go to the devil. The other was the wife. She was a little older and rather pretty with a black silk dress and a red rose at her breast. Labrousse saw I was crazy about the 'young man' and told me I ought to try to seduce her. I ogled provocatively and she actually came over to our table and made me drink out of her glass."

"How do you ogle someone?" Françoise asked.

"Like this," said Xavière. She threw a veiled, provocative glance in the direction of the pitcher of orange juice. Again Françoise was embarrassed. It was not because Xavière proved so adept; it was because she seemed to do it with such zest and with such complete self-satisfaction.

"And then?" asked Françoise.

"And then we asked her to sit down."

The door opened noiselessly, and the young nurse with the olive skin came up to the bed.

"It's time for the injection," she said brightly.

Xavière stood up.

"You needn't go," said the nurse, as she filled a syringe with a green liquid. "It will only take me a minute."

Xavière gave Françoise an unhappy but faintly reproachful look.

"I don't scream, you know," Françoise said with a smile.

Xavière walked to the window and pressed her forehead against the pane. The nurse turned back the bedclothes and uncovered a bit of thigh. The skin was mottled with bruises, and underneath were a number of tiny hard lumps. With a quick stroke she inserted the needle, dexterously and painlessly.

"There, that's all," she said. She looked at Françoise a little severely. "You mustn't talk too much. You'll tire yourself."

"I'm not doing the talking."

The nurse gave her a smile and left the room.

"What a horrible creature!" Xavière exclaimed.

"She's nice," said Françoise, feeling a sentimental indulgence towards this thoughtful, skillful young woman who took such good care of her.

"How can anyone be a nurse?" cried Xavière. She threw a timorous but disgusted glance at Françoise.

"Did she hurt you?"

"Of course not. It doesn't hurt at all."

Xavière shuddered; she was really capable of shuddering at a thought.

"A needle pricking its way into my flesh is something I couldn't bear."

"If you were to take drugs . . ." said Françoise.

Xavière threw back her head and laughed a short scornful laugh. "Ah, then I'd be doing it to myself. I can do anything in the world to myself."

Françoise recognized that tone of superiority and malice. Xavière judged people far less by their acts than by the situations they happened to be in, even if it was through no fault of their own. She had been willing to ignore it this time because it was Françoise, but being ill was a serious fault; she suddenly remembered that.

"You'd have to bear it none the less," Françoise said, adding a little maliciously: "It may happen to you one of these days."

"Never," said Xavière. "I'd rather die than see a doctor." Her moral principles forbade the use of medicines, for it was contemptible to continue the struggle for life if life were failing. She loathed any kind of struggle on principle, regarding it as showing a lack of a proper nonchalance and pride.

She'd allow herself to be cared for like anyone else, thought Françoise, with annoyance; but that was a small consolation. For the moment, Xavière was there, fresh and free in her black suit; a high-necked plaid blouse set off the radiance of her face and the smooth luster of her hair. Françoise lay bound, at the mercy of nurses and doctors. She was thin and ugly, an invalid; she could hardly speak. Suddenly, she felt the illness in her as a humiliating blemish.

"Perhaps you'd like to tell me the rest of your story," she said.

"Won't she come in again and interrupt us?" Xavière asked irritably. "She doesn't even knock."

"I don't think she'll come back."

Making an effort, she went on with her story.

"Well! She waved to her friend, and they sat down beside us. The 'young man' finished her whisky and then suddenly collapsed on the table, with her arms spread out and her head resting on her arm like a small child. She was laughing and crying at the same time. Her hair was all tousled, she had drops of perspiration on her forehead, but all the same she was all clean and pure."

Xavière stopped speaking, she was watching the scene in her mind's eye.

"It's magnificent—when someone goes to the very limit in something, really to the limit," she said. For a moment, she looked off into space, then she began again excitedly. "The other girl shook her. She was determined to get her home. She looked like a maternal whore, you know, those whores who don't want anything to happen to their little pimps, for the sake of their own interests and out of a possessive instinct, as well as from some disgusting sort of pity."

"I see," said Françoise. One might have thought that Xavière had spent years among prostitutes. "Didn't someone knock?" she added, listening. "Would you mind telling them to come in?"

"Come in," said Xavière in a clear voice; a shadow of displeasure came into her eyes.

The door opened.

"Greetings," said Gerbert. Looking a little embarrassed he shook hands with Xavière. "Greetings," he repeated as he walked over to the bed.

"How nice of you to come." Françoise had not dared to hope for his visit, but she was surprised and delighted to see him. It seemed as if a fresh breeze had come into the room, sweeping away the odor of illness and the staleness of the air.

"You do look funny," said Gerbert, laughing sympathetically. "You look like a Red Indian chief. Are you feeling better?"

"Completely cured," said Françoise. "These things reach the crisis in nine days; either you croak or the fever subsides. Do sit down."

Gerbert took off his muffler, a glaringly white woollen muffler with wide ribbing. He sat down on a hassock in the middle of the room and turned from Françoise to Xavière with a slightly persecuted look.

"The fever has subsided, but I'm still wobbly," said Françoise. "In a little while, I'm to be X-rayed, and I think it will give me a funny feeling to put my feet out of bed. They're going to examine my lungs to find out precisely what condition they're in. The doctor told me when I came here that my right lung was like a piece of liver and that the other one, too, was slowly beginning to turn into liver." She had a brief fit of coughing. "I hope they've gone back to a decent condition. Can you imagine me having to spend years in a sanatorium?"

"That wouldn't be much fun," said Gerbert. His eyes wandered over the room in search of inspiration. "Just look at all your flowers! It looks like a bridal chamber!"

"The basket is from the students at the school, the pot of azaleas from Tedesco and Ramblin; Paula Berger sent the anemones."

Another coughing fit shook her.

"You see, you're coughing," said Xavière with a compassion that was just a shade too eager. "You were forbidden to talk."

"You're a perfect nurse," Françoise said. "I'll stop."

There was a short silence.

"And then what happened to these women?" she asked.

"They left. That's all," said Xavière, suddenly grown taciturn.

With a look of heroic resolve, Gerbert tossed back the lock of hair that was falling over his face.

"I hope you'll be well in time to come and see my marionettes," he said. "It's going well, you know, the show will be ready in about two weeks."

"But you'll put on others during the year, won't you?"

"Yes, now that we have a place. They're decent fellows, the *Images* boys. I don't care much for what they're doing, but they're obliging all the same."

"Are you satisfied?"

"Oh, I'm as pleased as can be."

"Xavière told me that your marionettes are lovely."

"Darn it!" he suddenly exclaimed. "I should have brought you one. There they have marionettes on strings, but we use dolls like a Punch and Judy show—the ones you work on your hand. It's much harder. They're made of oilcloth with big flared skirts that hide your whole arm. You slip them on like gloves."

"Did you make them?" Françoise asked.

"Mollier and I. . . . But all the ideas were mine," Gerbert said proudly. He was so wrapped up in his subject that he forgot his shyness.

"It's not so easy to manage, you know, because the movements have to have rhythm and expression; but I'm beginning to learn how to do it. You can't possibly imagine all the small problems of production involved. Just think," he raised his hands, "you have a doll on each hand. If you want to send one to the edge of the stage, you have to find an excuse for moving the other at the same time. That requires some ingenuity."

"I'd love to see a rehearsal," Françoise said.

"We've been working every day, from five to eight. We're doing three sketches and a play with five characters. I've had them in my head now for a long time!" He turned to Xavière. "We were more or less counting on you last night. Doesn't the part interest you?"

"Of course! I think it's great fun," Xavière rejoined in an offended tone.

"Well, then, come along with me later. Yesterday, Chanaud read the part, but she was terrible. She enunciates as if she were on a stage. It's very hard to find the proper pitch," he said to Françoise. "The voice has to sound as if it were coming from the dolls."

"But I'm afraid I won't do it right," said Xavière.

"Of course you will. The four cues you gave the other day were perfect." Gerbert smiled coaxingly. "And you know we're dividing the proceeds among the actors. With a little luck, you'll certainly get something like five or six francs."

Françoise dropped back against the pillows; she was happy that they were now talking to each other. She had begun to feel tired. She wanted to stretch out her legs, but the slightest movement required elaborate strategy; she was sitting on a rubber ring sprinkled with talcum powder and there was rubber under her heels, while a kind of wicker hoop held the sheets away from her knees, otherwise the friction would have irritated her skin. She managed to extend her feet. *When Xavière and Gerbert leave, and if Pierre does not come in immediately, I will sleep a little.* Her mind was blank. She heard Xavière saying: "The fat woman suddenly changed into a female Montgolfier, her skirts were pulled up to form the basket of the balloon and away she floated into the air." She was talking about the marionettes she had seen at a fair in Rouen.

"When I was in Palermo, I saw *Orlando Furioso*," Françoise said.

She didn't go on, she didn't feel like describing it all. It was in a tiny little street near a grape-vendor's; Pierre had bought her a huge bunch of sticky muscat grapes. Seats were five sous and the audience was made up only of children—the width of the benches was just right for their small behinds. Between the acts, a fellow went around with a tray filled with glasses of cold water which he sold for one sou each, and then he sat down on a bench near the stage. He held a long pole in his hand with which he poked children who made noise during the performance. On the walls were large paper drawings portraying the story of Roland. The dolls were superb and very stiff in their knight's armor. Françoise closed her eyes. It had been only two years before, but it already seemed to belong to a prehistoric age. Everything had now become so complicated—feelings, life, Europe. To her it made no difference, because she was drifting passively like flotsam; but there were dark reefs everywhere on the horizon. She was drifting on a gray ocean, and all around her stretched tarry, sulphurous waters, and she was floating, thinking of nothing, fearing nothing, desiring nothing. She opened her eyes again.

The conversation had stopped. Xavière was looking at the tips of her shoes and Gerbert was intently staring at the pot of azaleas.

"What are you working on now?" he said at last.

"Merimée's *l'Occasion*," Xavière said.

She still had not been able to make up her mind to rehearse the scene with Pierre.

"And you?"

"Octave in *Les Caprices de Marianne*, but only so that I can give Canzetti her cue."

Again there was a silence.

"Is Canzetti any good as Marianne?"

"I don't think it's her kind of part," Gerbert said.

"She's common," Xavière said with conviction.

There was an embarrassed silence.

With a shake of his head, Gerbert tossed back his hair. "You know, I might do a marionette number at Dominique Oryol's? It would be marvellous, because the place seems to have got off to a good start."

"Elisabeth mentioned it to me," Françoise said.

"It was she who introduced me. She's got tremendous pull there." He looked delighted and a little shocked. "She's really flying high these days, it's unbelievable!"

"She has money to burn. People are talking about her. It's changing her life," said Françoise. "She's become quite elegant."

"I don't like the way she dresses." Gerbert was frankly prejudiced.

It was strange to think that out there, in Paris, the days were not all alike; things were happening, they moved, they changed. But all these far-off eddies, these jumbled flickerings, awakened no desire in Françoise.

"I have to be at the Impasse Jules-Chaplain at five o'clock," said Gerbert. "I've got to go."

He looked at Xavière.

"Well, are you coming with me? Otherwise Chanaud won't ever give up the part."

"I'm coming." She put on her raincoat and carefully tied her scarf under her chin.

"Will you be staying here much longer?" Gerbert asked.

"Not more than a week, I hope," said Françoise, "and then I'll go home."

"Good-bye, until tomorrow," Xavière said a little coldly.

"Until tomorrow."

She smiled at Gerbert who raised his hand in a little farewell salute. He opened the door and stepped back to let Xavière pass; he must have been wondering what he could possibly talk to her about. Françoise dropped back against the pillows. It delighted her to think that Gerbert was fond of her. Naturally, he was far less fond of her than of Labrousse, but it was a personal affection that was really meant for her. She, too, was very fond of him. She could think of no more delightful relationship than this friendship, devoid of any demands and always so satisfying. She closed her eyes; she was at ease; years in a sanatorium . . . even this thought inspired no rebellion in her. In a few moments, she would know. She felt prepared to accept any verdict whatsoever.

The door opened softly.

"How do you feel?" said Pierre.

The blood rushed to Françoise's cheeks; it was something more than pleasure that Pierre's presence brought her. Only with him her calm indifference disappeared.

"I'm getting better and better," she said, holding his hand in hers.

"They're going to X-ray you in a little while, aren't they?"

"Yes. But you know, the doctor thinks that my lungs are completely healed."

"I only hope it won't tire you."

"I'm fit as a fiddle today," she said.

Her heart was filled with tenderness. How unfair she had been comparing Pierre's love to an old whited sepulcher! Thanks to this illness, she had tangible proof of its living abundance. It was not only his constant presence, his telephone calls, his attentions, for which she was grateful to him. What had been unforgettably sweet to her was that, over and above his avowed tenderness, she had seen in him a passionate anxiety which had had nothing to do with choice, but which had simply overwhelmed him. At this moment, the face looking toward her was utterly without reserve; it was useless to tell him over and over that the X-ray was hardly more than a formality. Worry had affected him deeply. He put a bundle of books on the bed.

"Look what I've chosen for you! Are they all right?"

Françoise looked at the titles—two detective stories, an American novel, a few magazines.

"I should say they are! You're a darling."

Pierre took off his overcoat. "I passed Gerbert and Xavière in the garden."

"He was taking her to rehearse a marionette show," Françoise said. "It's dreadfully funny to see them together. They pass from the wildest glibness to the bleakest silence."

"Yes," said Pierre, "they are amusing." He took a step toward the door. "I think someone's coming."

"Four o'clock. That's it."

The nurse entered, walking with an air of importance ahead of two orderlies who were carrying a huge armchair.

"How's our patient?" she asked. "I hope she's going to take her little expedition nicely."

"She looks well," Pierre said.

"I feel very well."

To cross the threshold of this room, after her long imprisonment, was a real adventure. She was lifted up, wrapped in blankets and settled in the armchair. It was strange to find herself sitting in a chair; it was not the same as sitting up in bed; it made her somewhat dizzy.

"All right?" asked the nurse, turning the door handle.

"Fine," said Françoise.

She looked with slightly shocked surprise at this door that was opening to the outside world; normally, it opened to let people in; now it had suddenly changed direction and was transformed into an exit. And the room, too, was shocking, with its empty bed. It was no longer the heart of the hospital, to which all corridors and stairs led; now it was the corridor, laid with sound-deadening linoleum, that became the vital artery on to which a vague series of small cubicles opened. Françoise had the feeling of having come from the other side of the world. It was almost as strange as stepping through a looking glass.

The armchair was set down in a tiled room filled with complicated apparatus. It was terribly hot. Françoise half closed her eyes. This voyage into the beyond had tired her.

"Can you stand up for two minutes?" asked the doctor, who had just come in.

"I'll try." Françoise was no longer sure of her strength.

Strong arms helped her to a standing position and guided her among the apparatus; the ground swirled out from under her feet, it made her feel sick. She never imagined that it could be such an effort to walk; big beads of perspiration stood out on her forehead.

"Keep absolutely still," said a voice. She was placed against one of the machines and a wooden screen was pressed against her chest. She was choking; she would never be able to hold out for two minutes without suffocating. There was sudden darkness and silence; she heard nothing more than the short, quick wheeze of her breathing. Then, there was a click, a sharp noise, and everything went black. When she regained consciousness, she was again reclining in the armchair; the doctor was bending gently over her, and the nurse was sponging her dripping forehead.

"It's all over," he said. "Your lungs are in excellent condition. You can sleep in peace."

"Are you feeling better?" the nurse asked.

Françoise nodded ever so slightly; she was exhausted, she felt as if she would never regain her strength, she would have to remain in bed all her life. She flopped against the back of the armchair and was carried off down the corridors; her head was empty and heavy. She saw Pierre marching up and down in front of the door of her room. He gave her an anxious smile.

"It's all right," she murmured.

He started to move toward her.

"Just a second, please," said the nurse.

Françoise turned to him, and seeing him standing so firmly on his own legs, she was overcome with distress. How weak and helpless she was! Nothing more than an inert bundle which was being carried by the strength of men's arms.

"Now you're going to have a good rest," said the nurse. She settled the pillows and pulled up the sheets.

"Thank you so much." Françoise stretched herself out with delight. "Would you mind saying it's all right for him to come in?"

The nurse left the room. A short conference took place behind the door and Pierre entered. Françoise watched him enviously; it seemed so natural for him to move across the room.

"I'm so happy," he said. "It seems that you're as sound as a bell."

He leaned over her and kissed her. The joy in his smile warmed Françoise's heart; he had not created it intentionally as a gift for her, he lived it freely for its own sake. His love had again become a glistening reality.

"How unapproachable you looked in that sedan chair," he said tenderly.

"I very nearly fainted," Françoise said.

Pierre took a cigarette from his pocket.

"You may smoke your pipe, you know."

"Certainly not," he said. He looked longingly at the cigarette. "I shouldn't even smoke this."

"No, no, my lungs are completely cured," Françoise rejoined happily.

Pierre lit his cigarette. "And now we'll soon be taking you home; you'll see what a pleasant convalescence you'll have. I'll get you a phonograph and records, you'll have visitors, you'll be in clover."

"Tomorrow, I'll ask the doctor when I can leave." She sighed. "But I feel as if I shall never be able to walk again."

"Oh! That will soon come back," he said. "We'll put you in your armchair for a little while every day, and then we'll have you stand up for a few minutes, and you'll soon be taking real walks."

Françoise smiled at him trustingly.

"It seems you had a wonderful time last night, you and Xavière," she said.

"We found a rather amusing place."

He suddenly became glum. Françoise felt that she had all at once thrust him back into a world of unpleasant thoughts.

"She told me about it with her eyes popping out of her head," she said, with disappointment in her voice.

Pierre shrugged his shoulders.

"What is it?" she asked. "What's worrying you?"

"Oh! It's of no interest," Pierre said with a reticent smile.

"How strange you are! Everything interests me," said Françoise, a little anxiously.

Pierre hesitated.

"Well?" She looked at him. "Please tell me what's in your mind."

Pierre still hesitated, then he seemed to take the plunge. "I wonder if she isn't in love with Gerbert."

Françoise stared at him dumbfounded. "What do you mean?"

"Just what I said. It would be only natural. Gerbert is young and charming. He has the sort of charm that appeals to Xavière." He looked vacantly at the window. "It's even more than likely," he said.

"But Xavière is much too absorbed in you," Françoise said. "She was in raptures over last night."

Pierre thrust his lip forward and Françoise saw, with a feeling of uneasiness, that sharp and slightly pedantic look she had not seen for a long time.

"Naturally," he said arrogantly, "I can always give someone a wonderful time if I want to take the trouble. What does that prove?"

"I don't understand why you think that."

Pierre seemed hardly to hear her. "We are dealing with Xavière and not Elisabeth," he said. "It's quite clear that I have a certain intellectual attraction for her, but she doesn't confuse the two things, that's a cinch."

Françoise felt a slight jolt of dismay. It was Pierre's intellectual charm that had made her fall in love with him.

"She's sensual," he continued, "and her sensuality is unadulterated. She likes my conversation, but what she wants are the kisses of a handsome young man."

Françoise's dismay deepened; she liked Pierre's kisses, did he despise her for that? But she was not the person under discussion.

"I'm sure Gerbert isn't making love to her," she said. "First of all, he knows that you're interested in her."

"He doesn't know anything," Pierre said. "He only knows what he is told. Anyway, that's beside the point."

"But have you noticed anything between them, at least?"

"When I caught a glimpse of them in the garden just then, it struck me as obvious," he said, beginning to bite one of his nails. "You've never seen the way she looks at him when she thinks she's not being watched. She looks as if she'd like to eat him up."

Françoise recalled a particularly avid look on Xavière's face which she had caught sight of the night of the New Year's Eve party.

"Yes," she said, "but she was also in a trance over Paula Berger. Those are snapshots of passion, they don't really amount to feeling."

"And don't you remember how furious she was when we once joked about Aunt Christine and Gerbert?" If Pierre continued, he would gnaw his finger to the bone.

"That was the day she first met him," Françoise said. "You aren't going to suggest that she was already in love with him?"

"Why not?" rejoined Pierre. "He appealed to her at first sight."

Françoise thought for a moment. She had left Xavière alone with Gerbert that evening, and when she had seen her again, Xavière had been in a strange fury. Françoise had wondered if Gerbert had been rude to her, but perhaps it had been quite the contrary, and Xavière became angry with him because she was too attracted by him. And then several days later, she had committed that strange indiscretion. . . .

"What are you thinking?" Pierre asked nervously.

"I'm trying to remember."

"You see, you're hesitating." His tone was importunate. "Oh! There are any number of indications. What did she have in mind when she deliberately went and told him that we had gone out without him?"

"You thought then that it was a dawning feeling for you?"

"There was something of that in it—she was beginning to take an interest in me; but it must have been more complicated than that. Perhaps she was really sorry not to have spent the evening with him; perhaps she wanted to feel a momentary complicity with him against us. Or, she may have wanted to take revenge on him for the desire he made her feel."

"In any case, that gives no indication one way or the other," said Françoise. "It's all too ambiguous."

She raised herself a little on the pillows; this discussion was tiring her, the perspiration was beginning to ooze out in the small of her back and the palms of her hands. And she had believed that they were finished once and for all with these interpretations and analyses. Pierre could keep turning them over and over again for hours on end. She would have liked to have remained peaceful and detached, but Pierre's feverish agitation was infecting her.

"She didn't give me that impression a little while ago," she said.

Pierre's lip was again thrust forward. He had a strange expression, as if he were congratulating himself on keeping back the spiteful words he was, in fact, saying, "You see only what you want to see."

Françoise flushed. "I've been away from the world for three weeks now."

"But there had been many signs already."

"Which ones do you mean?"

"All those we've just mentioned," Pierre said vaguely.

"That's not very much," said Françoise.

Pierre looked annoyed. "I tell you I know what's up," he said.

"Then don't ask me." Françoise's voice quivered a little. Faced with this unexpected harshness in Pierre, she felt too weak and utterly miserable.

Pierre looked at her with remorse. "I'm tiring you with my talk," he said, in a burst of tenderness.

"How can you think that?" said Françoise. He seemed so tormented, she longed to help him. "Frankly, your evidence seems to me to be a little weak."

"At Dominique's, on the opening night, she danced just once with him, and when he put his arm round her, she shivered from head to foot, and there was no mistaking that smile on her face."

"Why didn't you tell me?"

"I don't know." He thought for a moment. "Yes, I know. It's the most unpleasant memory I have, the one that carries the most weight with me. In a way, I was afraid that telling you, and sharing my evidence with you, would make it that much more conclusive." He smiled. "I never thought I'd come to that."

Françoise recalled Xavière's face when she was talking about Pierre, her caressing lips, her tender look. "It doesn't seem to me to be that conclusive."

"I'll speak to her tonight," Pierre said.

"She'll get angry."

Pierre smiled, with a somewhat irritating air.

"Of course not, she loves me to talk to her about herself. She thinks I appreciate all her subtleties. In fact, that's my greatest attraction in her eyes."

"She's very fond of you," Françoise said. "I think Gerbert appeals to her for the moment, but it doesn't go any further than that."

Pierre's face brightened a little, but he remained tense.

"Are you sure of what you're saying?"

"Sure? No, one can never be sure."

"You see, you're not sure," and Pierre looked at her almost threateningly; just a few soothing words from her, and he would feel reassured as if by magic. Françoise set her teeth. She did not want to treat Pierre like a child.

"I'm not an oracle," she said.

"What are the odds, in your opinion, that she's in love with Gerbert?"

"They can't be calculated," Françoise replied rather impatiently. It was painful to her that Pierre could be so puerile; she refused to be his accomplice.

"Still, you can take a guess," Pierre insisted.

Her temperature had probably risen considerably during the course of the afternoon; she felt her whole body dissolving in sweat.

"I don't know. Ten to one," she said in an offhand way.

"No more than ten to one?"

"How on earth should I know?"

"You're not even making an effort," Pierre said tartly.

Françoise felt a lump rise in her throat. She felt like crying; it would be easy to say what he wanted to hear, to give in. But an obstinate resistance once more came to life in her, again things had meaning and value and were worth struggling for. Only, she was not equal to the struggle.

"It's stupid," said Pierre. "You're right. Why should I come and pester you with all this?" His face cleared. "You realize I want nothing more from Xavière than what I have, but I could not bear the thought of anyone else having more."

"I fully understand," Françoise said.

She smiled, but peace did not return; Pierre had broken into her isolation and her repose. She was beginning to catch sight of a world filled with riches and obstacles, a world in which she wanted to join him, that she might desire and fear at his side.

"I'll speak to her this evening," he repeated. "Tomorrow, I'll tell you everything that happens, but I won't torment you any more, I promise."

"You haven't been tormenting me. It was I who made you talk. You didn't want to."

"It was a sore point," he said with a smile. "I was certain that I'd be incapable of discussing it coolly. It wasn't that I didn't want to talk to you about it, but when I came in and saw you with your pathetic thin face, everything else seemed ridiculous to me."

"I'm no longer ill," Françoise said. "You don't have to handle me with care."

"But you see very clearly that I'm not particularly careful how I handle you." Pierre smiled. "I'm really ashamed. All I do is talk about myself."

"Well, one could hardly call you the repressed type!" Françoise said. "In fact, you're amazingly honest. You may be a complete sophist in discussions, but you never cheat yourself."

"I don't deserve any credit for that," he said. "You know that I never feel involved in what goes on in me." He looked up at Françoise. "I was struck by something you told me the other day—that I put my feelings beyond time, beyond space, and that in order to keep them intact, I did not live them. That was a little unfair. But where I myself am concerned, it seems to me that I do behave rather in that way; I always think that I'm elsewhere, and that the moment is of no importance."

"That's true. You always think that you're above anything that happens to you."

"And can therefore do anything I want to. I take refuge in the notion that I am the man who is accomplishing a certain work, the man who, with you, has achieved so perfect a love. But that's too convenient. Everything else exists too."

"Yes, the rest does exist," Françoise said.

"You see, my honesty is still a means of cheating myself. It's amazing how cunning one can be," Pierre added with an air of conviction.

"Oh! We'll foil your tricks!" She smiled at him. What was she uneasy about? He might cross-examine himself, he might question the world, but she knew she had nothing to fear from this freedom that separated him from her. Nothing would ever change their love.

Françoise rested her head against the pillow. Noon. She still had a long period of solitude before her, but it was no longer the steady white solitude of the morning. A warm anxiety had crept into the room; the flowers had lost their brilliance, the orange juice its freshness; the walls and the polished furniture seemed naked. Xavière . . . Pierre . . . Her eyes, no matter where they rested, were only conscious of absences. Françoise closed them. For the first time in weeks, she felt the stirring of anxiety again. How had the night gone? Pierre's indiscreet questions probably hurt Xavière. Perhaps, in a little while, they would be reconciled at Françoise's bedside. And then what? She became aware of that burning in her throat, that feverish beating of her heart. Pierre had brought her back from the depths of limbo and she didn't want to return; she didn't want to remain here any longer. This hospital was now nothing but an exile. Even illness had not been able to give her back her solitary destiny. The future that now loomed ahead of her was her future beside Pierre—*our* future. She listened. During the past days, settled peacefully in her invalid's life, she welcomed visits as a simple distraction. Today, it was different. Pierre and Xavière were approaching, step by step, along the corridor. They had climbed the stairs. They were coming from the station, from Paris, from the center of their life; it was a portion of this life that they would spend here. The steps halted outside the door.

"May we come in?" asked Pierre, as he opened the door. There he was, and Xavière was with him. The transition from their absence to their presence had, as always, been imperceptible.

"The nurse told us that you had slept well."

"Yes, and as soon as the injections are finished, I'll be able to leave."

"Provided you behave and don't get too excited," Pierre said. "Relax and don't talk. We'll do the talking." He smiled at Xavière. "We have lots of things to tell you."

He sat down on a chair beside the bed, and Xavière sat on the big square hassock; she had washed her hair that morning, and her face was framed in a thick golden foam; her eyes and her pale mouth had a caressing and secretive expression.

"Everything went very well at the theater last night," Pierre began. "The house was responsive, and we had a great many curtain calls. But for some unknown reason I was in a lousy mood after the performance."

"You were nervous in the afternoon." Françoise gave him a little smile.

"Yes, and then I was probably feeling the lack of sleep—I don't know. Whatever it was, while we were walking along the rue de la Gaieté, I suddenly became impossible."

Xavière gave a queer little pout. "He was like a hissing and poisonous little snake," she said. "I was very cheerful when I arrived. I had rehearsed the Chinese princess very nicely for two hours. And," she added reproachfully, "I'd taken a nap on purpose to be fresh."

"And I, feeling mean as ever, did nothing but find excuses to lose my temper with her! Crossing the boulevard Montparnasse, she had the misfortune to let go of my arm . . ."

"Because of the traffic," Xavière quickly explained, "it was impossible to walk in step. It wasn't at all convenient."

"I took that as a deliberate insult," Pierre said, "and I was shaken by a fit of temper that made my bones rattle."

Xavière looked with consternation at Françoise.

"It was terrible. He wouldn't talk to me, except that now and then he would make an acidly polite remark. I didn't know what to do with myself. I felt so unjustly attacked."

"I can well imagine it," Françoise said, smiling.

"We had decided to go to the Dôme, because we had not been there for so long. Xavière seemed happy to be back there, and I thought that it was her way of depreciating the recent evenings we had spent together looking for adventure. That added to my fury, and for nearly an hour I sat, bursting with rage, over my glass of beer."

"I tried various topics of conversation," Xavière put in.

"Her patience was really angelic," Pierre said contritely, "but all her efforts at conciliation only made me the more furious. When you're in a state like that you know perfectly well that you can snap out of it if you want to, but you never see any reason to want to. I ended up by bursting into accusations. I told her that she was as inconsistent as the wind; that it was certain that if anyone spent one pleasant evening with her, the next would be execrable."

Françoise burst out laughing. "But what came over you to make you so unreasonable?"

"I sincerely believed that she had been cold and reserved when we met. I believed it because, out of surliness, I had made up my mind in advance that she would be on the defensive."

"Yes," said Xavière querulously. "He explained that he was in that charming temper because he was afraid that he might not spend as perfect an evening with me as the night before."

They smiled at one another with affectionate understanding. It seemed that Gerbert had not entered into it; in the end, of course, Pierre had not dared to talk about him, and he had got out of it with half-truths.

"She looked so pathetically shocked," Pierre said, "that I was promptly disarmed. I felt completely ashamed. I told her everything that had gone through my mind from the time we had left the theater," then smiling at Xavière, "and she was magnanimous enough to forgive me."

Xavière returned his smile. There was a brief silence.

"And then we agreed that for a long time all our evenings had been perfect," said Pierre. "Xavière was kind enough to tell me that never once had she been bored with me, and I told her that the moments I had spent with her counted among the most precious of my life." He added quickly, in a playful tone that did not ring quite true, "and we agreed that this was not so surprising considering the fact that, after all, we were in love with each other."

Despite the gaiety in his voice, the last word fell heavily on the room and silence closed over it. Xavière wore a forced smile. Françoise composed her features with difficulty; it was only a matter of a single word, it was a long time since things had reached this stage, but it was a decisive word and before saying it, Pierre really might have talked it over with her. She was not jealous of him, but she would not give up without a struggle this little sleek, golden girl whom she had adopted early one chilly morning.

Pierre continued easily and calmly, "Xavière told me that until that moment she had never been conscious that it was love." He smiled. "She knew well enough that the moments we spent together were happy and important ones, but she had not realized that it was owing to my presence."

Françoise glanced at Xavière, who was gazing non-committally at the floor. Françoise knew she was being unfair, Pierre had talked it over with her; she had been the first to tell him a long time ago: "You may fall in love with her." The night of the New Year's Eve party he had offered to give up Xavière. He had every right to feel his conscience clear.

"It seemed like a magical coincidence, I suppose?" said Françoise clumsily.

Xavière quickly looked up. "Of course not," she said, looking at Pierre. "I knew quite well that it was thanks to you, but I thought that it was simply because you were so interesting and so pleasant. Not because—not because of anything else."

"But what do you think now? You haven't changed your mind since yesterday?" Pierre asked with a winning smile which betrayed a slight uneasiness.

"Certainly not, I'm not a weather vane," Xavière said stiffly.

"You might have made a mistake," Pierre's voice wavered between curtness and gentleness. "Perhaps in a moment of exaltation, you mistook friendship for love."

"Did I look exalted last night?" Xavière asked with a constrained smile.

"You seemed caught up by the moment," said Pierre.

"No more than usual." She began to play with a strand of her hair, squinting at it with a stupid, venomous look. "The trouble is," she drawled, "that big words immediately make everything so oppressive."

Pierre's face froze. "If the words are apt, why be afraid of them?"

"Naturally," Xavière said, continuing to squint atrociously.

"Love is not a shameful secret," Pierre insisted, "and to me, it's weakness to refuse to look squarely at what goes on inside you."

Xavière shrugged her shoulders. "You can't change your nature," she said. "My soul is not for display."

Pierre looked so helpless and unhappy that Françoise's heart ached for him; he could be so vulnerable, if he chose to cast away all his defenses and all his weapons.

"Do you find it disagreeable for all three of us to discuss the matter?"

he said. "But that's what we decided yesterday evening. Perhaps it might have been better had we each talked alone with Françoise." He looked hesitatingly at Xavière. She threw him an angry glance.

"It's all the same to me whether we're two or three or a whole crowd," she said. "What seems strange to me is to hear you talk to me about my own feelings." She began to laugh nervously. "It's so strange, I can hardly believe it. Am I actually the person you're talking about? Is it me you've been dissecting? And do you expect me to put up with it?"

"Why not? It's you and I who are involved," Pierre said. He smiled timidly. "It seemed quite natural to you last night."

"Last night . . ." cried Xavière, her lips curling. "Last night you seemed to be living for once, and not just talking."

"You're being extremely unpleasant," Pierre said.

Xavière clutched at her hair and pressed it down over her forehead.

"It's absolutely insane to talk about yourself as if you were a piece of wood," she said fiercely.

"You only let yourself feel things in the dark and in secret," said Pierre in a rasping voice. "You're incapable of enjoying them in broad daylight. It's not the words that upset you. What irritates you is that, today, I'm asking you to agree, of your own free will, to what you were surprised into agreeing to last night."

Xavière's face fell, and she glanced at Pierre with a trapped look. Françoise would have liked to stop Pierre. She could easily understand how anyone might be afraid of, and want to escape from, this domineering tenseness which hardened his features. He himself was not happy at this moment either, but despite his vulnerability, Françoise could not help seeing him as a man bent on his masculine triumph.

"You've just let me say that you loved me," Pierre said. "It's not too late for you to change your mind. It would not surprise me in the least to discover that you feel nothing deeper than passing emotions." He gave Xavière a nasty look. "Go ahead, tell me frankly that you don't love me."

Xavière threw a desperate glance at Françoise.

"Oh! I wish none of this had ever happened," she said, in distress. "Everything was going so well before! Why must you spoil it all?"

Pierre seemed moved by this outburst. He looked first at Xavière, then at Françoise, unable to make up his mind.

"Give her time," said Françoise, "stop badgering her."

To love, not to love—how laconic and rational Pierre was becoming in his thirst for certainty! Françoise had a sisterly understanding of Xavière's bewilderment. How could she herself have described her own feelings in words? Everything was in such confusion within her.

"Forgive me," said Pierre. "I was wrong to lose my temper. It's all over. I don't want you to think that anything is spoiled between us."

"But it is spoiled, you can see that!" Xavière's lips were trembling, her nerves were on edge. Suddenly, she buried her face in her hands. "Oh! What can we do now? What can we do?" she said in a whisper.

Pierre bent towards her. "No, no, nothing has happened. Nothing has changed," he said insistently.

Xavière let her hands fall to her lap. "Everything's so heavy now. It's like a strait-jacket around me." She was trembling from head to foot. "It's so heavy."

"Don't you think that I expect anything further. I ask nothing more of you. It's just as it was before," Pierre insisted.

"Look what's happened already," said Xavière. She sat herself upright and threw her head back to check her tears. Her throat swelled convulsively. "It's a disaster, I'm sure of it. I'm not up to it," she said in a broken voice.

Françoise looked at her, helpless and pained; it was like that time at the Dôme; now, however, it was less permissible for Pierre to make a move, for it would have seemed not only brazen on his part but also presumptuous. Françoise wished she could put her arms around those trembling shoulders and find something to say, but she lay helpless between the sheets. No contact was possible; she could only utter brittle words which were doomed not to ring true. With no one to turn to, Xavière was struggling alone against dangers she saw surrounding her as if in a nightmare.

"There's no disaster to fear among the three of us," Françoise said. "You must have confidence. What are you afraid of?"

"I'm afraid," said Xavière.

"Pierre is a little snake, but his hiss is worse than his bite, and besides we'll tame him. You'll let yourself be tamed, won't you?"

"I won't even hiss any more. I swear it."

"Well?" said Françoise.

Xavière took a deep breath. "I'm afraid," she repeated in a wary tone. Just as the evening before, at the same time, the door opened softly and the nurse entered, a syringe in her hand. Xavière jumped up and walked to the window.

"It won't take a minute," said the nurse.

Pierre got up and took a step forward as if he intended to join Xavière, but he stopped in front of the fireplace.

"Is this the last injection?" Françoise asked.

"We'll give you one more tomorrow."

"And after that, I can just as well convalesce at home?"

"Are you in such a hurry to leave us? You'll have to wait until you're a little stronger, before you can be moved."

"How long? Another week?"

"A week or ten days."

The nurse inserted the needle.

"There, that's all," she said. She pulled up the sheets and left the room with an expansive smile.

Xavière whirled around on her heel. "I loathe her, with her honeyed voice," she said with bitter hatred. For a moment she stood motionless at the far end of the room; then she walked to the armchair on which she had thrown her raincoat.

"What are you doing?" said Françoise.

"I'm going out to get a little air. I'm suffocating in here." Pierre started toward her. "I must be alone," she said fiercely.

"Xavière! Don't be obstinate!" Pierre said. "Come back and sit down and let's talk sensibly."

"Talk! We've already talked too much!" She quickly put on her coat and walked toward the door.

"Don't go like this," Pierre said gently. He put out his hand and lightly touched her arm. Xavière started back.

"You're not going to give me orders now," she said tonelessly.

"Go and get some air," said Françoise, "but come back and see me late in the afternoon. Will you do that?"

Xavière looked at her. "I'd like to," she said docilely.

"Shall I be seeing you at midnight?" Pierre asked, in a curt tone.

"I don't know," Xavière replied almost in a whisper. She suddenly opened the door and went out closing it behind her.

Pierre walked to the window and for a moment remained motionless, his forehead leaning against the glass. He watched her leave the building.

"Now we're in a fine mess," he said, walking back to the bed.

"How tactless can you be!" Françoise said nervously, "What ever possessed you? The last thing in the world you should have done was to come back like that with Xavière and tell me all about it so soon. The situation was embarrassing for everyone. Even a less sensitive girl could not have stood it."

"Well! What else could I have done?" said Pierre. "I suggested that she come and see you alone, but of course she felt that that was more than she could cope with. She said that it would be far better for us to come together. And as for me, there was never any question of my speaking to you without her. We would have looked like a couple of grownups making plans for a child without consulting her."

"I don't deny it," Françoise said. "It was a very delicate matter." She added with a strange obstinate pleasure, "In any case, your solution was not a happy one."

"Last night it seemed so simple," Pierre said with a faraway look. "We discovered our love. We came to tell it to you as a beautiful story that had happened to us."

The blood rushed to Françoise's cheeks and her heart was filled with resentment. She hated this role of a dispassionate benevolent divinity which they obliged her to play, to suit their own convenience, on the thin pretext of revering her.

"Yes, and the story was hallowed in advance," said Françoise. "I quite understand; it was even more important for Xavière than for you to think that I'd be told about last night." She recalled their delighted look of mutual understanding when they came into her room; they were bringing her their love, like a beautiful gift, that she might return it to them transformed into virtue. "Only, Xavière can never imagine things in detail. She hadn't realized that words would have to be used. She was horrified as soon as you opened your mouth. I am not surprised that she was, but you should have foreseen it."

Pierre shrugged his shoulders.

"I didn't think I had to be on my guard," he said. "I had no suspicion. That little fiend! If you could have seen how submissive and yielding she was last night. When I said the word 'love,' she trembled a little, but her face was all acquiescence. I took her home."

He smiled, but he seemed not to feel that he was smiling. His eyes remained vague.

"When I was about to leave her, I took her in my arms and she held her lips up to mine. It was a completely chaste kiss, but there was so much tenderness in her gesture."

The picture scared Françoise like a sharp burn. Xavière—her black suit, her plaid blouse and her white neck; Xavière—supple and warm in Pierre's arms, her eyes half closed, her mouth proffered. Never would she see that face. She made a determined effort; she was about to be unfair, she would not let herself be submerged in this growing resentment.

"You're not offering her an easy love," she said. "It was only natural for her to be frightened for a moment. We don't usually look at her from that point of view; but after all, she's a young girl and she has never loved. That does count, after all."

"I only hope she doesn't do anything foolish," Pierre said.

"What do you think she might do?"

"With her, you never know. She was in such a state." He looked anxiously at Françoise. "Will you try to reassure her? Explain everything. You're the only one who can put matters right."

"I'll try."

She looked at him, and their conversation of the previous evening flashed back to her mind. She had loved him too blindly, and for too long, for what she received from him; but she had promised herself to love him for himself, even if he availed himself of that freedom to escape from her; she would not be daunted by the first obstacle. She smiled at him.

"What I shall try to make her understand," she said, "is that you are not one man between two women, but that all three of us form something very special, something difficult, perhaps, but something which could be beautiful and satisfying."

"I wonder if she'll meet me tonight," he said. "She was so unlike herself."

"I'll do my best to persuade her," Françoise promised. "It isn't really so serious." There was a short silence. "And Gerbert?" asked Françoise. "He doesn't figure in all this?"

"We hardly mentioned him," said Pierre, "but I think you were right. He attracts her for the moment, and a minute later she no longer gives him a thought." He rolled a cigarette between his fingers. "Still, that was what brought the whole thing to a head. I found our relationship delightful, as it was. I wouldn't have tried to change a thing if jealousy hadn't aroused my damned need of domination. It's chronic, as soon as I feel I'm being met with resistance, I lose my head."

It was true that there was this dangerous mechanism in him of which he was not master. Françoise felt a tightening in her throat.

"You'll end up by sleeping with her," she said. No sooner were the words out of her mouth than she was overwhelmed by an unbearable certainty—Pierre, with his caressing masculine hands, would turn this black pearl, this austere angel, into an impassioned woman. He had already pressed his lips to her soft lips. She looked at him with a kind of horror.

"You know that I'm no sensualist," said Pierre. "All I want, is to be able to make her look at me whenever I choose the way she looked at me last night when nobody in the world existed for her but me."

"But it's more or less inevitable," Françoise said. "Your domineering isn't going to be content with half measures. To make sure that she always loves you as much, you'll ask a little more of her each time."

In her voice was a harsh hostility that wounded Pierre. He made a slight grimace.

"You're going to disgust me with myself," he said.

"It always seems sacrilege to me," Françoise said more gently, "to think of Xavière as a sexual woman."

"But it does me, too," he agreed, lighting a cigarette. "The point is, I won't tolerate her sleeping with another man."

Again Françoise felt that unbearable sensation in her heart. "That's just why you'll be brought to sleeping with her," she said. "I don't say at once, but in six months, in a year."

She saw each step along the fatal path that led from kisses to caresses, from caresses to complete surrender. Through Pierre's fault, Xavière would end up like anyone else. For a moment she frankly hated him.

"Do you know what you are going to do now?" she asked, controlling her voice. "You're going to sit down in your corner, as you did the other day, and work. I'll rest for a while."

"I tire you, I know," Pierre said. "I keep forgetting you're ill."

"It's not you."

She closed her eyes. She was suffering an evil pain. Exactly what did she want? What could she want? She did not know; but it was absurd her imagining that she could escape by renunciation; she was too fond of Pierre and of Xavière; she was too involved. A thousand painful recollections whirled through her head, lacerated her heart; she felt as if the blood coursing through her veins had been poisoned. She turned to the wall and began to cry silently.

Pierre left Françoise at seven o'clock. She had finished her supper and she was too tired to read; she could do nothing but wait for Xavière. But would she come? It was terrible to be dependent on that capricious will, and yet powerless to influence it. A prisoner. Françoise looked at the bare walls; the room smelled of fever and night; the nurse had taken away the flowers and turned off the ceiling light. There was only the lamp on the table beside her that formed a cage of light around her bed.

"What do I want?" Françoise asked herself again in anguish. All she knew was how to cling obstinately to the past; she had let Pierre go forward alone. And now that she had let go of her hold, he had gone too far ahead for her to reach him. It was too late. *And if it weren't too late?* she thought. If in the end she were to decide to throw all her reserves into action instead of standing stock-still, her arms hanging empty at her sides? She pulled herself up a little on the pillows. She, too, must give herself without reservation, that was her only chance; perhaps then she, in her turn, would be caught up by this new future which Pierre and Xavière had already entered without her. She looked excitedly at the door. She would do it; she had made up her mind; there was absolutely nothing else to do. If only Xavière would come! Half-past seven. It was no longer Xavière she was awaiting, her hands moist and her throat dry; it was her life, her future, and the resurrection of her happiness.

There was a soft knock.

"Come in," said Françoise.

Nothing happened. Xavière was afraid that Pierre was still there.

"Come in," Françoise cried, as loudly as she could; but her voice was choked. Xavière might go away without hearing her, and she had no way of calling her back.

Xavière came in. "I'm not disturbing you?" she asked.

"Certainly not, I was looking forward to seeing you."

Xavière sat down beside the bed.

"Where have you been all this time?" Françoise asked gently.

"I've been for a walk."

"How upset you were. Why do you torment yourself like that? What are you afraid of? There's no reason for it."

Xavière lowered her head; she seemed to be completely worn out.

"I was perfectly foul just then," she said, and added timidly, "Was Labrousse very angry?"

"Of course not," said Françoise. "He was just worried." She smiled. "But you'll reassure him."

Xavière stared at Françoise with a look of terror. "I don't dare go and see him."

"But that's absurd," Françoise said. "Just because of that scene?"

"Because of everything."

"You've worked yourself up over a word, but a word doesn't change anything. You don't think he'll feel he has any rights over you?"

"You saw just now," said Xavière. "It's already caused a row."

"It was you who made the row, because you became panic-stricken." Françoise smiled. "Anything new always upsets you. You were afraid to come to Paris, afraid of the theater. And after all, so far, nothing very terrible has happened to you."

"No," said Xavière with a shadow of a smile.

Her face, drawn with fatigue and anguish, seemed more impalpable than ever; still, it was made of soft flesh which Pierre's lips had touched. For a while Françoise gazed with a lover's eyes at this woman whom Pierre loved.

"On the contrary, everything could be so easy," she said. "A closely united couple is something beautiful enough, but how much more wonderful are three persons who love each other with all their being." She waited a while. Now the moment had come for her, too, to commit herself and to take her risks. "Because, after all, it is certainly a kind of love that exists between you and me."

Xavière threw her a quick glance.

"Yes," she said in a low voice. Suddenly, an expression of childlike tenderness softened her face and impulsively she leaned toward Françoise and kissed her.

"How hot you are," she said. "You're feverish."

"I'm always a little feverish at night." She smiled. "But I'm happy to have you with me."

It was so simple; this love, which was filling her heart with sweetness, had always been within her reach; she had only to stretch out her hand, her timid and avaricious hand.

"You see, if there is also love between you and Labrousse, what a beautiful well-balanced trio that makes," she said. "It's not a recognized way of living, but I don't think it will be too difficult for us. Don't you think so, too?"

"Oh yes." She suddenly seized Françoise's hand and squeezed it.

"Just let me get well, and you'll see what a beautiful life we'll have, the three of us," said Françoise.

"You'll be back at the end of a week?"

"If all goes well."

Suddenly Françoise felt a painful stiffening of her whole body. No, she would not stay in this hospital any longer, this was the end of her peaceful detachment; she had regained her keen zest for happiness.

"That hotel is so dismal without you," Xavière said. "In the old days, even when I didn't see you for a whole day, I felt you were up there above me and I could hear your step on the stairway. It's so empty now."

"But I'll be coming back," said Françoise, with emotion. She had never suspected that Xavière was so conscious of whether she was there or not. How she had misjudged her! How she would love her, to make up for all the time she had lost! She squeezed Xavière's hand and looked at her in silence. Now, when her temples were throbbing with fever and her throat was dry, she understood at last the miracle that had entered her life. She had been slowly drying up in the security of those patiently constructed theories and leaden thoughts. And now, in a burst of purity and liberation, all that too human world had crumbled into dust. One open, childlike look from Xavière had sufficed to destroy that prison, and now, on this liberated earth, a thousand marvels would come to life, thanks to this exacting young angel. A sad angel with gentle feminine hands, as red as those of a peasant woman, with lips perfumed with honey, tobacco and green tea.

"My precious Xavière," said Françoise.

Part Two

1

ELISABETH'S eyes ran over the upholstered walls, and came to rest on the miniature theater, painted red, at the far end of the room. For a time she had thought with pride: "This is my work." But it was not so very much to be proud of; it had, after all, to be the work of somebody.

"I must go home," she said. "Pierre is coming to supper with Françoise and the Pagès girl."

"Ah! So Pagès is walking out on me," said Gerbert looking a trifle disappointed.

He had not taken the trouble to remove his make-up; with his green eyelids and the thick layer of ocher covering his cheeks, he looked much more handsome than he actually was. Elisabeth had brought him and Dominique together, and made Dominique engage him and his marionette number. She had played an important part in the organization of the night club. She smiled bitterly. During the discussions, aided and abetted by liquor and tobacco, she had had the intoxicating sensation of being an active agent, but it was like the rest of her life—factitious activity. This she had understood, during these three gloomy days; nothing that happened to her was ever real. Sometimes, through the fog, it was possible to catch a glimpse of something which faintly resembled an event or an act; people could be taken in by it, yet it was nothing but a crude optical illusion.

"She'll walk out on you more often than not," she said.

In Xavière's absence, Lise had taken over her part and, in Elisabeth's opinion, played it at least as well, yet Gerbert appeared put out. Elisabeth studied him closely.

"That child has some talent," she continued, "but she seems to lack conviction in whatever she does, and that's a pity."

"I can understand that it isn't much fun for her having to come here every night," said Gerbert, slightly on the defensive, a fact not lost on Elisabeth. She had for a long time suspected that Gerbert had a soft spot for Xavière. It was amusing. Did Françoise suspect this?"

"What about your portrait?" she asked. "Tuesday evening? I only want to make a few sketches."

What she wanted very much to know was what Xavière thought of Gerbert. One way or the other Xavière could not think much about him, the way they held on to her; still, her eyes had had a strange sparkle that opening night while she was dancing with him. If Gerbert were to make advances, how would she react?

"Tuesday, if you like," he said.

He was so shy. He would never dare take the initiative; he did not even suspect that he stood a chance.

Elisabeth pecked lightly at Dominique's forehead.

"Good-bye, darling."

She went out into the street. It was late; she would have to walk quickly if she wanted to get there before them; she had put off as long as possible the moment when she'd be alone again. She would manage to speak to Pierre somehow; the game was lost in advance, but she wanted to take this last chance. She compressed her lips. Suzanne was triumphant; Nanteuil had just accepted *Partage* for next winter, and Claude was oozing fatuous satisfaction from every pore. Never had he been so tender as during the past three days, and never had she hated him more. He was a careerist—vain and weak; he was eternally bound to Suzanne, and eternally Elisabeth would remain the tolerated and clandestine mistress. During these past few days, the truth, in all its unbearable crudity, had become obvious to her; she had nursed her vain hopes out of cowardice, she could expect nothing of Claude; and yet she would put up with anything to keep him, for she could not live without him. She had not even the excuse of a generous love, her suffering and bitterness had killed all love. Had she really ever loved him? Was she capable of loving? She quickened her pace. There had been Pierre. If he had devoted his life to her, perhaps she would never have grown up so full of inner discord and falsehood. Perhaps for her, too, the world would have been complete and she would have known peace in her heart. But that was all in the past. She was hurrying to him with nothing in her heart but a desperate desire to hurt him.

She climbed the stairs and turned on the light. Before going out she had set the table, and the supper looked really very attractive. She, too, looked attractive with her pleated skirt, plaid jacket, and careful make-up. Anyone looking at this whole scene in a mirror could well imagine that it was an old dream come true. When she was twenty, in her dreary little bedroom, she used to prepare mincemeat sandwiches and bottles of cheap red wine for Pierre, pretending that it was a choice supper with foie gras and old Burgundy. Now the foie gras was on the table, together with caviar canapés, and there was sherry and vodka in the bottles; now she had money, any number of connections, and a dawning reputation. And yet, she continued to feel herself on the fringe of society; this supper was only a counterfeit supper in a pseudo-elegant studio, and she was only a living caricature of the woman she pretended to be. She crumbled a petit four between her fingers. The pretense used to be fun in the old days; it was the anticipation of a brilliant future. Now she no longer had a future. She knew that in no way would she ever reach the authentic ideal of which her present self was only a copy. Never would she know anything other than these shams. It was the curse which had been cast upon her; everything she touched turned into papier-mâché.

The doorbell shattered the silence. Did they know that everything was spurious? Surely they knew. She gave a final glance at the table and at her face. She opened the door. Françoise was framed in the doorway, a bunch of anemones in her hand. It was Elisabeth's favorite flower— at least that was what Elisabeth had decided ten years ago.

"These are for you, I found them at Banneau's just now," said Françoise.

"How sweet of you," Elisabeth exclaimed, "they're lovely." Something softened in her. Besides, it wasn't Françoise she hated.

"Do come in," she said, as she led them into the studio.

Hidden behind Pierre was Xavière, with that timid, foolish expression on her face. Elisabeth was prepared for it, but it irritated her none the less. They were making fools of themselves, dragging this child with them wherever they went.

"Oh, how pretty!" cried Xavière. She stared at the room and then at Elisabeth with undisguised astonishment. She had a look which said: "I would never have expected this of her."

"This studio is a dream, isn't it?" Françoise said as she took off her coat and sat down.

Pierre turned to Xavière, "Take off your coat, you'll be cold when you leave."

"I'd rather wear it."

"It's very warm in here," Françoise objected.

"I assure you I'm not too warm," Xavière replied with gentle persistence. They both stared at her unhappily and then looked questioningly at each other. Elisabeth repressed a shrug. Xavière would never know how to dress; she was wearing an old lady's coat, much too big and drab for her.

"I hope you're hungry and thirsty," said Elisabeth hospitably. "Help yourselves. You've got to do justice to my supper."

"I'm famished," Pierre said. "Besides, I make no bones about my atrocious appetite." He smiled, and the others smiled too. All three of them looked hilarious and conspiratorial. They almost seemed drunk.

"Sherry or vodka?"

"Vodka," they said in chorus.

She knew very well that Pierre and Françoise preferred sherry; had Xavière gone so far as to impose her tastes on them? She filled the glasses. Pierre was certainly sleeping with Xavière, she was sure of that. And the two women? It was quite possible—they made such a perfectly symmetrical triangle. Sometimes they were to be seen in pairs—they must have arranged a rotation—but most often all three of them were to be seen arm in arm, walking in step.

"I saw you yesterday crossing the boulevard Montparnasse," she said. She smiled slightly. "You looked so funny."

"Why funny?" asked Pierre.

"You were holding each other by the arm, and you were hopping from one foot to the other, the three of you together." When he becomes infatuated with someone or something, she thought, he loses all sense of proportion; he has always been that way. What does he see in Xavière?—with her yellow hair, her expressionless face, her red hands—there is nothing attractive about her.

She turned to Xavière. "Don't you want to eat anything?"

Xavière examined the plates suspiciously.

"Try one of these caviar canapés," Pierre suggested. "It's all so delicious. Elisabeth, you're entertaining us royally."

"And she's dressed like a princess," Françoise put in. "It certainly becomes you to be elegant."

"It's becoming to everyone," Elisabeth rejoined. Françoise surely had more than adequate means to be just as chic, if she wanted to go to the trouble.

"I think I'll try the caviar," Xavière said after due consideration, and she took a sandwich and bit into it. Pierre and Françoise were watching her with passionate interest.

"How do you like it?" Françoise asked.

Xavière took her time. "It's good," she said emphatically.

The two faces relaxed. In view of their behavior, it was obviously not this child's fault if she considered herself a goddess.

"Are you really all right now?" Elisabeth asked Françoise.

"I've never felt so full of energy. My illness obliged me to take a good long rest, and that has done me a world of good."

She had even put on a little weight. She looked blossoming. With an air of doubt, Elisabeth watched her devour a foie-gras canapé. Was there really no flaw in this happiness which they were so ostentatiously exhibiting?

"Could I see your latest canvases? I'd like to very much," Pierre asked her. "It's such a long time since I've seen anything of yours. Françoise has told me that you've changed your style."

"I'm in the very middle of a transition," said Elisabeth, with ironic pretentiousness. Her pictures! Pigment spread on canvas so as to give the appearance of pictures; she spent her days painting in order to convince herself that she was a painter, but it was still nothing but a lugubrious game.

She took out one of her canvases, put it on an easel, and turned on a blue light. There, that was part of the ritual! She would show them her fraudulent paintings and they would bestow fraudulent praise. They would not know that she knew: this time they were the dupes.

"Well, yes, that's a radical change!" Pierre said.

He studied the picture with a look of genuine interest. It was a section of a Spanish arena with a bull's head in one corner, and rifles and corpses in the middle.

"That's not in the least like your first sketch," Françoise said. "You ought to show that to Pierre too, so that he can see the development."

Elisabeth took out her "Firing Squad."

"That's interesting," said Pierre, "but it's not as good as the other. I think you're quite right to avoid any kind of realism in the treatment of such subjects."

Elisabeth turned searching eyes on him, but he seemed genuinely sincere.

"As you have seen, this is the line along which I'm now working," she said. "I'm trying to use the incoherence and freedom of the sur-realists, but giving them direction."

She took out "Concentration Camp," "Fascist Landscape," and "The Night of the Pogrom," which Pierre examined approvingly. Elisabeth threw a puzzled look at her pictures. After all, wasn't it only a public she lacked to become a real artist? The real artist was one whose work was real. In a sense, Claude was not completely wrong when he panted to have his play put on. A work of art only became real by becoming known. She chose one of her most recent canvases, "The Game of Massacre." As she was putting it on the easel, she caught the look of dismay Xavière had turned toward Françoise.

"Don't you care for pictures?" she asked with a tight-lipped smile.

"I don't understand anything about it," Xavière said apologetically.

Pierre turned to her quickly with an uneasy look, and Elisabeth felt a sudden wave of anger. They probably had warned Xavière that this was to be an inevitable part of the evening's entertainment, but she was beginning to grow restless, and her slightest whim was more im-portant to them than Elisabeth's entire fate.

"What do you think of it?" she asked.

It was a daring and complex painting which called for considerable comment. Pierre glanced at it hastily.

"I like it very much, too," he said.

It was obvious that he only wanted to get it over and done with. Elisabeth took away the canvas. "That's enough for today," she said. "We mustn't make a martyr of this child."

Xavière gave her a somber look; she understood perfectly well that Elisabeth was not blind where she was concerned.

"You know, if you want to put on a record," Elisabeth said to Fran-çoise, "it's all right. Only take a fine needle, because of the tenant under me."

"Oh, yes!" cried Xavière eagerly.

"Why don't you try exhibiting this year?" said Pierre, lighting his pipe. "I'm sure you'd interest a large public."

"It's not the right moment. In these uncertain times it would be madness to launch a new name."

"Still, theaters are doing very well."

Elisabeth looked at him, hesitated, then said point-blank, "Did you know that Nanteuil has taken Claude's play?"

"Oh, yes," he said, looking vague. "Is Claude pleased?"

"Not terribly." Slowly Elisabeth inhaled the smoke of her cigarette. "I'm absolutely heartbroken. It's one of those snap decisions that can ruin a man permanently." She took her courage in both hands. "Oh, if only you had taken *Partage*. Claude would have been made."

Pierre looked embarrassed; he disliked refusing anyone a favor. However he generally managed to squirm out of such situations.

"Listen," he said, "would you like me to talk to Berger about it again? It so happens we're lunching with them tomorrow."

Xavière had put her arm around Françoise and was teaching her to dance a rumba and Françoise's face wore an expression of agonized concentration, as if her soul's salvation depended on her prowess.

"Berger won't go back on his rejection," Elisabeth said. A flash of absurd hope struck her. "But Berger isn't the right man; it's you. Listen, you're putting on your play next winter; but not until October. If only you would put on *Partage* for a few weeks!"

She waited, her heart pounding. Pierre puffed at his pipe. He seemed uncomfortable.

"You know what's most likely to happen," he said at last, "is that next year we'll go on an extended tour."

"Bernheim's famous plan?" said Elisabeth skeptically. "But I thought you didn't want to have anything to do with it." She was defeated, but she would not let Pierre get out of it so easily.

"It's quite tempting," Pierre said. "We'll make money. We'll see the world." He glanced at Françoise. "Of course, it's not finally settled."

Elisabeth thought a moment. Obviously, they would take Xavière with them. Pierre seemed capable of doing anything for a smile from her. Perhaps he was even ready to give up his work to treat himself to a triangular idyll traveling round the Mediterranean for a year.

"But if you didn't go?" she continued.

"If we didn't go . . ." Pierre repeated irresolutely.

"Yes, would you put on *Partage* in October?" She wanted to force a definite reply from him. He never liked to go back on his word.

Pierre drew at his pipe a few times. "After all, why not?" he said without conviction.

"Do you mean that seriously?"

"Of course," he said in a more decided tone. "If we stay, we can very easily open the season with *Partage*."

He had agreed very quickly; he must be absolutely certain of going on that tour. But still it was a little rash. If he did not carry out this plan, he would be committed.

"That would be absolutely marvelous for Claude!" she said. "When will you be quite certain?"

"In another month or two."

There was a silence.

If there were some way of preventing their going, thought Elisabeth excitedly.

Françoise, who had been watching them out of the corner of her eye for some time, quickly joined them.

"It's your turn to dance," she said to Pierre. "Xavière never tires, but I'm worn out."

"You danced very well," Xavière said. She smiled good-naturedly. "You see, all that was needed was the desire to do it."

"I think you have enough for two," Françoise rejoined gaily.

"And we are going to try it again," Xavière persisted in a gently threatening tone.

This highly affected badinage they adopted among themselves was really too irritating.

"Excuse me a moment," said Pierre. He went with Xavière to choose a record. She had finally decided to take off her coat. She had a slender body, but the experienced eye of the painter could detect a tendency to put on flesh; she would soon be fat if she didn't keep herself on a strict diet.

"She's quite right to watch herself," Elisabeth said. "She could easily get too fat."

"Xavière?" Françoise laughed. "She's a reed."

"Do you think it's quite fortuitous that she eats nothing?"

"It's certainly not because of her figure," said Françoise. She seemed to find the idea completely ridiculous. She had been lucid about Xavière for a while, but now she had become as complacently foolish as Pierre. As if Xavière were not a woman like any other! Elisabeth had seen through her. Behind the mask of a golden-haired virgin, she saw her capable of every human weakness.

"Pierre told me that you may go on a tour next winter," she said. "Is that serious?"

"There's some talk of it," Françoise admitted; she seemed embarrassed. She had no idea what Pierre had said and didn't want to commit herself.

Elisabeth filled two glasses with vodka.

"What are you going to do with that child?" she asked, shaking her head. "I very much wonder!"

"Do with her?" Françoise seemed dumbfounded. "She's on the stage, you know."

"First of all, she isn't," said Elisabeth, "and besides, that isn't what I mean." She half emptied her glass. "She isn't going to spend her life hanging on to your coattails, I suppose?"

"No, probably not."

"Hasn't she any desire for a life of her own—love, adventure?"

Françoise gave her a crooked smile. "I don't think she's giving it much thought for the moment."

"Not for the moment, naturally," said Elisabeth.

Xavière was dancing with Pierre. She danced very well. She had such a shamelessly provocative smile on her face that it was actually indecent. How could Françoise tolerate it? A coquette, a sensualist, Elisabeth had seen it clearly. Certainly she was in love with Pierre, but she was a sly, fickle girl; she was capable of sacrificing everything to the pleasure of the moment. That was the fly in the ointment.

"What's become of your lover?" Françoise asked.

"Moreau? We had a terrible row. About pacifism. I teased him and then he got angry. He ended up by almost strangling me." She rummaged in her bag. "Here, look at his last letter."

"I don't think he's so stupid," said Françoise. "The things you've said to me against him!"

"Everyone thinks a lot of him." Elisabeth had found him interesting in the beginning, and she had enjoyed encouraging his love. Why was she so completely disgusted with him? She emptied out the contents of her bag. It was because he was in love with her. That was the best way to lose value in her eyes. She had enough pride left to be able to despise the ridiculous feelings she inspired.

"His letter is most correct," said Françoise. "What did you answer?"

"I was really embarrassed. It was very difficult to explain to him that I had never for a moment taken this affair seriously. Besides . . ." She shrugged her shoulders. How could she know what to think? She herself was bewildered. This sham friendship, which she had created for lack of anything better to do, could lay claim to as much reality as her painting, her politics, or her rows with Claude. It was just like everything else—pointless play acting.

She continued, "He followed me as far as Dominique's, pale as a ghost, his eyes popping out of his head. He was furious. There was no one in the street. I was terrified." She gave a short laugh. She could not help talking about it, but she had not been in the least frightened, and there had been no scene. Just a poor fellow at his wits' end, trying to express himself in words and awkward gestures.

"Just imagine, he pinned me against a lamppost, grabbed me by the throat, while he shouted dramatically, 'I'll have you, Elisabeth, or I'll kill you.' "

"He actually tried to strangle you?" Françoise asked incredulously. "I didn't think you meant literally."

"Oh yes," said Elisabeth. "He really seemed on the point of murder." It was exasperating; if you told things just as they happened, people didn't believe they had happened at all; and as soon as they began to believe you, they believed something entirely different from what had actually taken place. She remembered his glassy eyes quite close to her face, and his pale lips coming nearer and nearer to her mouth.

"I said to him, 'Strangle me, but don't kiss me,' and his hands tightened around my neck."

"Well, my God!" said Françoise, "that would have been a fine *crime passionel.*"

"Oh! he let go at once. I merely said, 'This is ridiculous,' and he let go." She had almost felt disappointed, but even had he tightened his grip, held on until she collapsed, it would not really have been a crime. Just a clumsy accident. Never, never did anything really positive happen to her.

"Was it because of his passion for pacifism that he wanted to murder you?"

"He was incensed when I said that war was the only way of getting out of the mess we're in."

"I feel for him in that," said Françoise. "I'd be afraid that the cure might be worse than the disease."

"Why?" asked Elisabeth. She shrugged her shoulders. War. Why were they all so afraid of it? War at least was something solid; it did not turn into papier-mâché in your hand. Something real. At last, real deeds would be possible. In preparation for the revolution, she had begun to learn Russian just in case. Perhaps at last she would be able to show what she had in her; perhaps it was circumstances that had never yet measured up to her capacities.

Pierre had joined them. "Are you quite sure that war will lead to revolution?" he asked. "And even then, don't you think it would be a very high price to pay?"

"It's because she's a fanatic," Françoise said with an affectionate smile. "She would plunge Europe into a blood bath to serve the cause."

Elisabeth smiled. "A fanatic . . ." she said modestly; and her smile fell abruptly. Surely they weren't fooled. They knew: she was quite hollow; there was no conviction except in words, and they, too, were artificial and theatrical.

"A fanatic!" she repeated, bursting into a strident laugh. That was a good one!

"What's the matter?" Pierre asked with a look of annoyance.

"Nothing," said Elisabeth. She was silent. She had gone too far. Too far—but then that, too, had been done deliberately, hadn't it?—that cynical disgust with herself?—and this contempt for that trumped-up disgust, wasn't that also theatrical? And this doubt about the contempt . . . It became maddening, if you began being sincere—was there really no way to stop?

"We're going to say good-bye," said Françoise. "We must run along."

Elisabeth started. They were all three standing there in front of her and they seemed uncomfortable: she must have had a strange look on her face during that silence.

"Good-bye. I'll drop into the theater one of these evenings," she said as she accompanied them to the door. When they were gone she went back to her studio. She walked to the table and poured out a large glass of vodka and drank it off. What if she had gone on laughing? If she had shouted at them, "I know, I know that you know!" They would have been astonished. But what use was it? Tears and revulsions—they would have been theatrical, too, but more tiring and just as futile. There was no way out. Nowhere in the world, or in herself, had a vestige of truth been allotted her.

She looked at the dirty plates, at the empty glasses, at the ashtray filled with cigarette ends. They wouldn't always be so triumphant; there was something that could be done, something to do with Gerbert. She sat down on the edge of the couch. She remembered Xavière's pearly cheeks and fair hair, and Pierre's blissful smile while he was dancing with her. It was all whirling madly through her head, but tomorrow she would be able to sort out all these thoughts. Something could be done; an authentic act that would make genuine tears flow. Perhaps at that moment, she would feel that she, too, was really living. Then, they would not go on tour; they would put on Claude's play. Then . . .

"I'm drunk," she murmured.

There was nothing to do but sleep and wait for the morning.

2

"Two BLACK coffees, and one light, with croissants, please," Pierre said to the waiter. He smiled at Xavière. "You're not too tired?"

"I'm never tired when I'm enjoying myself." She had put down in front of her a bag of pink shrimps, two huge bananas and three raw artichokes. None of them had wanted to go home to bed after leaving Elisabeth's. They had gone to the rue Montorgueil to have some onion soup and then, to Xavière's delight, they had walked all around les Halles.

"How pleasant the Dôme is at this hour," said Françoise. The café was almost empty. A man in blue overalls was kneeling on the floor scrubbing the soapy tiles, and it made the place smell like a laundry. As the waiter was placing their order on the table, a tall American woman in evening dress threw a paper pellet at his head.

"It's wonderful to see American women drunk," Xavière remarked very seriously. "They're the only people who can get dead drunk without at once going to pieces."

She took two lumps of sugar, held them uncertainly for a moment above her glass, and then dropped them into her coffee.

"What are you doing, you little wretch?" cried Pierre. "Now you won't be able to drink it."

"But I did it on purpose, to neutralize it." She looked at Françoise and Pierre disapprovingly. "You don't seem to know that you're poisoning yourselves with all the coffee you drink."

"You're a nice one to talk," said Françoise. "You're always guzzling tea; that's still worse!"

"Ah, but I'm systematic," Xavière explained, shaking her head. "But you, you drink that stuff without even thinking about it, just like water."

She really looked refreshed. Her hair was lustrous, her eyes shone like enamels. Françoise noticed that the clear iris was surrounded by a dark blue ring; she was always discovering something new in this face. Xavière was a perpetual surprise.

"Just listen to them!" said Pierre.

A couple near the window were talking in low voices. The young woman was coquettishly fingering her black hair, which was imprisoned in a hair net. "That's how it is," she was saying, "nobody has ever seen my hair. It belongs only to me."

"But why?" asked the young man in a passionate voice.

"Those women!" Xavière said scornfully. "They feel so cheap they naturally have to invent something to make themselves seem precious."

"That's true," said Françoise. "This girl withholds her hair. With Éloy it's her virginity, and with Canzetti her art. It enables them to throw the rest to the four winds."

Xavière smiled faintly and Françoise watched the smile with a little envy; it must give one a sense of power to feel so precious to oneself.

Pierre had been staring at the bottom of his glass for some time. His muscles had sagged, his eyes were clouded and a look of idiotic suffering had spread over his features.

"Don't you feel a little better than you did earlier?" asked Xavière.

"No," he said. "No, poor Pierre doesn't feel any better."

They had started this game in the taxi. Françoise was always amused when he improvised an act, but she took only a minor part for herself.

"Pierre isn't poor. Pierre feels very well," said Xavière with gentle authority. She thrust a threatening face very close to his.

"You do feel well, don't you?"

"Yes, I feel well," Pierre said quickly.

"Then smile," said Xavière.

Pierre's lips flattened out till they were stretched almost from ear to ear; at the same time his eyes became wild, and around his smile his face took on the look of someone under torture; it was amazing what he could do with his face. Suddenly, as if a spring had broken, his smile collapsed into a tearful grimace. Xavière almost choked with laughter, and then, with all the pompous seriousness of a hypnotist, she passed her hand over Pierre's face from forehead to chin. The smile came back. With a sly look, Pierre moved his finger downward across his mouth and the smile vanished. Xavière shook with laughter until tears came to her eyes.

"Exactly what method do you use, Mademoiselle?" Françoise asked.

"A method all my own," Xavière replied modestly. "A mixture of suggestion, intimidation and reasoning."

"And you obtain good results?"

"Amazing! If only you knew what a state he was in when I first took him in hand!"

"Yes, yes, of course," Françoise said, "it's most important to pay the strictest attention to the initial symptoms." At this moment, the patient appeared to be very far gone. He was greedily munching tobacco straight from his pipe, like a donkey from its manger; his eyes were popping out of their sockets and he was really chewing the tobacco.

"Good God!" said Xavière in horror. Then she adopted a level tone of voice. "Listen carefully," she said, "you ought to eat only what is edible. Pipe tobacco is not edible, therefore you are making a big mistake by eating tobacco."

Pierre listened obediently, then he began eating from his pipe again.

"It's good," he said earnestly.

"We'll have to try psychoanalysis," Françoise said. "Perhaps his father whipped him with an elder branch when he was a child?"

"What's that got to do with it?" asked Xavière.

"Took a hiding, took to hiding—in other words a smoke screen," Françoise explained solemnly. "He eats tobacco to sublimate the hiding. The tobacco also represents the pith of the elder which he destroys, through symbolic assimilation."

Pierre's face was changing dangerously. It had become very red. His cheeks were swelling visibly and a pinkish blur was beginning to spread over his eyes.

"It's no longer good," he said angrily.

"Stop that," Xavière said. She took the pipe out of his hands.

"Oh!" said Pierre. He looked at his empty hands. "Oh! oh, oh," he wailed. He snivelled, and quite suddenly tears rolled down his cheeks. "Oh! I'm so unhappy!"

"You frighten me," Xavière said. "Stop it."

"Oh! I'm so unhappy." He was bawling, lustily now with a terrible childlike face.

"Stop," cried Xavière, her features distorted with fright. Pierre began to laugh and wiped his eyes.

"What a poetic idiot you'd make," Françoise said. "One could fall in love with an idiot with a face like that."

"You still have a chance," Pierre said.

"Aren't there ever any idiot's parts on the stage?" Xavière asked.

"I know of one superb one, in a play by Valle Inclan, but it's a silent part."

"What a pity," said Xavière with gentle irony.

"Did Elisabeth pester you again about Claude's play?" Françoise asked. "I thought I understood that you dodged it by saying we were going on tour next winter."

"Yes," Pierre said, looking thoughtful, as he stirred the remains of his coffee. "And after all, why the devil are you so set against this plan? If we don't go on tour next year, I'm very much afraid that we never shall."

Françoise had a feeling of displeasure, but so slight that she was surprised. Everything felt blurred and dulled in her, as if an injection of cocaine had anesthetized her soul.

"But there's also the risk that your play will never be produced," she said.

"We'll probably be able to go on working when it's no longer possible to leave France," Pierre said insincerely. He shrugged his shoulders. "And besides, my play is not an end in itself. We've spent our lives working so hard, wouldn't you like a little change?"

Just at the very moment when they were nearing their goal! In the course of next year she would finish her novel, and Pierre would at last reap the fruits of ten years' work. She realized that a year's absence would be disastrous, but she realized it with listless indifference.

"Oh! as far as I'm concerned, you know how much I like traveling," she said. It wasn't even worth the struggle, she knew she was defeated in advance; not by Pierre, however, but by herself. The faint spark of resistance which still survived in her was not strong enough to give her any hope of carrying the fight to a finish.

"Doesn't it thrill you to think of the three of us watching the coast of Greece draw nearer and nearer as we stand on the deck of the *Cairo-City!*" He smiled at Xavière. "You can see the Acropolis in the distance, looking like any silly little monument. We'll jump into a taxi and go jolting into Athens; the road is very bumpy."

"And then we'll have dinner in the Zapeion Gardens," Françoise said. She looked happily at Xavière. "She's quite capable of loving the grilled shrimps and lamb tripe, and even the resinous wine."

"Of course I'll love them," Xavière said. "What disgusts me is the sensible cooking here in France. But there, I'll eat like an ogre, you'll see."

"As far as that goes, it's nearly as abominable as the food in that Chinese restaurant where you stuffed yourself," Françoise said.

"Will we stay in one of those districts with nothing but little wood and corrugated-iron huts?"

"We can't, there's no hotel," Pierre said. "They're just emigrant quarters. But we'll spend a lot of time there."

It would be fun to see all that with Xavière, her eyes transfiguring the most insignificant object. Just then, when they were showing her around les Halles—all the little bistros, the mounds of carrots, the tramps—Françoise felt she was seeing them for the first time. She took a handful of shrimps and began shelling them. Through Xavière's eyes, the swarming docks of Piraeus, the blue boats, the dirty children, the taverns smelling of olive oil and grilled meat, would reveal undreamed riches. She looked at Xavière, then at Pierre. She loved them; they loved each other; they loved her. For weeks all three of them had been living in happy enchantment. And how precious was this moment, with the light of dawn on the empty banquettes of the Dôme, the smell of the soapy tiles, and this faint flavor of fresh fish!

"Berger has some superb photographs of Greece," Pierre said. "I must ask him for them later."

"That's right, you're going to lunch with those people," Xavière said, with a tender sulkiness.

"If it were only Paula, we would take you with us," Françoise said. "But with Berger there, it becomes formal."

"We'll leave the whole company in Athens," Pierre went on, "and we'll make a grand tour across the Peloponnesus."

"On mules?" asked Xavière.

"Partly on mules."

"And we'll have lots of adventures," said Françoise.

"We'll kidnap a beautiful little Greek girl." Pierre turned to Françoise. "Do you remember that little girl at Tripolis, the one we felt so sorry for?"

"Of course I remember her. It's terrible to think that she'll probably spend the whole of her natural life stagnating in that kind of desert crossroads."

Xavière was beginning to look sullen. "And after that, we'll have to drag her about with us. That'll be an awful nuisance."

"We'll send her off to Paris," said Françoise.

"But she'd be there when we got back."

"Do you mean to say," Françoise asked her, "that if you found out that in some corner of the world someone very nice indeed was living in utter misery and unable to escape, you wouldn't lift a finger to rescue him?"

"No," said Xavière with a stubborn look, "it wouldn't matter to me." She looked at Pierre and Françoise, and suddenly added with bitterness, "I don't want anyone else with us."

It was childish, but Françoise felt as if she were being wrapped around her shoulders with a heavy cope. She thought she ought to feel free after all those renunciations, and yet she had never been less free than during these last few weeks. For the moment she seemed to be bound hand and foot.

"You're right," Pierre agreed. "We three have enough to do as it is. Now that we've achieved a perfectly harmonious trio, we've got to take advantage of it without bothering about anything else."

"Still, supposing one of us met with something really exciting?" Françoise insisted. "It might well be to the common good; it's always a pity to limit oneself."

"But what we've just built up is still so new," said Pierre. "We must first put a good long period behind us; after that any of us will be able to have adventures, leave for America, or adopt a Chinese child. But not before . . . let's say five years."

"Yes," Xavière said excitedly.

"Shake hands on that, it's a pact. For five years each of us will devote himself exclusively to the trio." He put his hand palm up on the table. "I forgot that you don't like that gesture," he said smiling.

"But I do," Xavière said solemnly, "it's a pact." She put her hand on Pierre's.

"Agreed," said Françoise, putting her hand out too.

Five years! How heavy those words sounded! She had never been afraid to commit herself to the future; but now that the future had changed character, she no longer felt the free urge of her whole being. She could not think, "my future," because she could not separate herself from Pierre and Xavière. But it was no longer possible to say, "our future," for that implied a future with Pierre alone. Together they had planned the same future for both; planned one life, one work, one love. But with Xavière there, all that became meaningless. It was not possible to live with her, but only beside her. Despite the sweetness of the past few weeks, Françoise was gripped with fear at the thought of the long unchanging years ahead. Strange and fateful, they stretched into infinity like a black tunnel in which the twists and bends would have to be blindly endured. This was not a proper future—it was a shapeless and unpeopled extension of time.

"It seems odd to be making plans at this late date," she said. "We've grown so used to living from day to day."

"But you've never really believed there's going to be a war," Pierre said. He smiled. "Don't start now that things seem just about settled."

"I don't actually think about it," Françoise said, "but the future seems completely shut off." It was not so much because of war, but it didn't matter. She was glad enough, thanks to this ambiguity, that she could seem to explain; she had long since ceased to be scrupulously honest.

"It's true that imperceptibly we've begun to live without thinking of a tomorrow," Pierre said. "I believe almost everyone has reached that stage, even the most extreme optimists."

"It puts a blight on everything," Françoise said. "Nothing extends beyond the present."

"Oh, but I don't agree," Pierre rejoined eagerly. "On the contrary, things are more precious to me because they are threatened on all sides."

"To me everything seems pointless. How can I explain? In the old days, whatever I did, I had the impression of being thoroughly involved in things—for instance, my novel. It existed. It insisted upon being written. Now, writing is simply piling up pages."

She pushed away the mound of tiny pink shells she had emptied. The young woman with her precious hair at the other table was now alone with two empty glasses; she had lost her animated look and was thoughtfully applying lipstick to her mouth.

"The point is that we've been torn from our own personal history," said Pierre, "but that seems to me to be all to the good."

"Of course," Françoise said, smiling at him. "Even if there is a war, you'll still find a way of getting something out of it."

"But how can such a thing possibly happen?" Xavière suddenly exclaimed with an air of superiority. "Surely people aren't crazy enough to want to get themselves killed."

"Nobody asks their opinion," said Françoise.

"All the same, it's the public who decides, and they're not fools," Xavière said with angry contempt. Conversations about war or politics always irritated her, because of their uselessness. Nevertheless, Françoise was surprised by her aggressive tone.

"They're not all fools," said Pierre, "but they're fickle. Society is a strange machine; nobody can control it."

"Well! I don't understand why people let themselves be crushed by the machine."

"What do you want them to do?" Françoise asked.

"Not to act like a lot of sheep."

"Then you must join a political party."

Xavière interrupted her. "Good God! I wouldn't want to dirty my hands."

"In that case, you'll be one of the sheep," Pierre said. "It's always the same. You can't fight society except by social means."

"In that case," Xavière said, her face suddenly crimson with rage, "if I were a man, I'd refuse to go when they came to get me."

"That would be a great help," said Françoise. "They'd march you off between two policemen, and if you were stubborn about it, they'd shove you up against a wall and shoot you."

A faraway look came into Xavière's eyes. "Does it really seem to you so terrible to die?" she said.

She must have been in a blind rage to argue with such complete bad faith. Françoise felt that this outburst had been directed particularly at her, but she had no notion what fault she had committed. She looked at Xavière with horror. What venomous thoughts had suddenly changed that face, which a moment ago was all sweetness and tenderness? Malignantly they blossomed beneath her stubborn little forehead, under the shelter of her silky hair, and Françoise was defenseless against them. She loved Xavière. She could no longer stand her hatred.

"You said a little while ago that it was disgusting to let yourself be killed," she said.

"But it's not the same if you die voluntarily."

"Killing yourself in order not to be killed is not dying voluntarily!"

"In any case, I would prefer it," she said, and added with a distant, weary air, "Besides, there are other ways. It's always possible to desert."

"That's not so easy, you know," Pierre said.

Xavière's eyes softened, and she gave Pierre an ingratiating smile. "Would you do it, if it were possible?" she asked.

"No," said Pierre, "for a thousand reasons. First of all, I'd have to give up the idea of ever returning to France, and that's where I have my theater, my public; that's where my work has a meaning and a chance of leaving some mark."

Xavière sighed. "That's true," she said with a sad and disappointed expression. "You drag so much deadwood about with you."

Françoise shuddered. Xavière's words always held a double meaning. Did she also include Françoise in that deadwood? Did she resent Pierre's still loving her? Françoise had at times noticed sudden silences whenever she happened to break into one of Xavière's tête-à-tête's with Pierre, or short spells of surliness if Pierre talked to her a little too long. These she had disregarded; but today, they seemed obvious. Xavière would have liked to feel that Pierre was free and belonged to her alone.

"The deadwood," said Pierre, "why, it's myself! You can't differentiate between a man and what he feels and loves, and the life he himself has shaped."

Xavière's eyes were glistening. "Well, as far as I'm concerned," she said with a slightly theatrical shiver, "I'd go anywhere, any time. One should never be bound to a country or a profession; or," she concluded impetuously, "to anybody or anything."

"But that's because you don't understand that what a person does and what a person is, are one and the same thing," Pierre said.

"That depends on who the person is." She was smiling to herself and bristling with defiance; she did nothing and she was Xavière; she was irrevocably Xavière.

After a short silence she said with a modesty that betrayed her bitter hatred, "Of course, you know more about these things than I."

"But you think that a little common sense is worth more than all this knowledge?" Pierre cheerfully rejoined. "Why did you suddenly decide to hate us?"

"I, hate you?" she exclaimed, staring with wide-eyed innocence, but her mouth remained tight. "I'd have to be insane."

"It irritated you, didn't it, to hear us driveling on again about war, when we'd just been busy making such pleasant plans?"

"You surely have a right to talk about whatever you choose," Xavière said.

"You think we enjoy creating a tragedy out of nothing, but I assure you that it's not so. The situation demands careful consideration; the course of events is equally important to us and to you."

"I know," said Xavière with some embarrassment. "But what good does it do to talk about it?"

"So that we'll be ready for anything," Pierre answered. He smiled. "It's not bourgeois prudence. But if you really have a horror of being browbeaten, if you don't want to be one of the sheep, then there's no better way to begin than by weighing your position very carefully."

"But I don't understand anything about it," said Xavière in a plaintive voice.

"No one can begin to understand in one day. First of all, you'll have to start reading the newspapers."

Xavière pressed her hands against her temples. "Oh! They're so boring," she said. "I can't make head or tail of them."

"It's true," Françoise said. "If you're not already well informed it all seems meaningless." Her heart was heavy with pain and anger; it was jealousy that made Xavière hate these adult conversations in which she was unable to participate. All this fuss, merely because she could not bear Pierre's attention to be directed toward anybody but herself, even for a moment.

"Well, I know what I'll do," said Pierre. "One of these days, I'll give you a long lecture on politics, and after that I'll keep you regularly informed. It's really not so complicated, you know."

"I'd like you to do that," Xavière agreed happily. She leaned over closer to them. "Have you noticed Éloy? She's taken a table near the door, so that she can wheedle a few words out of you when you pass her."

Éloy was dipping a croissant into her cup of coffee, and she was not made up. She looked shy and lonely, and the effect was not unpleasing.

"Anyone seeing her like that and not knowing her, would think her attractive," said Françoise.

"I feel sure that she comes here for breakfast with the express purpose of meeting you."

"She's quite capable of that," Pierre said.

The café had been filling up. At a nearby table, a woman was writing letters with one eye on the cashier's counter, obviously haunted by the fear that a waiter should discover her and insist on her ordering something. But no waiter put in an appearance, even though a man near the window was rapping on his table with increasing impatience.

Pierre looked at the clock.

"We'll have to go home," he said. "I still have a hundred and one things to do before lunching with Berger."

"Of course, now you've got to go, just when everything's coming right again," Xavière said resentfully.

"But everything has always been all right," Pierre said. "What's a momentary cloud compared with this stupendous night?"

Xavière smiled shyly, and they left the Dôme, waving a brief greeting to Éloy from a distance. Françoise found little pleasure in the thought of going to Berger's for lunch, but she was happy for the chance to be alone with Pierre for a while, or at least to be with him without Xavière. It was a brief glimpse of the outside world. She was beginning to feel stifled in this trio, which was in danger of becoming hermetically sealed.

Xavière amiably linked her arms with Françoise and Pierre, but her face was still downcast, and they walked to the hotel without exchanging a word. There was a special-delivery letter in Françoise's box.

"It looks like Paula's handwriting," Françoise said, as she opened the envelope.

"She's put us off," she said. "She has invited us to supper on the sixteenth instead."

"Oh! What a godsend!" cried Xavière, her eyes sparkling.

"It's a real bit of luck," said Pierre.

Françoise said nothing. She kept turning the paper over in her hand. If only she had not opened it in front of Xavière, she might have withheld its message and spent the day alone with Pierre. Now it was too late.

"We'll go upstairs and freshen up a bit, and meet at the Dôme later," she said.

"It's Saturday," Pierre said. "We can go to the flea-market, and have lunch in the big blue shed."

"Oh, yes! That will be wonderful! What a godsend!" Xavière repeated with delight. There was something almost nasty in her joyous insistence.

They went upstairs. Xavière left them at her door, and Pierre followed Françoise up to her room.

"Aren't you sleepy?" he asked.

"No, when we walk like that, a sleepless night isn't too tiring."

She began to wipe off her make-up. A cold bath and she would feel completely refreshed.

"The weather is perfect, we'll have a wonderful day," Pierre said.

"That is, if Xavière is in a good humor."

"She will be; she always gets sullen when she thinks we're going to leave her behind."

"That wasn't the only reason." She hesitated, she was afraid that Pierre might find her accusation outrageous. "I think she was angry because we had five minutes' conversation together." Again she hesitated. "I think she's a little jealous."

"She's terribly jealous," Pierre said. "Have you only just noticed it?"

"I was wondering if I mightn't be wrong." It always shocked her to see Pierre welcome with approval the very feelings she was fighting with all her might. "She's jealous of me," she added.

"She's jealous of everything. Of Éloy, of Berger, of the theater, of politics, of the fact that we think about war. She feels that it's disloyal of us. We're not supposed to worry about anything but her."

"She was angry with me today," Françoise said.

"Yes, because you expressed reservations about our future plans. She's jealous of you, not only because of me, but of you yourself."

"I know."

If Pierre had the intention of making her feel better, he was going about it in the wrong way. She felt more and more oppressed.

"I find it deplorable," she said, "for it means a love without friendship. It makes you feel that you are being loved in defiance of yourself and not for yourself."

"That is her way of loving," said Pierre.

He was adjusting himself very nicely to this love. He even felt he had gained a victory over Xavière, while Françoise felt painfully at the mercy of that passionate, touchy soul. She seemed to exist only through Xavière's capricious feelings for her. It was as if a voodoo sorceress had taken possession of her through the medium of a waxen image and was subjecting her to the most horrible tortures. At that moment, Françoise was an untouchable, a wasted and shriveled up soul. She had to wait for a smile from Xavière before she could hope to regain some self-respect.

"Well, we'll soon see what sort of mood she's in."

But it was true agony to feel that her happiness and even her intrinsic being was dependent to such an extent on this strange, rebellious spirit.

Joylessly, Françoise bit into a thick slice of chocolate cake; every mouthful stuck in her throat; she was furious with Pierre. He knew that Xavière, weary after a night without sleep, would be sure to go to bed early; and he might have guessed that, after the morning's misunderstanding, Françoise was eager to spend some time with her alone. When Françoise had recovered from her illness, they had drawn up certain hard and fast rules. On alternate days, she was to go out with Xavière from seven in the evening until midnight; and every other day Pierre was to see Xavière from two till seven. Each was free to spend the rest of the time as desired, but any tête-à-tête with Xavière was taboo. Françoise, at least, kept scrupulously to this program; Pierre was more apt to suit his convenience. Today he had really gone too far; he had asked in a plaintive if not playful tone not to be sent away before he had to go back to the theater; he seemed to have no feeling of guilt. Perched on a high stool next to Xavière, he was telling her the story of Rimbaud's life with great animation. This story had been in the telling ever since they had been to the flea-market, but it had been interspersed with so many digressions that Rimbaud had not yet met Verlaine. Pierre was speaking. His words were describing Rimbaud, but his voice seemed rich in countless intimate allusions, and Xavière was watching him with a kind of voluptuous docility. Their relationship was virtually chaste, yet a few kisses and light caresses had been enough to establish between them a sensual understanding, quite apparent beneath their reserve. Françoise looked away; she, as a rule, loved Pierre's storytelling, but tonight neither the inflections of his voice, nor his enchanting figures of speech, nor his unexpected turns of phrase affected her; she felt too much bitterness toward him. He was careful to explain to her almost daily that Xavière was as fond of her as she was of him, but he deliberately behaved as if this feminine friendship seemed unimportant to him. It was certain that he easily held first place, but that was no excuse for his tactlessness. Of course, there was no question of refusing him what he asked; he would have become angry, and perhaps Xavière too. Yet, by cheerfully accepting Pierre's presence, Françoise seemed to set too little store by Xavière. Françoise glanced into the mirror that covered the whole wall behind the bar; Xavière was smiling at Pierre; she was obviously pleased that he was trying to monopolize her, but that did not mean she did not resent Françoise's giving him that chance.

"Ah! I can just imagine how furious Madame Verlaine was," said Xavière with a burst of laughter.

Françoise felt miserable. Did Xavière always hate her? She had been amiable throughout the afternoon, but only in a superficial way, because the weather was heavenly and the flea-market enchanted her; it meant absolutely nothing. *And what can I do if she does hate me?* thought Françoise. She lifted her glass to her lips and noticed that her hands were trembling; she had drunk too much coffee during the day, and impatience was making her jittery. She could do nothing, she had no real hold on this stubborn little soul, not even on the beautiful living body protecting it; a warm, lithe body, accessible to masculine hands, but which confronted Françoise like a rigid suit of armor. She could only wait quietly for the verdict that would acquit or condemn her; and she had now been waiting ten hours.

It's disgusting! she thought suddenly.

She had spent the day watching Xavière's every frown, listening to every intonation; at this moment, she was still exclusively absorbed in this despicable anguish, and in these pleasant surroundings reflected by the mirror, separated from Pierre, separated from herself.

And if she hates me, what then? she thought defiantly. Was it not possible to consider Xavière's hatred exactly as she did those cakes lying on a plate? They were a beautiful pale yellow, decorated with pink arabesques; she might have also been tempted to eat one, had she not known their sourish, new-born-baby taste. Xavière's small, round head did not occupy much more space in the world, one glance encompassed it; and if those fumes of hatred issuing from it could only be forced back into their container, then they, too, could be kept under control. One word, and the hatred would thunderously collapse, dissolving into a cloud of smoke that would exactly fill Xavière's body, becoming as harmless as the familiar taste hidden under the yellow cream of the cakes; Xavière felt that she existed, but it didn't matter. She was writhing in contortions of rage all in vain; one could just barely make out a few faint eddies, passing over her defenseless face, as unexpected and orderly as clouds in the sky. *They're simply thoughts in her head,* Françoise thought. For a moment she thought the words had taken effect, for only the faintest vignettes were now flitting in disorder beneath that blonde head and were almost instantly gone.

"Unfortunately, I've got to go! Look here, I'm late already," Pierre said. He jumped down from his stool and put on his trench coat. He had given up wearing his distinguished looking soft silk scarf, and he now looked very young and gay. Françoise put out her hand to him with tenderness, but it was a tenderness as lonely as her rancor. He was smiling, and his smile hung poised before her eyes without mingling with the beat of her heart.

"I'll see you tomorrow; ten o'clock at the Dôme," he said.

"Good, until tomorrow then." Indifferently, she shook his hand, and then she saw it close round Xavière's hand. And she could see from Xavière's smile that the pressure of his fingers was a caress.

Pierre departed and Xavière turned to Françoise. *Thoughts in her head. . . .* That was easy to say, but Françoise did not believe in what she had said, it was all sham; the magic word would have had to spring from the depths of her soul, but her soul was too numbed. A harmful mist still remained suspended across the world, poisoning sounds and lights, and penetrating to the very marrow of her bones. She would have to wait until it dissipated by itself; wait, and watch, and suffer, sordidly.

"What shall we do?" she asked.

"Whatever you like," Xavière said with a charming smile.

"Would you prefer a walk or shall we go some place?"

Xavière hesitated. She must have had a very definite idea in the back of her mind.

"What would you say to going to the Negro dance hall?" she asked.

"Why, that's a wonderful idea. It's ages since we've been there."

They left the restaurant and Françoise took Xavière's arm. This suggestion of Xavière's marked the evening as a gala occasion; whenever she wanted particularly to show her affection for Françoise she made a point of inviting her to dance. It was also possible that she was quite simply thinking of her own amusement.

"Shall we walk a little?" Françoise suggested.

"Yes, let's go up the boulevard Montparnasse," said Xavière. She disengaged her arm. "I'd rather I gave you my arm," she explained.

Françoise complied submissively, and as Xavière's fingers touched her, she gently squeezed them; the velvety suède-gloved hand surrendered to hers with tender trust. Like a new dawn, happiness returned, but Françoise was not yet sure whether to believe in it.

"Look, there's the beautiful dark girl with her Hercules," said Xavière.

They were holding hands; the wrestler's head looked minute on top of his tremendous shoulders; the girl was laughing merrily.

"I'm beginning to feel at home," Xavière said, as she glanced with pleasure over the sidewalk tables of the Dôme.

"You've taken your time."

Xavière breathed a faint sigh. "Oh! But when I think of the old streets in Rouen—in the evening—all around the Cathedral, my heart breaks!"

"You weren't so fond of it when you were there," said Françoise.

"It was so poetic."

"Are you going back to see your family?"

"Of course. I'm definitely going there this summer." Her aunt wrote to her every week. In all, they had taken things far better than could have been expected. Suddenly, the corners of Xavière's mouth drooped, and she had the tired look of a much older woman. "I knew how to live alone in those days. I'm amazed when I think how I used to feel things."

Xavière's regrets always covered up some resentment. Françoise put herself on the defensive.

"And yet I can remember that even then you complained of being dried up," Françoise said.

"It wasn't the way it is now," said Xavière in a hollow voice. She looked down and murmured, "Now, I'm diluted."

Before Françoise could reply she gaily squeezed her arm. "Why don't you buy some of those lovely candies?" she said, stopping in front of a shop as pink and shiny as a sugared almond.

"In the window, a huge wooden tray was turning on its own axis, proffering stuffed dates, glazed nuts, and chocolate truffles.

"Do buy some for yourself," said Xavière.

"If this is to be a wonderful gala evening I mustn't make myself sick, as I did the last time," Françoise objected.

"Oh! One or two pieces of candy," said Xavière, "would be quite safe."

She smiled. "This shop has such lovely colors, I feel as if I'm walking into an animated cartoon."

They went in. "Don't you want anything?" Françoise asked.

"I'd like some Turkish Delight." Xavière studied the sweets with a look of enchantment. "Suppose we take some of those too," she said pointing to some lollypops wrapped in transparent paper. "It has such an amusing name."

"Two of those clear candies, one Turkish Delight, and a half pound of 'fairy fingers,' " said Françoise.

The shop assistant put the candy into a crinkly paper bag tied with a pink ribbon run through the top as a drawstring.

"I'd buy the candy just for the bag," said Xavière. "It looks like an alms-purse. I've got half a dozen of them already," she added proudly.

She offered Françoise a clear candy, and then bit into one of the little gelatinous squares.

"We're like two little old women offering each other goodies," Françoise said. "It's shameful."

"When we're eighty, we'll go tottering down to the shop and stand for two hours in front of the window arguing about the flavor of Turkish Delight and drooling a little. The people of the neighborhood will point their fingers at us."

"And we'll shake our heads and say, 'These aren't like the candies we used to buy!' " said Françoise laughing. "I'm sure we won't be walking any slower than we are now."

They smiled at each other. Whenever they strolled along the boulevard, they were apt to slow down to an octogenarian pace.

"Would it bore you to look at those hats?" Xavière asked, stopping in front of a milliner's shop.

"Would you by any chance like to buy one?"

Xavière laughed. "It's not that I dislike them, it's my face that objects. No, I was looking for you."

"Would you like me to wear a hat?"

"You'd look so lovely in one of those little sailor hats," Xavière said in a pleading tone. "Just think of your face under it. And when you go to an elegant party you could put on a big veil and tie it in a huge bow at the back." Her eyes were shining. "Oh! Do promise that you'll do it."

"A veil! I'd be petrified," Françoise laughed.

"But you can wear anything," Xavière insisted. "Ah! If only you'd let me choose your clothes!"

"Well!" Françoise rejoined gaily. "You'll choose my spring wardrobe.

I'll put myself in your hands." She squeezed Xavière's hand. How delightful she could be sometimes! One had to excuse her abrupt changes of mood; the situation was by no means an easy one, and she was so young. Françoise looked at her with tenderness. She did so want Xavière to have a beautiful, happy life.

"What exactly did you mean just then when you complained you were being diluted?" she asked softly.

"Oh! No more than that," Xavière said.

"But what did you mean?"

"Just that."

"I do so want you to be satisfied with your life."

Xavière did not reply. All her gaiety had suddenly vanished.

"Do you find that by living so intimately with other people you lose something of yourself?" Françoise asked.

"Yes," said Xavière. "You become a parasite."

Her voice had been deliberately cutting. But in point of fact, Françoise thought, Xavière didn't seem to find it so disagreeable being with other people. She even got angry whenever Pierre and Françoise went out without her.

"And yet you still have a great many moments alone," she said.

"But it's not the same," Xavière said. "It isn't really being alone."

"I understand. Now, these are only blank intervals, while before they were filled."

"That's just it," Xavière sadly agreed.

Françoise thought for a moment. "But don't you think it would be different if you tried to make something of yourself? That's the best way of not becoming diluted."

"And what am I to do?"

She looked quite crestfallen. Françoise wanted with all her heart to help her; but it was difficult to help Xavière. She smiled.

"Become an actress, for example," she said.

"An actress!"

"I'm so sure you could, if only you would work," Françoise insisted warmly.

"Oh! no," Xavière said wearily.

"You can't be certain."

"That's just it. It's so pointless to work without knowing." Xavière shrugged her shoulders. "Even the most insignificant of those girls believes that she will be an actress."

"It doesn't prove that you won't be one."

"The chances are one in a hundred."

Françoise squeezed her arm more tightly. "What strange reasoning," she said. "Listen, I don't think it's possible to calculate your chances. On the one hand, there's everything to gain, and on the other, nothing to lose. You must bank on success."

"Yes, you've already told me that," Xavière said. She shook her head mistrustfully. "I don't like acts of faith."

"It's not an act of faith. It's a bet."

"It's all the same to me." Xavière made a little face. "That's how Canzetti and Éloy console themselves."

"Yes, they make up compensatory myths; it's nauseating. But it's not a question of dreaming, it's a question of willing. That's different!"

"Elisabeth wants to be a great artist," Xavière said. "What a laugh!"

"I wonder," said Françoise. "I have a feeling she puts the myth into action the better to believe in it, but that she's really incapable of willing anything." She thought for a moment. "You seem to think that people are what they are once and for all, but I don't. I think you make yourself what you are of your own free will. It wasn't pure chance that Pierre was so ambitious in his youth. You know what was said about Victor Hugo? That he was a lunatic who thought he was Victor Hugo."

"I can't bear Victor Hugo," Xavière said. She quickened her pace. "Couldn't we walk a little faster? It's cold, don't you think?"

"All right, let's walk faster," Françoise said and continued, "I do so want to convince you. Why do you have so little confidence in yourself?"

"I don't want to lie to myself," Xavière said. "I think it's disgraceful to have blind faith; nothing is certain except what you can touch."

She looked at her closed fist with a queer bitter sneer. Françoise studied her uneasily. What was going on in that head of hers? Certainly, during these weeks of peaceful happiness she had not been asleep. Behind her smiles a thousand things had been going on in her. She had forgotten none of them; they were all there, tucked away, and one fine day, after a few sparks, there would be an explosion.

They turned the corner of the rue Blomet. The big red cigar of the café-tobacco shop came into view.

"Have a candy," Françoise said.

"No, I don't like them."

Françoise was holding one of the thin clear lollipops in her hand. "I think they have a pleasant taste," she said. "A nice, pure taste."

"But I loathe purity," Xavière said, screwing up her mouth.

Again Françoise felt a stab of anguish. What was too pure? The life in which they were imprisoning Xavière? Pierre's kisses? She herself? "You have such a pure profile," Xavière had often said. They had reached a door on which was written in bold white letters, *Bal Colonial*. They went in. A crowd was surging around the pay booth—black, pale yellow, and café-au-lait faces. Françoise got in line to buy two tickets—seven francs for ladies, nine francs for men. The rumba on the other side of the wooden partition threw her thoughts into confusion. What precisely had happened? Naturally, it was not enough to explain Xavière's reactions on the basis of a momentary caprice. To find the key she would have to think back over the events of these past two months. The old, carefully buried grievances never came to life except through some fresh irritation of the moment. Françoise tried to remember. Walking along the boulevard Montparnasse, the conversation had been light and easy; and then, Françoise had suddenly jumped to serious subjects. It was prompted by tenderness, but did it mean that she was capable of tenderness in words only, even with Xavière's velvety hand nestling in hers and her fragrant hair brushing against her cheek? Was it her awkward purity? Was it that?

"Look, there's Dominique's whole crowd," Xavière said as they walked into the dance hall.

There was the Chanaud girl, Lise Malan, Dourdin, Chaillet. . . . Françoise nodded to them and smiled, while Xavière cast a veiled glance in their direction; she had not let go of Françoise's arm, for she did not dislike having people take them for Lesbians when they entered a public place; it was the kind of shocking behavior that amused her.

"Let's take that table over there," she said.

"I'll have a Martinique punch," Françoise announced.

"I'm going to have one too," Xavière said. Then she added contemptuously, "I can't understand how people can stare with such cowlike rudeness. And anyway I don't give a damn."

Françoise experienced real pleasure at feeling herself included in the stupid spite of this bunch of gossips; she felt as if she and Xavière were being cut away from the rest of the world and imprisoned in an impassioned intimacy.

"You know, I'll dance as soon as you like," Françoise said. "I feel inspired this evening." Except for the rumba, she danced well enough not to look foolish. Xavière's face brightened.

"Really? It won't bore you?"

Xavière put her arm firmly around her. There was an absent expression on Xavière's face when she danced and she never looked around her. But she was not as absorbed as she seemed. She knew how to see without seeming to; it was even a talent in which she took great pride. She certainly enjoyed attracting attention and was deliberately holding Françoise tighter than usual, and smiling at her with flagrant coquetry. Françoise returned her smile. Dancing made her head spin a little. She felt Xavière's beautiful warm breasts against her, she inhaled her sweet breath. Was this desire? But what did she desire? Her lips against hers? This body unresisting in her arms? She could think of nothing. It was only a confused need to keep this amorous face forever turned toward hers, and to be able to say with passion, "She is mine."

"You danced extremely well," Xavière said as they reached their table.

She remained standing. The orchestra had struck up a rumba and a mulatoo came over and bowed to her with a courteous smile. Françoise sat down at the table and took a sip of her sirupy punch. In this huge room, decorated with pale frescoes and resembling, in its banality, a private banquet hall, most of the faces were colored; from ebony to pinkish ocher, every shade of skin could be found here. These Negroes danced with unrestrained obscenity, but their movements had such pure rhythm that, in its elemental simplicity, the rumba kept the sacred character of a primitive rite. The whites who mingled with them were by no means as successful; the women, in particular, either danced like inflexible machines or looked as if they were having hysterical fits. Xavière alone with her perfect grace defied both obscenity and decorum.

Xavière refused a second invitation with a shake of her head and came back to their table.

"They're bewitched, these Negresses," she said angrily. "I'll never be able to dance like that."

She touched her glass with her lips. "Oh! How sweet it is! I can't drink it."

"You dance devilishly well, you know," Françoise said.

"Yes, for a civilized person," said Xavière scornfully. She was staring at something in the middle of the dance floor. "Look, she is still dancing with that little Creole." Her eyes indicated Lise Malan. "She hasn't let go of him since we arrived." She added dolefully, "He's disgracefully pretty."

It was quite true. He was charming, looking so slender in his tight-fitting, fawn-pink jacket. An even more doleful groan escaped from Xavière's lips.

"Ah!" she said, "I'd give one year of my life to be that Negress for just one hour."

"She's beautiful," Françoise agreed. "Her features are not in the least Negroid. Don't you think she must have Indian blood?"

"I don't know," Xavière said, looking miserable. Admiration had brought a gleam of hatred to her eyes.

"Or else, I'd have to be rich enough to buy her and keep her locked up. Baudelaire did that, didn't he? Imagine coming home and, instead of a dog or a cat, finding this magnificent creature purring in front of the fireplace!"

A naked, black body stretched out in front of a log fire. . . . Was that what Xavière was dreaming of? How far did her dreams go?

"I loathe purity." How could Françoise help not recognizing the sensuality of that nose and mouth? The avid eyes, the hands, the sharp teeth visible between her partly opened lips, in search of something to seize, something tangible. Xavière did not yet know what; sounds, colors, perfumes, bodies, everything was her prey. Or did she know?

"Come, let's dance," she said suddenly.

Her hands grasped hold of Françoise, but it was not Françoise and her well-meaning tenderness they coveted. The very first evening they had met, there had been a delirious light in Xavière's eyes. It had died. It would never come back. *How could she love me?* thought Françoise in despair. Delicate and cool, like the scorned taste of the clear candy, with stern, too placid features, a transparently pure soul, Olympian—as Elisabeth used to say—Xavière would never offer even an hour of her life to feel in herself this cold perfection she so piously worshipped. *That's what I am,* thought Françoise with some disgust. In the past, when she had taken no notice of it, this awkward fumbling barely existed. Now it pervaded her whole person; and her gestures— her thoughts even—were angular and sharp, cutting; her perfectly adjusted equilibrium had turned into empty sterility. This mass of bare and translucent whiteness with its jagged edges was, for all she might think to the contrary, irrevocably herself.

"You aren't tired?" she asked when they came back to their table. There were faint circles under Xavière's eyes.

"Yes, I am tired," said Xavière. "I'm getting old." She pouted. "And what about you?"

"A little," Françoise said. Dancing, lack of sleep and the sweet taste of rum were making her feel a little nauseous.

"Of course we only see each other in the evening," said Xavière. "We can't be fresh."

"That's true," Françoise agreed, adding hesitantly, "Labrousse is never free in the evening. We have to keep the afternoons for him."

"Yes, naturally," said Xavière, her face clouding.

Françoise looked at her with a sudden hope, more painful than her regrets. Did Xavière resent her discreet self-effacement? Had she hoped that Françoise would vindicate her right, compel recognition of her love? Still, she should have understood that Françoise was not wantonly resigning herself to the fact that Pierre was preferred to her.

"We could perhaps make other arrangements," she suggested.

Xavière cut her short. "No, everything's fine just as it is," she said quickly.

She frowned. This idea of making arrangements was loathsome to her; she would have liked to have Pierre and Françoise completely at her beck and call, without any program at all. But that, after all, was asking too much. Suddenly Xavière smiled.

"Ah! He's fallen for it," she cried.

Lise Malan's Creole was coming toward them with a shy, engaging air.

"Have you been flirting with him?"

"Oh! Not for his good looks," Xavière said. "I did it just to annoy Lise."

She got up and followed her victim to the middle of the dance floor. It had been discreetly accomplished, for Françoise had not noticed the slightest glance or the faintest smile. Xavière never ceased to astonish her.

She picked up the glass Xavière had barely touched and drank half of it; if only it could have revealed the thoughts in that mind! Was she angry because Françoise had accepted her love for Pierre? . . . *Yet I did not ask her to love him,* she thought with resentment. Xavière had made a free choice. What exactly had she chosen? What was the truth beneath all her coquetry, her tenderness, her jealousies? Was there indeed any truth? Françoise suddenly felt she was on the verge of hating her. Dazzling in her white blouse with its wide sleeves, a tinge of color in her cheeks, she danced; and her face, glowing with pleasure, was turned toward her Creole. She was beautiful. Beautiful, alone, carefree. She was living her own life, with a sweetness or cruelty dictated by each instant; her life to which Françoise was irrevocably bound. And Françoise struggled helplessly in front of her, while she smiled contemptuously or approvingly. What exactly did she want? Françoise could only guess; she had to guess everything—what Pierre felt, what was good, what was evil, and what she herself really and truly wanted. She emptied her glass. She saw nothing clearly any more, nothing at all. Shapeless wreckage lay all about her, within her emptiness and the darkness around it.

The orchestra stopped playing for a minute, and then the dancing was resumed. Xavière stood facing her Creole, a few inches away from him. They were not touching one another, and yet a single shudder seemed to pass through both their bodies. At that moment, Xavière wanted to be no one other than herself; her own charm filled her to the brim. And suddenly, Françoise felt that she, too, was replete. She was nothing, a woman lost in a crowd, a minute particle of the world, wholly drawn toward this infinitesimal golden head which she was unable to seize; but now, in this abject state, she was vouchsafed what she had vainly desired six months earlier at the height of her happiness, for this music, these faces, these lights, had been transformed into regret, into waiting, into love. They were one with her, and gave an irreplaceable meaning to each beat of her heart. Her happiness was shattered, but it was falling all round her in a shower of impassioned moments.

Xavière came back to the table, staggering a little. "He dances divinely," she said. She leaned back in her chair and suddenly her expression changed. "Oh! I'm so tired!"

"Do you want to go home?"

"Oh, yes! I do so want to," she said in an imploring voice.

They left the dance hall and got into a taxi. Xavière collapsed on the seat and Françoise slipped her arm round her; as she closed her hand over Xavière's small, limp hand, she felt flooded with joy. Whether she wanted or not, Xavière was bound to her by a bond stronger than hatred or love; Françoise was not her prey along with the rest, she was the very substance of her life, and all the moments of passion, of pleasure, of desire could not have existed without this firm web that supported them. Whatever happened to Xavière, happened through Françoise, and Xavière, whether she liked it or not, belonged to her.

The taxi stopped in front of the hotel, and they hurried upstairs. Despite her weariness, Xavière's walk had lost none of its spring. She opened the door of her room.

"I'll come in for a moment," Françoise said.

"Just being home makes me feel less tired." She took off her jacket and sat down beside Françoise, and suddenly all Françoise's precarious calm was shattered. Xavière was sitting there, bolt upright, in her dazzling blouse, close beside her and smiling, yet out of reach. She was fettered by no bond except the ones she decided to forge for herself. She could only be held by her own consent.

"It was a delightful evening," Françoise said.

"Yes," said Xavière. "We'll have to do that again."

Françoise looked around her anxiously; solitude would close in on Xavière, the solitude of her room, of her sleep, and of her dreams. There would be no way of breaking in.

"You'll soon be dancing as well as the Negress."

"Oh no! That's impossible," said Xavière.

Silence fell again, heavily, words were powerless. Paralyzed by the frightening grace of this beautiful body she could not even desire. She was at a loss for a gesture.

Xavière's eyes closed and she smothered a childlike yawn. "I think I'm falling asleep right here," she said.

"I'll leave you now." Françoise stood up; she had a lump in her throat, but there was nothing else to do; she had not known what else to do.

"Good night," she said.

She was standing near the door. Impulsively, she took Xavière in her arms.

"Good night, dear Xavière," she said, brushing Xavière's cheeks with her lips.

Xavière yielded, and for a moment she remained very still and soft against Françoise's shoulder. What was she waiting for? For Françoise to let her go, or for her arms to close more tightly around her. Quickly the girl disengaged herself.

"Good night," she said in a completely natural voice.

It was all over. Françoise climbed the stairs to her room. She was ashamed of that futile gesture of tenderness. She let herself sink down on her bed with a heavy heart.

3

"APRIL, May, June, July, August, September, six months' training and I'll be ready for the slaughter," thought Gerbert.

He stood planted in front of the bathroom mirror, adjusting the wings of the magnificent bow tie he had just borrowed from Péclard. He wished he knew whether or not he would be afraid, but in a situation like that you could never tell; the cold—that was probably the worst . . . taking off your shoes to see if your toes were still there.

"There's no more hope this time," he thought with resignation. It seemed unbelievable that people were crazy enough to decide in cold blood to set the whole world on fire. But the fact remained that German troops had entered Czechoslovakia, and England was being rather obstinate on the subject.

With an expression of satisfaction, Gerbert studied the beautiful bow he had just tied. In general he disapproved of neckties, but he had no idea where Labrousse and Françoise would take him for dinner. They both had a vicious passion for cream sauces, and no matter what Françoise said, one did attract attention when one wore a sweater in any of those restaurants with checkered tablecloths. He put on his jacket and went into the living room. He was alone in the apartment. He carefully selected two cigars from Péclard's desk and then went into Jacqueline's bedroom. Gloves, handkerchiefs, rouge, Lanvin's arpège—an entire family could have been fed on the money paid for these frivolities. Gerbert stuffed a pack of Greys and a bag of chocolates in his pocket; Françoise's only weakness was her passion for sweets; one could allow her that. Gerbert was grateful to her for so often unashamedly wear-

253

ing worn out shoes and stockings with runs in them. In her room at the hotel, no studied elegance affronted the eye; she owned neither knick-knacks nor embroideries, nor even a tea service; and besides, you never had to play up to her. She was not given to coquetry, to headaches, to abrupt changes of mood; she demanded no special consideration; you could even remain blissfully silent with her.

Gerbert slammed the door behind him and dashed down the three flights of stairs at top speed—forty seconds—Labrousse could never have precipitated himself down that dark, winding staircase as quickly as that. Sometimes he did win the race unfairly by a stroke of luck. Forty seconds. Labrousse would surely accuse him of exaggerating. "I'll say thirty seconds," Gerbert decided. "In that way, we can work back to the truth." He crossed the Place Saint Germain des Prés. They had arranged to meet him at the Café de Flore; they liked the place because they did not go there very often, but as far as he was concerned, he was fed up with the intellectual élite. "Next year I'll have a change of air," he said fiercely. "If Labrousse arranges that tour, it will be great." He looked quite determined. Gerbert pushed open the door. Next year, he'd be in the trenches, there was no more question about it. He walked through the café smiling vaguely around him, then his smile broadened. Taken singly, each one of the three was slightly comic, but when you saw them together, it was really a scream.

"What are you splitting your face about?" asked Labrousse.

Gerbert waved his hand helplessly.

"The sight of the three of you," he said.

They were sitting in a row on a banquette, with Françoise and Pierre on either side of Pagès. He sat down opposite them.

"Are we so comical?" Françoise asked.

"You've no idea."

Labrousse looked at him out of the corner of his eye. "Well, how does the idea of a lively little holiday along the Rhine strike you?"

"Lousy," said Gerbert. "And you were so sure, saying everything was calming down."

"This last blow has come as a complete surprise."

"We're in for it this time, that's certain," Gerbert said.

"I think we have far less chance of getting out of it now than we had in September. England explicitly guaranteed Czechoslovakia. She can't back out."

There was a short silence. Gerbert always felt embarrassed in Pagès's presence. Even Labrousse and Françoise seemed ill at ease. Gerbert pulled the cigars out of his pocket and handed them to Labrousse.

"Here," he said. "They're big ones."

Labrousse gave a low whistle of approval.

"Péclard does all right for himself! We'll smoke them after dinner."

"Here's something for you," Gerbert said, putting down the cigarettes and chocolate in front of Françoise.

"Oh! How nice." The smile on her face was like the one she gave Labrousse at tender moments. It made Gerbert feel happy; there were moments when he almost thought Françoise was fond of him. Yet she hadn't seen him for so long; she hardly gave him a thought. She thought of no one but Labrousse.

"Help yourself," she said, offering the bag to the table at large.

Xavière shook her head with an air of reserve.

"Not before dinner," said Pierre. "You'll spoil your appetite."

Françoise took a piece of chocolate; she could probably finish them in no time. It was fantastic, the quantity of sweets she could eat without making herself sick.

"What will you have?" Labrousse asked Gerbert.

"A Pernod."

"Why do you drink Pernod when you don't like it?"

"I don't like Pernod, but I like drinking Pernod," Gerbert explained.

"That's just like you," Françoise said laughing.

Again silence fell. Gerbert had lighted his pipe; he bent over his empty glass and slowly blew smoke into it.

"Do you know how to do that?" he challenged Labrousse. The glass was filled with creamy, curling spirals.

"It looks like ectoplasm," Françoise remarked.

"You've only to blow gently," Pierre said. He took a drag at his pipe and bent over with an air of concentration.

"Very good," Gerbert said with condescension. "Here's to you." He clinked his glass against Pierre's and in one gulp inhaled the smoke.

"You're proud of yourself, aren't you?" Françoise said, smiling at Pierre whose face was beaming with satisfaction. She looked regretfully at the remains of the chocolates, then resolutely put them in her bag.

"You know, if we want to have enough time to eat, we ought to leave now," she said.

Again, Gerbert wondered why people usually thought she looked stern and intimidating; she did not try to act girlish, but her face was full of gaiety, life and healthy appetites; she seemed so completely at ease that it made you feel at ease when you were with her.

Labrousse turned to Xavière and looked at her anxiously. "You did understand? You are to take a taxi and say to the driver: 'To the Apollo, rue Blanche.' He'll put you there right in front of the theater and all you have to do is go inside."

"Is it really a cowboy film?" Xavière asked suspiciously.

"It's super," Françoise said. "It's full of the most wonderful galloping horses."

"And shootings, and terrific free-for-alls," said Labrousse.

They were leaning toward Xavière like two tempting demons, and their voices had a ring of supplication. Gerbert made a heroic effort to suppress a burst of laughter which he could barely restrain. He took a sip of Pernod; every time he hoped that by some miracle he would suddenly find this taste of aniseed agreeable, but every time it gave him the same nauseating shiver.

"Is the hero handsome?" Xavière asked.

"He's most attractive," Françoise assured her.

"But he's not handsome," she insisted obstinately.

"It's not the usual sort of good looks," Labrousse admitted.

Xavière pouted disappointedly. "I don't trust you. The one you took me to see the other day looked like a seal. That was unfair."

"You mean William Powell?"

"Oh, but this one's quite different," Labrousse said imploringly. "He's young, and well built and utterly primitive."

"Well, all right, I'll go see it," she said with an air of resignation.

"Will you be at Dominique's at midnight?" Gerbert asked.

"Of course," Xavière said with an offended look.

Gerbert took her answer skeptically, for she hardly ever turned up.

"I'll stay five minutes longer," she said as Françoise rose.

"Have a nice evening," Françoise said warmly.

"Enjoy yourself too." Xavière's face had a queer expression and she quickly looked down.

"I wonder if she'll go to the movies," Françoise said as they left the café. "It's too silly of her; I'm sure she'd love it."

"Did you see?" Labrousse said. "She did her best to remain pleasant, but she didn't hold out till the end. She's annoyed with us."

"Why?" Gerbert asked.

"For not spending the evening with her."

"Well, then, why not take her along?" He found it very unpleasant that this dinner should seem such a complicated affair to Labrousse and Françoise.

"Certainly not," Françoise said. "It wouldn't be at all the same thing."

"The girl is a little tyrant, but we do manage to keep our ends up," said Pierre cheerfully.

Gerbert's serenity returned, but he would have liked very much to know just what Xavière meant to Labrousse. Was it out of affection for Françoise that he was fond of her? Or what? He would never dare ask him. He was very pleased when Labrousse happened to give him a little bit of himself, but it was not his place to question him.

Labrousse stopped a taxi.

"What do you say to dinner at the Grille?" Françoise proposed.

"Fine," said Gerbert. "Maybe they've still got some of their great ham and beans." He suddenly noticed that he was hungry, and he slapped his hand to his forehead. "Ah! I knew I'd forgotten something."

"What?" asked Labrousse.

"At lunch, I forgot to take a second helping of beef. What an idiot!"

The taxi pulled up in front of the little restaurant; a heavy grill covered the front windows; inside, to the right of the entrance, was a zinc-topped bar with a number of tempting bottles on it; the dining room was empty. The proprietor and the cashier, with napkins around their necks, were eating their dinner together at one of the marble-topped tables.

"Ah!" cried Gerbert, tapping his forehead again.

"You frighten me," Françoise said. "What else have you forgotten?"

"I forgot to tell you that I went down my stairs in thirty seconds."

"You're a liar," said Labrousse.

"I was sure you wouldn't believe it. Exactly thirty seconds."

"You'll have to do it again, with me there as witness. Anyway, I did beat you down the Montmartre steps."

"I slipped," Gerbert said. He picked up the menu: ham and beans was on it.

"This place is certainly deserted," Françoise remarked.

"It's too early. And besides, you know people stay home whenever things take a bad turn. We'll play to an audience of ten tonight." Pierre had ordered egg mayonnaise, and was zealously squashing the yolks into the dressing: he called this making *oeufs Mimosa*.

"I'd rather it would happen and get over with," said Gerbert. "It's no life, every day thinking it's going to happen tomorrow."

"But there's always that much time gained," Françoise said.

"That's what everyone said at the time of Munich," Pierre said. "But I'm convinced that it was a stupid blunder. Backing down won't do any good." He picked up the bottle of Beaujolais already on the table and filled their glasses. "No, these avoiding actions can't go on forever."

"After all, why not?" Gerbert said.

Françoise hesitated. "Isn't anything better than war?"

Labrousse shrugged his shoulders. "I don't know."

"If it gets too ghastly here, you can always take off to America," Gerbert said. "You'd certainly get a welcome there. You've already made a name for yourself."

"And what would I do there?" asked Pierre.

"I think a lot of Americans speak French," Françoise said. "And besides, you'd learn English. You'd produce your plays in English."

"That wouldn't interest me in the least. What meaning would it have for me to work in exile? If you want to leave your mark on the world, all your interest must be bound up in it."

"America is a world, too," Françoise said.

"But it's not mine."

"It will be, the day you adopt it."

Labrousse shook his head. "You're talking like Xavière. But I can't, I'm too involved in this one."

"You're still young," Françoise insisted.

"Yes, but don't you see, creating a new theater for Americans is a task that doesn't appeal to me. What interests me is to complete my own work, the work I began in that wretched room near the Gobelins on the money I wheedled out of Aunt Christine and with the sweat of my body." Labrousse looked at Françoise. "Don't you understand that?"

"I do," said Françoise.

She was listening to Labrousse with an attention so passionate that it filled Gerbert with a kind of regret. He had often seen women turn ardent faces toward Pierre; it had always embarrassed him. Such fulsome tenderness seemed to him either indecent or tyrannical. But the love blazing in Françoise's eyes was neither defenseless nor despotic. It almost made him wish he might inspire such a love himself.

"I've been molded by my past life," Labrousse continued. "The Ballets Russes, the Vieux Colombier, Picasso, surrealism—I'd be nothing without all of that. Of course I hope that art will gain a fresh inspiration from me, but I want it to be a continuation of that tradition. It's impossible to work in a vacuum, it leads nowhere."

"Obviously, to emigrate, to work for a development that is not yours, would hardly be satisfying," Françoise admitted.

"Personally, I'd rather go and put up barbed wire somewhere in Lorraine than eat corn-on-the-cob in New York."

"Just the same, I'd prefer the corn-on-the-cob, especially if it's broiled," she said.

"Well," said Gerbert, "I assure you that if there were any way of getting the hell out of here to Venezuela, or to Santo Domingo . . ."

"If war breaks out, I wouldn't want to miss it," Labrousse said. "I must even confess I feel a sort of curiosity."

"What depravity!" said Gerbert. He had been thinking about war all day, but it chilled him to the marrow to hear Labrousse talk about it so calmly, as if it were already there. It was already there, as a matter of fact, tucked away between the roaring stove and the zinc-topped bar with its yellow reflections. And this meal was a funeral feast. Helmets, tanks, uniforms, gray-green trucks—a vast muddy tide was breaking over the world. The earth was being submerged in this blackish quagmire, in which everyone was sucked down wearing clothes as heavy as lead and reeking like wet dogs, while sinister lights flashed in the sky.

"I wouldn't either," said Françoise. "I wouldn't like something important to happen without me."

"In that case, he should have joined up in Spain, or even gone to China."

"That's not the same thing," Labrousse objected.

"I don't see why not."

"It seems to me that it's a question of where you are," Françoise said. "I remember when I was at the Pointe du Raz, and Pierre tried to force me to leave before the storm, I was in despair; I felt that it was wrong to give in. Whereas, at this moment, I wouldn't care if all the storms in the world were raging there without me."

"There you are, that's exactly it. This particular war is part of my own personal history, and that's why I would not bring myself to miss it."

His face was beaming with pleasure. Gerbert looked enviously at both of them; it must give them a sense of security to feel so important to each other. Perhaps he himself, if he were really of very great importance to someone, would count for a little more in his own eyes; he could not seem to feel that either his life or his thoughts were of any great value.

"Just imagine," he said. "Péclard knows a doctor who went completely potty from cutting men up. While he was operating on one, the next guy would pass out. There was one—all the time they were hacking at him—never stopped yelling, 'Oh! the pain in my knee! Oh! the pain in my knee!' That couldn't have been very funny."

"When you've reached that point, there's nothing to do but yell," Labrousse said. "But, you know, I don't find even that too bad. It's just something you've got to put up with in life."

"If you take that line, anything can be justified. All you have to do is just sit back."

"Oh, no. To put up with something doesn't mean accepting life blindly. I'd be willing to live through almost anything, precisely because I'd always have it in me to live freely."

"A strange kind of freedom. You wouldn't be able to do any of the things that interested you."

Labrousse smiled. "You know, I've changed. I no longer have the same superstition about art. I can easily imagine other activities."

Gerbert thoughtfully drained his glass. It was strange to think that Labrousse could change. Gerbert had always regarded him as being immutable. He had an answer to every question; it was hard to imagine that there were still questions left that he could ask himself.

"Well, then, nothing stands in the way of your going to America," he said.

"For the moment," Labrousse said, "it seems to me that the best use to which I can put my freedom is to defend a civilization that is bound up with all the values that mean a lot to me."

"Still, Gerbert is right," Françoise said. "You'd regard any world justified in which there was a place for you." She smiled. "I've always suspected you of thinking you're God the Father."

They both looked elated. It always amazed Gerbert to see them becoming so excited over words. What difference did it make? What power had all these words over this glowing sensation from the Beaujolais he was drinking, against the gas that would stain his lungs green, the fear clutching at his throat?

"Just what are you objecting to about us?" Pierre asked.

Gerbert shuddered. He had not expected to be caught in the act of thinking. "Why, nothing at all," he said.

"You had your judicial look," said Françoise. She handed him the menu. "Don't you want any dessert?"

"I don't like desserts."

"There's a tart," Françoise suggested. "You like tarts."

"Yes, I do, but I'm too lazy."

They burst out laughing.

"Are you too tired to drink a glass of marc?" Labrousse asked.

"No, that's always easy to drink."

Labrousse ordered three liqueurs and the waitress brought a big, dust-coated bottle. Gerbert took out his pipe. This was awful; even Labrousse had to invent something to which he could cling! Gerbert could not believe that his calmness was completely sincere; Pierre valued his ideas in the way that Péclard valued his furniture. And Françoise leaned on Labrousse. In that way, people managed to surround themselves with an impervious world in which their lives had meaning, but there was always a little cheating at the bottom of it all. If you looked carefully, without trying to deceive yourself, you would find beneath all these imposing appearances nothing but a sprinkling of small, futile impressions—the yellow light on the bar-top, the taste of rotten medlars at the bottom of the glass of marc; it couldn't be caught in words, it had to be borne in silence and then it disappeared without leaving any trace, and something else, equally elusive, took its place. Nothing but sand and water, and it was silly to try to build anything on it. Even death did not deserve all the fuss that was made over it. Of course it was terrifying, but only because you couldn't imagine how you would feel.

"Being killed, that wouldn't be so bad," Gerbert said, "but you might also have to go on living with a bashed-in face."

"I'd sooner lose a leg," said Labrousse.

"I'd prefer an arm. I saw a young Englishman in Marseilles who had a hook instead of a hand; believe it or not, but it really looked distinguished."

"An artificial leg isn't so obvious," said Labrousse. "An arm would be impossible to disguise."

"It's true that in our profession we can't afford to go too far. Having your ear torn off would ruin your whole career."

"No, no, it's not possible!" Françoise broke in. Her voice was choking, her face had changed, and quite suddenly tears rose to her eyes. Gerbert thought she looked almost beautiful.

"It's also possible to come back without a scratch," Labrousse said soothingly. "And besides, we haven't gone yet." He smiled at Françoise. "You mustn't start having nightmares now."

With an effort, Françoise also smiled. "The one thing quite certain, is that you'll be playing to an empty house tonight."

"Yes," Pierre said. His eyes wandered over the deserted restaurant. "I must go all the same. I ought to be there now."

"I'm going home to do some work." She shrugged her shoulders. "Though I don't know how much enthusiasm I'll have for it."

They went out and Labrousse hailed a taxi.

"No, I'd rather walk home," Françoise said. She shook hands with Labrousse and then with Gerbert.

Gerbert watched her walk away with long, somewhat awkward strides, her hands in her pockets. He would probably not see her again for the best part of a month.

"Get in," Labrousse said, pushing him into the taxi.

When Gerbert reached his dressing room he found Guimiot and Mercaton already at their dressing tables, their arms and necks daubed with ocher; he absent-mindedly shook hands with them. The small, over-heated room reeked with the nauseating smell of cold cream and brilliantine. Guimiot stubbornly insisted on keeping the windows closed, he was afraid of catching cold. Gerbert walked to the window with marked determination.

If he says anything, I'll smash that little pansy's face, he thought.

He would have liked nothing better than to start a fight, it would have eased the strain, but Guimiot never turned a hair; he was dabbing his face with a huge mauve puff and the powder was flying all around him; he sneezed twice, looking utterly miserable. Gerbert was so glum, that even this didn't make him laugh. He began to undress—coat, tie, shoes, socks; and in a little while they would all have to be put on again. He was fed up by the mere thought of it, and besides, he did not like to exhibit his naked body in front of other fellows.

What the hell am I doing here! he suddenly asked himself, looking around him with an astonishment that almost felt like physical pain. He knew these states of mind all too well, they were sometimes terribly unpleasant, as if everything inside of him became stagnant water; he used to have these attacks during his childhood, especially when he saw his mother bent over a steaming washtub. In a few days, he would be polishing a gun; he would be marching in formation around the barrack square; and then they'd send him to mount guard in some icy hole; it was absurd. But meanwhile, he was smearing his thighs with a coat of coppery pigment, which was no end of trouble to scrape off; and that was no less absurd.

"Oh! Hell!" he said aloud. He had suddenly remembered that Elisabeth was coming to sketch him that evening. She certainly had picked a good day!

The door opened and Ramblin's head appeared. "Has anyone got some spirit-gum?"

"I have," said Guimiot eagerly. He regarded Ramblin as a wealthy and influential person, and shamelessly licked his boots.

"Thanks," said Ramblin coldly. He took the jar of quivering pink jelly and turned to Gerbert. "It's going to be dead tonight! There are three stray cats in the orchestra stalls, and about as many in the dress circle." He suddenly burst out laughing and Gerbert laughed with him. He liked Ramblin's sudden outbursts of solitary gaiety, and besides he was grateful to him, homosexual as he was, for never having tried to make him.

"Tedesco's in a blue funk," Ramblin said. "He believes all foreigners are going to be clapped into concentration camps. Canzetti is holding his hand and sobbing. Chanaud has already called her a dirty wop and is now ranting that French women will know how to do their duty. It's well worth seeing, I can assure you."

He was carefully sticking on the curls around his face, smiling at himself in the glass with an approving and quizzical expression.

Éloy poked her head through the door, "Gerbert, darling, would you give me a little of your blue pencil?" She always managed to think of some excuse to come into the men's dressing room when they were naked. She was half undressed herself, a transparent shawl barely concealing her enormous breasts.

"Scram, we're not presentable," Gerbert said.

"And cover those up," Ramblin added giving her shawl a tug. He watched her leave with disgust. "She says she's going to volunteer as a nurse. What a treat for the poor defenseless devils who fall into her clutches!"

He disappeared. Gerbert put on his Roman costume and began to make up his face. This was much more amusing, he loved detailed work; he had discovered a new way of making up his eyes by lengthening the line of the lids with a kind of star that had a most charming effect. He cast a satisfied last-minute glance in the mirror and went downstairs. He found Elisabeth sitting on a bench in the greenroom with her portfolio under her arm.

"Have I come too early?" she said in her best society manner. She was very elegant, there was no denying it; her jacket had certainly been cut by an expert tailor—Gerbert was a connoisseur.

"I'll be with you in ten minutes."

He took a look at the set. Everything was in place and the props were all arranged within reach. Through a slit in the curtains he studied the audience—there were no more than twenty people; that spelled disaster. Giving a little whistle between his teeth he proceeded along the passages to summon the actors; then he went back and sat down resignedly in front of Elisabeth.

"Are you sure this isn't going to disturb you?" she asked, starting to unwrap her drawing paper.

"Oh no, I just have to be here to see that no one makes any noise."

The three strokes on the gong reverberated in the silence with ominous solemnity. The curtain rose. Caesar's procession was gathered near the door opening on to the stage. Labrousse, draped in his white toga, came into the greenroom.

"Hello! You here?" he said to his sister.

"As you can see," said Elisabeth.

"But I thought you weren't doing portraits these days," he said, looking over her shoulder.

"This is just a study. If I did nothing but composition, I'd lose my touch."

"Come and see me later." He went on through the door and the procession fell in behind him.

"It's strange to watch a play from the wings," said Elisabeth. "You can see how it's put together."

She shrugged her shoulders and Gerbert looked at her in embarrassment. He was always ill at ease with her, he never knew very clearly what she expected of him; sometimes he felt that she was slightly crazy.

"Stay just that way. Don't move," she said. "Is that pose too tiring?"

"No," said Gerbert.

It was not tiring in the least, but it certainly made him feel a damned fool. As Ramblin walked through the greenroom he gave him a quizzical look. Silence ensued. All the doors were closed and not a sound could be heard. On stage, the actors were playing to an empty house. Elisabeth was obstinately sketching in order not to lose her touch, and Gerbert was there, looking like a fool. *What's the sense of it all*, he thought in a rage. As in his dressing room a short while before, he felt an emptiness in the pit of his stomach. One memory always came back to him when he was in this mood—a fat spider he had seen one evening in Provence while on a hike. Attached to its thread, it hung dangling from a tree; it would climb, then let itself drop back in sharp jerks, and climb up again with harrowing patience, one wondered where it got its stubborn courage, it seemed so terribly alone in the world.

"Is your marionette show going to last a while longer?" Elisabeth asked.

"Dominique said until the end of the week."

"Did Pagès finally turn down the part?"

"She promised me she'd come tonight."

Pencil in air, Elisabeth raised her head and looked Gerbert in the eye. "What do you think of Pagès?"

"She's all right," he said.

"Anything else?" She had a curious, insistent smile; she looked as if she were putting him through an examination.

"I don't know her very well."

Elisabeth laughed candidly. "Well, of course, if you're as shy as she is . . ."

She bent over her sketch and began to work with an air of concentration.

"I'm not shy," Gerbert said. He felt, with anger, that he was blushing; it was ridiculous, but he hated anyone to talk to him about himself, and he could not even move to hide his face.

"I can't help thinking you are," Elisabeth said with evident amusement.

"Why?"

"Because otherwise it wouldn't have been very hard for you to become better acquainted with her." Elisabeth looked up at Gerbert with genuine curiosity. "You really haven't noticed anything? Or are you pretending?"

"I don't know what you mean," said Gerbert, put out of countenance.

"You're really delightful. This shrinking, violet modesty is so rare." She rattled on confidently. Perhaps she really was on the verge of insanity.

"But Pagès doesn't give me a thought," said Gerbert.

"You think so?" Elisabeth rejoined with a touch of irony.

Gerbert did not answer. It was true that Pagès had sometimes acted strangely when they were together, but that did not prove much; she took no interest in anyone, except in Françoise and Labrousse. Elisabeth was probably making fun of him; she had an irritating way of sucking the point of her pencil.

"Doesn't she appeal to you?" she asked.

Gerbert shrugged his shoulders. "You've got things wrong," he said.

He looked around in embarrassment. Elisabeth had always been tactless. She talked irresponsibly, just for the pleasure of talking. But this time, really, she was going too far.

"Five minutes," he said, getting up. "It's time for the acclamations."

The members of the crowd had come in and sat down at the other end of the greenroom. He motioned to them and slowly opened the door to the stage. The actors' voices could not be heard, but Gerbert took his cue from the muted music which accompanied the dialogue between Cassius and Casca. Every evening he felt the same excitement while he waited for the theme indicating that the people were offering the crown to Caesar. He almost believed in the deceptive and dubious solemnity of this moment. He raised his hand and a great outcry drowned the last chords of the piano. Once more he watched in the silence emphasized by a faraway murmur of voices, then the short melody was heard again and a shout rose from every throat; the third time, a few words barely outlined the theme and the voices rose with redoubled volume.

"Now, we'll be undisturbed for a while," said Gerbert, resuming his pose. He was intrigued, even if he did not admit it. He knew that he was likable; he was even too likable, but Pagès!—that would be flattering!

"I saw Pagès this evening," he said after a pause. "I can assure you she didn't seem to feel too kindly toward me."

"How was that?" asked Elisabeth.

"She was furious because I was going to dine with Françoise and Labrousse."

"Ah! I see. She's as jealous as a cat, that young woman. She must really have hated you, but that doesn't prove anything." Elisabeth made a few pencil strokes in silence. Gerbert wanted to question her more closely, but he could not think of a question which did not seem indiscreet.

"It's a nuisance to have a child like that in one's life," Elisabeth said. "Devoted as Françoise and Labrousse may be, she's a burden to them just the same."

Gerbert remembered the incident that had occurred that evening, and Labrousse's good-natured tone. *"That girl is a little tyrant, but we do manage to keep our ends up."*

He remembered people's faces and intonations very clearly, only he was unable to go further and grasp what they were thinking; the incident stood out before him, distinct and precise, without his being able to arrive at any clear idea. He hesitated. This was a heaven-sent opportunity to gather a little information.

"I don't understand very clearly just how they feel about her," he said.

"You know what they're like," said Elisabeth. "They're so taken up with one another that their relationships with other people have become superficial or else a game." She bent over her sketch with a look of complete absorption. "They enjoy having an adopted daughter, but I think that it's also beginning to poison them."

Gerbert hesitated a moment. "Labrousse stares at Pagès with such solicitude at times."

Elisabeth laughed. "Surely you don't think Pierre is in love with her?"

"Of course not," he said. He was choking with rage. This woman was a real bitch with her elder-sister act.

"Just watch her," said Elisabeth, becoming serious again. "I'm certain of what I'm saying. You'd only have to lift a finger." Then she added with heavy irony, "It's true though, you'd have to lift your finger."

Dominique's cabaret was as deserted as *Les Tréteaux*; the show had been performed in front of six gloomy-faced habitués, and Gerbert felt a lump rise in his throat as he laid the little oilcloth princess in a suitcase; this was perhaps the last evening. Tomorrow, a rain of gray dust would descend over Europe, drowning the fragile dolls, the settings, the bistro bars, and all those rainbows of light glowing in the streets of Montparnasse. His hand rested for a moment on the cool, smooth face— a real funeral.

"She looks almost like a corpse," Xavière said.

Gerbert shuddered. Xavière was tying a silk handkerchief under her chin as her eyes rested on the tiny cold bodies laid out on the bottom of their box.

"It was nice of you to come tonight," he said. "It goes so much better when you're here."

"But I said that I would come," she said with offended dignity.

She had arrived just as the show was about to begin, and they had had no time to exchange even a few words. Gerbert glanced at her; if only he could find something to say to her, he was very anxious to keep her with him for a while. After all, she was not as intimidating as all that. With the handkerchief over her head, she even looked lovable.

"Did you go to the movies?" he asked.

"No," she said. She was twisting the fringe of her scarf. "It was too far."

Gerbert laughed. "By taxi it's a lot nearer."

"Oh!" said Xavière with a knowing look, "I don't trust them." She smiled amiably. "Did you have a good dinner?"

"I had ham and beans which was really a treat," Gerbert began with enthusiasm. He stopped, embarrassed. "But, talking about food nauseates you, doesn't it."

Xavière raised her eyebrows, which then looked as if they had been put on with a paint brush, as on a Japanese mask.

"Who told you that? It's a ridiculous myth."

Gerbert thought with satisfaction that he was becoming a psychologist, for it seemed clear to him that Xavière was still furious with Françoise and Labrousse.

"You're not going to pretend you're a glutton?" he said, laughing.

"It's because I'm a blonde," Xavière protested with a hurt look. "It makes everyone think I'm ethereal."

"But I bet you won't come and eat a hamburger with me?" he said without thinking, and he was suddenly aghast at his boldness.

Xavière's eyes sparkled. "Bet you I will," she said.

"Well, let's go." He stepped back to let her pass. *What in the world can I say to her?* he thought uneasily. Still, he was quite proud of himself, no one could say he had not lifted a finger. This was really the first time he had taken the initiative so boldly. Usually, he found he had been left behind.

"Oh! How cold it is!"

"Let's go to the Coupole. It's only a five-minute walk," Gerbert suggested.

Xavière looked around miserably. "Isn't there any place nearer?"

"Hamburgers are eaten at the Coupole," Gerbert said firmly. Women were all alike, they were always too hot or too cold, they required too much attention to be good companions. Gerbert had been fond of some of them because he liked to be liked, but it was hopeless, he felt bored in their company. If he had had the good fortune of being a homosexual, he would have only associated with men. On top of that, it was hell trying to get rid of a woman, especially if you did not like to hurt anyone's feelings. They understood in the long run, but they took their sweet time about it. Annie was beginning to understand; this was now the third time he had failed to keep an appointment without letting her know. Gerbert looked fondly at the façade of the Coupole. The play of the lights gave him as great a melancholy thrill as a jazz melody.

"You see, it wasn't far," he said.

"That's because you have long legs," retorted Xavière, glancing at him approvingly. "I like people who walk fast."

Before pushing the revolving door, Gerbert turned to her. "Do you still feel like a hamburger?" he asked.

Xavière hesitated. "To tell the truth, I don't really and truly want one. But I am thirsty."

She looked at him apologetically. She was really attractive with her glowing cheeks and her childish bangs showing under her handkerchief. A daring notion struck Gerbert.

"In that case, shall we go downstairs where there's dancing?" he said. He ventured a timid smile which was usually effective. "I'll give you a lesson in tap-dancing."

"Oh! That would be wonderful!" Xavière cried, with such enthusiasm that he was a little surprised. She tore the handkerchief off her head and dashed down the red stairs two at a time. Gerbert wondered in amazement whether there was not some truth in Elisabeth's insinuations. Xavière was always so reserved with people! But tonight she welcomed the slightest advance with the greatest alacrity.

"We can sit here," he said, pointing to a table.

"Yes, that will be just perfect." She looked around her with delight. It seemed that, faced with the threat of possible disaster, a dance hall was considered a better refuge than art theaters, for there were several couples on the floor.

"Oh! I adore this kind of decoration," Xavière exclaimed, wrinkling up her nose. Her facial expressions often struck him as being so funny he found it difficult to keep a straight face.

"At Dominique's everything's so niggardly—what they call good taste." She pouted a little and gave him a conspiratorial look. "Don't you think it has a miserly look? Their humor too, their jokes, the whole thing seems so cut and dried."

"Oh, yes," said Gerbert. "Even their laughter is strictly regulated. They remind me of that philosopher Labrousse told me about, who laughed when he saw a line drawn tangent to a circle, because it looked like an angle and it wasn't one."

"Now you're making fun of me!"

"I assure you," said Gerbert, "to him it seemed screamingly funny, but he was the dullest of the dull."

"Yet you can't say he missed a single chance to enjoy himself."

Gerbert began to laugh. "Did you ever hear Charpini? Now there's a fellow I call funny, especially when he sings *Carmen*. 'My mother, yes, I see her,' while Brancanto looks all over the place. 'Where? Here? Where is she, poor woman?' I laugh till I cry every time."

"No," Xavière said disconsolately. "I've never heard anything really funny. I'd so love to."

"Well, we'll have to go there some time. And Georgius? You don't know Georgius?"

"No," Xavière said, looking at him wretchedly.

"Perhaps you'd find him a bore," Gerbert said hesitantly. "His songs are full of coarse wisecracks and even puns." He could hardly imagine Xavière listening to Georgius with pleasure.

"I'm sure I'd love it," she said eagerly.

"What would you like to drink?" Gerbert asked.

"A whisky."

"Two whiskies, then," Gerbert said to the waiter. "You like whisky?"

"No." Xavière made a face. "It smells like iodine."

"But you like drinking it; it's just like me with Pernod," he said. "But I really like whisky," he added honestly. He smiled boldly. "Shall we dance this tango?"

"Surely," said Xavière. She got up and smoothed her skirt with the palm of her hand. Gerbert put his arm around her. He remembered how well she danced, better than Annie, better than Canzetti, but tonight, the perfection of her movements seemed miraculous to him. A light and delicate perfume rose from her fair hair, and for a moment Gerbert stopped thinking and yielded to the rhythm of the dance, to the singing of the guitars, to the orange haze of the lights, to the pleasure of holding a lithe body in his arms.

I've been a fool, he thought suddenly. He should have asked her to go out with him weeks ago, and now the army was waiting for him. It was too late, this evening would have no tomorrow. He was filled with regret. In his life, nothing had ever had a tomorrow. He had admired all beautiful and passionate love affairs from afar; but a great love was like ambition, possible only in a world where things were important, in which the words one spoke and the things one did left their mark; and Gerbert felt as if he had been parked in a waiting room with no exit for him into the future. Suddenly, as the orchestra paused, the anguish which had hung over him all evening changed to panic. All these years that had slipped through his fingers had never seemed anything but a wasted period of marking time, but they made up his sole existence, and he would never know any other. When he was stretched out in a field, stiff and muddy, with his identification disc on his wrist, then indeed there would be absolutely nothing more.

"Come on, let's have another whisky," he said.

Xavière smiled at him submissively. As they were returning to their table, Gerbert noticed a flower girl holding out a basket with flowers. He stopped and picked out a red rose. He laid it down in front of Xavière, and she took it and pinned it to her blouse.

4

FRANÇOISE gave one last fleeting glance at the mirror and, for once, no single detail displeased her. She had carefully plucked her eyebrows and brushed her hair straight up from the nape, thus accentuating the clear line of her neck, and her nails shone like rubies. She was looking forward to this evening. She was very fond of Paula Berger and always enjoyed herself when they went out together. Paula had agreed to take them to a Spanish night club, an exact replica of a cabaret in Seville, and Françoise was elated at the thought of a few hours' escape from the strained, passionate, cloying atmosphere in which Pierre and Xavière had imprisoned her. She felt fresh and full of life and ready to enjoy, at their proper value, Paula's beauty, all the attractions the place offered, and the poetry of Seville, which the music of guitars and the taste of Manzanilla would soon bring to life.

Five minutes to midnight; she could not wait any longer; if the evening was not to be spoiled, she had to go down and knock at Xavière's door. Pierre was expecting them at the theater at midnight, and he would be fuming if they did not arrive on time. She glanced once more at the pink slip of paper on which Xavière had scribbled in green ink: "*Please let me off this afternoon, I want to rest so as to be fresh for this evening. I shall be in your room at eleven-thirty. Much love, Xavière.*"

Françoise had found this note under her door in the morning and she, together with Pierre, had anxiously speculated on what Xavière could possibly have been up to the night before to want to sleep all day. "Much love," did not mean anything, it was an empty formula. When they had left her at the Flore, the previous evening, before going to dinner with Gerbert, Xavière had been very much on edge and it was impossible to foresee her present mood. Françoise threw a new, light wool cape over her shoulders. She gathered up her bag and the beautiful pair of gloves her mother had given her and went downstairs. Even if Xavière turned out to be in a sullen mood, and Pierre took it badly, she was determined not to let their quarrelling affect her. She knocked. From the other side of the door came a faint rustling; it seemed almost as if she were listening to the vibrations of the secret thoughts which Xavière indulged in when alone.

"What is it?" asked a sleepy voice.

"It's Françoise." This time there was not the slightest sound. In spite of her joyous resolutions, Françoise felt with a sinking heart the same anguish she always felt whenever waiting for Xavière to appear. Would Xavière be smiling or scowling? Whichever it might be, the course of the evening, the course of the entire world that night, depended on the light in her eyes. A minute passed before the door opened.

"I'm not nearly ready," Xavière said, in a dismal voice.

It was the same story every time, and every time it was just as disconcerting. Xavière was in her dressing gown; her tousled hair fell over a puffy, yellowish face. Behind her the unmade bed still looked warm, and it was obvious that the shutters had not been opened all day. The room was filled with smoke and the acrid smell of the alcohol stove. But what made this air so unbreathable, even more than the alcohol and tobacco, were all the unsatisfied desires, the boredom and bitterness accumulated in the course of hours—in the course of days, of weeks— between these walls with their nightmarish wallpaper.

"I'll wait for you," Françoise said irresolutely.

"But I'm not dressed." She shrugged her shoulders with an air of hopeless resignation. "No," she said, "you'd better go without me."

Françoise remained standing in the doorway, inert and appalled. Since she had watched the growth of jealousy and hatred in Xavière's heart, this place of refuge frightened her. It was not only a sanctuary where Xavière celebrated her own worship; it was a hothouse in which flourished a luxuriant and poisonous vegetation; it was like a cell in an insane asylum, in which the dank atmosphere adhered to the body.

"Look," she said, "I'll go and fetch Labrousse and in twenty minutes we'll come and pick you up. You can be ready in twenty minutes, can't you?"

Xavière's face suddenly showed signs of animation. "Of course I can. You'll see, I can hurry when I want to."

Françoise went down the last two flights. This was annoying—the evening was starting badly. For several days there had been a storm brewing and now it was coming to a head; it was particularly between Xavière and Françoise that things were not going well. That clumsy burst of affection on Saturday, after the Negro dance hall, had in no way cleared the air. Françoise walked faster. Things happened almost imperceptibly; a misplaced smile, an equivocal phrase, was sufficient to ruin any happy evening. This evening she would again pretend not to notice anything, but she knew that Xavière let nothing slip unintentionally.

It was barely ten past twelve when Françoise walked into Pierre's dressing room. He had already put on his overcoat and was sitting on the edge of the couch, smoking his pipe. He looked up and stared at Françoise with angry suspicion.

"Are you alone?" he asked.

"Xavière is waiting for us. She wasn't quite ready." Although she had steeled herself, a lump rose in her throat. Pierre had not even given her a smile; never before had he welcomed her in this way.

"Have you seen her? How was she?"

She stared at him in astonishment. Why did he seem so distraught? As far as he was concerned, things were progressing favorably. Whatever the quarrels Xavière might pick with him, they were never more than lovers' tiffs.

"She looked depressed and tired. She's spent the day in her room, sleeping, smoking and drinking tea."

Pierre got up. "Do you know what she was doing last night?" he said.

"What?" Françoise stiffened. Something unpleasant was coming.

"She was out dancing with Gerbert until five o'clock this morning," Pierre announced, almost in triumph.

"Oh!" She was upset. This was the first time that Gerbert and Xavière had gone out together, and in this feverish and complicated life, maintained in precarious equilibrium, the slightest change was pregnant with threats.

"Gerbert looked delighted, even slightly smug," Pierre continued.

"What did he say?" Françoise asked. She could not define this equivocal feeling that had just come upon her, but its gloomy quality did not surprise her. There was a musty flavor in all her pleasures these days, and her worst difficulties gave her a kind of enjoyment that set her teeth on edge.

"He thinks she dances magnificently and that she's quite likable,"

Pierre said dryly. He looked deeply chagrined, and Françoise was relieved to think that his uncivil greeting was not without excuse.

"She went into retirement all day," Pierre continued. "That's what she always does when she's been stirred up by something. She shuts herself up in order to have plenty of time to ruminate at leisure."

He closed the door to his dressing room and they left the theater.

"Why don't you tell Gerbert that you're fond of her?" suggested Françoise, after a silence. "A word would be enough."

Pierre's profile sharpened. "I really think he tried to sound me out," he said, with an unpleasant laugh. "He looked embarrassed, as if feeling his way, which I found slightly amusing." Pierre added on an even more rasping note, "I showered encouragement upon him."

"Well, then, naturally? How can you expect him to guess? You always put on such an air of indifference when he's about."

"You surely can't expect me to hang a sign on Xavière's back saying, 'No Trespassing'," Pierre said in a scathing tone. He started to bite one of his fingernails. "He should have guessed."

The blood rushed to Françoise's face. Pierre took pride in being a good sport, but there was nothing of the sportsman about him now. At this moment he was perverse and unfair, and she respected him too much not to hate him for this weakness.

"You know very well that he's no psychologist," she said. "And besides," she added bitterly, "you yourself told me, in connection with our own relationship, that when you respect someone deeply, you refuse to pry into their soul without their permission."

"But I'm not blaming anyone for anything," Pierre said icily. "Everything's all right as it is."

She looked at him with bitterness. He was deeply troubled, but his suffering was too manifestly aggressive to inspire pity. Nevertheless, she tried to be understanding.

"I wonder whether Xavière was nice to him largely because she was angry with us," she said.

"Perhaps, but the fact remains that she had no desire to return home before dawn and that she put herself out for him." He angrily shrugged his shoulders. "And now we'll have Paula on our hands and we won't even be able to have it out with Xavière."

Françoise felt her heart sink. Whenever Pierre was forced to brood over his misgivings and grievances in silent thought, he had the power of transforming the passage of time into a slow and refined torture; nothing was more dreadful than these suppressed accusations. This evening, to which she had been looking forward, was no longer a pleasure. With a few words, Pierre had already changed it into an onerous chore.

"Stay here, I'll go up and get Xavière," she said, as they arrived at the hotel.

She hurried up the two flights. Was no escape to freedom ever to be possible again? Would she once more be allowed only furtive glances at the people and things around her? She felt the wish to break this magic circle in which she found herself confined with Pierre and Xavière and which cut her off from the rest of the world.

Françoise knocked. The door opened immediately.

"You see. I did hurry," said Xavière. It was difficult to believe that this was the yellow-faced and feverish recluse of a short while before. Her face was smooth and clear; her hair fell in even waves on her shoulders. She was wearing her blue dress and pinned to the waist was a slightly faded rose.

"I think it's such fun to go to a Spanish night club," she said brightly. "We'll see real Spaniards, won't we?"

"Of course," Françoise said. "There'll be beautiful dancers, and guitarists, and castanets."

"Let's hurry," said Xavière. She lightly touched Françoise's wrap. "I do love this cape," she said. "It makes me think of a domino at a masked ball. You look beautiful," she added with admiration.

Françoise gave her an embarrassed smile; Xavière was completely out of tune, she was going to be painfully surprised when she caught sight of Pierre's stony face. She was now bounding joyously down the stairs.

"And now I've kept you waiting," she said gaily, as she shook hands with Pierre.

"It doesn't matter in the least," Pierre said, so curtly that Xavière looked at him in astonishment. He turned away and signaled a taxi.

"First we'll pick up Paula," said Françoise. "She has to take us as it's very hard to find the place if you've never been there."

Xavière sat down beside her on the back seat.

"You can sit between us, there's lots of room," Françoise said to Pierre with a smile.

Pierre pulled down the folding seat. "Thanks," he said. "I'm all right here."

Françoise's smile vanished. If he was going to be stubborn and sulk, there was nothing to do but leave him alone; she would not let him ruin this evening for her. She turned to Xavière.

"Well, I hear you were out dancing last night. Did you have a good time?"

"Oh, yes! Gerbert dances magnificently," said Xavière, in a completely natural tone. "We went to the Coupole, downstairs. Did he tell you? There was a wonderful orchestra." Her eyelids flickered, and she moved her lips a little as if she were going to smile at Pierre. "Your movies frightened me," she said. "I stayed at the Flore until midnight."

Pierre eyed her malevolently. "But you were quite free to do so."

Xavière was bewildered for a moment. Then a haughty tremor ran over her face and once more she turned her eyes toward Françoise.

"We must go there," she said. "After all, it's quite all right for women to dance together. At the Negro dance hall on Saturday, it was great fun."

"I'd very much like to," Françoise said, looking at her gaily. "You're getting quite debauched! This will make two nights running without any sleep."

"That's just why I rested all day," Xavière said. "I wanted to be fresh to go out with you."

Françoise met Pierre's sarcastic look without turning a hair. Really he was overdoing it. There was no reaon for him to look that way because Xavière had enjoyed dancing with Gerbert. Besides, he knew he was in the wrong; but he was taking refuge in a peevish superiority, from which eminence he assumed the right to trample on good faith, good manners, and every moral value.

Françoise had made up her mind to love him even in his freedom, but she detected too easy an optimism in such a resolution. If Pierre was free, it no longer depended on her alone to love him, for he was also free to make himself detestable. At this moment that was just what he was doing.

The taxi stopped.

"Do you want to come up to Paula's with us?" Françoise asked Xavière.

"Oh yes! You told me her apartment was so lovely."

Françoise opened the taxi door.

"You two go up. I'll wait for you," said Pierre.

"As you like."

Xavière took her arm and they entered the building.

"I'm so excited to see her beautiful apartment."

She looked like a happy little girl. Françoise squeezed her arm. Even if this tenderness arose from spite against Pierre, it was good to feel it. Moreover, during this long day of seclusion, Xavière had perhaps purified her heart. From the joy given by this hope, Françoise gauged to what extent Xavière's hostility had wounded her.

She rang the bell. A maid opened the door and conducted them into a huge high-ceilinged room.

"I will tell Madame that you are here," she said.

Xavière slowly turned around and said ecstatically, "How beautiful it is!"

Her eyes rested in turn on the multicolored chandeliers, on the pirate's chest studded with tarnished copper nails, on the state-bed covered with old red silk, embroidered with blue caravels, on the Venetian mirror hanging at the back of the alcove. Around the polished surface of this mirror curled glass arabesques, bright and capricious as the blossoming of hoarfrost. A vague sense of envy seized Françoise. It was a wonderful gift to be able to write one's personality in silk, spun glass, and precious wood; for permeating these judiciously disparate objects, which her unerring taste had brought together, was the personality of Paula Berger. It was she whom Xavière was rapturously studying when she looked at the Japanese masks, the small greenish decanters, the shell dolls rigid under a glass dome. By contrast, Françoise felt as she had before—at the Negro dance hall and at the New Year's Eve party— as smooth and naked as the faceless heads in a di Chirico painting.

"Good evening, I'm so glad to see you." With both hands held out, Paula came toward them with a brisk step that contrasted with the majesty of her long black dress. A knot of dark velvet flowers, tinged with yellow, accentuated her waist. With arms outstretched, she seized Xavière's hands and held them for a moment in her own.

"She looks more and more like a Fra Angelico," she said.

Xavière looked down in embarrassment. Paula dropped her hands.

"I'm quite ready," she said, throwing a short silver-fox coat over her shoulders.

They went downstairs. As Paula approached, Pierre managed to force a smile.

"Did you have much of a house tonight?" asked Paula, as the taxi was driving off.

"Twenty-five people," Pierre replied. "We're going to close. In any case, they have to start rehearsals on *Monsieur le Vent*, and we're supposed to end the run a week from today."

"We're less fortunate," said Paula. "The play was about to open. Don't you think it's a little strange how people retire into their shells as soon as things look ominous? Even the woman who sells violets near my house told me that she hadn't sold three bunches in the last two days."

The taxi stopped in a steep, narrow street. Paula and Xavière walked ahead a few paces while Pierre paid the driver. Xavière was studying Paula with a look of fascination.

"I'll be quite a spectacle walking into this place flanked by three women," muttered Pierre between his teeth.

He looked resentfully at the ill-lit blind-alley into which Paula was going. All the houses seemed asleep. At the far end, on a small wooden door, in weather-worn lettering, was painted the word, *Sevillana*.

"I telephoned to ask them to keep a good table for us," said Paula. She went in first and walked swiftly up to a dark-skinned man who must have been the proprietor, and they smilingly exchanged a few words. The main room was small. In the middle of the ceiling was a spotlight that cast a rosy glow on the crowded dance floor. The rest of the room was plunged in shadow. Paula walked toward a table in one of the booths against the wall.

"How nice it is here," Françoise said. "It's just like Seville."

She was on the point of turning to Pierre. She remembered the wonderful evenings they had spent, two years earlier, in a cabaret near Alameda, but Pierre was in no mood to conjure up memories. He cheerlessly ordered a bottle of Manzanilla. Françoise looked around her. She loved these first moments, when surroundings and people were blended in a vague mass, half hidden in tobacco smoke. It was a pleasure to think that this confused scene would slowly begin to focus and reveal its innumerable separate details and enthralling episodes.

"What I love about this place," said Paula, "is that there's no artificial quaintness."

"Yes, it couldn't be more authentic," Françoise agreed.

The tables were of rough wood, as were the stools used in place of chairs, and the bar had kegs of Spanish wine stacked behind it. Nothing held the eye, except the balcony with the piano and the beautiful shining guitars which the musicians, dressed in light colors, were holding across their knees.

"You ought to take off your coat," Paula said, touching Xavière's shoulder.

Xavière smiled. Ever since they had stepped into the taxi, she had not taken her eyes off Paula. She took off her coat with the docility of a sleepwalker.

"What a lovely dress!" Paula exclaimed.

Pierre turned a piercing look on Xavière. "Why do you keep that rose? It's wilted," he said tersely.

Xavière stared at him. Slowly she unpinned the rose and put it in the glass of Manzanilla the waiter had just brought.

"Do you think that will revive it?" Françoise asked.

"Why not?" Xavière said, gazing out of the corner of her eye at the drooping flower.

"The guitarists are good, aren't they?" said Paula. "They have the real flamenco style. They create the whole atmosphere." She looked at the bar. "I was afraid it might be empty, but the Spaniards aren't so affected by events."

"These women are amazing," Françoise said. "They're covered with layers of make-up and yet it doesn't make them look artificial; their faces are still completely alive and sensual."

One by one she was studying the short, fat, Spanish women, their heavily painted faces crowned with thick black hair. They were all like the women of Seville who, on summer evenings, wore clusters of heavily scented spikenard flowers behind their ears.

"And how they dance!" said Paula. "I often come here to admire them. When they're standing still, they look rather dumpy and short-legged. They appear clumsy, but as soon as they begin to move, their bodies become so light and so full of grace."

Françoise took a sip from her glass. The flavor of dried nuts brought back at once the merciful shade of the Seville bars where she and Pierre had stuffed themselves with olives and anchovies, while the sun beat down pitilessly on the streets. She turned to look at him, she wanted him to join her in recalling that wonderful holiday. But Pierre kept a malevolent eye fixed on Xavière.

"Well, it didn't take long," he said.

The rose was drooping sadly on its stem, as if it had been poisoned; it had turned yellow and its petals were tinged with brown. Xavière picked it up gently.

"Yes, I think it's quite dead," she said.

She tossed it on the table and then looked at Pierre defiantly. She seized her glass and drained it at one draft. Paula gaped in astonishment.

"Does the soul of a rose have a pleasant taste?" Pierre asked.

Xavière leaned back and lighted a cigarette without answering. There was an awkward silence. Paula smiled at Françoise.

"Would you like to try this paso doble?" she asked, obviously trying to change the subject.

"When I dance with you, I almost have the illusion of knowing how," said Françoise, rising.

Pierre and Xavière sat side by side without exchanging a word. Xavière was staring at the smoke of her cigarette as if spellbound.

"How far advanced are the plans for your recital?" Françoise asked, after a moment.

"If the situation clears up I'll try something in May."

"It will certainly be a success," Françoise said.

"Perhaps." A shadow passed over Paula's face. "But that does not particularly interest me. I would so like to find a way of introducing my conceptions of the dance in the theater."

"But you're doing that already to a certain extent," said Françoise. "Your plasticity is so perfect."

"That's not enough," Paula said. "I'm sure there must be something else to discover, something really new." Again her face clouded over. "Only I would have to feel my way, take risks. . . ."

Françoise looked at her with a warm feeling of sympathy. When Paula had renounced her past to throw herself into Berger's arms, she thought she was starting upon an adventurous, heroic life at his side; and now Berger, like a good businessman, was doing nothing more than exploit an established reputation. Paula had sacrificed too much for him to admit her disappointment, even to herself. But Françoise could guess the painful flaws in this love, in this happiness which she continued to defend. Something bitter rose in her throat. In the booth where she had left them, Pierre and Xavière were still not speaking. Pierre was smoking, his head slightly bowed. Xavière was staring at him with a furtive and woebegone expression. How free she was!

Free in heart, free in thought, free to suffer, to doubt, to hate. No past, no pledge, no loyalty to herself to shackle her.

The music of the guitars died away. Paula and Françoise came back to their places. Paula noticed a little anxiously that the bottle of Manzanilla was empty, and that Xavière's eyes had a too brilliant luster beneath their blue-tinged lashes.

"You're going to see the dancer," Paula said. "I think she rates with the best."

A plump, mature woman, in Spanish costume, was moving toward the middle of the dance floor. Her perfectly round face, beneath the black hair, parted in the middle and surmounted by a comb as red as her shawl, suddenly lighted up. She smiled to everyone around her while the guitarist plucked out a few staccato notes on his instrument. He began to play. Slowly the woman straightened her torso, and slowly she raised her two beautiful arms. Her fingers clicked the castanets, and her body began moving with the lightness of a child. The wide flowered skirt whirled about her muscular legs.

"How beautiful she's suddenly become," Françoise said, turning to Xavière.

Xavière did not reply. In her enraptured contemplation, no one else existed. Her cheeks were flushed, her features were no longer under control and her eyes followed the movements of the dancer in dazed ecstasy. Françoise emptied her glass. Although she knew that no one could ever be at one with Xavière in any thought or action, it was hard, after the joy she had felt earlier at regaining her affection, not to exist for her any longer. She again turned her attention to the dancer, who was now smiling at an imaginary gallant. She enticed him; she spurned him; finally, she fell into his arms. Then she became a sorceress, every movement suggesting dangerous mystery. Following that dance, she mimed a joyful peasant girl at some village festivity, whirling dizzily, with delirious uplifted face and frenzied eyes. All the youth and reckless gaiety evoked by her dancing acquired a moving purity as it sprang, transmuted, from her no longer youthful body. Françoise could not help taking a surreptitious glance at Xavière: she gave a start of amazement. Xavière was no longer watching, her head was lowered. In her right hand she held a half-smoked cigarette which she was slowly moving toward her left hand. Françoise barely suppressed a scream. The girl was pressing the lighted end against her skin, a bitter smile curling her lips. It was an intimate, solitary smile, like that of a half-wit; the voluptuous, tortured smile of a woman possessed of some secret pleasure. The sight of it was almost unbearable, it concealed something horrible.

The dancer had finished her repertoire and was bowing amid applause. Paula had turned toward the table, and now gazed speechlessly with questioning eyes. Pierre had noticed Xavière's performance some time before. Since no one thought fit to speak, Françoise held her tongue; and yet what was going on was intolerable. With her lips rounded coquettishly Xavière was gently blowing on the burnt skin which covered her wound. When she had blown away this little protective layer, she once more pressed the glowing end of her cigarette against the open wound. Françoise flinched. It was not only her flesh that rose up in revolt, but she felt herself attacked in a more profound and irreparable way, and to the very center of her being. Behind that maniacal grin, was a danger more positive than any she had ever imagined. Something was there that hungrily hugged itself, that unquestionably existed for its own sake. Approach to it was impossible, even in thought. Just as she seemed to be getting near it, the thought dissolved. This was nothing tangible, but an incessant flux, a never-ending escape, only comprehensible to itself, and forever occult. Eternally excluded she could only continue to circle around it.

"That's idiotic," she said. "You will burn yourself to the bone."

Xavière raised her head and gazed about her with a vaguely wild expression in her eyes. "It doesn't hurt," she said.

Paula took her wrist. "In a few moments it's going to hurt terribly," she said to her. "How childish!"

The burn was about the size of a dime and seemed to be very deep.

"I assure you I don't feel it at all," Xavière said, pulling her hand away and looking at Paula in a self-satisfied and mysterious way. "It's a voluptuous feeling, a burn."

The dancer came to the table. In one hand she was holding a plate, and, in the other, one of those double-necked *porrons* from which the Spaniards drink on festive occasions.

"Who wants to drink my health?" she asked.

Pierre put a note on the plate and Paula took the *porron* between her hands. She said a few words to the woman in Spanish. She threw back her head and skillfully directed a jet of red wine into her mouth, and then cut off the flow with a quick jerk.

"Your turn," she said to Pierre.

Pierre took the object and examined it warily. Then he tilted his head back, bringing the nozzle to the very edge of his lips.

"No, not like that," the woman said.

With a steady hand, she drew the *porron* away. For a moment Pierre let the wine run into his mouth, and then, in an effort to catch his breath, he moved and the liquid spilled on his tie.

"Damn it!" he said furiously.

The dancer laughed and began to taunt him in Spanish. He looked so upset that Paula burst out laughing, and her grave features softened, making her look younger.

Françoise barely achieved a strained smile. Fear had taken possession of her and she could think of nothing else. This time she felt that the peril involved more than her happiness.

"We're staying on for a while, aren't we?" Pierre asked.

"If it doesn't bore you," Xavière said timidly.

Paula had just left. It was to her calm gaiety that this evening owed all its charm. She had initiated each of them to the more unusual steps of the paso doble and the tango. She had invited the dancer to their table and had induced her to sing some beautiful folk songs for them, which the whole audience took up in chorus. They had drunk a considerable amount of Manzanilla. Pierre had finally brightened up and had fully regained his good humor. Xavière did not seem to be suffering from her burn; innumerable violent and contradictory feelings had been successively reflected in her face. Only for Françoise had the time passed slowly. Music, songs, dancing—nothing had succeeded in allaying the anguish that paralyzed her. From the moment Xavière had burned her hand, she had been unable to free her thoughts from the image of that tortured, ecstatic face, and she felt herself shuddering. She turned to Pierre; she needed to regain contact with him, but she had separated herself too completely. She could not succeed in attuning herself to him. She was alone. Pierre and Xavière were talking and their voices seemed to be coming from across a very great distance.

"Why did you do that?" Pierre was saying as he touched Xavière's hand.

Xavière looked at him in supplication; her whole expression was one of tender pleading. It was because of her that Françoise had hardened her heart against Pierre to such an extent that even now she was unable to smile at him; and yet Xavière had already silently made up with him, and seemed prepared to fall into his arms.

"Why?" he asked again. He stared for a moment at the injured hand. "I'd be willing to swear it's a consecrated burn."

Xavière was smiling, as she turned a guileless face towards him.

"A penitential burn," he continued.

"Yes," Xavière said. "I was so disgustingly sentimental about that rose. I was ashamed of it."

"You wanted to bury deep within you the memory of last night, didn't you?" Pierre's tone was friendly, but he was tense.

Xavière stared with admiring eyes. "How did you know?" she asked. She seemed spellbound by this sorcery.

"That wilted rose. It was easy to guess."

"That was a ridiculous, theatrical gesture," Xavière said. "But it was you who provoked me," she added smiling warmly.

Her smile was like a kiss, and Françoise wondered uncomfortably what she was doing there, witnessing this amorous tête-à-tête. She did not belong there; but where did she belong? Surely nowhere else. At this moment she felt erased from the face of the world.

"I!" said Pierre.

"You were looking sarcastic, and you were staring at me threateningly," Xavière said tenderly.

"Yes, I was unpleasant. I apologize. But it was because I felt that you were interested in everything in the world but us."

"You must have antennae," she said. "You were bristling before I even opened my mouth," she shook her head, "only your antennae are not very good ones."

"I at once suspected that you'd become infatuated with Gerbert," Pierre said bluntly.

"Infatuated?" She frowned. "But what on earth did that young man tell you?"

Pierre had not done it intentionally. He was incapable of anything so contemptible, but his words carried an unpleasant insinuation against Gerbert.

"He didn't tell me anything," said Pierre. "But he was charmed with his evening, and it's not very often that you take the trouble to charm anyone."

"I might have guessed as much," said Xavière with rage. "No sooner

am I a little civil to a fellow than he gets ideas! God knows what he's
gone and concocted in that empty little brain of his!"

"And besides, if you stayed shut up all day," Pierre continued, "it
was surely to ruminate over last evening's romance."

Xavière shrugged her shoulders. "It was romantic hot air," she said
testily.

"That's how it seems to you now."

"Not at all. I knew it all the time," Xavière insisted impatiently. She
looked straight at Pierre. "I wanted last night to seem wonderful to
me," she said. "Do you understand?"

There was a silence. No one would ever precisely know what Gerbert
had been to her during those twenty-four hours, and she herself had
already forgotten. What was certain was that she was now sincere in
repudiating him.

"It was to revenge yourself on us," Pierre said.

"Yes," Xavière said in a low voice.

"But we hadn't had dinner with Gerbert for ages. We have to see
him occasionally." Pierre was apologetic.

"I know," said Xavière, "but it always annoys me when you allow
yourselves to be preyed upon by all these people."

"You're a possessive little person."

"I can't help it," Xavière admitted dejectedly.

"Don't try," said Pierre tenderly. "Your possessiveness is not petty
jealousy. It goes with your inflexibility, with the violence of your feelings. You'd no longer be the same person if it were taken away from
you."

"Ah! It would be so nice if we three were alone in the world!"
Xavière said. Her eyes had a passionate gleam. "Only the three of us!"

Françoise's smile was forced. She had often been hurt by this sort of
secret understanding between Pierre and Xavière, but tonight she
detected her own condemnation in it. Jealousy and resentment were
feelings she had always spurned, yet this pair were now discussing them
as if they were beautiful objects, encumbering but precious, to be
handled with respectful care. She, too, might have enshrined these
disturbing riches within herself. Why had she instead preferred the
old, empty precepts which Xavière brazenly rejected? On many occasions she had been stabbed by jealousy. She had been tempted to hate
Pierre, to wish Xavière ill; but, under the futile pretext of keeping herself pure, she had created a void within herself. In contrast, Xavière,

with calm audacity, chose to assert herself to the utmost. As recompense she had a definite place in the world, and Pierre turned to her with passionate interest. Françoise had not dared to be herself, and she understood, in a passion of suffering, that this hypocritical cowardice had led her to being nothing at all.

She looked up. Xavière was speaking.

"I like you when you look tired," she was saying; "you become very ethereal." She gave Pierre a quick smile. "You look like your ghost. You were beautiful as a ghost."

Françoise studied Pierre. It was true that he was pale. That nervous fragility, reflected now in his drawn features, had often moved her to tears, but she was too detached from him to be touched by it tonight. It was only through Xavière's smile that she could sense its romantic charm.

"But I don't want to be a ghost any more, you know."

"Ah! But a ghost isn't a corpse," said Xavière. "It's a living thing, only it gets its body from its soul. It hasn't any unnecessary flesh; it doesn't get hungry, thirsty, or sleepy." Her eyes rested on Pierre's forehead, then on his hands, long, firm, slender hands, that Françoise had often lovingly touched, but never thought to look at. "And besides, what I find most poetic is that a ghost is not earth-bound. Wherever it may be, it is also somewhere else at the same time."

"I'm nowhere else but here," Pierre said.

He smiled fondly at Xavière. Françoise recalled the joy with which she had so often received such smiles, yet she was now incapable of even desiring one.

"Yes," said Xavière, "but I don't know how to put it exactly; you are here because you want to be. You don't look caged."

"Do I often look caged?"

Xavière hesitated. "Sometimes," she smiled coquettishly. "When you talk with dull old fogies, you almost seem to be one of them yourself."

"I remember when you met me, you were inclined to take me for a tiresome pompous ass!"

"You've changed," Xavière said.

She ran her eyes over him with a proud and happy look of possession. She thought she had changed him. Could it be true? It was no longer for Françoise to judge. Tonight the most precious treasures of her arid heart were sinking in indifference; she felt obliged to trust this intense fervor that shone with new brilliance in Xavière's eyes.

"You look completely worn out," Pierre said.

Françoise shuddered. He was speaking to her, and he seemed worried. She tried to control her voice.

"I think I've drunk too much," she said. The words stuck in her throat.

Pierre looked at her with distress. "You've thought me completely hateful this evening, haven't you?" he said remorsefully.

Spontaneously he laid his hand on hers. She managed to smile at him. She was touched by his solicitude, but even this tenderness that he was reawakening in her could not tear her from her solitary anguish.

"You were rather impossible," she said, taking his hand.

"I'm sorry," Pierre said, "for losing control." He seemed so upset at having hurt her, that if their love alone had been at stake Françoise would have been at peace again. "Now I've spoiled your evening for you," he said, "and you were so looking forward to it."

"Nothing's been spoiled," Françoise said, and with an effort she added more cheerfully, "We still have some time ahead of us. It's delightful to be here." She turned to Xavière. "Isn't it? Paula was not exaggerating. It's a wonderful place."

Xavière wore a peculiar smile. "Don't you think we look a little like American tourists seeing the night life of Paris? We're sitting by ourselves so that we won't be contaminated, and we're sight-seeing without coming into contact with anything. . . ."

Pierre's face clouded over. "What! Do you want us to snap our fingers and shout '*Olle!*' What do you expect?"

"I don't expect anything," Xavière replied coldly. "I'm stating a fact."

It was beginning all over again. Hatred like a dense vapor, as corrosive as an acid, was once more emanating from Xavière, and there was no defense against its excruciating bite. There was nothing to do but endure it and wait. But Françoise felt completely exhausted. Pierre was not so resigned. Xavière did not frighten him.

"Why do you suddenly hate us?" he said harshly.

Xavière burst into a strident laugh. "No, no! You're not going to begin all over again," she said. Her cheeks were aflame and her mouth was set. She seemed on the point of exasperation. "I don't spend my time hating you. I'm listening to the music."

"You do hate us," Pierre insisted.

"Definitely not," Xavière said. She caught her breath. "It's not the first time I've been astonished at the pleasure you take in looking at things from outside, as if they were stage sets." She touched her breast. "I," she continued with an impassioned smile, "I'm made of flesh and blood. Do you understand?"

Pierre threw a despairing glance at Françoise. He hesitated, then seemed to be trying to get control of himself.

"What happened?" he asked, in a conciliatory tone.

"Nothing happened," said Xavière.

"You thought Françoise and I were behaving like lovers?"

Xavière looked him in the eye. "Precisely," she said arrogantly.

Françoise clenched her teeth. She was struck with a wild desire to thrash Xavière, to trample her underfoot. She spent hours listening patiently to her duets with Pierre, and Xavière had the nerve to refuse her the right to exchange the slightest token of friendship with him! That was too much. It could not go on like this. She would endure it no longer.

"You're utterly unfair," Pierre said angrily. "If Françoise was depressed it was because of my behavior toward you. I don't think that can be called behaving like lovers."

Without answering, Xavière leaned forward. At a neighboring table, a young woman had just sprung to her feet and in a raucous voice was beginning to recite a Spanish poem. A great silence fell, and every eye was turned toward her. Even without full knowledge of the meaning of the words, her impassioned accent, and her face, illuminated by emotional fervor, were deeply moving. The poem was about hatred and death, about hope, too, perhaps, and in its surges of sudden violence and of lamentation the fate of ravaged Spain was vividly evoked to every mind. Fire and sword had driven the guitars from the streets, gone were the songs, the dazzling shawls, and the spikenard blossoms. The cabarets had been leveled, and the bombs had ripped open the goatskin bottles of wine; in the warm sweetness of the evening, fear and hunger stalked. The flamenco songs and the taste of the intoxicating wines they were drinking were now no more than funerary evocations of a dead past. For a little while, her eyes fixed on the red and tragic mouth, Françoise yielded to the power of the desolate pictures called up by this bitter incantation. She longed to lose herself, body and soul, in these desperate cries, in the nostalgia throbbing beneath these mysterious intonations. She turned her head. She could stop thinking about herself, but she could not forget that Xavière was beside her.

Xavière was no longer watching the woman; she was staring into space. She was holding a lighted cigarette which had burned down to the point where the lighted end was almost touching her fingers, without her apparently being aware of it; she seemed to be in the grip of an hysterical ecstasy. Françoise passed her hand across her forehead, she was dripping with perspiration. The atmosphere was stifling, and her thoughts burned like fire. This hostile presence, which had betrayed itself earlier in a mad smile, was approaching closer and closer; there was now no way of escaping this terrifying revelation. Day after day, minute after minute, Françoise had fled the danger; but the worst had happened, and she had at last come face to face with this insurmountable obstacle, which she had sensed, under vague forms, since her earliest childhood. Behind Xavière's maniacal pleasure, behind her hatred and jealousy, the abomination loomed, as monstrous and definite as death. Before Françoise's very eyes, yet apart from her, existed something like a condemnation with no appeal: detached, absolute, unalterable, an alien conscience was rising. It was like death, a total negation, an eternal absence, and yet, by a staggering contradiction, this abyss of nothingness could make itself present to itself and make itself fully exist for itself. The entire universe was engulfed in it, and Françoise, forever excluded from the world, was herself dissolved in this void, the infinity of which no word, no image could encompass.

"Look out!" said Pierre.

He bent over Xavière, and lifted the red-hot stub from her fingers. She stared at him as if having been awakened from a nightmare, then looked at Françoise, and abruptly took each of them by the hand. The palms of her hands were burning. Françoise shuddered when she came in contact with these feverish fingers which tightened on hers; she wanted to withdraw her hand, but she was now unable to move. Riveted to Xavière, she contemplated in amazement this body which allowed itself to be touched, and this beautiful face behind which the abomination was concealed. For a long time Xavière had been only a fragment of Françoise's life, and suddenly she had become the only sovereign reality, and Françoise had no more consistency than a pale reflection.

Why should it be she rather than I? thought Françoise, with anger. She need only have said one word, she need only say, "It is I." But she would have had to believe it; she would have had to choose herself. For many weeks Françoise had no longer been able to dissolve Xavière's hatred, her affection, her thoughts to harmless vapors. She had let them bite into her; she had turned herself into a prey. Freely, through her moments of resistance and revolt, she had been busy destroying herself. She was witnessing the course of her own life like an indifferent spectator, without ever daring to assert herself, whereas Xavière, from head to foot, was nothing but a living assertion of herself. She made herself exist with so sure a power, that Françoise, spellbound, had let herself be charmed into preferring Xavière to herself, thus obliterating herself. She had begun to see everything through Xavière's eyes—places, people and Pierre's smiles. She had reached the point of no longer knowing herself, except through Xavière's feelings for her, and now she was trying to merge with Xavière. But in this hopeless effort she was only succeeding in destroying herself.

The guitars kept up their monotonous thrumming and the air felt like a fiery sirocco. Xavière's hands had not let go their prey; her set face was expressionless. Pierre had not moved either. It was as if the same spell had transformed all three of them into marble. Pictures kept flashing through Françoise's mind—an old jacket, a deserted glade, a corner of the Pôle Nord where Pierre and Xavière were carrying on a mysterious tête-à-tête far removed from her. She had felt before, as she did this night, her own being dissolving itself in favor of other inaccessible beings; but never had she realized with such perfect lucidity her own annihilation. If only there were nothing left in her; but there still remained, among an infinity of deceptive will-o'-the-wisps, a faint phosphorescence hovering over the surface of things. The tension that had held her in its grip all evening suddenly snapped and she burst into silent sobs.

The spell was broken. Xavière withdrew her hands. Pierre spoke.

"Suppose we leave," he said.

Françoise rose. In a flash she was drained of all thought, and her body submissively set itself in motion. She put her cape over her arm and crossed the room. The cold outdoor air dried her tears, but her inner trembling never ceased. Pierre touched her shoulder.

"You aren't well," he said anxiously.

Françoise gave an apologetic smile. "I've definitely drunk too much," she said.

Xavière was walking a few paces ahead of them, as stiff as an automaton.

"She's also had all she can hold," Pierre said. "We'll take her home, and then we can talk undisturbed."

"Yes," said Françoise.

The cool of the night and Pierre's tenderness helped to restore her calm. They caught up with Xavière and each took her by an arm.

"I think it would do us good to walk a bit," Pierre said.

Xavière said nothing. Against a livid face, her lips were set in a stony grin. They walked down the street in silence; day was dawning. Xavière stopped suddenly.

"Where are we?" she asked.

"At the Trinité."

"Ah!" she said. "I think I was a little tipsy."

"I think so too," said Pierre cheerfully. "How do you feel?"

"I don't know. I don't know what's happened." She frowned miserably. "I remember a very beautiful woman who was talking in Spanish; after that there's a blank."

"You watched her for a while," Pierre said. "You were smoking cigarette after cigarette, and I had to take the stubs from between your fingers. You were letting them burn you without feeling anything. And then you seemed to wake up a little. You took our hands."

"Ah! Yes," said Xavière. She shuddered. "We were in the depths of hell. I began to think we'd never get out again."

"You sat there for some time, as if you'd been turned into a statue. And then Françoise began to cry."

"I remember," Xavière said, with a vague smile. She lowered her eyelids and said, in a faraway voice, "I was so glad when she cried, for that's just what I wanted to do."

For a second Françoise looked with horror at this delicate but implacable face in which she had not once seen any of her own joys and sorrows reflected. Not for one minute during the whole evening had Xavière given a thought to her distress. She had seen her tears only to rejoice at them. Françoise snatched her arm away from Xavière's, and began to run on ahead as if suddenly carried away by a tornado. Sobs of revulsion shook her. Her anguish, her tears, this night of torture, belonged to her and she would not let Xavière rob her of them. She would flee to the end of the world to escape the avid tentacles with which Xavière wanted to drain her of her life-blood. She heard hurrying steps behind her and felt a firm hand on her arm.

"What is it?" asked Pierre. "Please, Françoise, calm yourself."

"I don't want to," she cried. "I don't want to." Weeping, she fell against his shoulder. When she looked up she saw Xavière, who had caught up with them and was now looking at her with dismayed curiosity. But Françoise had lost all sense of shame, and nothing could affect her now. Pierre pushed them both into a taxi and she continued to weep without restraint.

When they reached the hotel, Françoise rushed upstairs without looking back, and threw herself on the couch. Her head ached. There was a sound of voices on the floor below, and almost immediately the door opened.

"What happened?" cried Pierre. Quickly he came to her and took her in his arms. She clung to him, and for a while there was nothing but emptiness and darkness, and a caress that lightly touched her hair.

"My dear love, what happened to you? Speak to me," Pierre's voice murmured.

She opened her eyes. In the light of dawn the room looked strangely fresh; she felt that it had not come under the influence of the night. With surprise she found herself once more in the presence of familiar shapes which her eyes could observe with composure. The thought of her continuing to reject this reality now seemed as untenable as the thought of death. She must return to the full consciousness of material objects and of herself. But she was as overwhelmed as if she had risen from the grave. It was something she would never forget.

"I don't know," she said. She smiled at him feebly. "Everything was unbearable."

"Did I hurt you?"

She seized his hands. "No," she said.

"Is it because of Xavière?"

Françoise shrugged her shoulders helplessly. It was too difficult to explain, and her head ached too much.

"It was hateful for you to witness her jealousy." There was a touch of remorse in his voice. "I myself found her insufferable. This can't go on; I shall speak to her tomorrow."

Françoise started. "You can't do that," she said. "She'll hate you."

"I don't care." He got up, took a few steps around the room, then came back to her.

"I feel guilty," he said. "I stupidly relied on the good feelings she has for me, but there was never any question of this just being a lousy attempt at seduction. We wanted to build a real trio, a well-balanced life for three, in which no one was sacrificed. Perhaps it was taking a risk, but at least it was worth trying! But if Xavière wants to behave like a jealous little bitch, and you have to be the unfortunate victim, while I play the gallant lover, it becomes nothing but a dirty business." His face was stern and his voice harsh. "I shall speak to her."

Françoise looked at him tenderly. He judged the weakness he had shown as severely as she had. Once more he was himself, in his strength, in his clarity of thought, and in this proud rejection of anything base. But even a return to the perfect agreement between them would not give her back her happiness. She felt exhausted and cowardly at the thought of new complications.

"Don't tell me that out of love for you she's going to admit being jealous of me?" she said warily.

"I'll no doubt look like a conceited ass and she will be insanely angry," Pierre said, "but I'll take my chance."

"No," said Françoise. If Pierre were to love Xavière, she in her turn would feel unbearably guilty. "No, please. Besides, that wasn't why I cried."

"Why did you, then?"

"You'll laugh at me," she said, with a weak smile. There was a glimmer of hope; perhaps if she managed to put her anguish into words she might be rid of it. "It's because I discovered that she has a conscience like mine. Have you ever felt someone else's conscience in yourself?" Again she was trembling, the words were not releasing her. "It's intolerable, you know."

Pierre was looking at her a little incredulously.

"You think I'm drunk," she said. "In a way I am, but it makes no difference. Why are you so astounded?" She rose suddenly. "If I were to tell you that I'm afraid of death, you would understand. Well, this thing is just as real and just as terrifying. Of course, we all know we're not alone in the world; we say these things, just as we say that we'll die some day. But when we begin to believe it . . ."

She leaned against the wall, the room was swirling round her. Pierre took her by the arm.

"Listen, don't you think you ought to rest? I am not making light of what you're telling me, but it would be better to talk about it calmly after you've slept a little."

"There's nothing to say about it," Françoise said. She began to cry again. She was dead tired.

He laid her on the bed, took off her shoes and threw a blanket over her.

"I'd like to get a breath of air," he said, "but I'll stay until you've fallen asleep."

He sat down beside her, and she pressed his hand against her cheek. Tonight Pierre's love no longer sufficed to bring her peace, he could not defend her against this thing that had been revealed to her during the day and evening. It was beyond reach. Françoise no longer even felt its mysterious touch, and yet it continued inexorably to exist. The weariness, the worries, even the disasters, brought by Xavière when she came to Paris, all these Françoise had accepted wholeheartedly because they were moments of her own life. But what had happened during the course of this night was something utterly different. She could not absorb it. It seemed as if the world now stood before her, preparing her excommunication, and that the bankruptcy of her very existence had just been completed.

5

FRANÇOISE smiled at the concierge and walked on across the court-yard, where the old scenery had been left to rot, and ran up the little green steps. During the past few days the theater had suspended per-formances and she was looking forward to having a long evening with Pierre; twenty-four hours had passed since she had last seen him, and a slight anxiety tempered her impatience. She never succeeded in wait-ing unmoved for the account of his excursions with Xavière, yet they were all alike: there were kisses, quarrels, tender reconciliations, ardent conversations, and lengthy silences. Françoise opened his door. Pierre was bending over a chest of drawers, rummaging about among bundles of papers.

He hurried toward her. "Ah! How slowly the time has passed without you!" he said. "How I cursed Bernheim and his business luncheons! They didn't let me go until rehearsal time." He took Françoise by the shoulders. "What have you been doing with yourself?"

"I've a hundred and one things to tell you," she said.

She touched his hair and the nape of his neck. Every time she saw him again, she liked to make certain that he was made of flesh and blood.

"What were you doing? House cleaning?"

"Oh! I give up. It's hopeless." Pierre cast a vindictive glance at the chest of drawers. "Anyhow, it's not so urgent now."

"The atmosphere was certainly much less tense at the dress rehearsal," Françoise said.

"Yes, I believe we've escaped again; for how long, is another matter." Pierre rubbed his pipe against his nose to make it shine. "Was it a success?"

"People laughed a lot. I'm not sure that was the effect intended; but in any case, I really enjoyed myself. Blanche Bouguet wanted me to stay for supper, but I got away with Ramblin. He trotted me around to I don't know how many bars. I kept my end up, and it hasn't stopped me from working hard all day."

"You must give me a detailed account of the play, and of Bouguet and Ramblin. Would you like something to drink?"

"Give me a little whisky," said Françoise. "And then you tell me first what you've been doing. Did you spend a pleasant evening with Xavière?"

"Whew!" said Pierre. He threw up his hands. "You never saw such a battle royal. Luckily, it's all over, but for two hours, we sat side by side in a corner at the Pôle Nord, quivering with hatred. We never before indulged in such high tragedy."

He took a bottle of Vat 69 from his cupboard, and half filled two glasses.

"What happened?"

"Well, I finally broached the question of her jealousy toward you," Pierre said.

"You shouldn't have."

"I told you that I had made up my mind to do it."

"How did you lead up to it?"

"We talked about her exclusiveness, and I told her that, on the whole, it was something strong and estimable in her, but that there was one place where it did not fit, and that was within the trio. She willingly agreed with me, but when I added that she was nevertheless showing signs of being jealous of you, she turned scarlet with surprise and anger."

"You were in a difficult position," said Françoise.

"Yes. I might easily have appeared ridiculous or obnoxious to her. But her mind's not petty—it was only the basis of the accusation that bowled her over. She fought like a tigress, but I didn't budge. I pointed out to her a number of instances. She wept with rage. She hated me so much that it frightened me. I thought she was going to die of suffocation."

Françoise looked at him anxiously. "Are you at least quite sure she doesn't bear you any grudge?"

"Absolutely sure. I lost my temper, too, at the beginning. But later,

I made it abundantly clear that I was only trying to help her because she was becoming odious in your eyes. I told her that what we had set our minds on, the three of us, was something difficult to achieve, and that it required the complete good will of each one of us. When she was quite convinced that my words carried no censure, and that I'd only warned her against a danger, she stopped being angry with me. I believe that not only did she forgive me, but that she has decided to try her utmost to control herself."

"If it's true, it does her great credit," Françoise said. She felt a sudden surge of confidence.

"We talked far more sincerely than usual. And I had the feeling that this conversation had released something in her. You know that look she has, of always withholding the best of herself, that had disappeared. She seemed to be completely tractable and without reservation, as if she saw no further objection to loving me openly."

"By honestly acknowledging her jealousy, she was perhaps delivered from it," Françoise said. She took a cigarette and looked fondly at Pierre.

"Why are you smiling?" Pierre asked.

"I'm always amused at how you take anyone's favorable opinion of you as a sign of grace. It's one more way of seeing yourself as God in person."

"There's something in that," Pierre admitted with a little confusion. He smiled abstractedly, and his face took on a kind of happy innocence that it usually had only in sleep. "She invited me to have tea with her, and for the first time, when I kissed her, she returned my kisses. Until three o'clock in the morning she lay in my arms in a state of complete surrender."

Françoise felt a stab in her heart. She, too, would have to learn to master herself. It was always painful to think that Pierre could embrace that body, whose bestowal she had not even known how to accept.

"I told you you'd end up by sleeping with her." She tried to mitigate the brutality of these words by smiling.

Pierre made an evasive gesture. "It will depend on her," he said. "Naturally I . . . but I wouldn't want to make her do anything that might be distasteful to her."

"She hasn't the temperament of a virgin," Françoise said.

The moment she uttered them, these words struck her painfully, and she blushed. She hated to look upon Xavière as a woman with a woman's desires, but the truth forced itself upon her. "I loathe purity. I'm made of flesh and blood." With all the strength at her command, Xavière was in revolt against this uneasy chastity to which she had been sentenced. In her bad moods, her bitter resentment was apparent.

"Certainly not," Pierre said. "And I even go so far as to think that she'll never be happy until she has achieved a well-balanced sexual life. Don't you think she's in a state of crisis at the moment?"

"Yes, I believe it implicitly," Françoise agreed.

Perhaps Pierre's kisses, his caresses, were precisely what had awakened Xavière's senses. Certainly, matters could not rest at their present stage. Françoise was carefully examining her fingers; she would grow accustomed to this idea in the end, already it was beginning to seem a little less painful. Since she was certain of Pierre's love and of Xavière's tenderness, no image could harm her any longer.

"What we're demanding of her is most unusual," Pierre said. "We were able to envisage such a way of living only because of the exceptional love between us two, and she can only conform to it because she herself is exceptional. It's quite understandable that she should have moments of uncertainty and even revolt."

"Yes, you must give us time," said Françoise.

She got up, walked over to the drawer Pierre had left open and plunged her hands among the scattered papers. She herself had sinned through mistrust. She had not forgiven Pierre his shortcomings which were frequently very minor. She had kept to herself a mass of thoughts she should have shared with him, and often, she had sought less to understand him than to oppose him. She picked out an old photograph and smiled. Dressed in a Greek tunic and wearing a curled wig, Pierre was gazing at the heavens with a youthful and stern expression.

"That's how you looked when I first set eyes on you," she said. "You've hardly aged at all."

"Neither have you." He came and stood beside her and bent over the drawer.

"I'd like to go through all that with you," said Françoise.

"Yes. It's full of amusing things." He straightened up and ran his hand along Françoise's arm. "Do you think we were wrong to embark on this affair?" he asked anxiously. "Do you think we'll succeed in carrying it through?"

"I've sometimes had my doubts," Françoise replied. "But this evening hope is returning." She walked away from the chest of drawers and went back to sit down by her glass of whisky.

"And where have you got to?" Pierre asked, sitting down beside her.

"I?" asked Françoise. When she was in her ordinary state of mind, it always frightened her a little to talk about herself.

"Yes. Do you still feel that there is something scandalous about Xavière's existence?"

"But it only comes to me in flashes, you know."

"But still it does recur from time to time?" Pierre insisted.

"It's bound to," said Françoise.

"You're amazing. You're the only living being I know who's capable of shedding tears on discovering in someone else a conscience similar to your own."

"Do you consider that stupid?"

"Of course not," said Pierre. "It's quite true that everyone experiences his own conscience as an absolute. How can several absolutes be compatible? The problem is as great a mystery as birth or death, in fact, it's such a problem that philosophers break their heads over it."

"Well, then, why are you amazed?"

"What surprises me, is that you should be affected in such a concrete manner by a metaphysical problem."

"But it is something concrete," Françoise said. "The whole meaning of my life is at stake."

"I don't say it isn't," said Pierre. He surveyed her with curiosity. "Nevertheless, this power you have to live an idea, body and soul, is unusual."

"But to me, an idea is not a question of theory. It can be tested or, if it remains theoretical, it has no value." She smiled. "Otherwise, I wouldn't have waited for Xavière's arrival to find out that my conscience is not unique in this world."

Pierre ran his finger thoughtfully over his lower lip. "I can readily understand your making this discovery apropos of Xavière," he said.

"Yes, I've never had any difficulty with you, because I barely distinguish you from myself."

"And besides, between us there's reciprocation."

"How do you mean?"

"The moment you acknowledge my conscience, you know that I acknowledge one in you, too. That makes all the difference."

"Perhaps," said Françoise. She stared in momentary perplexity at the bottom of her glass. "In short, that is friendship. Each renounces his pre-eminence. But what if either one refuses to renounce it?"

"In that case, friendship is impossible," said Pierre.

"Well, then, what can be done about it?"

"I don't know."

Xavière never renounced any part of herself. No matter how high she placed someone else, even if it amounted to worship, that person remained an object to her.

"There's no remedy," Françoise said. She smiled. One would have to kill Xavière. . . . She rose and walked to the window. Tonight, Xavière did not weigh heavily on her mind. She drew back the curtain. She loved this small peaceful square where the people of the neighborhood came to get a breath of fresh air. An old man seated on a bench was taking some food out of a paper bag; a child was running around a tree, each leaf carved with metallic clarity by a street lamp. Pierre was free. She was alone. But, within this separateness, they could re-establish a union as essential as the one she used to dream of too easily.

"What are you thinking about?" Pierre asked.

She took his face between her hands and, without answering, kissed it again and again.

"What a wonderful evening we've had," Françoise said. She squeezed Pierre's arm happily. They had looked at old photographs together, reread old letters, and then made a grand tour along the river, past the Châtelet and through the Halles, discussing Françoise's novel, and their youth, and the future of Europe. It was the first time in weeks that they had had such a long, unrestricted, and objective conversation. At last the circle of passion and anxiety, in which Xavière's sorcery held them as prisoners, had been broken, and they found themselves once more together at the heart of the immense world. Behind them stretched the limitless past; continents and oceans were spread out in vast expanses over the surface of the globe, and the miraculous certainty of existing amid this incalculable wealth even overflowed the narrow bounds of space and time.

"Look, there's a light in Xavière's room," Pierre said.

Françoise shuddered. After that untrammeled flight, she came down to earth with a painful shock in this dark little street, in front of her hotel. It was two o'clock in the morning. Pierre, like a detective on the alert, was staring at a lighted window in the black façade.

"What's so surprising about that?" Françoise asked.

"Nothing," said Pierre. He opened the door and hurried up the stairs. On the third-floor landing he stopped. A murmur of voices broke the silence.

"Someone's talking in her room," Pierre said. He stood still, listening. A few paces behind, her hand on the banister, Françoise also remained motionless. "Who on earth can it be?" he said.

"Who was she going out with tonight?" Françoise asked.

"She had no plans." He took a step forward. "I want to know who it is." He took another step and a floor-board creaked.

"They'll hear you," Françoise warned him.

Pierre hesitated. Then he bent down and began to untie his shoe laces. Françoise was overwhelmed by a despair more bitter than any she had ever known. Pierre had begun to tiptoe along between the yellow walls of the hall. He pressed his ear to the door. With one stroke, the happy evening, Françoise herself, the whole world, everything vanished. There was nothing but the silent landing, the wooden door, and those whispering voices beyond it. Françoise looked at him in distress. In those mad, hunted features, she could scarcely recognize the beloved face that had been smiling so tenderly at her only a short while ago. She mounted the last few steps. She felt as if he were a madman under the influence of some temporary lucidity, who with a touch would fall back into delirium. Those rational hours of relaxation had been merely a temporary suspension of his madness. There would never be a cure. Pierre tiptoed back to her.

"It's Gerbert," he said in a low voice. "I suspected as much."

Shoes in hand, he climbed up to the next floor.

"Well, there's nothing so mysterious about that," said Françoise, walking into her room. "They went out together, and he came home with her."

"She didn't tell me she was going to see him. Why did she hide it from me? Or else she decided on the spur of the moment."

Françoise had taken off her coat. She slipped out of her dress and put on her dressing gown.

"They must have run into each other," she said.

"They no longer go to Dominique's. No, she must have deliberately gone to look for him."

"Unless it was he," Françoise said.

"He would never have dared ask her to go out with him at the last minute." Pierre was sitting on the edge of the couch, gazing at his stockinged feet in apparent perplexity.

"In all probability she suddenly felt like going out to dance," Françoise said.

"Yes, so great an urge that she rang him up, when she's scared to death of a telephone! Or else she went all the way to Saint Germain des Prés, although she's incapable of taking three steps away from Montparnasse!" Pierre kept staring at his feet. The right sock had a hole in it, and the protruding tip of his toe seemed to fascinate him. "There's something behind all this," he said.

"What should there be?" Françoise was resignedly brushing her hair. How long was this indefinite and perpetually new discussion to last? What has Xavière done? What would she do? What was she thinking? Why? How? Evening after evening, the obsession was revived, always as harassing, always as futile, and the same feverish taste in her mouth, the same desolation in her heart, the same weariness in her sleepy body. When these questions had finally been answered, a new series of identical questions would take up their relentless round. What does Xavière want? What will she say? How? Why? There was no way of putting a stop to them.

"I don't understand," Pierre said. "She was so affectionate last night, so yielding, so trusting."

"Well, who says that she's changed? Whatever you may say, going out with Gerbert is not a crime."

"No one, except you or me, has ever entered her room," Pierre said. "If she did invite Gerbert, it's either in revenge, which means that she's begun to hate me; or else she had a sudden desire for him to come up to her room. And that means that he attracts her very strongly." He was swinging his feet and looking perplexed. "It could be both."

"Probably it's a mere whim," Françoise said without conviction. Last night's reconciliation with Pierre had certainly been sincere; that was one kind of pretense of which Xavière was incapable. But, with her, the last smiles were not to be trusted, they were only the signs of a lull between storms. As soon as she had parted from anyone, Xavière immediately began to review the situation, and it very often happened that having left her after a calm, reasonable, and affectionate talk, one returned only to find her blazing with hatred.

Pierre shrugged his shoulders. "You know very well that it isn't a whim," he said.

Françoise took a step toward him. "Do you think she's angry with you because of that conversation? I really am sorry."

"There's nothing for you to be sorry about," Pierre said brusquely. "She ought to be able to stand hearing someone tell her the truth."

He got up and took a few steps across the room. Françoise had often seen him worried, but this time he seemed to be fighting some intolerable suffering. She longed to come to his relief; the bitter defiance, which she usually felt toward him when he was suffering from self-inflicted anxieties and worries, had dissolved before the distress on his face. But nothing depended on her any more.

"Aren't you going to bed?" she asked.

"Yes," said Pierre.

She stepped behind the screen and rubbed some orange-scented cream on her face. Pierre's anxiety was infecting her. Directly below her, separated only by a few boards and a little plaster, was Xavière's unpredictable face, with Gerbert watching it. Xavière had probably switched on the bedside lamp, a faint glow beneath its blood-red shade, and muffled words were finding their way through the smoky half-light. What were they saying? Were they sitting side by side? Were they touching each other? It was easy to imagine Gerbert's face, he was always the same, always himself; but what had he become in Xavière's heart? Was he desirable, touching, cruel, indifferent? Was he a beautiful object to be admired, was he an enemy or a prey? Their voices could not reach her room; she heard only the rustle of clothes on the other side of the screen and the ticking of the alarm clock, amplified in the silence, as if heard through a haze of fever.

"Are you ready?" Françoise asked.

"Yes," said Pierre. Barefoot and in pajamas, he was beside the door. He opened it softly. "You can't hear anything now," he said. "I wonder if Gerbert is still there."

Françoise walked over to him. "No, you can't hear a thing."

"I'll go and see," said Pierre.

Françoise laid her hand on his arm. "Be careful. It would be so unpleasant if they were to find you there."

"Don't worry."

For a moment Françoise watched him through the half-open door. Then she picked up a wad of cotton-wool and a bottle of nail-polish remover, and began meticulously cleaning her nails. First one finger, then another; round each cuticle there were still a few specks of pink. If it were possible to lose oneself in each minute, tragedy could never force its way through to one's heart; it would have to have assistance. Françoise gave a start. Two bare feet were padding across the floor.

"Well?" she said.

"There was absolutely no sound." He stood leaning against the door. "They are certainly necking."

"Or were necking; probably Gerbert has left," said Françoise.

"No, if the door had opened or closed, I would have heard it."

"In any case, they could be quiet without necking," Françoise said.

"If she did bring him home with her, it's because that's what she wanted."

"Not necessarily."

"I'm sure of it," said Pierre.

This peremptory tone was not usual with him. Françoise stiffened.

"I can't see Xavière bringing a man home to make love with him; or if she did, he'd have to be unconscious. Why, she'd go mad if she thought Gerbert suspected that she had fallen for him! You saw how she decided to hate him when she thought he'd been a little bit too cocky."

Pierre gave Françoise a queer look.

"Can't you trust my psychological sense? I tell you that they were necking."

"You're not infallible," said Françoise.

"That may be, but where Xavière is concerned, you are wrong every time."

"That remains to be proven," Françoise said.

Pierre gave her a sly, almost spiteful smile. "What if I were to tell you that I saw them?"

Françoise was taken aback. Why had he been so underhanded with her? "You saw them?" she asked in an unsteady voice.

"Yes, I looked through the keyhole. They were on the couch and they were kissing."

Françoise felt more and more uncomfortable. There was something shamefaced and shifty in Pierre's expression.

"Why didn't you tell me so at once?"

"I wanted to know if you'd take my word for it," Pierre said with a short, unpleasant laugh.

Françoise could hardly hold back her tears. Pierre had deliberately tried to put her in the wrong. All this strange maneuvering implied a hostility she had never suspected. Was it possible that he was nursing secret resentments against her?

"You seem to think you're an oracle," she said curtly.

She got into bed and Pierre disappeared behind the screen. Her throat ached. After such an evening of mutual understanding and tenderness this sudden burst of hatred was inconceivable. But was he really the same man? Was he the man who a short while before was talking to her about herself with such solicitude, or was he this furtive Peeping Tom bending over a keyhole with the smirk of a jealous lover? She could not restrain a feeling of real horror in the face of this stubborn, hot-headed indiscretion. Lying on her back, with her arms folded under her head, she held back her thoughts as one holds one's breath in an attempt to postpone the moment of suffering, but this precarious tension was worse than a definite, unrelieved pain. She turned her eyes to Pierre who was now ready for bed. Fatigue softened the flesh of his face without making his features any gentler; beneath that hard stubborn face, the whiteness of his neck seemed almost obscene. She turned toward the wall. Pierre lay down beside her and put out his hand to turn off the light. For the first time in their life together, they were about to go to sleep as enemies. Françoise kept her eyes open. She was afraid of what might happen when she gave way to sleep.

"Aren't you sleepy?"

She did not stir. "No," she said.

"What are you thinking?"

She did not answer. She could not utter another word without beginning to cry.

"You think I'm hateful," Pierre said.

She controlled herself. "I think that you're well on the way to hating me."

"I!" he cried. She felt his hand on her shoulder and saw that the face he was turning toward her was full of distress. "I don't want you even to think such a thing; that would be the bitterest blow."

"It began to look like it," she said in a choking voice.

"How could you believe such a thing? That I could hate you!"

His tone betrayed a poignant despair, and suddenly, with a spasm of joy and pain, Françoise saw that there were tears in his eyes. She threw herself toward him without trying to restrain her sobs. Never had she seen Pierre cry.

"No, I don't believe it," she said. "It would be so horrible."

Pierre hugged her to him. "I love you," he said in a low voice.

"And I love you, too."

Lying against his shoulder she continued to weep, but now her tears were sweet. She would never forget how Pierre's eyes had filled with tears because of her.

"You know," said Pierre, "I lied to you just then."

"When?"

"It wasn't true that I wanted to put you to the test. I was ashamed for having looked. That's why I didn't tell you at once."

"Ah!" Françoise said, "that's why you looked so shifty!"

"I wanted you to know that they were in each other's arms, but I thought you'd take my word for it. I was angry with you for forcing the truth out of me."

"I thought you were acting out of pure spite," said Françoise, "and that seemed appalling to me." Gently, she ran her hand over his forehead. "It's funny, I never thought you could feel ashamed."

"You can't imagine how low I felt, creeping along the hall in my pajamas and peeping through the keyhole."

"I know; passion is sordid," Françoise said.

Her calm was restored. Pierre no longer seemed a monster to her, since he was capable of so lucidly passing judgment on himself.

"It is sordid," he repeated, staring at the ceiling. "I can't bear the thought that she's kissing Gerbert."

"I understand," Françoise said. She pressed her cheek against his. Until tonight, she had always tried to keep outside Pierre's predicaments. Perhaps it had been instinctive prudence on her part, because now that she was trying to live his distress with him, the suffering which was closing in upon her was unbearable.

"We ought to try to sleep," Pierre said.

"Yes." She closed her eyes. She knew that Pierre had no desire to sleep, nor could she take her thoughts from the couch in the room below her, where Gerbert and Xavière were locked in each other's arms, mouth to mouth. What was Xavière trying to find in his arms? Revenge against Pierre? Sensual satisfaction? Was it by chance that she had chosen this prey rather than another? Or when she so savagely demanded something to touch, was she thinking of him? Françoise's eyelids were growing heavy. In a sudden flash, she recalled Gerbert's face, his bronzed cheeks, his long girlish eyelashes. Was he in love with Xavière? Was he capable of being in love? Would he have loved her, Françoise, if she had been willing? Why had he been unable to take the initiative? How hollow seemed all those old reasons! Or was it she who could no longer fathom their difficult meaning? In any case, it was Xavière he was embracing. Her eyes became as hard as stone. For a moment or two, she still heard the even breathing beside her; then nothing.

Suddenly, Françoise regained consciousness. There was a thick layer of fog behind her; she felt that she had slept for a long time. She opened her eyes. In the room, night had given way to morning. Pierre was sitting up in bed; he looked wide awake.

"What time is it?" she asked.

"It's five o'clock."

"Didn't you sleep?"

"Yes, a little." He looked at the door. "I'd like to know if Gerbert has gone."

"He couldn't have stayed all night," Françoise said.

"I'm going to have a look."

He threw back the covers and got out of bed. This time Françoise did not try to hold him back; she, too, wanted to know. She got up and followed him on to the landing. A gray light had filtered into the stairwell; the whole house was still asleep. She leaned over the banister; her heart was thumping. What would happen now?

A moment later Pierre reappeared at the foot of the stairs and beckoned to her. She went down to him.

"The key is in the lock; you can't see anything, but I think she's alone. She seems to be crying."

Françoise went up to the door. She heard the faint clink of china, as if Xavière had put a cup down on a saucer. This was followed by a muffled sound and a sob; then another louder sob, then a torrent of desperate, unrestrained sobbing. Xavière had no doubt fallen on her knees in front of the couch or thrown herself full length on the floor. She was always so circumspect even when she was most miserable, that it was impossible to believe that this animal groan came from her body.

"You don't think she's drunk?" Alcohol was the only thing that could have made Xavière lose control of herself so completely.

"I suppose she must be," said Pierre.

They stood in front of the door, anguished and helpless. There was no pretext for knocking at this hour of the morning, and yet it was agonizing to think of Xavière prostrate and sobbing, a prey to all the nightmares of drunkenness and loneliness.

"We mustn't stay here," Françoise said, at last. The sobs had subsided; they had changed into short, painful gasps. "We'll know everything in a few hours."

Slowly, they went upstairs to their room. Neither of them had the strength to propose fresh conjectures. Words would not serve to free them from this nebulous fear in which Xavière's wailing could be heard echoing. What was wrong with her? Could she be healed? Françoise threw herself on the bed, and unresistingly let herself sink into the depths of weariness, fear and grief.

When Françoise awoke, daylight was filtering through the shutters. It was ten o'clock. Pierre was asleep, with his arms above his head, looking angelic and defenseless. Françoise propped herself up on her elbow. From under the door there protruded a scrap of pink paper. Suddenly, the whole night came back to her, its feverish comings and goings, and its throbbing uncertainties. She jumped out of bed. The sheet of paper had been torn in half, on one of the pieces were scrawled words in large, untidy, overlapping strokes. Françoise deciphered the beginning of the note. "*I am so disgusted with myself—I ought to have jumped out of the window—but I shan't have the courage. Don't forgive me. Tomorrow morning you ought to kill me yourself if I've been too cowardly to do it.*" The last sentences were totally illegible. At the bottom of the sheet, in huge shaky letters, was written: "*No forgiveness.*"

"What is it?" asked Pierre. He was sitting on the edge of the bed, his hair tousled, his eyes still heavy with sleep; but through the fog of waking an acute anxiety appeared.

Françoise handed him the paper. "She was plain drunk," she said. "Look at the writing."

" 'No forgiveness,' " Pierre read aloud. He glanced hastily over the scrawl. "Quick, go and see what's happening to her. Knock on her door." There was panic in his eyes.

"I'm going." She put on her slippers and hurried downstairs. Her legs were shaking. What if Xavière had suddenly become insane? Would she be stretched out, lifeless, behind her door? Or huddled wild-eyed in a corner?

There was a pink patch on the door. Françoise hurried up to it. A piece of paper had been pinned up with a thumbtack. It was the other half of the torn sheet.

Xavière had written in large letters, "No forgiveness," and beneath it was a jumbled mass of illegible scribbles. Françoise bent over the key-hole, but the key blocked the aperture; she knocked. There was a faint creaking, but no one answered. Xavière was probably asleep.

Françoise hesitated a moment. Then she tore down the paper and went back to her room.

"I didn't dare knock," she said. "I think she's asleep. Look what she had pinned to her door."

"It's illegible," said Pierre, as he studied the mysterious marks for a moment. "There's the word 'unworthy.' One thing is certain, she was completely beside herself." He thought for a moment. "Was she already drunk when she kissed Gerbert? Did she deliberately get drunk to give herself courage, so that she could play me a dirty trick? Or did they get drunk together without premeditation?"

"She must have cried, then written this note, and after that she must have fallen asleep," Françoise said. She wished she could be sure that Xavière was lying peacefully in her bed.

She opened the shutters and daylight poured into the room. With amazement, she looked down for a moment on the busy, sane street where everything had its normal appearance. And then she turned back into the anguish-ridden room in which all thoughts continued their endless round.

"I'll go and knock all the same," she said. "It's impossible to stay like this without knowing for certain. Supposing she's swallowed some drug! God knows what state she's in."

"Yes, knock until she answers," Pierre urged.

Françoise went downstairs again. For hours she had never stopped going up and down those stairs, either in reality or in thought. The sobs she had heard still echoed in her brain. Xavière had probably lain prone for a long time, and then gone over to lean out of the window; the frenzy of disgust that had wrung her heart was frightful to imagine. Françoise knocked. Her heart was racing; but there was no answer. She knocked louder.

A muffled voice murmured, "Who's there?"

"It's I, Françoise."

"What is it?" said the voice.

"I wanted to know if you were ill."

"No," said Xavière. "I was asleep."

Françoise felt extremely awkward. It was broad daylight, Xavière was in bed in her own room, and she was speaking in a voice which was very much alive. It was a normal morning in which the tragic memories of the night seemed entirely out of place.

"It's because of last night," Françoise said. "Do you really feel all right?"

"Of course I feel all right, I want to sleep," Xavière rejoined crossly.

Françoise hesitated a moment longer. Devastated by this cataclysmic night, these sullen replies, far from bringing relief, left her with a strange flat feeling of disappointment. She could not very well insist further, so she went back to her room. After those despairing moans and pathetic pleas, she found it hard to resign herself to facing a dull and ordinary day.

"She was asleep," she said to Pierre. "She seemed to think it quite un-called for that I should come and wake her up."

"Didn't she open her door to you?" Pierre asked.

"No," said Françoise.

"I wonder if she'll keep her appointment at noon? I don't think so."

"I don't think so, either."

They dressed in silence. There was no point in putting into words thoughts that led nowhere. When they were ready, they left the room and, by mutual consent, started off for the Dôme.

"You know the thing to do," Pierre said, "is to telephone Gerbert and ask him to come and meet us. He'll be able to tell us what went on."

"On what pretext?"

"Tell him exactly what's happened; that Xavière has written us a fantastic note, and is now barricading herself in her room; that we're worried and would like to be enlightened."

"Good. I'll go and phone," Françoise said, as they reached the café. "Order me a black coffee."

She went downstairs and gave the telephone girl Gerbert's number; she felt as nervous as Pierre. What exactly had taken place last night? Only kisses? What did they want from each other? What was going to happen?

"Hello?" said the telephone girl. "Hold on. Here's your number."

Françoise stepped into the booth. "Hello. May I speak to Monsieur Gerbert, please."

"Speaking," said Gerbert. "Who's this?"

"It's Françoise. Could you come and meet us at the Dôme? We'll explain why."

"Sure thing," said Gerbert. "I'll be there in ten minutes."

"Good," said Françoise. She dropped some money on the plate and went up to the café. At one of the tables at the back of the room sat Elisabeth, with the daily papers spread out in front of her and a cigarette between her lips. Pierre was sitting beside her, frowning with annoyance.

"Well! What a surprise!" said Françoise. Elisabeth knew that this is where they came almost every morning, and she had certainly come to spy on them. Did she know something?

"I came to read the papers and write a few letters," she said, adding with a hint of satisfaction: "Things look pretty grim."

"Yes," Françoise said. She noticed that Pierre had not ordered anything; obviously he wanted to get away as soon as possible.

Elisabeth gave an amused laugh. "What's the matter with the two of you this morning? You look like a pair of mutes."

Françoise hesitated.

"Xavière got drunk last night," Pierre said. "She wrote a demented note saying that she wanted to kill herself, and now she refuses to open her door to us." He shrugged his shoulders. "She's capable of any kind of idiocy."

"In fact, we must get back to the hotel as quickly as possible. I don't feel at all easy."

"Nonsense! She won't kill herself," Elisabeth said. She stared at the tip of her cigarette. "I met her last night on the boulevard Raspail; she was skipping along with Gerbert. I can assure you that she had no thoughts of suicide."

"Did she seem to be drunk then?" Françoise asked.

"She always looks more or less doped up," said Elisabeth. "I couldn't say." She shook her head. "You take her far too seriously. I know what she really needs. You ought to make her join an athletic club, where she'd be obliged to do eight hours' exercise a day and eat steaks. She'd feel a lot better, believe me."

"We'll go back and see what's happening to her," said Pierre, getting up.

They shook hands with Elisabeth and left the café.

"I told her we'd only come to telephone," Pierre explained.

"Yes, but I told Gerbert to meet us here."

"We'll wait for him outside, and catch him as he arrives."

They began to walk up and down the pavement in silence.

"What if Elisabeth comes out and finds us here, what will we look like?"

"Oh! to hell with her!" Pierre said irritably.

"She ran into them last night, and she came along to find out what's going on. How she hates us!"

Pierre did not answer. His eyes never left the subway exit. Françoise was apprehensively watching the café terrace. She had no wish to be caught by Elisabeth in this moment of agitation.

"There he is," said Pierre.

Gerbert was coming toward them with a smile. The dark circles under his eyes seemed to cover half his face. Pierre's face brightened.

"Greetings. We've got to make a quick getaway," he said with a pleasant smile. "Elisabeth's watching us from in there. We'll go and hide in the café across the street."

"It wasn't inconvenient for you to come, I hope?" Françoise asked him. She was embarrassed. Gerbert would think the step they had taken very odd. He already looked constrained.

"No, not at all," he said.

They sat down at a table and Pierre ordered three coffees. He alone seemed perfectly at his ease.

"Look at what we found under our door this morning," he said, taking Xavière's message from his pocket. "Françoise knocked at her door and she refused to open it. Perhaps you can enlighten us. We heard your voice last night. Was she drunk, or what? What condition was she in when you left her?"

"She wasn't drunk," Gerbert said. "But we brought back a bottle of whisky with us. Maybe she drank it afterward." He paused and tossed back his hair, looking embarrassed. "I'll have to tell you. I slept with her last night," he said.

There was a brief silence.

"That's no reason for her wanting to jump out of the window," Pierre said with energy.

Françoise looked at him almost with admiration. How well he could act! She might almost have been taken in herself.

"It's easy to understand that from her point of view it is a world-shaking event," she said with constraint. This news had certainly not taken Pierre unawares; he no doubt had sworn to himself that he would put a good face on it. But when Gerbert left them, what anger, what an outburst of suffering might come!

"She came looking for me at the Deux Magots," said Gerbert. "We talked for a while, then she asked me to come back to her room. After we got there, I don't know any longer just how it happened, but suddenly she was kissing me, and finally—well, we slept together." He was staring fixedly at the bottom of his glass looking sheepish and somewhat annoyed.

"Has this been brewing for some time?" Pierre asked.

"And you think that she attacked the whisky after you left?" said Françoise.

"Probably," Gerbert said. He raised his head. "She threw me out, and yet I swear that it wasn't I who had gone looking for it," he said defiantly. His face relaxed. "How she cursed me! I was petrified! You'd have thought I'd raped her."

"That's just what she would do," Françoise said.

Gerbert looked at Pierre with sudden timidity. "You don't blame me?"

"For what?"

"I don't know," said Gerbert with embarrassment. "She's young. I don't know," he concluded with a faint blush.

"Don't make her pregnant, that's all I ask of you," Pierre said.

Françoise crushed her cigarette in the saucer. She was ill at ease. Pierre's duplicity made her uncomfortable. It was more than play acting. He was sneering at himself and at everything that meant most to him; but this fierce calm was achieved only at the cost of a strain painful to imagine.

"Oh! You can rest assured of that," said Gerbert. He added with a preoccupied look, "I wonder if she'll come back."

"If she'll come back—where to?" asked Françoise.

"I told her when I left that she'd know where to find me, but that I wouldn't go to get her," Gerbert said with dignity.

"Oh! you'll go all the same," said Françoise.

"Certainly not," Gerbert rejoined indignantly. "She's not going to get the idea into her head that she can run me."

"Don't get excited. She'll come back," Pierre said. "She's proud when it suits her, but she has no consistent principles. If she feels like seeing you, she'll rake up some good excuse." He puffed at his pipe.

"Do you think she's in love with you, or what?"

"I can't quite make it out. I've kissed her now and then, but she didn't always seem to like it."

"You ought to go and see what's happening to her," Pierre said to Françoise.

"But she's already sent me flying."

"Well, never mind that. Go on insisting until she lets you in. She mustn't be left alone. God knows what ideas she's got in her head." Pierre smiled. "I'd gladly go myself, but I don't think it would be wise."

"Don't tell her you have seen me," said Gerbert anxiously.

"Don't worry."

"And remind her that we're expecting her at noon," Pierre said.

Françoise left the café and turned into the rue Delambre. She detested this role of go-between which Pierre and Xavière had all too often forced her play, and which made her hateful to each of them in turn. But today, she had made up her mind to throw herself into it wholeheartedly. She was really frightened for them.

She went upstairs and knocked. Xavière opened the door. Her skin was yellow, her eyelids swollen, but she had dressed carefully. She had put lipstick on her mouth and mascara on her eyelashes.

"I've come to find out how you are," Françoise said gaily.

Xavière cast a gloomy look in her direction. "How I am? I'm not ill."

"You wrote me a note that gave me a terrible fright."

"I wrote you?"

"Look," said Françoise, handing her the pink slip.

"Ah! I vaguely remember." She sat down on the couch beside Françoise. "I got disgracefully drunk," she said.

"I thought you really intended to commit suicide," Françoise said. "That's why I knocked this morning."

Xavière stared at the paper in disgust.

"I must have been even more drunk than I thought," she said. She passed her hand across her forehead. "I met Gerbert at the Deux Magots, and I don't really remember why, but we came back to my room with a bottle of whisky. We had a few drinks together, and after he left, I finished the bottle." She was staring into space, her mouth partly opened in a faint sneer. "Yes, I remember now. I stayed at the window for a long time thinking I ought to jump out. And then I felt cold."

"Well! It would have been cheerful if they'd brought your little corpse back to me," Françoise said.

Xavière shivered. "In any case, that's not the way I'd kill myself," she said.

Her face fell. Françoise had never seen her look so miserable. She felt her heart go out to her. She so much wanted to help her! But Xavière would have to want to accept her help.

"Why did you think of committing suicide?" she asked gently. "Are you so unhappy?"

Suddenly Xavière's eyes rolled back, and her face was transfigured by an ecstacy of suffering. Françoise felt all at once torn out of herself and consumed by this unbearable pain. She put her arms around Xavière and hugged her.

"My darling little Xavière, what's the matter? Tell me."

Xavière fell limply against her shoulder and burst into sobs.

"What is it?" repeated Françoise.

"I'm ashamed," she said.

"Why ashamed? Because you got drunk?"

Xavière swallowed her tears and said in a childish voice: "Because of that, because of everything. I don't know how to behave. I quarreled with Gerbert. I threw him out. I was loathsome. And then I wrote that stupid letter. And then. . . ." She moaned and began to weep again.

"And then what?" said Françoise.

"And then nothing. Don't you think that's enough? I feel filthy," she said, and blew her nose miserably.

"All that isn't so serious," Françoise said. The beautiful, generous suffering which had, for a moment, filled her heart, had become cramped and bitter. Even in the midst of despair, Xavière was keeping herself under absolute control. . . . With what abandon she lied!

"You mustn't get so upset."

"I'm sorry," said Xavière. She dried her eyes, and said in rage, "I'll never get drunk again."

It had been folly hoping for a moment that Xavière would turn to Françoise, as to a friend, in order to unburden her heart; she had too much pride and too little courage. Silence ensued. Françoise was filled with compassion at the thought of the inevitable future that now threatened Xavière and that no one could avert. She would undoubtedly lose Pierre forever and her relationship with Françoise would itself be affected by such a rupture. Françoise would not succeed in saving them if Xavière spurned all her advances.

"Labrousse is expecting us for lunch."

Xavière drew back. "Oh! I don't want to go."

"Why?"

"I feel so depressed and so tired."

"That's no reason."

"I don't want to." She pushed Françoise away from her with a persecuted look. "I don't want to see Labrousse just now."

Françoise put her arm around her. How she wished she might drag the truth from her! Xavière did not suspect how much she needed help.

"What are you afraid of?" she asked.

"He'll think that I got drunk on purpose, because of the night before, because I was so intimate with him," Xavière said. "There'll be more explanations, and I've had enough, enough, enough!" She burst into tears.

Françoise hugged her tighter, and said noncommittally: "There's nothing to explain."

"Yes, there's everything to explain." Xavière said. The tears were pouring down her cheeks and her face was the picture of human misery.

"Whenever I see Gerbert, Labrousse thinks that I've turned against him, and he gets angry with me. I can't bear it any more. I never want to see him again," she cried in a paroxysm of despair.

"On the contrary, if you were to see him," Françoise said, "if you were to speak to him yourself, I'm sure everything would be cleared up."

"No, it's hopeless," said Xavière. "Everything's finished. He'll hate me." She let her head sink on Françoise's knees. She was sobbing violently. How unhappy she would be! And how Pierre was suffering at this very moment. . . .

Françoise felt utterly miserable and tears came to her eyes. Why was all their love put to no better use than torturing one another? A black hell now lay in wait for them.

Xavière raised her head and looked at Françoise in amazement.

"You're crying because of me," she said. "You're crying! Oh! I don't want you to."

Impulsively, she took Françoise's face between her hands and began to kiss her with fanatical devotion. They were sacred kisses, purifying Xavière of all her defilement and restoring her self-respect. With these soft lips on her face, Françoise felt so noble, so ethereal, so sublime, that it sickened her heart; she longed for a human friendship, and not this fanatical and imperious worship of which she was forced to be the docile idol.

"I don't deserve your crying over me," Xavière said. "When I see what you are and what I am! If you only knew what I am! And it's because of me you're crying!"

Françoise returned her kisses. Despite everything, this violent tenderness and humility were intended for her. On Xavière's cheeks, mixed with the salty taste of tears, she found the memory of those hours in a sleepy little café, when she had vowed to make her happy. She had not succeeded, but if only Xavière were to consent, she could, whatever the cost, protect her from the entire world.

"I don't want any harm to come to you," she said passionately.

Xavière shook her head. "You don't know me. You're wrong to love me."

"I do love you. I can't help it," Françoise said with a smile.

"You're wrong," repeated Xavière sobbing.

"You find life so difficult. Let me help you."

She wanted to say to Xavière, "*I know everything, and it doesn't make any difference,*" but she could not speak without betraying Gerbert. She remained encumbered by her useless mercy, which could find no sin to forgive. If only Xavière would confess, she would be able to console her and reassure her. She would protect her even from Pierre himself.

"Tell me what is upsetting you so much," she said in an urgent tone. "Tell me."

In Xavière's face something wavered. Françoise was waiting, hanging on her lips, for just one sentence; Xavière was on the verge of bringing about what Françoise had so long desired: a complete union, which would encompass their joys, their worries, their torments.

"I can't tell you," Xavière said in despair. She recovered her breath and added more calmly, "There's nothing to tell."

Françoise's frustration flared into anger and she felt like taking that obstinate little head in her hands and tearing it open. Was there no way of breaking into Xavière's secret retreat? For all her sweetness, for all her vehemence, she remained obstinately entrenched behind her aggressive reserve. An avalanche was about to crash down on her, and Françoise was condemned to remain in the background, a helpless witness.

"I could help you, I'm sure," she said in a voice trembling with anger.

"No one can help me," Xavière said. She threw back her head, smoothing her hair with her finger tips. "I've already told you that I'm worthless, I warned you," she added impatiently. Her wild, faraway look had returned.

Françoise could not insist any further without being indiscreet. She had felt ready to give herself to Xavière unreservedly, and had this gift been accepted, she would have been freed both from herself and from this woeful alien presence which constantly barred her path. But Xavière had repelled her. She was willing to weep in Françoise's presence, yet not permit her to share her tears. Françoise was alone, faced by a solitary and stubborn conscience. Her finger brushed lightly over Xavière's hand still disfigured by a large sore.

"Is the burn quite healed?" she asked.

"Yes, it's all right now," Xavière said. She looked at her hand. "I would never have thought that it could hurt so."

"No wonder! You gave it a queer treatment." In her dejection, Françoise could find nothing more to say. Then she added, "I'll have to go. Are you sure you don't want to come with me?"

"No," said Xavière.

"What shall I tell Labrousse?"

Xavière shrugged her shoulders, as if the question were none of her concern. "Whatever you like."

Françoise got up. "I'll try to manage something," she said. "Good-bye."

"Good-bye," said Xavière.

Françoise did not let go of her hand.

"It makes me very sad to leave you here so tired out and despondent."

Xavière smiled feebly. "Hangovers are always like that," she said. She remained seated on the edge of the couch as if made of stone, and Françoise left the room.

Despite everything, she would try to protect Xavière. It would be a solitary and joyless struggle, since Xavière herself was refusing to stand by her, and she anticipated—not without some apprehension—the hostility she would arouse in Pierre by protecting Xavière from him. But she felt tied to Xavière by a bond she had not chosen. With slow steps, she went down the street. She wanted to press her forehead against a lamppost and cry.

Pierre was sitting where she had left him. He was alone.

"Well, did you see her?" he asked.

"I saw her. She sobbed without stopping. She was terribly upset."

"Is she coming?"

"No, she's frightened to death of seeing you." Françoise looked at Pierre and chose her words carefully. "I think she's afraid that you might guess everything, and it's the thought of losing you that's making her so desperate."

Pierre sneered. "She's not going to lose me before we've had a nice little explanation. I've got a thing or two to say to that girl. She, of course, told you nothing?"

"No, nothing. She only said that Gerbert had come to her room, that she had thrown him out, and that she got drunk after he left." Françoise shrugged her shoulders dejectedly. "For a moment, I thought she was going to talk."

"I'll try to make her come out with the truth, all right," Pierre said.

"Be careful," said Françoise. "As much of a sorcerer she may believe you to be, she'll suspect that you know if you insist too much."

Pierre's face froze. "I'll manage," he said. "If need be, I'll tell her that I looked through the keyhole."

Françoise lit a cigarette to maintain her composure; her hand was unsteady. She pictured with horror Xavière's humiliation if she believed that Pierre had seen her. He would know only too well how to find ruthless words.

"Don't drive her too hard," she said. "She'll do something desperate."

"Oh no, she's much too cowardly."

"I don't say she'll commit suicide, but she'll go back to Rouen and her life will be ruined."

"She can do what she pleases," Pierre said angrily. "But I swear to you that I'll pay her back in her own coin."

Françoise looked down. Xavière was guilty toward Pierre; she had wounded him to the depths of his soul, and Françoise keenly felt this wound. Had she been able to concentrate solely on that, everything would have been much simpler. But she also thought of Xavière's contorted face.

"You can't imagine," Pierre went on more calmly, "how tender she was with me. Nothing obliged her to put on that amorous act." His voice hardened again. "She's nothing but undiluted coquetry, caprice, and treachery. Her sleeping with Gerbert was due solely to another wave of hatred, to make our reconciliation worthless, to fool me, and to get her revenge. She didn't fail, but it's going to cost her something!"

"Listen," said Françoise, "I can't prevent you from doing as you please, but promise me one thing. Don't tell her that I know, for in that case she couldn't bear to live near me any more."

Pierre looked at her. "All right," he said. "I'll pretend not to have told a soul."

Françoise put her hand on his arm, and she was overcome with anguish. She loved him, and to save Xavière, with whom no love was possible, she was confronting him as a stranger; tomorrow, perhaps, he would become her enemy. He would suffer, avenge himself, and hate, without her, and even in spite of her. She was casting him back into his solitude, she who had never desired anything but to be united with him! She withdrew her hand. He was staring into space. She had already lost him.

6

FRANÇOISE cast a final glance at the stage where Éloy and Tedesco were in the middle of a passionate scene.

"I'm going," she whispered.

"Will you speak to Xavière?" Pierre asked.

"Yes, I promised I would."

She looked unhappily at Pierre. Xavière was stubbornly avoiding him, and he insisted on having an explanation with her; his nervous tension had increased steadily during these past three days. When he wasn't finding fault with Xavière, he would fall into moods of black silence; the hours passed so slowly in his company that Françoise had welcomed this afternoon's rehearsal with relief, as providing a kind of alibi.

"How shall I know if she accepts?" Pierre asked.

"At eight o'clock you'll see whether or not she's there."

"But it will be unbearable to wait without knowing."

Françoise shrugged her shoulders helplessly. She was almost certain that this step would be futile, but if she said that to Pierre, he would doubt her sincerity.

"Where are you meeting her?" he asked.

"At the Deux Magots."

"Well, I'll telephone in an hour's time. You can tell me what she's decided."

Françoise stifled a protest; she had too many occasions these days for contradicting Pierre, and even in their most trifling discussions there was something bitter and mistrustful that wrung her heart.

"Very well," she said.

She rose and went to the center aisle. The dress rehearsal would take place the day after next. She hardly gave it a thought—or Pierre, for that matter; eight months before, in this same theater, they were finishing the rehearsal of *Julius Caesar*; in the semidarkness, she could make out the same heads, dark ones and fair ones; Pierre was sitting in the same seat, his eyes fixed on the stage, lit by the same spotlights. But everything was now so different! Not very long ago, a smile from Canzetti, a gesture from Paula, the fold of a dress, would have been the inspiration or the source of a fascinating story; the inflection of a voice, the color of a shrub, would stand out with feverish sharpness against a vast horizon of hope, and in the shadow of the red seats a whole future lay hidden. Françoise left the theater. Passion had drained the past of its wealth, and, in this arid present, there was nothing left to love, nothing more to think about. The streets had stolen the memories and the promises which, in the past, had protracted their existence into infinity. Beneath the overcast sky broken by brief glimpses of blue, the streets were now nothing but distances to be covered.

Françoise sat down at the terrace of the café. A moist aroma of walnut cordial hung in the air, this was the season when, in other years, they began to think about sun-baked roads and shadowy mountain tops. Françoise thought of Gerbert's sunburnt face, his tall body bent under a rucksack. Where did he stand with Xavière? Françoise knew that she had gone to meet him the very evening after that tragic night, and that they had made it up between them. While affecting total indifference toward Gerbert, Xavière admitted that she saw him often. How did he feel about her?

"Greetings," said Xavière gaily. She sat down and laid a small bunch of lilies-of-the-valley in front of Françoise. "This is for you," she said.

"How sweet of you!"

"You must pin them to your dress."

Françoise obeyed with a smile. She knew that this trustful affection she saw in Xavière's laughing eyes was only a mirage. Xavière hardly gave her a thought and unhesitatingly lied to her. Behind those ingratiating smiles, there was perhaps remorse and certainly delicious satisfaction at the idea of Françoise's being fooled so easily; and Xavière was no doubt also seeking an ally against Pierre. But however false her heart, Françoise was susceptible to the seduction of her perfidious face. In her plaid blouse, with its bright colors, Xavière looked very springlike, and a limpid gaiety enlivened her features now devoid of mystery.

"What lovely weather," she said. "I'm very proud of myself. I walked for two hours, just like a man, and I'm not the least bit tired."

"It's really awful," Françoise rejoined. "I've hardly profited by the sun at all. I spent the afternoon at the theater."

Her heart contracted. She wished she could abandon herself to the delightful illusions that Xavière was so graciously creating for her. They would tell each other stories, they would walk down to the Seine, sauntering slowly and exchanging fond words. But she was denied even this fragile sweetness. She must at once lead up to a thorny discussion that would change Xavière's smiles and make her seethe with incalculable hidden venom.

"Are things going well?" Xavière asked eagerly.

"Pretty well. I think it'll keep up for three or four weeks—enough to finish the season."

Françoise took a cigarette and rolled it between her fingers. "Why don't you come to the rehearsals? Labrousse asked me again if you'd made up your mind not to see him any more."

Xavière's face clouded. She gave a slight shrug. "Why should he think that? It's stupid."

"You've been avoiding him for the last three days," said Françoise.

"I'm not avoiding him. I cut one appointment because I was mistaken about the time."

"And another because you were tired. He wanted me to ask you if you could meet him at the theater at eight o'clock."

Xavière turned away. "At eight o'clock, I shan't be free," she said.

Apprehensively, Françoise studied the sullen and averted profile and the thick fair hair.

"Are you sure?" she said.

Gerbert was not going out with Xavière that night. Pierre had made sure of that before setting the time.

"Yes, I'm free," Xavière said. "But I'd like to go to bed early."

"You can see Labrousse at eight o'clock and still go to bed early."

Xavière looked up, and rage flashed in her eyes. "You know very well I couldn't! I'll have to argue until four o'clock in the morning!"

Françoise shrugged her shoulders. "Why don't you admit frankly that you don't want to see him?" she said. "But at least give him your reasons."

"He'll scold me again. I'm sure he hates me now."

It was true that Pierre wanted this meeting only so that he could dramatically break off with Xavière; but perhaps if she agreed to see him, she might quell his anger. By evading him again, she would completely exasperate him.

"I don't really think he feels very pleased with your behavior," Françoise said. "But in any case, you're not gaining anything by burrowing into the ground. He'll be able to find you. You'd far better go and speak to him this very evening." She looked impatiently at Xavière. "Make an effort."

Xavière's face fell. "I'm afraid of him," she said.

"Look," said Françoise, putting her hand on Xavière's arm, "you don't want Labrousse to stop seeing you altogether, do you?"

"Doesn't he ever want to see me again?" Xavière asked.

"He certainly won't want to if you go on being obstinate."

Xavière lowered her head despondently. How many times had Françoise looked dispiritedly down on that golden head into which it was so hard to force any sense!

"He'll telephone me at any moment now," she continued. "Let me make the appointment."

Xavière did not answer.

"If you like, I'll go and see him before you do. I'll try to explain."

"No," cried Xavière vehemently, "I'm fed up with all your fussing. I don't want to go."

"You prefer a complete break?" Françoise said. "Think it over, because that's what you're headed for."

"Then it can't be helped," said Xavière dramatically.

Françoise snapped the stalk of one of the lilies-of-the-valley with her fingers. She could get nothing from Xavière. Her cowardice only aggravated her treachery; but she was deluding herself if she thought she could escape Pierre; he was capable of coming to her door in the middle of the night.

"You're saying it can't be helped because you never think seriously of the future."

"Oh!" said Xavière. "At any rate, we wouldn't get anywhere, Labrousse and I."

With a sudden movement she pushed back her bangs, baring her smooth forehead. Her face seemed to swell in a burst of violent hatred and suffering. Her mouth was partly open in a smile, like a gash in an overripe fruit; and this open wound in the venomous pulp was exposed to the sunlight. It was impossible to get anywhere. It was the whole of Pierre that Xavière coveted, and since she could not have him without sharing him, she renounced him with an infuriated bitterness which enveloped Françoise together with him.

Françoise was silent. Xavière was adding difficulties to the battle Françoise had vowed to fight for her. Unmasked and powerless, Xavière's jealousy had lost none of its violence. She would have only granted Françoise a little real affection, if she had succeeded in taking Pierre from her, body and soul.

"Telephone for Mademoiselle Miquel!"

Françoise rose to her feet. "Say yes," she urged.

Xavière threw her an imploring look and shook her head.

Françoise went downstairs to the booth and picked up the receiver. "Hello," she said.

"Well," asked Pierre, "is she coming or not?"

"It's still the same old story. She's too afraid. I couldn't manage to convince her. She seemed frightfully upset when I told her that you'd wind up breaking with her."

"All right," said Pierre. "She won't miss anything."

"I did everything I could."

"I know. You're very kind," Pierre said. His voice was sharp. He hung up.

Françoise came back and sat down beside Xavière who greeted her with a flippant smile.

"You know," she said, "no hat ever looked so well on you as that little sailor hat."

Françoise smiled without conviction. "You must always choose my hats for me," she said.

"Greta was watching you and looking thoroughly annoyed. It makes her ill to see another woman dressed as well as she is."

"Her own suit is charming," said Françoise.

She almost felt a sense of relief. The die had been cast. By stubbornly refusing her support and her advice, Xavière had relieved her of the heavy responsibility of ensuring her happinesss. Her eyes glanced over the terrace, where light-colored coats, summery jackets, and straw hats were making their first timid appearance. And suddenly, as in other years, she felt a violent desire for sun, for forests, and for strenuous mountain walks.

Xavière glanced at her furtively with an insinuating smile.

"Did you notice that little girl in her first communion dress? Flat-chested girls of that age are so depressing."

She seemed determined to turn Françoise's thoughts away from painful preoccupations which were not entirely concerned with her. She gave the impression of a carefree and good-natured serenity. Françoise glanced obediently at the family that was passing by, dressed in their Sunday best.

"Did you ever make your first communion?" she asked.

"I should say so," Xavière said, and she laughed a little too vivaciously. "I insisted on having roses embroidered on my dress from top to bottom. My poor father finally gave in."

She stopped short. Françoise followed the direction of her glance and saw Pierre closing the door of a taxi. The blood rushed to her face. Had Pierre forgotten his promise? If he spoke to Xavière in her presence, he could not pretend to have kept the secret of his shameful discovery.

"Greetings!" said Pierre. He pulled up a chair and nonchalantly sat down. "I hear that you're not free again tonight," he said to Xavière.

Xavière kept staring at him as though bewitched.

"I thought we ought to break this evil spell that's been hanging over our appointments." Pierre wore a very friendly smile. "Why have you been avoiding me for three days?"

Françoise rose. She did not want Pierre to humiliate Xavière in her presence and, beneath his politeness, she recognized a merciless determination.

"I think it would be better if you talked things over without me," she said.

Xavière clutched her arm. "No, stay," she said in a lifeless voice.

"Let me go," Françoise said gently. "What Pierre has to say to you does not concern me."

"Stay, or I'll go," said Xavière, through clenched teeth.

"Well, stay then," Pierre said impatiently. "You can see she's about to have a fit of hysterics."

He turned to Xavière. There was now no trace of politeness in his face. "I would like to know just why I terrify you so much?"

Françoise sat down again and Xavière let go of her arm. She swallowed and then seemed to regain her full composure.

"You don't terrify me," she said.

"It certainly looks as if I do." He stared into Xavière's eyes. "What's more, I can tell you why."

"Then don't ask me," Xavière retorted.

"I wanted to hear it from your own lips." He paused a little theatrically and, without taking his eyes off her, continued: "You're afraid that I might read into your heart and tell you out loud what I see there."

Xavière's face contracted. "I know that your head is full of filthy thoughts. They're repulsive to me and I don't want to know what they are," she said with disgust.

"It's not my fault if the thoughts you inspire are filthy," Pierre said.

"In any case, keep them to yourself."

"I'm sorry, but I came for the express purpose of telling them to you."

He was taking his time. Now that he held Xavière in his power he seemed calm and almost amused at the notion of directing the scene as he pleased. His voice, his smile, his pauses, everything was so carefully calculated that Françoise had a gleam of hope. His object was to put Xavière at his mercy, but if he succeeded effortlessly, perhaps he would spare her the too harsh truths, and perhaps he would let himself be persuaded not to break with her.

"You seem not to wish to see me any more," he continued. "You will doubtless be pleased to hear that I, too, have no desire to continue our relationship. However, I am not in the habit of dropping people without giving them my reasons."

Abruptly, Xavière's brittle composure crumbled. Her eyes were popping, her half-open mouth now expressed nothing but incredulous surprise. It was impossible that Pierre should not be affected by the sincerity of her anguish.

"But what have I done to you?" she asked.

"You have done nothing to me," said Pierre. "What's more, you owe me nothing. I never assumed any rights over you." His manner became crisp and detached. "No, it's simply that I have finally discovered what you are, and the whole affair has ceased to interest me."

Xavière looked all around her, as if seeking help. Her hands were clenched. Apparently she was desperately anxious to fight, to defend herself, but everything she thought to say must have seemed full of pitfalls. Françoise wanted to prompt her. She was sure now that Pierre was not bent on burning his bridges behind him, was hoping that his very severity would wrench from Xavière words that would make him relent.

"Is it because of the appointments I failed to keep?" Xavière finally asked, almost in tears.

"It's because of the reasons that caused you to fail to keep them," said Pierre. He waited a moment, but Xavière made no comment. "You were ashamed of yourself," he continued.

"I was not ashamed, but I was certain that you were furious with me. You're always furious when I see Gerbert, and since I got drunk with him . . ." She shrugged her shoulders disdainfully.

"But I would thoroughly approve of your being friendly with Gerbert, or even loving him," he said. "You couldn't make a better choice." This time he did not try to curb the threat of his voice. "But you're incapable of any clean feeling. You've never seen anything in him but an instrument to soothe your pride, to appease your anger." He checked a protest from Xavière. "You yourself admitted that when you put on that little romantic act with him, it was out of jealousy. And it wasn't for nothing you brought him home the other night."

"I was sure you'd think that," Xavière said. "I was sure of it." She clenched her teeth and two tears of rage ran down her cheeks.

"Because you know that it's true," said Pierre, "I'll tell you myself what happened. When I forced you to acknowledge your infernal jealousy, you trembled with rage. There is no limit to the vileness you'll allow yourself, provided that it remains concealed. You were disconcerted because all your flirting failed to conceal the baseness of your little soul from me. What you demand of people is blind admiration. And truth offends you."

Françoise looked at him apprehensively, she wanted to stop him. He seemed carried away by his own words, and he was losing control. The stern expression on his face was no longer play acting.

"That's too unfair," Xavière said. "I stopped hating you immediately."

"You certainly did not," said Pierre. "I'd have to be very innocent to believe that. You've never stopped. Only, to indulge in hate body and soul, you'd have to be less lazy than you are. Hate takes it out of you, so you took a breather. You felt quite safe, knowing that as soon as it suited you, you'd recover all your bitterness. So you set it aside for a few hours, because you felt like being kissed."

Xavière's face became contorted.

"I had no desire to be kissed by you," she said sharply.

"That's possible," Pierre said. There was a set smile on his face. "But you felt like being kissed and I happened to be there." He surveyed her up and down before adding in a more vulgar tone: "Now understand, I'm not complaining; it's very pleasant to kiss you, and I got as much out of it as you did."

Xavière gasped. She looked at Pierre with such sheer horror that she appeared almost soothed, but silent tears belied the hysterical calm of her features.

"What you're saying is outrageous," she whispered.

"What *is* outrageous," Pierre said vehemently, "is your behavior. Your entire relationship with me has been nothing but jealousy, pride, and treachery. You could not rest until you had me at your feet. You still have no feeling of friendship for me except in your childish exclusiveness. Out of spite, you tried to start a quarrel between Gerbert and me. In addition, you were jealous of Françoise to the point of jeopardizing your own friendship with her. When I begged you to try and build a human relationship with us, unselfishly, without capriciousness, you could only hate me. And finally, with your heart full of this hatred, you threw yourself into my arms because you were in need of sensations."

"You're lying," Xavière said. "You've invented everything."

"Why did you kiss me?" Pierre continued. "It wasn't to please me. That presupposes generosity, and no one has ever seen the slightest trace of it in you. And besides, I didn't ask that much of you."

"Oh! How I regret those kisses," Xavière cried, gritting her teeth.

"I should imagine you do," Pierre said with a vicious smile. "Only you couldn't resist them, because you never deny yourself anything. You wanted to hate me that night, but my love was precious to you." He shrugged his shoulders. "To think that I could have taken those ravings for the sign of a complex nature!"

"I was trying to be polite," Xavière said.

She had intended to be insulting, but she no longer had control of her voice, now shaking with sobs. Françoise wanted to stop this slaughter; it had gone far enough. Xavière would never again be able to hold her head up in front of Pierre. But Pierre was now being stubborn; he would see it to the finish.

"That's carrying politeness too far," he said. "The truth is that you were unscrupulously leading me on. Our relationship continued to please you, so you intended to keep it intact, and you reserved the right to hate me under the surface. I know you well. You aren't even capable of following a line of your own. You yourself are betrayed by your own cunning."

Xavière gave a short laugh. "Your beautiful theories are very easy to construct. I wasn't at all as passionate as you say I was that night, and, what's more, I didn't hate you." She looked at Pierre with a little more self-assurance; she no doubt had begun to think that his assertions were not based on fact. "You're the one who's inventing this story of my hating you, because you always choose the worst possible interpretation."

"I'm not talking at random," Pierre said in a somewhat menacing tone. "I know what I'm saying. You hated me without ever daring to formulate your thoughts in my presence. As soon as you'd left me, infuriated by your own weakness, you immediately looked for some means of getting back at me; but, coward that you are, you were only capable of doing so in an underhand way."

"What do you mean?" Xavière asked.

"It was very well contrived. I would have gone on adoring you unsuspectingly, and you would have accepted my devotion and at the same time made a fool of me; that's just the sort of triumph you revel in. The trouble is that you're too ineffective to carry out a brilliant lie. You think you're clever, but your tricks are obvious, you can be read like a book. You don't even know how to take elementary precautions to conceal your treachery."

Abject terror spread over Xavière's face.

"I don't understand," she said.

"You don't understand?"

There was a silence. Françoise threw him an imploring look, but, at this moment, his feelings for her were by no means friendly. If he did remember his promise, he would not hesitate deliberately to cast it aside.

"Do you think you're going to make me believe that you brought Gerbert home with you by chance?" Pierre said. "You deliberately made him get drunk, because you had decided, cold-bloodedly, to sleep with him in order to take revenge on me."

"Ah! So that's it!" said Xavière. "That's just the sort of calumny you're capable of imagining!"

"Don't bother to deny it. I'm not imagining anything. I know."

Xavière stared at him with the sly and triumphant look of a lunatic. "Do you dare to suggest that Gerbert invented such filth?"

Again, Françoise silently made a desperate appeal to Pierre. He must not crush Xavière so cruelly! He must not betray Gerbert's naïve confidences! Pierre hesitated.

"Of course, Gerbert told me nothing," he said finally.

"So?" said Xavière. "You see . . ."

"But I have eyes and ears," Pierre said, "and I use them whenever I have occasion. It's easy to look through a keyhole."

"You . . ." Xavière put her hand to her throat. She felt as if she were about to choke. "You didn't do that!" she said.

"No! I'd be ashamed to do such a thing I suppose," he said with a sneer. "With someone like you, any behavior is permissible."

Xavière looked at Pierre, then at Françoise, in a frenzy of impotent rage. She was gasping. Françoise searched in vain for a word or a gesture. She was afraid that Xavière might begin screaming or smashing glasses in front of everyone.

"I saw you," Pierre said.

"Oh! That's enough," said Françoise.

Xavière rose. She put her hands to her temples. Tears were pouring down her cheeks. Suddenly she rushed blindly away.

"I'll go with her," Françoise said.

"If you like."

He leaned back affectedly, and pulled his pipe out of his pocket. Françoise ran across the street. Xavière was walking very rapidly, her body erect, her head thrown back. Françoise caught up with her, and they walked along the rue de Rennes in silence. Xavière suddenly turned to Françoise.

"Leave me alone!" she said in a strangled voice.

"No," said Françoise. "I won't leave you."

"I want to go home."

"I'll go with you." She stopped a taxi. "Get in," she said firmly.

Xavière obeyed. She leaned her head back against the cushion and stared at the roof. Her upper lip curled back in something like a sneer.

"That man—I'll get even with him," she said.

Françoise touched her arm. "Xavière," she whispered.

Xavière shuddered, and jerked away. "Don't touch me," she said vehemently.

She stared at Françoise with a wild look, as if a new thought had struck her.

"You knew about it," she said. "You knew everything."

Françoise said nothing. The taxi stopped. She paid the driver and hurried up the stairs after Xavière. Xavière had left the door to her room ajar. She was leaning with her back against the washbasin, her eyes swollen, her hair dishevelled, her cheeks blotched with red. She seemed possessed by an enraged demon whose convulsions were torturing her frail body.

"So, all these days you've let me talk, and you knew that I was lying!"

"It wasn't my fault if Pierre told me everything, and I wanted to disregard it," Françoise said.

"How you must have laughed at me!"

"Xavière! The idea never entered my mind," said Françoise, taking a step toward her.

"Don't come near me," Xavière screamed. "I never want to see you again. I want to go away, for good."

"Do calm down. All this is stupid. Nothing's happened between us, these misunderstandings with Labrousse have nothing to do with me."

Xavière had seized a towel and was fiercely tugging at the fringe. "I'm accepting your money," she said, "I'm letting you support me! Do you realize that?"

"You're raving," Françoise said. "I'll come back when you're yourself again."

Xavière dropped the towel. "Yes," she cried. "Go away."

She went over and threw herself down on the couch, sobbing.

Françoise hesitated. Then she walked softly out of the room, closed the door, and went upstairs. She was not very worried. Xavière was still more apathetic than proud, and she would not have the absurd courage to ruin her life by going back to Rouen. But she would never forgive Françoise for the indisputable superiority she had gained over her; that would be one more grievance, in addition to so many others. Françoise took off her hat and looked at herself in the glass. At this moment she did not even have the strength to feel worn out; she no longer regretted an impossible friendship; she found no bitterness in herself toward Pierre. All she could do now was to try patiently, sadly, to save the poor remnants of a way of living in which she had taken so much pride. She would persuade Xavière to remain in Paris and she would try to win back Pierre's confidence. She smiled weakly at her reflection. After all these years of passionate demands, of triumphant serenity and avidity for happiness, was she, like so many others, about to become a woman resigned to her fate?

7

FRANÇOISE crushed the stub of her cigarette in her saucer.

"Will you have enough energy to work in this heat?" she asked.

"It doesn't bother me," said Pierre. "What are you going to do this afternoon?"

They were sitting on the balcony outside Pierre's dressing room where they had just had lunch. Below them, the little square in front of the theater looked as though it were being crushed under the heavy blue sky.

"I'm going to the Ursulines, with Xavière. There's a Charlie Chaplin festival."

Pierre's lip jutted out. "You never leave her side nowadays," he said.

"She's her own worst enemy," said Françoise.

Xavière had not returned to Rouen and, although Françoise gave her a great deal of attention, and she saw Gerbert frequently, for the past month she had dragged herself about, like a soulless body, through the blazing summer heat.

"I'll come for you at six o'clock," Françoise said. "Will that be all right?"

"Fine," said Pierre. With a forced smile, he added, "Have a good time."

Françoise returned his smile, but as soon as she left the room, all her shallow cheerfulness vanished; for when she was alone, nowadays, her heart was always sad. To be sure, Pierre did not blame her, even in thought, for having kept Xavière to herself, yet nothing henceforth could prevent him from feeling that she was shadowed by a hated presence; it was Xavière whom Pierre continually saw hovering in the background.

336

The clock at the Vavin crossing pointed to two thirty. Françoise quickened her pace. She saw Xavière sitting on the terrace of the Dôme, wearing her dazzling white blouse, her hair shining; from a distance she looked radiant, but her face was lifeless and her eyes dull.

"I'm late," said Françoise.

"I've just arrived," Xavière rejoined.

"How are you?"

"It's hot," said Xavière with a sigh.

Françoise sat down beside her; with amazement she noticed, in addition to the usual odor of tobacco and tea peculiar to Xavière, a strange new medicinal smell.

"Did you sleep well last night?" she asked.

"We didn't go dancing—I was too worn out," Xaxière said, pouting, "and Gerbert had a headache."

She readily talked about Gerbert, but Françoise would not let herself be taken in by that. It was not from any feelings of friendship that Xavière occasionally confided in her; it was to counteract any impression of solidarity with Gerbert. She was no doubt greatly attracted to him physically, and she took an easy revenge by criticizing him harshly.

"I went for a long walk with Labrousse along the Seine. It was a gorgeous night." She stopped. Xavière was not even pretending to be interested; she was staring into space with a worried expression.

"We'll have to leave now if we're really going to a movie."

"Yes," said Xavière.

She rose and took Françoise's arm. It was a mechanical gesture, and she did not appear to feel any presence at her side. Françoise fell into step with her. At this moment, in the oppressive heat of his dressing room, Pierre was busy working. Françoise herself could have stayed on peacefully in her room and done some writing. In the old days, she would never have missed the chance of avidly seizing upon these long unoccupied hours; the theater was closed, she had time, plenty of leisure, yet she could do nothing but waste it. It was not even a case of thinking that she was already on vacation; she had totally lost her old sense of discipline.

"Do you still want to go to the movies?" she asked.

"I don't know," Xavière said. "I think I'd much rather go for a walk."

Françoise recoiled, frightened at the prospect of the desert of tepid boredom that was suddenly stretching out before her; she would have to get through this great waste of time with no relief! Xavière was in no mood to talk; but because of her presence it was impossible for Françoise to enjoy a real silence in which she could be alone with her own thoughts.

"Well then, let's walk," she said.

The streets smelled of tar, and it stuck to one's feet. These first hot days, with thunder in the air, always took one by surprise. Françoise felt like a tasteless wad of cotton.

"Are you still tired today?" she asked in an affectionate tone.

"I'm always tired," Xavière said. "I'm growing old." She cast a sleepy glance at Françoise. "I'm sorry, I'm not good company."

"Don't be silly! You know I'm always happy to be with you."

Xavière did not return her smile; she had already withdrawn into herself. Françoise would never be able to make her understand that she did not expect Xavière to display for her either the grace of her body or the attractions of her mind, but that she wanted only to be allowed to participate in her life. All through the past month, she had tried persistently to get closer to her, but Xavière stubbornly remained a stranger whose negative presence cast a threatening shadow over Françoise. There were moments when Françoise was absorbed in herself, others when she gave herself entirely to Xavière; but she would often recall with anguish that second personality, revealed to her one evening in a maniacal smile. The only way to destroy its abominable reality would have been to sink her own personality with Xavière's in a single friendship. During these long weeks, Françoise had felt the need of this more and more keenly; but Xavière would never relinquish any part of herself.

A strange sobbing sound came to them through the hot sticky air. At a deserted street corner, a man was seated on a folding chair, holding a saw between his knees; and to the wailing of this instrument his voice droned out the mournful words:

> *"This evening in the rain,*
> *My sad heart full of pa-ain*
> *I listen, but in va-ain*
> *For the echo of your step."*

Françoise pressed Xavière's arm. The sickly music in this scorching solitude seemed to her the very reflection of her heart. The arm remained on hers, unresisting but insensible. Even through this beautiful tangible body it was not possible to reach Xavière. Françoise longed to sit down on the curbstone and never move again.

"Supposing we go to some place," she said, "it's too hot for walking." She no longer had the strength to wander about aimlessly under this relentless sky.

"Oh, yes! I'd like to sit down," said Xavière. "But where shall we go?"

"Would you like to go back to the Moorish café where we enjoyed ourselves so much? It's quite close."

"Okay, let's go."

They turned the corner; it was already a relief to be walking toward some definite goal.

"That was the first time we spent a really long happy day together," Françoise said. "Do you remember?"

"It seems such ages ago," said Xavière. "How young I was then!"

"It's not even a year ago."

Françoise, too, had aged since that not so distant winter. In those days she used to live without asking herself any questions, the world all around her was wide and rich, and it belonged to her; she loved Pierre, and Pierre loved her; from time to time, she even used to indulge in the luxury of thinking her happiness monotonous. She pushed open the door and recognized the same wool rugs, the copper trays, the multicolored lanterns: the place had not changed. The dancer and the musicians, squatting on their heels in a recess at the back, were talking among themselves.

"How dismal it looks now," said Xavière.

"That's because it's still early. It will probably fill up later on. Would you rather go somewhere else?"

"Oh, no. Let's stay here."

They sat down on the rough cushions in the same place as before and ordered mint tea. Again, as she sat beside Xavière, Françoise caught a whiff of the unusual smell that had intrigued her at the Dôme.

"What did you wash your hair with today?" she asked.

Xavière ran her fingers through her silky bangs. "I didn't wash my hair," she said with surprise.

"It smells like a pharmacy."

Xavière gave a knowing smile, which she immediately repressed. "I didn't touch it," she said.

Her face darkened, and she lit a cigarette in a slightly theatrical manner. Françoise gently laid her hand on her arm.

"You're depressed," she said. "You mustn't let yourself go like this!"

"What can I do? I'm not happy."

"But you're not making the slightest effort. Why didn't you take the books which I put out for you?"

"I can't read when I'm in a gloomy mood," said Xavière.

"Why don't you work with Gerbert? The finest cure for you would be to work out a good act."

Xavière shrugged her shoulders. "It's impossible to work with Gerbert! He just acts his own part, he's incapable of suggesting anything. I might as well work with a brick wall." She added in a cutting tone, "And besides, I don't like what he's doing, it's so trivial."

"You're unfair," said Françoise. "He may be a bit lacking in temperament, but he's sensitive and intelligent."

"That's not enough." Her face contracted. "I loathe mediocrity," she said furiously.

"He's young, and he hasn't had much experience. But I think he'll do something yet."

Xavière shook her head. "If at least he were downright bad, there'd be hope, but he's nothing. He can just about manage to reproduce correctly what Labrousse has taught him."

Xavière had a great many grievances against Gerbert, but one of the most bitter was certainly his admiration for Labrousse. Gerbert always said that Xavière was never more peevish with him than when he had just seen Pierre or even Françoise.

"That's a pity," said Françoise. "It would change your outlook on life if you were to do a little work." She looked wearily at Xavière. She did not really know what anyone could do for her. Suddenly she could name the strange new smell she had noticed.

"Why, you smell of ether," she said with astonishment.

Xavière turned away without answering.

"What were you doing with ether?"

"Nothing," said Xavière.

"What else?"

"I inhaled a little. It's pleasant."

"Is this the first time you've taken it, or have you done it before?"

"Oh! I've taken it occasionally," Xavière answered with studied rudeness.

Françoise got the impression that Xavière was not sorry at having her secret discovered.

"Be careful," Françoise said, "you're going to dull your faculties or completely wreck yourself."

"I have nothing to lose," said Xavière.

"Why do you do it?"

"I can't get drunk any more. It makes me ill."

"Well, ether will make you much more ill."

"Just think," Xavière said, "all you have to do is put a piece of cotton to your nose, and then you're practically unconscious for hours."

Françoise took her hand.

"Are you really so unhappy?" she said. "What's the matter? Tell me."

She knew why Xavière was suffering, but she could not make her admit it point-blank.

"Except for your work, are you getting along well with Gerbert?" she continued. She watched for the reply with an interest prompted not by concern for Xavière alone.

"Oh, Gerbert! Yes," Xavière shrugged her shoulders. "He doesn't matter much, you know."

"Still, you're very fond of him."

"I'm always fond of what belongs to me," said Xavière. She added with a fierce look, "It's restful to have someone entirely to yourself." Her voice softened. "But after all, it's just something pleasant in my existence, nothing more."

Françoise turned cold. She felt personally insulted by Xavière's disdainful tone.

"Then it's not because of him that you're depressed?"

"No," said Xavière.

She had such a defenseless and pitiful look that Françoise's wave of hostility subsided.

"And it's not my fault either?" she asked. "Are you satisfied with our relationship?"

"Oh, yes." She had a brief sweet smile that was gone immediately. Suddenly her face livened. "I'm bored," she said passionately. "I'm disgustingly bored."

Françoise did not answer. It was Pierre's absence which was causing such a void in Xavière's existence; he would have to be returned to her, but Françoise was very much afraid that this was impossible. She had finished her glass of tea. The café had been filling up; for some time the musicians had been playing their reedy flutes. The dancing-girl advanced to the middle of the room and a quiver ran through her body.

"What big hips she has," Xavière said with disgust. "She's put on weight."

"She's always been stout."

"Possibly," said Xavière. "I was so easily dazzled in the old days." She let her eyes wander slowly over the wall. "I've changed a great deal."

"The truth is," said Françoise, "that's plain nonsense. You now like only what's really beautiful, and that's nothing to feel sorry about."

"No, no," said Xavière. "Nothing whatever moves me now!" She blinked a few times, and then she drawled, "I'm worn out."

"You like to think so," Françoise rejoined with annoyance, "but they're just words. You're not worn out. You're simply moody."

Xavière gave her an unhappy look.

"You give in to yourself," Françoise went on more gently. "You mustn't go on in this way. Listen, first of all you're going to promise me not to take any more ether."

"But you don't understand," said Xavière. "These endless days are horrible."

"It's serious, you know. You're going to wreck yourself completely, if you don't stop."

"That won't hurt anyone."

"In any case it would hurt me," Françoise said tenderly.

"Oh!" said Xavière skeptically.

"What does that mean?" Françoise insisted.

"You can't still have a very high opinion of me."

Françoise was unpleasantly surprised. Xavière did not often seem touched by her tenderness, but at least she had never seemed to question it.

"What!" said Françoise. "You know I've always had the highest regard for you."

"In the old days, yes. You thought well of me then."

"Why should I think less of you now?"

"It's just an idea I have," Xavière said listlessly.

"And yet, we've never seen more of each other. I've never sought greater intimacy with you," Françoise was disconcerted.

"Because you feel sorry for me." She gave an unhappy laugh. "That's what I've come to! I'm somebody people feel sorry for!"

"But you're wrong," Françoise said. "Whatever put that notion into your head?"

Xavière stared stubbornly at the end of her cigarette.

"Tell me," said Françoise. "People don't say things like that without good reason."

Xavière hesitated, and again Françoise had the unpleasant feeling that, by her reticences and silences, it was Xavière who had been responsible for the course of their conversation.

"It's only natural that you should be disgusted with me," Xavière said. "You have good reason to despise me."

"It's always the same old story. But we've thrashed all that out already! I thoroughly understood that you did not want to talk to me about your relations with Gerbert, and you agreed that, in my place, you would have kept silent just as I did."

"Yes," Xavière said.

Françoise knew that with her no explanation was ever final. Xavière no doubt still woke up at night in a fury, remembering with what ease Françoise had deceived her for three days.

"You and Labrousse always think so exactly alike," continued Xavière. "And he holds such a wretchedly low opinion of me."

"That's entirely his own business," Françoise said. These words cost her an effort—they were a kind of repudiation of Pierre—and yet they only expressed the truth. She had once and for all refused to take his part.

"You think me far too easily influenced," she said. "Actually, he hardly ever talks to me about you."

"He must hate me so," said Xavière sadly.

There was a silence.

"And what about you? Do you hate him?"

Her heart sank. The whole of this conversation had had no other aim than to prompt this question. She began to catch a glimpse of the goal toward which she was moving.

"I?" said Xavière. She cast a pleading glance at Françoise. "I don't hate him," she said.

"He's convinced you do," said Françoise. Still under the influence of Xavière's desire, she continued. "Would you agree to see him again?"

Xavière shrugged her shoulders. "He has no great wish to see me."

"I don't know. If he knew that you miss him, it would make a difference."

"Of course I miss him," said Xavière slowly. She added in a clumsy attempt to seem offhand, "You know, Labrousse is not somebody you can stop seeing without regrets."

For a moment Françoise looked thoughtfully at that broad, pale face which exhaled an aroma of pharmaceutical fumes. The pride that Xavière maintained in her distress was so pitiful that Françoise said, almost in spite of herself, "I could perhaps try to talk to him."

"Oh! That wouldn't do any good," Xavière said.

"I wouldn't be too sure."

It was done. The decision was made of its own accord, and Françoise knew that she could no longer keep from acting upon it. Pierre would listen to her with a scowl. He would answer her discourteously, and his cutting words would reveal to himself the extent of his hostility toward her. She bent her head, sick at heart.

"What will you tell him?" Xavière asked in an insinuating tone.

"That we talked about him," said Françoise. "That you showed no hatred, quite the contrary. That if only he would forget his grievances, you for your part would be happy to regain his friendship."

She stared vaguely at one of the gaudy hangings. Pierre pretended not to be interested in Xavière, but whenever her name was mentioned, Françoise could sense that he was all attention. He had passed her once in the rue Delambre, and in his eyes Françoise had noticed a wild desire to run after her. Perhaps he would agree to see her again so that he might torment her at closer range; perhaps, if that happened, he would again be won over by her. But neither the appeasement of his bitterness nor the resurrection of his troubled love would bring him close to Françoise again. The only possible hope of reconciliation would have been to send Xavière back to Rouen, and start life afresh without her.

Xavière shook her head. "It's not worth the effort," she said with woeful resignation.

"I can always try."

Xavière shrugged her shoulders as if declining all responsibility. "Oh! Do as you like," she said.

Françoise felt angry. It was Xavière who had brought her to this, with her smell of ether and her woebegone looks, and now she withdrew, as she always did, into a haughty indifference, thus sparing herself the shame of a failure or the obligation of gratitude.

"I'm going to try."

She no longer had any hope of achieving that friendship with Xavière which alone could have saved her, but at least she would do everything to deserve it.

"I'll speak to Pierre at once," she said.

When Françoise entered Pierre's dressing room, he was still seated at his desk, his pipe in his mouth, his face unshaven and looking happy.

"How industrious you are," she said. "You haven't budged all this time?"

"You'll see. I think I've done a good piece of work." He swivelled round on his chair. "And what about you? Did you have a good time? Was it a good program?"

"Oh! We didn't go to the movies. That was to be expected. We dawdled along the streets and it was outrageously hot." Françoise sat down on a cushion on the doorstep of the balcony. The air had cooled off a little, and the tops of the plane trees were gently quivering. "I'm glad to be going on this walking tour with Gerbert. I'm fed up with Paris."

"And I'll hang on here, shaking in my shoes," Pierre said. "You'll be a good girl and send me a telegram every evening: 'I'm still alive.' "

Françoise smiled at him. Pierre was satisfied with his day's work; his face was gay and affectionate. There were moments like this when it might have seemed that nothing had changed since the summer before.

"There's nothing to be afraid of," said Françoise. "It's much too early to do any real mountain climbing. We'll go to the Cevennes or to Cantal."

"You're not going to spend the evening making plans!" Pierre said apprehensively.

"Don't worry, we'll spare you." She smiled. "You and I will also have some plans of our own to make soon."

"That's true. We'll be leaving in less than a month."

"We really must make up our minds where we're going."

"I think we'll stay in France, whatever happens," Pierre said. "We must expect a period of tension toward the middle of August, and even if nothing happens, it wouldn't be very pleasant to find ourselves at the other end of the world."

"We've talked about Cordes and the Midi," said Françoise, adding with a laugh, "Of course there would be some landscapes, but we'd see small towns galore. You do love small towns, don't you?"

She looked hopefully at Pierre. When just the two of them were alone, far from Paris, perhaps he would never lose this friendly and relaxed look. How she longed to take him away with her for weeks without end.

"I'd love to wander with you all around Albi, Cordes, and Toulouse,"

Pierre said. "You'll see, I'll even go for a long walk every once in a while."

"And I'll stay in cafés as much as you like without complaining," rejoined Françoise with a laugh.

"What will you do with Xavière?"

"Her family is quite willing to have her for the holidays. She'll go to Rouen. It won't do her any harm to get her health back."

Françoise looked away. If Pierre became reconciled with Xavière, what would become of all these happy plans? His passion for her might return and he might revive the trio. They would have to take her with them on their trip. A lump rose in her throat. Never had she desired anything so keenly as this long period alone with him.

"Is she ill?" Pierre asked coldly.

"She's in a rather bad state."

She must not speak; she must let Pierre's hatred die slowly of indifference. He was already on the way to being cured. One more month and, under the sun of the Midi, this feverish year would be nothing more than a memory. She need add nothing, but simply change the subject. Pierre had already opened his mouth. He was going to talk about something else, but Françoise forestalled him.

"Do you know her latest? She's begun to take ether."

"Ingenious," said Pierre. "What's the idea?"

"She's terribly unhappy." In spite of herself, Françoise was irresistibly drawn toward the danger she dreaded. She never had been able to play for safety.

"Poor child!" Pierre said with heavy irony. "What can be the matter with her?"

Françoise began to roll her handkerchief between her moist hands. "You left a void in her life," she said in a bantering tone, which sounded false.

Pierre's face hardened. "Don't make me cry," he said. "And what would you like me to do about it?"

Françoise squeezed her handkerchief tighter. How raw the wound still was! No sooner had she opened her mouth than Pierre was on the defensive. She was now no longer talking to a friend. She gathered up her courage.

"You don't consider the possibility of seeing her again?"

Pierre gave her an icy look. "Ah!" he said. "She's asked you to sound me out?"

Françoise's voice hardened in turn. "I was the one to suggest it," she said, "when I understood how terribly she missed you."

"I see," Pierre said. "She broke your heart with her ether-addict act."

Françoise blushed. She was aware of the complacency behind Xavière's tragic air; she knew that she had allowed herself to be out-maneuvered, but before Pierre's cutting tone she was determined to make a stand.

"That's too easy," Françoise said. "If you don't give a damn what happens to Xavière—all right; but the fact remains that she's down in the depths, and it's because of you!"

"Because of me!" said Pierre. "Well, you certainly have nerve." He got up and planted himself in front of Françoise with a sneer. "Do you expect me to lead her by the hand to Gerbert's bed every night? Isn't that what she needs for the peace of her mangy little soul?"

Françoise kept a tight hold on herself. There was nothing to be gained by getting angry.

"You know very well that when you left her, you said such cruel things that even someone with less pride than she would never have recovered. You're the only person who can wipe those things away."

"I beg your pardon," Pierre said. "I'm not preventing you from forgiving wrongs, but I don't happen to have the vocation of a sister of charity."

Françoise felt cut to the quick by this scornful tone.

"After all, it wasn't such a crime to sleep with Gerbert. She was free, she hadn't promised you anything. It was painful to you, but you knew that you could accept it, if you wanted to." She threw herself into an armchair. "I find your bitterness toward her to be sexual and shabby. You're acting like a man who's furious with a woman he's never had. That, I think, is unworthy of you."

She waited nervously. The blow had struck home. Hatred flashed into Pierre's eyes.

"I hate her for having been a flirt and a traitor. Why did she let me kiss her? Why all those fond smiles? Why did she pretend to love me?"

"But she was sincere. She's fond of you," said Françoise. Harsh memories suddenly welled up in her heart. "And besides, it was you who demanded her love," she said. "You know she was bowled over the first time you mentioned the word."

"Are you insinuating that she didn't love me?" said Pierre. Never before had he looked at her with such decided hostility.

"I didn't say that. I do say that there is something forced in that love, in the sense in which one forces the flowering of a plant. You were always demanding more and more in the way of intimacy and intensity."

"You've certainly devised a strange reconstruction of the case," said Pierre with a malevolent smile. "It was she who finally proved to be so demanding that she had to be stopped, because she asked nothing less of me than to give you up."

Françoise suddenly broke down. It was true. It was out of loyalty to her that Pierre had lost Xavière. Had he come to regret it? Did he now hold a grievance against her for what he had done on so spontaneous an impulse?

"If she could have had me all to herself, she would have been ready to love me passionately," Pierre continued. "She slept with Gerbert to punish me for not having thrown you overboard. You must admit that all this is rather shabby. I'm amazed that you should take her part!"

"I'm not taking her part," said Françoise weakly. She felt her lips beginning to tremble: with one word, Pierre had awakened a stinging resentment in her. Why was she suddenly siding with Xavière? "She's so unhappy," she murmured.

She pressed her fingers against her eyelids. She did not want to cry, but she suddenly found herself plunged into bottomless despair. Nothing seemed clear to her any longer, and she was weary of trying to find a way out. All she knew was that she loved Pierre and him alone.

"Do you think I'm so very happy?" said Pierre.

Françoise was suddenly torn by such intolerable anguish that a cry rose to her lips. She clenched her teeth, but the tears sprang to her eyes. All Pierre's suffering surged back into her heart. Nothing else on earth counted but his love, and during the whole of this month, when he had needed her, she had let him struggle alone. It was too late to ask his pardon. She had withdrawn too far for his still wanting her help.

"Stop crying," said Pierre a little impatiently. He was staring at her coldly. She knew that after defying him she had no right again to inflict her tears on him, but she was now nothing but a chaotic mass of pain and remorse.

"Please calm yourself," Pierre said.

She could not calm herself, because it was by her own fault that she had lost him. Her life would not be long enough to mourn her loss.

She buried her face in her hands. Pierre was pacing up and down the room, but she was now not even concerned about him. She had lost all control over her body, and her thoughts kept on eluding her. She was an old, broken-down machine.

Suddenly, she felt Pierre's hand on her shoulder. She looked up.

"You hate me now," she said.

"Of course not, I don't hate you," he said with a forced smile.

She caught hold of his hand. "You know," she said in a broken voice, "I'm not so friendly with Xavière, but I feel such great responsibility. Ten months ago she was young, ardent, full of hope, and now she's a poor wreck."

"In Rouen, too, she was to be pitied. She was always talking about committing suicide."

"That was different," Françoise said. She sobbed again. It was torture. The moment she called to mind Xavière's pale face, she could no longer make up her mind to sacrifice her, even for Pierre's happiness. For an instant she remained motionless, her hand riveted to the hand resting inertly on her shoulder. Pierre was looking at her. Finally he said, "What do you want me to do?" His face was set.

Françoise let go of his hand and wiped her eyes. "I no longer want anything," she said.

"What did you want a little while ago?" he said, controlling his impatience with difficulty.

She rose and walked toward the balcony. She was afraid to ask anything of him. Whatever he might grant reluctantly would only separate them the more. She came back to him.

"I thought, that if you were to see her, perhaps you'd regain your friendship for her. You mean so much to her."

Pierre cut her short.

"Very good, I'll see her," he said.

He went out and leaned on the balcony railing, and Françoise followed him. He was looking down at the little park where a few pigeons were hopping about. Françoise stared at the curved nape of his neck and again she was overcome by remorse. At the very time when he was really trying so hard to find peace, she had thrown him back into the raging torrent. She recalled the happy smile with which he had greeted her. Now she had before her a man full of bitterness, preparing himself with rebellious obedience to submit to a demand he did not approve. She had often asked things of Pierre, but in the days when they were united, never could anything that one granted the other be felt as a sacrifice. This time she had put Pierre in the position of giving in to her with resentment. She pressed her hands against her temples. Her head ached and her eyes burned.

"What is she doing this evening?" Pierre suddenly asked.

Françoise started.

"Nothing that I know of."

"Well! Ring her up. While I'm about it, I'd prefer to settle this matter as soon as possible."

He began nervously biting his nails. Françoise walked to the telephone.

"And what about Gerbert?"

"You'll see him without me."

Françoise dialled the hotel number. She became aware of that hard iron band cutting across her stomach. All the old miseries would come back again. Pierre would never have a serene friendship with Xavière. Even now, his haste augured future storms.

"Hello! Would you call Mademoiselle Pagès, please?"

"Just a moment. Hold on."

She heard the click of heels on the stairs, and confused sounds. Someone shouted Xavière's name up the stairwell. Françoise's heart began racing. Pierre's nervousness was catching.

"Hello," said Xavière's unsteady voice. Pierre picked up his earphone.

"It's Françoise. Are you free this evening?"

"Yes, why?"

"Labrousse would like to know if he may come to see you."

There was no reply.

"Hello!" repeated Françoise.

"To see me now?"

"Would that be inconvenient?"

"No, it wouldn't."

Françoise sat for a moment not knowing what else to say.

"Well, that's settled," she said. "He'll come at once."

She hung up.

"You're putting me in a false position," Pierre said with a look of annoyance. "She was not at all anxious for me to come and see her."

"I think rather that she was overcome."

They were silent for a long while.

"I'm going," said Pierre.

"Come back and see me, and tell me how it went off."

"All right, I'll see you tonight," he said. "I think I'll be there early."

Françoise walked to the window and watched him cross the street. Then she came back and sat down in the armchair. She leaned back, exhausted. She felt that she had just made the final choice, and that it was calamity she had chosen. She jumped. There was a knock at the door.

"Come in," she said.

Gerbert entered. With amazement Françoise saw the fresh face framed in hair as black and smooth as that of a Chinese woman. Before the light of his smile, the shadows gathering in her heart were dissipated. She suddenly remembered that in this world there were other things to love that were neither Xavière nor Pierre. There were snow-capped peaks, sun-lit pines, roadside inns, people and stories. There were these laughing eyes that rested on her with friendliness.

Françoise opened her eyes and closed them again immediately. Dawn was already breaking. She was sure she had not slept, she had heard every hour strike, and yet she felt as if she had gone to bed only a few moments before. On her return at midnight, after having worked out with Gerbert a detailed plan of their walking tour, Pierre had not yet arrived. She had read for a little while, and then she had turned out the light and tried to sleep. It was only natural that the heart-to-heart talk with Xavière should have been protracted. She did not want to ask herself any questions about its outcome, she did not want to feel a vise grip her throat again, she did not want to wait. She had been unable to sleep, but she had fallen into a torpor filled with endlessly reverberating noises and images; it was like the feverish hours of her illness; the hours had seemed short to her. Perhaps she would manage to get through the remainder of the night without anguish.

She shuddered. She heard footsteps on the stairway; the treads creaked too loudly for it to be Pierre, and the steps were already continuing up the next flight. She turned to the wall. If she began to listen to all the night noises, to count the minutes, it would be hellish, and she wanted to remain calm. She was lucky to be lying comfortably in her bed, snug and warm. At this moment, there were tramps sleeping on the hard pavements of les Halles, and harassed travelers standing in the corridors of trains, and soldiers on guard at barracks gates.

She huddled more snugly under the sheets. During the course of those long hours, Pierre and Xavière had no doubt more than once experienced mutual hate, only, in turn, to become reconciled; but how was she to know whether, in this rising dawn, love or bitterness had finally triumphed? She could see a red table in a large, unpeopled room, and over empty glasses two faces, now in ecstasy, now enraged. She tried to concentrate on each expression in turn, but neither of them harbored any threat; as things were now, there was nothing left to be threatened. If only she could have decided upon one or the other. It was this empty uncertainty that finally threw her into panic.

The room was growing perceptibly lighter. At almost any moment Pierre would be there, but she could not project herself into that very moment which his presence would fill. She could not even feel she was being swept toward it, for its place in time had not yet been set. Françoise had experienced periods of waiting resembling mad gallops, but on this occasion she was marking time. Periods of waiting, moments of flight, the whole year had been spent in this way. And now, what was she to hope for? The happy equilibrium of their trio? Its final breakup? Neither one nor the other would ever be possible, for there was no way of uniting with Xavière, and no way of freeing oneself from her. Even exile would not obliterate this existence that refused to be joined. Françoise remembered how, through her indifference, she had at first spurned that existence; her indifference had been conquered, and now their friendship had failed. There was no salvation. She could flee, but she would have to return, and there would be other periods of waiting and other moments of flight, endlessly.

Françoise reached for her alarm clock—seven o'clock—it was daylight outside. Her whole body was already alert, and immobility changed into anxiety. She threw back the sheets and began her toilet. She noticed with surprise that, awake in broad daylight and with her head clear, she wanted to cry. She washed, applied her make-up and slowly put on her clothes. She did not feel nervous, but she did not know what to do with herself. When she had finished dressing, she again lay down on her bed. At this moment, there was no place for her anywhere in the world. Nothing drew her out of doors, and nothing held her here but an absence. She was no more than an empty longing, bereft of body and soul to the extent that the very walls of her room astonished her. Françoise stiffened. This time, she recognized the step. She composed her features and sprang toward the door. Pierre smiled at her.

"Are you up already?" he said. "I hope you weren't worrying."

"No," she said. "I knew that you had so many things to say to one another." She looked him up and down; it was clear that he was not returning from a void. In his high color, his lively look, his gestures, was reflected the fullness of the hours he had just lived. "Well?" she said.

Pierre assumed an embarrassed but happy look familiar to Françoise.

"Well, everything's starting afresh," he said. He touched her arm. "I'll tell you all the details, but Xavière's waiting for us for breakfast. I said that we'd come back at once."

Françoise put on her jacket. She had just lost her last chance of regaining a pure and peaceful intimacy with Pierre, but she had hardly dared believe in this chance even for a moment; she was now too weary for regret or for hope. She went downstairs. The idea of being once more in the trio roused in her hardly more than a resigned anxiety.

"Tell me in a few words what happened," she said.

"Well, I went to her hotel," Pierre began. "I felt at once that she was very much moved, and that moved me. We stayed there for a while talking stupidly about the weather, and then we went to the Pôle Nord and had a gigantic discussion." Pierre said nothing for a moment, and then he continued in that conceited, nervous tone always so painful to Françoise. "I have the feeling that it won't take much to make her drop Gerbert."

"Did you ask her to break it off?"

"I'm not a beggar," said Pierre.

Gerbert had never worried about the quarrel between Pierre and Xavière. To him their whole friendship had never seemed to rest on anything more than a whim, and he was going to be cruelly hurt when he learned the truth. Actually, Pierre would have done better to have been frank with him from the very beginning; Gerbert would willingly have given up trying to win Xavière. At the moment, he was not deeply attached to her, but it certainly would be unpleasant for him to lose her.

"When you have gone off on your trip," said Pierre, "I'll take Xavière in hand, and if by the end of the week the question isn't settled, I will ask her to make a choice."

"Yes," Françoise said. She hesitated. "You'll have to explain the whole story to Gerbert, otherwise you'll appear a perfect heel."

"I'll explain it to him," Pierre said quickly. "I'll tell him that I didn't want to use authority over him, but that I thought I had the right to compete as an equal." He looked at Françoise without much assurance. "Don't you agree with me?"

"There's something to be said for it," Françoise admitted.

In one sense, it was true that there was no reason for Pierre to sacrifice himself for Gerbert, but neither did Gerbert deserve the cruel disillusionment awaiting him. Françoise kicked along a little round pebble. Doubtless, she would have to relinquish the idea of finding the perfect solution to any problem. For some time it had seemed that, whatever decision she made, it turned out to be the wrong one. And besides, no one worried very much any more about knowing what was right or wrong. She herself took no interest in the question.

They walked into the Dôme. Xavière was seated at a table, her head bowed. Françoise touched her shoulder lightly.

"Good morning," she said with a smile.

Xavière shuddered and raised a surprised face to Françoise. Then she, too, smiled, but with restraint.

"I couldn't believe that it was you so soon," she said.

Françoise sat down beside her. Something in this greeting was painfully familiar to her.

"How fresh you look!" Pierre said.

Xavière had no doubt taken advantage of Pierre's absence to make her face up again with great care. Her complexion was smooth and clear, her eyes brilliant, her hair glossy.

"Yet I'm tired," she said. Her eyes rested first on Françoise and then on Pierre, and she put her hand to her mouth and stifled a little yawn. "In fact, I think I'd like to go home to sleep," she said with an embarrassed, affectionate look that was not directed at Françoise.

"Now?" said Pierre. "But you have the whole day ahead."

Xavière's face clouded over. "I feel very uncomfortable," she said. She shook her arms, making the wide sleeves of her blouse puff out. "It's unpleasant to wear the same clothes for hours on end."

"At least have a cup of coffee with us," said Pierre disappointedly.

"If you wish."

Pierre ordered three coffees. Françoise took a croissant and began nibbling at it. Her courage failed her and she made no attempt to speak a friendly word. She had already lived this scene more than twenty times. She was sickened in advance by the cheerful tone, the bright smiles she felt rising to her lips, and by her mounting irritation and resentment. Xavière was sleepily staring at her fingers. For some time no one spoke.

"What did you and Gerbert do?" Pierre asked, turning to Françoise.

"We had dinner at the Grille and we planned our walking tour. I think we'll leave the day after tomorrow."

"Are you really going to climb mountains?" Xavière asked in a dismal voice.

"Yes," said Françoise curtly. "You think that ridiculous?"

Xavière raised her eyebrows. "Well . . . if you enjoy it," she said.

Again silence fell. Pierre looked at them uneasily. "You both look sleepy," he said reproachfully.

"This isn't a very good time to look at people," said Xavière.

"Still, I can remember a very pleasant time we spent here at this same hour."

"Oh! It wasn't so pleasant," Xavière rejoined.

Françoise well remembered that morning and the soapy smell of the tiles. It was then, for the first time, that Xavière's jealousy had been openly declared. In spite of all efforts to conciliate her, Françoise found her today exactly as before. At this moment, it was not only Françoise's presence, it was her very existence that Xavière wanted to eradicate.

Xavière pushed away her glass. "I'm going home," she said firmly.

"Above all, get a good rest," Françoise said ironically.

Xavière shook her head without answering. She smiled vaguely at Pierre and hurried out of the café.

"It's a fiasco," said Françoise.

"Yes." He seemed vexed. "Still she looked very pleased when I asked her to wait for us."

"Doubtless she didn't want to leave you." She gave a little laugh. "But what a shock seeing me there in front of her."

"It's going to be hellish again," said Pierre. He stared dismally at the door through which Xavière had left. "I wonder if it's worth starting again. We'll never get out of it."

"How did she speak to you about me?"

Pierre hesitated. "She seemed to be friendly toward you," he said.

"And what else?" She looked with annoyance at Pierre's puzzled face. It was now he who felt bound to spare her. "Hasn't she got any little grievances?"

"She seems to be slightly angry with you," Pierre admitted. "I think she's come to the conclusion that you have no deep love for her."

Françoise stiffened. "What exactly did she say?"

"She told me that I was the only person who didn't try to throw cold water on her moods," he said. Beneath the indifference in his voice could be detected the faint satisfaction at feeling himself irreplaceable to such a degree. "And then at one point she said to me with delight, 'You and I are not moral beings; we are capable of doing vile things.' And when I protested, she added, 'It's because of Françoise that you're so bent on appearing moral, but deep down you're as treacherous as I am and your soul is just as black.'"

Françoise blushed, for she, too, was beginning to consider this legendary morality of hers, which people laughed at indulgently, as a ridiculous fault. Perhaps it would not take her long to shake it off. She looked at Pierre. His hesitant expression did not reflect a very clear conscience. It was obvious that Xavière's words had flattered him in some way.

"I suppose she considers my effort at reconciliation a proof of luke-warmness."

"I don't know," said Pierre.

"What else did she say? Let me have the full story," she added impatiently.

"Well, she made a bitter allusion to what she calls loves of devotion."

"What's that?"

"She explained her character to me, and she told me with hypocritical humility, 'I know that I'm often very disagreeable with people, but what can I do? I'm not made for loves of devotion.'"

Françoise was dumbfounded. This was a double-edged betrayal. Xavière blamed Pierre for remaining responsive to so wretched a love, while she herself fiercely rejected it. Françoise had been far from suspecting the degree of her hostility, made up as it was of jealousy and chagrin.

"Is that all?"

"I think so," he said.

That was not all, but Françoise was suddenly tired of asking questions. She knew enough to have on her lips the treacherous taste of this night, in which Xavière's triumphant rancor had wrenched from Pierre a thousand petty betrayals.

"Anyway, you know, I don't give a damn how she feels," she said.

It was true. Suddenly, at this culminating point of misery, nothing mattered. Because of Xavière, she had almost lost Pierre, and in return Xavière gave her only contempt and jealousy. No sooner was Xavière reconciled with Pierre, than she tried to establish between them an underhand complicity which he only half-heartedly disclaimed. Their dual rejection of Françoise left her in such a forlorn state of desolation that there was no room left for either anger or tears. Françoise hoped for nothing further from Pierre, and his indifference no longer affected her. As for Xavière, she joyfully felt stirring within her something black and bitter which she did not yet understand and which was almost a deliverance; something powerful and free was bursting at last. It was hate.

8

"I THINK we're almost there at last," Gerbert said.

"Yes, it's that little house we can see up there."

They had covered a considerable distance during the day, and for the past two hours it had been hard uphill going. Night was falling and it was cold. Françoise looked tenderly at Gerbert walking ahead of her up the steep path. They were both walking at the same pace; they both felt the same happy fatigue, and were together silently looking forward to the red wine, the supper, and the log fire they hoped to find up there. Whenever they arrived in these isolated villages, it was always something of an adventure. They could never be certain whether they were going to sit down at a noisy table in a peasant kitchen, or have their dinner alone in an empty inn, or end up in some small middle-class hotel already filled with tourists. Whichever it was, they would set their packs down in a corner and, with their muscles relaxed and their hearts content, spend quiet hours side by side, talking over the day they had just spent and making plans for the next. It was toward this warm intimacy that Françoise was hurrying, rather than to the succulent omelette and the raw, homemade spirits. A gust of wind whipped her face. They were reaching a pass that dominated a fan of valleys lost in the hazy dusk.

"We won't be able to pitch the tent," she said. "The ground is soaked."

"We'll probably find a barn," said Gerbert.

A barn. Françoise felt a sickening emptiness. Three nights earlier they had slept in a barn. They had gone to sleep a few feet from one another, but in his sleep Gerbert's body had rolled over and he had thrown his arms about her. With a vague regret she had thought, *He takes me for someone else,* and she had held her breath so as not to wake him. Then she dreamed; and in her dream she was in this same barn, and Gerbert, with his eyes wide open, had clasped her in his arms. She had yielded, her heart filled with sweetness and security, till anguish had undermined this state of tender well-being. "It's not true," she found herself saying. Gerbert had clasped her tighter, and exclaimed, "It is true. It would be too ridiculous if it weren't." Not many moments later a ray of light had fallen on her eyelids. She had awakened to find herself still lying in the hay, pressed close to Gerbert, and there had been no truth in it at all.

"You've been tossing your hair into my face all night," she had said with a laugh.

"Not at all, you've kept on poking your elbows into me," Gerbert replied indignantly.

She could not think of a similar awakening without a feeling of distress. Beneath the tent, huddled in a narrow space, she felt protected by the hardness of the earth, the discomfort, and the wooden tent-pole separating her from Gerbert; but she knew that, later that night, she would not have the courage to make up her bed far from his. It was useless trying to deny the vague yearning that had been hanging over her all these days. During the two hours of silent climbing, it had been persistently in her thoughts until it became at length a choking desire. Tonight, while Gerbert was innocently sleeping, she would dream again, regret and suffer, all to no purpose.

"Do you think this place is a café?" he asked.

On the wall of the house was a red sign bearing the word *B Y R R H* in huge letters, and stuck above the door was a handful of dried branches.

"It looks like one," Françoise said.

They walked up the three steps and into a large warm room that smelled of cooking and dried twigs. There were two women seated on a bench, peeling potatoes, and three peasants at a table with glasses of red wine before them.

"Good evening," said Gerbert.

Every eye turned toward him. He went up to the two women.

"Could you give us something to eat?" he asked.

The women looked at him suspiciously.

"And so you've come a long way?" the elder woman said.

"We've come up from Burzet," Françoise replied.

"That's a fairish distance," said the other woman.

"That's just why we're hungry."

"But you aren't from Burzet." The old woman spoke accusingly.

"No, we're from Paris," Gerbert admitted.

There was a silence. The women looked questioningly at each other.

"The trouble is that I haven't much to give you," the old woman said at last.

"Haven't you any eggs? Or a bit of cold meat paté? Anything at all . . ." Françoise asked.

The old woman shrugged her shoulders.

"Eggs, yes. We have plenty of eggs." She rose and wiped her hands on her blue apron. "Would you care to step inside?" she added somewhat reluctantly.

They followed her into a low-ceilinged room where a wood fire was burning. It looked like a middle-class provincial dining room. There was a round table, a wooden chest loaded with knickknacks, and on the armchairs, orange satin cushions trimmed with black velvet.

"But first, would you please bring us a bottle of red wine," said Gerbert.

He helped Françoise remove her rucksack and then put down his own.

"We're in luck," Gerbert said with a look of contentment.

"Yes, it's wonderfully comfortable."

Françoise walked up to the fire. She knew only too well what was lacking in this cozy evening. If only she had been able to touch Gerbert's hand, to smile at him tenderly, then the blazing logs, the smell of the dinner, the black velvet cats and the sparrows would have rejoiced her heart. But it all remained scattered around her, without touching her. It almost seemed absurd that she should be there.

The innkeeper returned with a bottle of thick, coarse wine.

"You don't by any chance happen to have a barn where we could spend the night?" Gerbert asked her.

The woman was setting the places on the oilcloth. She looked up.

"You aren't going to sleep in a barn?" she said, looking shocked. She thought for a moment. "You're out of luck. I would have had a room for you, but my son, who's a postman, just came home."

"We'd be very happy in the barn, if it isn't putting you out," Françoise assured her. "We have blankets." She pointed to the rucksacks. "But it's too cold to pitch our tent."

"Oh, it won't put me out," said the woman. She left the room and brought back a steaming soup tureen. "At least this will warm you up a bit," she said in a friendly tone.

Gerbert filled the soup bowls and Françoise sat down opposite him.

"She's getting tame," said Gerbert when they were alone again. "Everything's turning out splendidly."

"Splendidly," echoed Françoise with conviction.

She looked furtively at Gerbert. His face beamed with a gaiety that was very like tenderness. Was he really beyond reach? Or was it just that she had never dared to put out her hand to him? Who was holding her back? It was neither Pierre nor Xavière. She no longer owed anything to Xavière. Moreover, Xavière was preparing to give up Gerbert. They were alone, at the top of a wind-swept mountain pass, separated from the rest of the world, and their relations concerned no one but themselves.

"I'm about to do something that is going to disgust you," announced Gerbert in a threatening tone.

"What?"

"I am about to pour wine into my soup." As he spoke, he suited his action to his words.

"That must be horrid," Françoise said.

Gerbert put a spoonful of the reddish liquid to his mouth. "It's delicious," he said. "Try some."

"Not for anything in the world!"

She drank a little wine. Her palms were moist. She had always made a point of disregarding her own dreams and desires, but this self-effacing wisdom now revolted her. Why didn't she make up her mind to go after what she wanted?

"The view from the top of the pass was magnificent," she said. "I think we'll have good weather tomorrow."

Gerbert scowled at her. "Are you going to insist that we get up at dawn again?"

"Stop complaining. The real mountain climber is on the peak at five in the morning."

"They're all crazy," said Gerbert. "I'm a cocoon before eight o'clock."

"I know," Françoise smiled. "But, if you go to Greece, let me tell you, you'll have to be on your way before dawn."

"Yes, but there you take a nap in the afternoon," Gerbert rejoined. He thought for a moment. "I hope that plan for a tour doesn't collapse."

"If there's another crisis," Françoise said, "I'm afraid it will."

Gerbert resolutely cut himself a huge chunk of bread.

"In any case, I'll manage to find a way out. I'm not going to stay in France next year." His face lit up. "It seems you can make a fortune on Mauritus."

"Why Mauritus?"

"Ramblin told me about it. The place is full of millionaires who'll pay anything for a little amusement."

The door opened and the innkeeper came in. She was carrying a huge potato-omelette.

"Why, this is a feast," exclaimed Françoise. She helped herself and passed the platter to Gerbert. "Here, I'll leave you the largest portion."

"Is that all for me?"

"All for you."

"That's very honest of you," he said.

She glanced at him. "Am I not always honest with you?" There was a boldness in her voice that embarrassed her.

"Yes, I can't deny the fact," Gerbert answered without turning a hair.

Françoise was kneading a tiny pellet of bread between her fingers. She would have to cling fast to the decision she'd made on the spur of the moment. She did not know how, but something would have to happen before tomorrow.

"Would you want to go for a long time?" she asked.

"One or two years," said Gerbert.

"Xavière will never forgive you," she said insincerely. She rolled the tiny gray ball on the table and said casually, "Wouldn't you hate to leave her?"

"On the contrary."

Françoise looked down. There was such a burst of light within her, she was afraid it might be visible from without.

"Why? Is she such a burden to you? I thought you were really quite fond of her."

She was happy to think that if, at the end of this trip, Xavière were to break with him, Gerbert would hardly suffer at all. But that was not the reason for this immodest joy that had just blazed within her.

"She isn't a burden to me, when I think that it's soon going to end," Gerbert said. "But off and on, I wonder if this isn't the way people are drawn into living together. I'd loathe that."

"Even if you were in love with the person?" Françoise asked.

She held out her glass to him, and he filled it to the brim. She was in agony now. He was there, facing her, alone, unattached, absolutely free. Owing to his youth and the respect he had always shown Pierre and herself, she could hardly expect him to take the initiative. If she wanted something to happen, she could only count on herself.

"I don't think I'll ever love any woman," Gerbert said.

"Why?" asked Françoise. She was so tense that her hand was trembling. She leaned forward and drank a sip without touching the glass with her hand.

"I don't know," said Gerbert. "You can't do anything with a skirt. You can't go walking, you can't get drunk, or anything. They can't take a joke and then besides, you always have to make a fuss over them, and you always feel you're in the wrong." He added with conviction, "I like it when I can be just what I am with people."

"Don't mind me," Françoise said.

Gerbert burst out laughing. "Oh you! You're like a man!" he said warmly.

"That's right, you've never regarded me as a woman."

She felt a queer smile on her lips. Gerbert glanced at her curiously. She looked away and emptied her glass. She had made a bad start; she would be ashamed to treat Gerbert with clumsy flirtatiousness, she would have done better to be frank about it: *Would it surprise you if I were to suggest that you sleep with me?* or something of that sort. But her lips refused to form the words. She pointed to the empty platter.

"Do you think she's going to give us something else?" Her voice did not have the ring she would have liked.

"I don't suppose so."

The silence had already lasted too long. Something equivocal had slipped into the atmosphere.

"Well, we can always ask for more wine," she said.

Again Gerbert looked at her a little uneasily.

"A half bottle," he said.

She smiled. He loved simple situations. Had he guessed why she needed the help of intoxication?

"Madame, would you mind?" Gerbert called.

The old woman entered and placed a dish of boiled beef and vegetables on the table.

"What would you like after that? Some cheese? Some preserves?"

"I don't think we'll be hungry any more," Gerbert said. "But please get us a little more wine."

"Why did that old lunatic start off by telling us there was nothing to eat?"

"Most of the people round here are like that," said Gerbert. "I don't think they're very anxious to make twenty francs, and they're always afraid people are going to be a nuisance."

"It must be something like that," Françoise agreed.

The woman returned with a bottle. After thinking it over, Françoise decided to drink no more than a glass or two. She did not want Gerbert to attribute her behavior to the momentary stimulus of wine.

"On the whole," she said, "what you hold against love, is that you can't feel at ease. But don't you think that you seriously impoverish your life if you reject any close relationship with people?"

"But there are close relationships other than love," Gerbert said quickly. "I put friendship far above it. I'd be very well satisfied with a life in which there were nothing but friendships."

He looked at Françoise a little persistently. Was he, too, trying to make her understand something? That he had a true friendship for her, or that she was precious to him? He rarely talked at such length about himself. Tonight, there was a kind of receptiveness about him.

"As it happens, I can never love someone for whom I have not first had a feeling of friendship," Françoise said.

She had put the sentence in the present tense, but she had used an offhand and matter-of-fact tone. She wished she could have added something, but she couldn't bring herself to pronounce the words that were on the tip of her tongue. Finally, she said, "I think just friendship alone is barren."

"I don't think so," said Gerbert.

He was bristling a little. He was thinking of Pierre. He was thinking that it was impossible to be fonder of anyone than he was of Pierre.

"Yes, basically, you're right," Françoise said.

She put down her fork and went to sit by the fire. Gerbert rose, too, and picked up a big round log lying near the fireplace and skillfully laid it on the andirons.

"Now you can smoke your pipe," she said, adding with a spontaneous burst of affection, "I love to see you smoke a pipe."

She stretched out her hands to the fire. She felt content. Tonight, there was an almost avowed affection between Gerbert and herself. And why need she ask for more? His head was slightly lowered. He was studiously drawing on his pipe, and the fire gilded his face. She broke off a piece of dry wood and threw it on the fire. Nothing could quell her desire to hold his head between her hands.

"What are we going to do tomorrow?" Gerbert asked.

"We'll go up to Gerbier des Joncs, then to Mézanc." She rose and rummaged in her rucksack. "I don't know exactly the best way to go down." She spread out a map, opened the guidebook and lay flat on the floor.

"Do you want to look?"

"No, I trust you," he said.

She absently studied the network of tiny roads edged in green and dotted with blue marks indicating the best views. What would tomorrow bring? The answer was not on the map. She did not want this trip to end in regrets that would soon turn into remorse and then into self-hatred. She was about to speak. But did she even know whether Gerbert would find pleasure in kissing her? He had probably never thought about it. She could not bear the thought of his giving in to her out of friendly compliance. The blood rushed to her face; she remembered Elisabeth—a woman who takes—and she loathed the thought. She looked up at Gerbert and felt somewhat reassured. He had too much affection and too much esteem for her to laugh at her in secret. What she had to do was give him an opportunity for a frank refusal. But how was she to go about it?

She gave a start. The younger of the two women was standing in front of her, a big lantern swinging in her hand.

"If you want to go to bed, I'll show you the way."

"Yes, thank you very much," said Françoise.

Gerbert picked up the two rucksacks, and they went out of the house. It was a pitch-black night and a gale was blowing. The round, vacillating spot of light illuminated the muddy ground ahead of them.

"I don't know if you'll be very comfortable," the woman said. "One of the windows is broken and, besides, the cows in the stable alongside make noise."

"Oh! That won't bother us," Françoise assured her.

The woman stopped and pushed open a heavy wooden door. Françoise blissfully inhaled the smell of hay. It was a huge barn, and in among the piles of hay she caught a glimpse of stacks of logs, crates, and a wheelbarrow.

"You aren't using matches, are you?" the woman asked.

"No, I've got a searchlight," said Gerbert.

"Well, good night," she said.

Gerbert closed the door and bolted it.

"Where shall we settle down?" Françoise said, peering around.

Gerbert played a thin beam of light over the floor and the walls.

"In the corner at the back, don't you think? The hay is nice and deep and we'll be far from the door."

They walked forward carefully. Françoise's mouth was dry. It was now or never. She had about ten minutes left, for Gerbert always fell sound asleep almost the moment he lay down. And she had absolutely no idea how to approach the question directly.

"Listen to that wind," said Gerbert. "We'll be much better off here than under a tent." The walls of the barn were shaken by the squalls. Next door, a cow kicked at her stall and rattled her chains.

"You'll see what a swell set-up we'll have," said Gerbert.

He put the searchlight on a board on which he also carefully laid out his pipe, his watch, and his wallet. Françoise took out her sleeping bag and a pair of flannel pajamas from her rucksack. She walked a few paces away and began to undress in the dark. She hadn't a thought in her head, only that imperative desire gripping her stomach. She had no time to invent some roundabout way, but she did not give up. If the searchlight went out before she had spoken, she would call: "Gerbert," and she would say in one breath, "Has it never occurred to you that we might sleep together?" What happened afterward would be of no importance. She now had but one desire and that was to free herself of this obsession.

"How industrious you are," she said, coming back into the light.

Gerbert had laid out the sleeping bags side by side, and had fashioned pillows by stuffing two sweaters with hay. He walked away and Françoise slipped halfway into her sleeping bag. Her heart was pounding ready to burst. For a moment she wanted to give it all up and escape into sleep.

"How comfortable the hay is," said Gerbert as he lay down alongside her. He had put the searchlight on a beam behind them. Françoise looked at him and again she felt a violent desire to feel his lips against hers.

"We've had a wonderful day," he continued. "This is great country." He was now lying on his back, smiling. He seemed in no hurry to go to sleep.

"Yes, I loved our dinner and sitting in front of the wood fire talking like two old folk," Françoise said.

"Why like old folk?"

"We were talking about love and friendship, as if we were finished, dried up and out of the game."

In her voice there was a resentful irony that did not escape Gerbert. He looked at her in embarrassment.

"Have you made some good plans for tomorrow?" he asked after a brief silence.

"Yes, it wasn't very complicated."

She let the conversation drop. She felt pleased that the atmosphere was growing oppressive. Gerbert made another effort.

"This lake you were talking about, it would be nice if we could go and bathe in it."

"We probably can," Françoise said.

She withdrew into a stubborn silence. Usually, conversation between them did not flag. Surely Gerbert would finally sense something.

"Look what I can do," he said suddenly.

Raising his hands above his head, he moved his fingers, and the searchlight cast a vague animal silhouette on the opposite wall.

"How clever that is!"

"I can also make a judge," said Gerbert.

She was now sure that he was trying to put a bold face on the situation. She felt a lump in her throat. She watched him intently forming shadows of a rabbit, a camel, a giraffe. When he had exhausted his repertoire he lowered his hands.

"Shadow plays are fun," he began glibly, "they are almost as good as marionettes. Didn't you ever see the silhouettes Begramian designed? Only we didn't have a script. Next year we'll have to try it again."

He stopped short. He could no longer pretend not to see that Françoise was not listening. She had rolled over on to her stomach, and was staring at the light which was getting weaker.

"The battery is dying," he said. "It's going out."

Françoise did not reply. Despite the cold draught coming through the broken pane, she was perspiring. She felt as if she had come to a halt above an abyss, unable to advance or withdraw. She was without thought, without desire, and suddenly the situation seemed plainly absurd. She smiled nervously.

"Why are you smiling?" asked Gerbert.

"For no reason at all." Her lips began to tremble. With all her soul she had invited this question, and now she was afraid.

"Were you thinking about something?" Gerbert asked.

"No," she said. "It was nothing."

Suddenly, tears rose to her eyes. Her nerves were at the breaking point. Now she had gone too far. It was Gerbert himself who would force her to speak, and perhaps this delightful friendship between them would be ruined forever.

"Well, I know what you were thinking," Gerbert said challengingly.

"What?" asked Françoise.

"I won't tell you," Gerbert replied with dignity.

"Tell me, and I'll tell you if you're right."

"No, you tell me first," Gerbert insisted.

For a moment they surveyed each other like two enemies, Françoise became completely numb, but the words finally crossed her lips.

"I was smiling—wondering how you would look—you who loathe complications—if I suggested your sleeping with me."

"I thought you were thinking that I wanted to kiss you and didn't dare," Gerbert said.

"It never occurred to me that you wanted to kiss me," said Françoise stiffly. There was a silence. Her ears were ringing. Now it was done. She had spoken. "Well, answer me. How would you take it?" she said.

Gerbert shrunk back into his shell. He did not take his eyes off Françoise, but his whole face was on the defensive.

"It isn't that I wouldn't like to," he said. "I'd be too frightened."

Françoise caught her breath and managed to smile lightly.

"That's a clever answer," she said. She finally steadied her voice. "You're right. It would be artificial and embarrassing."

She reached for the light. She had to switch it off quickly and take refuge in the darkness; she would have a good cry, but at least she would no longer drag this obsession about with her. The only thing she feared was that their waking in the morning might be awkward.

"Good night," she said.

Gerbert continued to stare at her obstinately with a fierce, uncertain look.

"I was convinced, before going on this trip, that you had bet Labrousse that I'd try to kiss you."

Françoise pulled back her hand.

"I'm not as conceited as all that," she said. "I know you think of me as a man."

"That's not true," said Gerbert. His outburst stopped short, and once again a mistrustful shadow passed over his face. "I'd loathe to be in your life what people like Canzetti are for Labrousse."

Françoise hesitated. "You mean, to have an affair with me that I wouldn't take seriously?"

"Yes," said Gerbert.

"But I never take anything lightly."

Gerbert looked at her hesitatingly.

"I thought you had noticed it and that it amused you," he said.

"Saw what?"

"That I wanted to kiss you the other night in the barn and yesterday when we were standing beside that brook." He shrank back even more and said somewhat angrily, "I'd made up my mind that when we got back to Paris, I'd kiss you on the platform. Only I thought you'd laugh in my face."

"I!" said Françoise. Joy had brought a red glow to her cheeks.

"Otherwise, there would have been dozens of times I'd have wanted to. I'd love to kiss you."

He lay huddled up in his sleeping bag, motionless, like a trapped animal. Françoise gauged the distance separating them, and took the plunge.

"Well, kiss me, you silly little Gerbert," she said offering him her mouth.

A few moments later, Françoise incredulously ran her hand over this smooth, young, firm body that for so long had seemed beyond reach. This time she was not dreaming. She was actually holding him, wide awake, in her arms. Gerbert's hand caressed her back, the nape of her neck; it rested on her head and stayed there.

"I love the shape of your skull," Gerbert whispered. He added in a voice unfamiliar to her, "It seems strange that I should be kissing you."

The light went out. The wind was raging and a cold blast came in through the broken pane. Françoise rested her cheek against his shoul-

der; her body was relaxed now, lying against his, and she no longer felt
any embarrassment in talking to him.

"You know," she said, "it wasn't just sensuality that made me want to
be in your arms; above all it was affection."

"Is that true?" he said joyfully.

"Of course it's true. Have you never felt how fond I am of you?"

Gerbert's fingers tightened on her shoulder.

"That makes me happy," he said. "That makes me really happy."

"But wasn't it obvious?"

"Not at all," said Gerbert. "You were always as cool as a cucumber.
It even hurt me when I saw you give Labrousse or Xavière a certain
look. I thought you'd never look at me that way."

"It was you who were always so matter-of-fact with me," Françoise
said.

Gerbert cuddled up against her. "Still, I've always been crazy about
you," he said. "But really."

"You kept it well hidden," said Françoise. Her lips touched his long
eyelashes. "The first time I wanted to hold your head in my hands was
in my office the night before Pierre returned. Do you remember? You
were sleeping on my shoulder. You weren't paying any attention to me,
but all the same, I was happy to know you were there."

"Oh! I wasn't really asleep," Gerbert said. "And I liked to feel you
against me, too, but I thought you were giving me your shoulder the
way you might have given me a pillow."

"You were wrong," said Françoise. She ran her hands through his soft
black hair. "And you know that dream I told you about the other day,
in the barn, when you said to me, 'No, it's not a dream. It would be too
ridiculous if it weren't true . . .' I was lying to you. It wasn't because
we were wandering about in New York that I was afraid of waking up.
It was because I was in your arms, just as I am now."

"Really?" said Gerbert. He lowered his voice. "The next morning I
was quite afraid you'd suspected me of not really having been asleep.
I was only making believe so that I could hold you close to me. That
was dishonest, but I did so want to do it."

"Well! I certainly never suspected it," Françoise laughed. "We
might have played hide-and-seek for a long time. It was a good thing I
vulgarly threw myself at you."

"You?" Gerbert protested. "You didn't throw yourself at me. You
didn't want to say anything."

"Do you maintain that it's thanks to you that we finally got around to it?"

"I helped just as much as you. I left the light on, and I kept the conversation going to prevent you from going to sleep."

"How bold of you!" said Françoise. "If you knew how you looked at me during dinner, when I tried a few feeble advances."

"I thought you were beginning to get drunk."

Françoise pressed her cheek against his.

"I'm so glad I wasn't discouraged," she said.

"So am I."

He put his warm lips to her mouth and she felt his body cleave tightly to hers.

The taxi whisked along between the lines of chestnut trees on the boulevard Arago. Above the tall houses, the blue sky was as pure as the sky up in the mountains. With a timid smile, Gerbert put his arm round Françoise's shoulder. She leaned against him.

"Are you still happy?" she asked.

"Yes, I'm happy." He looked at her trustfully. "What delights me, is that I feel you're really fond of me. So it almost doesn't matter not being able to see you for a long time. That may not sound like a very nice thing to say, but it really is."

"I understand," Françoise said. She felt a lump in her throat. She recalled their breakfast at the inn after their first night; they had looked laughingly at each other with delighted, slightly embarrassed surprise; they had started off along the road with fingers intertwined like Swiss sweethearts; on a meadow, at the foot of Gerbier des Joncs, Gerbert had picked a small dark-blue flower and given it to Françoise.

"It's foolish," she said, "and all wrong, but I don't like to think that tonight someone else will be sleeping beside you."

"I don't like it either," said Gerbert in a low voice. He added with a kind of distress, "I wish you were the only person who loved me."

"I love you very much," Françoise said.

"I've never loved any woman the way I love you, nowhere near the way I love you."

Françoise's eyes became dim. Gerbert would never take root anywhere, he would never belong to anyone. But he was unreservedly giving her all that he was able to give of himself.

"My dear, darling Gerbert," she said kissing him.

The taxi stopped. She sat facing him for a moment, her eyes blurred, unable to let go of his fingers. She felt a physical anguish, as if she were being forced to jump into deep water.

"Good-bye," she said suddenly. "I'll see you tomorrow."

"Until tomorrow."

She went through the small door of the theater.

"Is Monsieur Labrousse upstairs?"

"Yes he is. He hasn't even rung yet," said the concierge.

"Would you please bring up two cafés-au-lait, and some toast."

She crossed the courtyard. Her heart was pounding with incredulous hope. The letter had been sent three days before. Pierre might have changed his mind, but it was characteristic of him, when once he had given up something, to feel completely detached from it. She knocked.

"Come in," said a sleepy voice.

She turned on the light. Pierre opened two sleepy eyes. He was tightly wrapped in the bedclothes. He had the blissful, lazy look of someone emerging from a huge cocoon.

"You certainly look as if you've been sleeping," she said gaily.

She sat down on the edge of the bed and kissed him.

"How warm you are. You make me feel like going to bed myself."

She had slept well on the train, stretched out full length on one of the seats, but these white sheets looked so inviting.

"Oh! I'm so glad you're here!" Pierre said. He rubbed his eyes. "Wait. I'll get up."

She walked to the window and pulled back the curtains, while he put on a superb red-velvet dressing gown made from an old costume.

"How well you look," Pierre said.

"I've had a good rest." She smiled. "Did you get my letter?"

"Yes." He too smiled. "You know, I wasn't very surprised."

"It wasn't so much sleeping with Gerbert that surprised me," Françoise said. "It's the kind of fondness he has for me."

"And what about you?" Pierre asked tenderly.

"I feel the same way!" Françoise said. "I'm very fond of him. And what really delights me, is that our relationship has become so close without losing its lightheartedness."

"Yes, that's a good job," said Pierre. "He's as lucky as you are." He smiled, but there was a shade of reticence in his voice.

"You don't see anything wrong in it?" Françoise asked.

"Of course not."

There was a knock.

"Here's your breakfast," said the concierge.

She put the tray on the table. Françoise took a piece of toast, it was all crisp on the surface and soft inside; she spread it with butter and poured coffee into the cups.

"Real café-au-lait," she said, "and real toast. This is wonderful. I wish you could have seen the black treacle Gerbert used to concoct for us."

"God forbid," said Pierre. He looked preoccupied.

"What are you thinking about?" Françoise asked a little uneasily.

"Oh! Nothing," said Pierre. He hesitated. "If I look a little perplexed it's because of Xavière. All this is going to be the devil for her!"

Françoise's heart stopped. "Xavière," she said. "I wouldn't allow myself to make one more sacrifice for her."

"Oh! Don't think I'd dream of reproaching you," said Pierre quickly. "But what dismays me a little, is that I've just convinced her that she must build a stable and decent relationship with Gerbert."

"Well, obviously, it's inopportune," Françoise said with a slight laugh. She looked him up and down. "Just where do you stand with her? How did things turn out?"

"Oh! It's very simple," said Pierre. He hesitated a second. "You remember when I left you, I wanted to force her to break off. Well, as soon as we spoke about Gerbert, I was aware of a far stronger resistance than I had expected. She's tremendously fond of him, whatever she may say, and that made me hesitate. Had I insisted, I think I would have won; but I wondered if I really wanted to."

"Yes?" said Françoise. She did not yet dare believe the promise in this reasonable voice and confident face.

"The first time I saw her again, I was shaken." Pierre shrugged his shoulders. "And then, when I had her at my disposal from night till morning, repentant, full of good will, almost loving, she suddenly lost all importance for me."

"Well, really, you are perverse," Françoise said cheerfully.

"Not at all," said Pierre. "You see, if she had thrown herself into my arms without reserve, I would almost certainly have been touched; or perhaps, if she had remained on the defensive, I'd have gone on out of sheer obstinacy. But seeing her eager to win me back, while determined at the same time not to sacrifice anything for me, I felt nothing but pity and disgust."

"And then?" said Françoise.

"For a while I was tempted to go on just the same," Pierre said. "But I felt so alienated from her, that it seemed dishonest, not only toward her, but toward you, and Gerbert." He stopped for a moment. "And besides, when an affair is over, it's over. There's nothing to be done about it. The fact that she slept with Gerbert, the scene we had, what I thought about her and about myself, all that is irreparable. The first morning at the Dôme, when she had another fit of jealousy, I became sick at the thought that everything was about to begin all over again."

Unashamedly, Françoise welcomed the evil joy pouring into her heart. She had formerly paid too high a price trying to keep her soul pure.

"But do you still see her?" she asked.

"Of course. We've even agreed that there's now an irreplaceable friendship between us."

"She wasn't angry with you when you told her you weren't passionately fond of her any longer?"

"Oh! I was clever about it," said Pierre. "I pretended that I was reluctant to withdraw, but at the same time, I convinced her that since she was disinclined to give up Gerbert, she ought to give herself fully to this love." He looked at Françoise. "I don't wish her any harm, you know. As you once said, it's not up to me to play the judge. If she was at fault, I was too."

"We all were," Françoise said.

"You and I have come out of this experience unharmed. I'd like to get her out of it as well." Thoughtfully, he began biting his nails. "You've rather upset my plans."

"That's too bad," said Françoise with indifference. "After all she needn't have shown such contempt for Gerbert."

"Would that have stopped you?" asked Pierre tenderly.

"He would have been fonder of her if she'd been more sincere," Françoise said. "That would have made all the difference. . . ."

"Well, what's done is done. Only we'll have to be careful not to let her suspect anything. You do see that? There'd be nothing left for her to do but drown herself."

"She won't suspect anything," Françoise said. She had no desire to drive Xavière to despair, and she could certainly be allotted a daily ration of soothing lies. Scorned, duped, she would no longer dispute Françoise's place in the world.

Françoise gazed at herself in the mirror. In the long run, capriciousness, intransigence, arrogant selfishness, all of these artificial values had revealed their weaknesses, and it was the old disdained virtues which triumphed.

I've won, thought Françoise triumphantly.

Once again she existed alone, with no obstacle at the heart of her destiny. Confined within her illusory and empty world, Xavière was now but a futile, living pulsation.

9

ELISABETH walked through the deserted hotel and out into the garden. There they were, both of them, sitting in the shade of the artificial stone grotto. Pierre was writing, Françoise was lying in a deck chair. Neither stirred; they looked like a *tableau vivant*. Elisabeth stood still, watching them from afar; as soon as they caught sight of her, their expressions would change, but she must not let them see her until she had deciphered their secret. Pierre looked up and smilingly spoke a few words to Françoise. What had he said? She was getting no further by studying his white sports shirt and bronzed skin. Beyond their gestures and their faces, the truth about their happiness remained concealed. This week of daily intimacy had been as deceptive, from Elisabeth's point of view, as had been her furtive glimpses in Paris.

"Are your suitcases packed?" she asked.

"Yes, I've reserved two seats on the bus," said Pierre. "We still have an hour."

Elisabeth put a finger on the sheets of paper in front of him. "What's this opus? Are you starting a novel?"

"It's a letter to Xavière," Françoise said with a smile.

"Well, she certainly can't feel neglected." She failed to understand how it was that Gerbert's presence had in no way altered the harmony of the trio. "Are you bringing her back to Paris this year?"

"Certainly," said Françoise. "Unless there's some real bombing."

Elisabeth looked all about her. The garden was spread out in the form of a terrace above a vast green and rose plain. It was quite small. Around each flower bed, a whimsical hand had planted sea shells and large misshapen stones; stuffed birds were nesting in the rock structures, and in among the flowers glittered metal balls, glass reflectors, and glossy paper figures. War seemed far away. One almost had to make an effort not to forget it.

"Your train is going to be packed," she said.

"Yes, everyone's clearing out. We're the only guests left."

"Oh dear," Françoise said. "I did so love our little hotel."

Pierre laid his hand on hers. "We'll come back. Even if war does break out, even if it lasts for a long time, it must end some day."

"How will it end?" Elisabeth asked thoughtfully.

The day was drawing to a close. There they were, three French intellectuals, meditating and chatting in the uneasy peacefulness of a French village, and war hanging over them. Beneath its deceptive simplicity, this moment had the grandeur of a page of history.

"Ah! Refreshments," said Françoise.

A maid had come out, carrying a tray loaded with beer, cordials, jams and biscuits.

"Would you like jam or honey?" Françoise asked gaily.

"I don't care," said Elisabeth irritably.

They seemed purposely to be avoiding serious conversation. In the long run, this kind of gallantry became aggravating. She looked at Françoise. In her linen dress, with her shoulder-length hair, she looked very young. Elisabeth suddenly wondered if the serenity for which she was admired was not partly due to thoughtlessness.

"We're going to have a funny sort of life," she continued.

"What I'm really afraid of is that we're going to be bored to death," said Françoise.

"Oh, no, on the contrary, it will be thrilling."

She did not know exactly what she would do; the German-Soviet pact had been a heavy blow; but she was sure that her energy would not be wasted.

Pierre bit into a slice of bread spread with honey and smiled at Françoise.

"It's funny to think that tomorrow we'll be in Paris," he said.

"I wonder if many people have gone back."

"In any case, Gerbert will be there." Pierre's face lit up. "Tomorrow night we simply must go to a movie. There are a lot of new American films playing."

Paris. On the café terraces of Saint Germain des Prés, women in summer frocks were drinking iced orangeade; huge, alluring posters were displayed all the way up the Champs-Élysées to the Étoile. Soon all this

nonchalant, pleasant life would disappear. Elisabeth's heart was sad: she
had not known how to enjoy it. It was Pierre who had made her loathe
frivolity; yet, in the conduct of his own life, he was not quite so strict.
That's what had been annoying her all week; while she lived with her
eyes riveted on them as on a pair of exacting paragons, they were calmly
yielding to their whims.

"I ought to go and pay the bill," Françoise said.

"I'll go," Pierre said. He rose. "Ouch," he said. "Damn those pebbles."
He picked up his sandals.

"Why do you always go barefoot?" Elisabeth asked.

"He says that his blisters haven't healed yet," said Françoise.

"They haven't. You made me do too much walking."

"Oh, we've had such a wonderful trip," Françoise sighed.

Pierre went off. In a few days they would be separated. In his army
uniform Pierre would be only an anonymous, lonely soldier. Françoise
would see the theater close and her friends scatter. And meanwhile,
Claude would vegetate at Limoges, out of range of Suzanne. Elisabeth
stared at the blue horizon where the pinks and the greens of the plain
finally merged. In the tragic light of history people were stripped of
their disquieting mystery. Everything was calm. The whole world was in
suspense, and in this period of universal waiting, Elisabeth, without
fear, without desire, felt herself in tune with the stillness of the evening.
She felt that she had at least been granted a long respite in which nothing more was required of her.

"Everything's ready," said Pierre. "The suitcases are in the bus." He
sat down.

He, too, with his cheeks bronzed by the sun, and his white sports
shirt, looked years younger. Suddenly, something unknown, something
forgotten, stirred in Elisabeth's heart. He was going away. Soon he
would be far away, deep in an inaccessible, dangerous zone, and she
was not going to see him again for a long time to come. Why had she
been unable to profit by his presence?

"Have some biscuits," Françoise said. "They're very good."

"No thanks," said Elisabeth. "I'm not hungry."

The pang that shot through her was unlike any she had known and
it was something merciless, it was something irremediable. *What if I
never see him again*, she thought. She felt herself growing pale. "You
have to report at Nancy don't you?" she asked.

"Yes, that's not a very dangerous place."

"But you won't stay there forever. You're not going to try any heroics, I hope?"

"You can trust me," Pierre said with a laugh.

Elisabeth looked at him with anguish. He might die. Pierre, my brother. I'm not going to let him leave without telling him. . . . What can I tell him? . . . This ironical man sitting opposite her had no need of her affection.

"I'll send you lovely packages," she said.

"That's right, I'll be getting packages," said Pierre. "How really delightful."

He smiled with an affectionate look in which she could read no ulterior meaning. He had often looked that way during the past week. Why was she so mistrustful. Why had she forever lost all the joys of friendship? What had she been seeking? What was the use of all these struggles and these hatreds? Pierre was going away.

"You know," Françoise said, "we ought to be going."

"Let's go," said Pierre.

They rose. Elisabeth followed them, with a lump in her throat. *I don't want him to be killed,* she thought in despair. She was walking beside him without even daring to take his arm. Why had she made all sincere words and gestures impossible? Now the spontaneous feelings in her heart seemed out of place, and yet she would have given her life for him.

"What a mob!" Françoise exclaimed.

There was a crowd around the gaudy little bus. The conductor was standing on the roof surrounded by suitcases, trunks and boxes. A man perched on a ladder at the back of the bus was handing him a bicycle. Françoise pressed her nose against the window and peered into the bus.

"We've got reserved seats," she said with satisfaction.

"On the train, though, I'm afraid you'll have to stand in the corridor," Elisabeth said.

"We've got plenty of sleep stored up," Pierre said.

They started to walk around the little bus. Only a few minutes left. No more than a word, a gesture. Let him know . . . I don't dare. Elisabeth looked at Pierre with despair. Couldn't everything have been different? Couldn't she have lived close to them all these years, with confidence and joy, instead of always having been on the defensive against an imaginary danger?

"All aboard," shouted the driver.

It's too late, thought Elisabeth in frenzy. She would have had to annihilate her whole past, her whole personality, to be able to rush toward Pierre and fall into his arms. She was no longer mistress of the present moment. Even her face did not obey her.

"See you soon," said Françoise.

She kissed Elisabeth and went back to her seat.

"Good-bye," Pierre said.

He hastily shook his sister's hand and smiled at her. She felt tears rising to her eyes. She seized him by the shoulders and put her lips to his cheek.

"You'll be very careful," she said.

"Don't worry."

He gave her a quick kiss and climbed into the bus. For a moment more his face was framed in the open window. Then the bus started off. He waved his hand. Elisabeth waved her handkerchief, and when the bus disappeared behind the wall, she turned on her heels.

"For nothing," she murmured. "All that for nothing."

She pressed her handkerchief to her lips and ran back to the hotel.

With eyes wide open, Françoise lay staring at the ceiling. Beside her, Pierre was sleeping, half dressed. Françoise had dozed a little, but down in the street a loud scream had pierced the night and wakened her; she was so afraid of nightmares that she had not closed her eyes again. The curtains were not drawn and moonlight streamed into the room. She was not suffering; she was not thinking about anything; she was only astonished at the ease with which the cataclysm was entering into the natural course of their lives. She leaned toward Pierre.

Pierre groaned and stretched. She turned on the light. Open suitcases, half-filled haversacks, cans of food, socks, were strewn in confusion all over the floor. Françoise stared at the full-blown red chrysanthemums on the wallpaper and was suddenly filled with anguish—tomorrow, they would still be flaunting themselves in the same place with the same passive obstinacy. The scene where she would live during Pierre's absence was already set. Until now the expected separation had remained an empty threat, but this room was the future materialized. It was here, fully present, in its unalterable desolation.

"Are you sure you have everything you'll need?" she said.

"I think so." He had put on his oldest suit and stuffed his wallet, his fountain pen, and his tobacco pouch in his pockets.

"When you think of it, it was stupid of me not to have bought you any walking shoes. I know what I'll do. I'll give you my ski shoes. You were very comfortable in them."

"I don't want to take your shoes."

"You can buy me a new pair when we go to winter sports again," she said sadly.

She took them from the back of a cupboard and handed them to him. Then she packed the underwear and food in a haversack.

"Aren't you taking your meerschaum pipe?"

"No, I'm saving that for my leaves," he said. "Take good care of it."

"Don't worry," she said.

The fine primrose-colored unsmoked pipe was lying in its case as if in a midget coffin. Françoise snapped down the lid and put it in a drawer. She turned to Pierre. He had put on her ski shoes. He was sitting on the edge of the bed, biting one of his nails. His eyes were bleary and his face had the idiotic expression that he was wont to assume in some of his games with Xavière. Françoise was standing in front of him without knowing what to do with herself. They had talked all day, but now there was nothing more to say. He was nibbling at his nail and she was watching him, tense, resigned and empty.

"Shall we be going?" she said at last.

"Let's go," he said.

He slung his two haversacks over his shoulders and walked out of the room. Françoise closed the door behind them, the door through which he would not pass again for months, and her legs trembled weakly as she went down the stairs.

"We have time for a drink at the Dôme," Pierre said. "But we'll have to be careful, because it won't be easy finding a taxi."

They left the hotel and for the last time set out on the way they'd taken so many times before. The moon was down and it was dark. For several nights now the sky over Paris had been dim; in the streets, there were only a few weak yellow lights with gleams that hugged the ground. The pink glow which from afar used to announce the Carrefour Montparnasse had vanished. Nevertheless, the café terraces still glimmered weakly.

"After tomorrow, everything closes at eleven o'clock," Françoise said. "This is the last pre-war night."

They sat down on the terrace. The café was filled with people, noise and smoke. One group of youths was singing; a host of uniformed officers had sprung up overnight and they were now scattered in groups around the tables. Women were tormenting them with laughter that gathered no response. The last night, the last hours. The nervous snatches of conversation contrasted strangely with the apathetic faces.

"Life will be strange here," Pierre said.

"Yes," said Françoise. "I'll write and tell you about everything."

"I hope Xavière won't be too much of a burden on you. Perhaps we shouldn't have made her come back so soon."

"No, it's better that you see her again. It really wouldn't have been worth the effort writing all those long letters if you were to destroy their effect with one blow. And besides, she must be near Gerbert these last days. She couldn't stay in Rouen."

Xavière. This name was hardly more than a memory, an address on an envelope, an insignificant fragment of the future. She could hardly believe that in a few hours she would see her in the flesh.

"As long as Gerbert is at Versailles, you'll be able to see him at least from time to time."

"Don't worry about me," Françoise said. "I'll always manage." She laid her hand on his. He was about to leave. Nothing else counted. They sat there for some time without saying a word, watching peace die.

"I wonder if there'll be a crowd," said Françoise rising.

"I don't think so. Three-quarters of the men have already been called up."

They strolled a short distance along the boulevard, till Pierre hailed a taxi.

"Gare de la Villette," he said to the driver.

They crossed Paris in silence. The last stars were growing pale. Pierre had a faint smile on his lips. He was not tense, rather he had the intent look of a child. Françoise felt a feverish calm within her.

"We're here already?" she said with surprise.

The taxi stopped at a small, round, deserted square. Two gendarmes, wearing silver-braided képis, were leaning against a post in the middle of the parking place. Pierre paid the taxi and walked up to them.

"Is this the mobilization depot?" he asked, handing them his military papers.

One of the gendarmes pointed to a small piece of paper tacked to the pole. "You have to go to the Gare de l'Est," he said.

Pierre seemed taken aback. Then looked at the gendarme with one of his unexpectedly naive expressions which always moved Françoise. "Have I time to walk?"

The gendarme laughed. "They're certainly not putting on a train especially for you. Don't be in such a hurry."

Pierre walked back to Françoise. He looked very small and ridiculous in this deserted place with his two haversacks and the ski shoes on his feet. Françoise felt that these ten years had not been long enough to let him know how immeasurably she loved him.

"We still have a little time," he said, and she saw by his smile that he knew everything there was to know.

They set off along the narrow streets as dawn was breaking. The air was mild; the clouds were already pink. It was the kind of walk they had so often taken after a night's hard work. They stopped at the top of the stairs leading down into the station. The glistening rails, submissively hedged in where they began between the asphalt platforms, suddenly escaped, became interlaced in their courses, and fled on out toward infinity. For a moment Françoise and Pierre looked at the long flat roofs of the trains lined up along the platforms, where the white hands of ten black clock-faces indicated five-thirty.

"This is where there's going to be a crowd," said Françoise a little apprehensively. She pictured gendarmes, officers, and all the civilian mob she'd seen in the newspapers. But the station entrance-hall was almost empty; there wasn't a uniform in sight. There were a few families seated among piles of bundles, and single figures carrying haversacks over their shoulders.

Pierre walked up to the ticket office, and then came back to Françoise.

"The first train leaves at six-nineteen. I'll get on at six o'clock to be sure of getting a seat." He took her arm. "We can still take a little walk," he said.

"This is a strange departure. I didn't think it would be like this. Everything seems so free and easy."

"Yes," said Pierre, "there seems to be no sign of regimentation anywhere; I didn't even receive a mobilization order. No one came to fetch me; I ask what time my train leaves, just like a civilian; I almost feel I'm leaving on my own initiative."

"And yet we know you can't stay behind; it seems almost as if an inner destiny were compelling you."

They went a few steps outside the station. The sky was cloudless and soft above the deserted avenues.

"There isn't a taxi to be seen," Pierre said, "and the subway isn't running. How are you going to get home?"

"I'll walk," said Françoise. "I'll go and see Xavière, and then I'll tidy up your office." Her voice died away. "You'll be sure to write to me at once?"

"From the train," Pierre promised. "But letters certainly won't reach you for some time. You'll be patient?"

"Oh! I think I have patience enough and some to spare," she said.

They went a little way along the boulevard. In the early morning, the calm of the streets seemed completely normal. There were no indications of war, except for the posters: one huge one trimmed with tricolor ribbons—an appeal to the French people—and one small, modest poster with black and white flags on a white background—the order of general mobilization.

"I'll go now," said Pierre.

They went back into the station. Above the gate was a notice stating that travelers only were admitted onto the platforms. Near the gate a few couples were clasped in each other's arms, and suddenly, when she looked at them, tears rose to Françoise's eyes. Once generalized, the experience she was now living became comprehensible. On these strangers' faces, in their trembling smiles, all the tragedy of separation was apparent. She turned to Pierre. She did not want to break down; she found herself once more plunged in a blurred moment, the bitter and fleeting taste of which was not even painful.

"Good-bye," said Pierre. He pressed her gently to him, looked at her for one last time and turned away.

He walked through the gate. She watched him disappear with a rapid and too determined step which bespoke the tenseness in his face. She, too, turned away. Two women turned away at the same time; suddenly, their faces sagged and one of them began to cry. Françoise straightened her back and walked toward the exit. Even if she cried for hours on end, she would still have as many tears to shed. She walked off with a long, even-paced stride—her hiking stride—across the unusual calm of Paris. Calamity was as yet nowhere in evidence, neither in the warmth of the air, nor in the gilded foliage of the trees, nor in the fresh smell of vegetables, coming from the Halles. So long as she kept walking, it would remain intangible; but she felt that, were she ever to stop, this insidious presence which she sensed all about her would surge back and her heart would burst.

She crossed the Place du Châtelet and retraced her steps up the boulevard Saint Michel. The Luxembourg fountain had been drained; its now-visible bed was covered with a slimy corrosion. At the rue Vavin, Françoise bought a newspaper. She would have to wait some time before she could knock at Xavière's door, and she decided to go and wait at the Dôme. She hardly gave Xavière a thought, but she was glad to have something definite to do with her morning.

She entered the café and suddenly the blood rushed to her face. At a table near the window, she caught sight of a fair head and a dark head. She hesitated, but it was too late to retreat. Gerbert and Xavière had already seen her. She was so limp and exhausted that a nervous shiver ran through her as she drew near their table.

"How are you?" she said to Xavière, holding out her hand.

"I'm all right," said Xavière in an assured tone. She surveyed Françoise. "But you look tired."

"I've just taken Labrousse to the train. I've had very little sleep."

Her heart was pounding. For weeks Xavière had been no more than a vague image. And here she was, suddenly resurrected, in an unfamiliar blue print dress with tiny flowers, her hair far fairer than she remembered it to be. Her lips, with their forgotten line, parted in a completely new smile; Xavière had not changed into a docile phantom. It was her presence in the flesh that once more had to be faced.

"I was out walking all night," Xavière said. "Those black streets were really beautiful. It was like the end of the world."

She had spent all these hours with Gerbert. For him, too, she had again become a tangible presence. How had he welcomed her in his heart? His face gave no clue.

"It will be still worse when the cafés are closed," Françoise said.

"Yes, that's dismal." Then her eyes lit up. "Do you think we'll really be bombed?"

"Perhaps," said Françoise.

"It must be terrific to hear the sirens at night and see people running from all sides like rats."

Françoise smiled stiffly. Xavière's deliberate childishness annoyed her.

"You'll have to take shelter in the cellar," she said.

"Oh! I won't go down."

There was a brief silence.

"I'll see you later," Françoise said. "You can meet me here. I'll be sitting at the back."

"See you later," said Xavière.

Françoise sat down at a table and took out a cigarette. Her hand was trembling, and she was astonished to find how violently upset she was. It was undoubtedly the tension of these last few hours that left her so defenseless. She felt herself thrown forward toward the unknown: uprooted, buffeted, without any resource to be looked for in herself. She had calmly accepted the idea of a denuded and uneasy life. But Xavière's existence had always threatened her, even beyond the limits of her life, and it was this old anguish that she recognized with terror.

10

"WHAT A pity, I'm out of oil," said Xavière.

She looked with dismay at the window half covered with a coat of blue paint.

"You've done a very nice job," Françoise said.

"Well, I'm sure Inès will never be able to see through her windows again."

Inès had hurriedly left Paris the day after the first false alert, and Françoise had subleased her flat. In her room at the Hotel Bayard the memory of Pierre was too present, and during these strange nights when Paris offered neither light nor escape, she felt the need for a home of her own.

"I must have some oil," Xavière said.

"There's none to be had anywhere."

She was in the midst of addressing, in capital letters, a package of books and tobacco that she was sending to Pierre.

"You can't get anything nowadays," Xavière said fiercely. She threw herself into an armchair. "Really, I might just as well have done nothing," she said in a sullen voice.

She was wrapped in a long dressing gown of thick brown wool with a cord tied around her waist; she buried her hands in the wide sleeves. With her hair neatly cut and falling perfectly straight around her face, she looked like a little monk.

Françoise put down her pen. The electric bulb, draped with a silk scarf, disseminated a feeble violet light over the room.

I ought to go and work, Françoise thought, but she did not have the energy. Her life had lost all of its cohesiveness. It had become a soft quicksandish mire in which she felt herself sinking at each step of the way, then bobbing back to the surface, but just long enough to go on a little farther where the same thing happened; she had a wavering hope of either sinking completely or of once more finding solid ground. There was no longer any future. The past alone was real, and it was in Xavière that the past was incarnate.

"Have you had any news from Gerbert?" Françoise asked. "How does he like army life?"

She had seen Gerbert again one Sunday afternoon ten days before, but it would not have seemed natural had she never asked about him.

"He doesn't seem bored," Xavière said. She had a faint, inward smile. "Especially since he loves grumbling." Her face reflected the fond certainty of complete possession.

"He must have plenty of opportunities."

"What's worrying him," said Xavière, with a self-satisfied, pleased air, "is whether he'll be scared or not."

"It's hard to imagine what things will be like."

"Oh! he's like me," Xavière said, "he imagines things."

There was silence.

"Did you know they put Bergmann into a concentration camp?" Françoise asked. "It's pretty awful how the political exiles are being treated."

"Oh, pooh!" said Xavière. "They're all spies."

"Not all. A great many genuine antifascists are being imprisoned in the name of an antifascist war."

Xavière looked contemptuous.

"Considering how interesting people are," she said, "it's not so tragic when they get their toes stepped on."

With a feeling of revulsion, Françoise looked at this young, cruel face.

"If you're not interested in people, I wonder what's left to be interested in."

"Oh! but we're not made the same way," Xavière said and her eyes swept over Françoise with a scornful, malicious look.

Françoise said nothing. Conversations with Xavière always degenerated into hate-ridden comparisons. What was revealed in Xavière's tone, in her shifty smiles, was something far worse than a childish or capricious hostility. It was true female hatred. She would never forgive Françoise for having kept Pierre's love.

"How about playing a record?" Françoise suggested.

"As you wish," said Xavière.

Françoise placed the first side of *Petrouchka* on the turntable.

"It's always the same thing," Xavière said angrily.

"There's no choice."

Xavière tapped her foot. "Is it going to last long?" she said through clenched teeth.

"What is?"

"The black streets, the empty shops, the cafés closing at eleven o'clock. The whole business," she added in a tremor of rage.

"It may last a long time," said Françoise.

Xavière buried her hands in her hair. "But I'll go mad," she said.

"People don't go mad that easily," Françoise assured her.

"I'm not the long-suffering kind," Xavière said in a tone of despair and hate. "I'm not content to contemplate events from the bottom of a tomb! It's not enough for me to tell myself that people on the other side of the world still exist, if I have no contact with them."

Françoise flushed. It was no use talking to Xavière. Whatever you said to her, she immediately turned it against you. Xavière looked at Françoise.

"You're lucky to be so sensible," she said with hypocritical humility.

"All that's necessary, is not to take oneself too tragically," Françoise rejoined curtly.

"Oh! It's a question of temperament," said Xavière.

Françoise looked at the bare walls and the blue panes that seemed to shroud the interior of a tomb. *I oughtn't to mind*, she thought unhappily. Still, to do herself justice, she had hardly left Xavière alone during these three weeks; she was going to continue to live with her till the war was over; she could no longer deny this alien presence which cast a baleful shadow over her and over the whole world.

A ring of the doorbell shattered the silence. Françoise went down the long passage.

"What is it?"

The concierge handed her an unstamped envelope addressed in a strange hand.

"A gentleman just left this."

"Thanks," said Françoise.

She tore open the letter. It was in Gerbert's handwriting: *"I'm in Paris. I'm waiting for you at the Café Rey. I have the whole evening."*

Françoise hid the note in her bag. She went into her room, took her coat and her gloves. Her heart blazed with pleasure. She tried to assume an appropriate expression, and returned to Xavière's room.

"My mother has asked me to make up a bridge-four," she said.

"Oh! You're going out," Xavière said reproachfully.

"I'll be back about midnight. Are you going to stay in all evening?"

"Where would I be going?"

"Well, see you later," said Françoise.

She groped her way down the unlighted stairs and dashed off along the street. Women were walking up and down the boulevard Montparnasse, the gray cases containing their gas-masks slung over their shoulders. An owl hooted behind the cemetery wall. Françoise stopped for a moment at the corner of the rue de la Gaieté to catch her breath. A somber red brazier shone out on the avenue du Maine. It was the Café Rey. All public places, with their drawn curtains and hidden lights, had the equivocal look of houses of ill-repute. Françoise drew aside the hangings over the door. Gerbert was sitting near the mechanical piano with a glass of marc in front of him. He had put his army cap on the table. His hair was cut short, and he looked ridiculously young in his khaki uniform.

"How marvelous that you were able to come!" said Françoise. She took his hand and their fingers linked together. "So, your scheme finally worked?"

"Yes," Gerbert said. "But I couldn't let you know in advance. I wasn't sure whether I'd manage it or not." He smiled. "I'm so pleased. It's very easy. I'll be able to do it again off and on."

"Then I can look forward to Sundays," Françoise said. "There are so few Sundays in a month." She looked at him regretfully. "Especially since you'll have to see Xavière."

"Yes, I'll have to," Gerbert said without enthusiasm.

"You know, I've got latest news from Labrousse. A long letter. He's living a completely bucolic life. He's rusticating in Lorraine in the home of a priest who stuffs him with plum tarts and creamed chicken."

"Damn it all!" said Gerbert. "I'll be way off somewhere when he gets his first leave. We won't see each other for ages."

"Yes. If it would only go on like this without any fighting."

She looked at the scarlet seats on which she had so often sat with Pierre. The bar and the tables were crowded, but the heavy blue cloth concealing the windows lent this swarming café something intimate and clandestine.

"I've no objection to going into action," Gerbert said. "It's probably not as boring as rotting away in barracks."

"Are you bored stiff, my poor lamb?"

"It's unbelievable how fed up you can get." He began to laugh. "Day before yesterday the captain sent for me. He wanted to know why I wasn't applying for a commission. He had found out that I used to eat every night at the Brasserie Chanteclerc. He just about told me: 'You have money; you belong with the officers.'"

"What did you answer?"

"I said I didn't like officers," Gerbert replied with dignity.

"That must have pleased him."

"And how!" said Gerbert. "When I left, he was purple. I mustn't tell Xavière," he said, shaking his head.

"Does she want you to become an officer?"

"Yes, she thinks we'd see more of each other. Women are enough to drive you insane," Gerbert said in a tone of conviction. "They seem to think that only love affairs are the things that count."

"You're the only one Xavière has left."

"I know," he said. "That's just what's getting me down." He smiled. "I was cut out to be a bachelor."

"Well, you've certainly got off to a bad start," Françoise laughed.

"Idiot," said Gerbert. "That doesn't apply to you." He looked at her lovingly. "What's so good about us is that there's friendship between us. I'm never uncomfortable with you. I can tell you anything and I feel perfectly free."

"Yes, it's wonderful for us to love one another so much and still remain free." She squeezed his hand. Even more precious to her than the pleasure of seeing and touching him, was his passionate confidence in her.

"I can't go to any swank places in this get-up," he said.

"No. But how would you like walking down to the Halles, having a steak at Benjamin's, and then coming back to the Dôme?"

"Fine," said Gerbert. "We'll have a Pernod on the way. It's amazing how I can take Pernod now." He rose and pulled aside the blue curtains to let Françoise pass. "Gosh! How you drink in the army! I get in soused every night."

The moon had risen, and was flooding trees and rooftops, a truly country moonlight. A car sped down the long deserted avenue, its blue headlights looking like enormous sapphires.

"This is beautiful," Gerbert said, looking at the night.

"Yes, these moonlit nights are beautiful. But when it's pitch black it isn't very pleasant. The best thing you can do is stay dug in at home." She nudged Gerbert. "Look, have you seen the policemen's beautiful new helmets?"

"They look very martial." He took her arm. "You poor thing, this life can't be very cheerful," he said. "Isn't there anyone in Paris nowadays?"

"There's Elisabeth. She'd gladly lend me her shoulder to cry on, but I avoid her as much as possible. It's funny, but she's never looked more flourishing. Claude is in Bordeaux. But as long as he's alone, away from Suzanne, I think she gets along very well without him."

"What do you do all day?" Gerbert asked. "Have you started working again?"

"Not yet. No. I trail around with Xavière from morning till night. We do some cooking, fuss with our hair, listen to old records. We've never been so intimate." Françoise shrugged her shoulders. "And I'm sure that she's never hated me more."

"Do you think so?"

"I'm sure of it," Françoise said. "Doesn't she ever talk to you about us?"

"Not often," said Gerbert. "She's on her guard. She thinks I'm on your side."

"Why?" Françoise asked. "Because you defend me when she attacks me?"

"Yes," said Gerbert. "We always start to quarrel when she talks to me about you."

Françoise felt a twinge in her heart. What on earth could Xavière have said about her?

"Well, what does she say?" she asked.

"Oh! any old thing."

"You can tell me, you know," said Françoise. "After all, there's nothing to hide between us."

"I was speaking in general," Gerbert said.

They walked a few steps in silence. A sharp whistle made them jump. A bearded air-raid warden directed his searchlight beam at a window showing a thin ray of light.

"These old boys are in their element," Gerbert said.

"I know. At the beginning they threatened to fire their revolvers at our windows. We've shaded all the lights, and now Xavière is painting the windows blue."

Xavière . . . Naturally . . . She talked about Françoise . . . And perhaps about Pierre . . . It was irritating to think of her complacently preening herself at the center of her little well-ordered universe.

"Has Xavière talked to you about Labrousse?"

"She's spoken about him," Gerbert said noncommittally.

"She's told you the whole story!"

"Yes," said Gerbert.

The blood rushed to Françoise's cheeks. My story! Within that blonde head, Françoise's thoughts had assumed an unalterable and unknown form, and it was in this alien form that Gerbert had had them confided to him.

"Then you know that Labrousse was quite hard hit?"

Gerbert did not answer.

"I'm so sorry," he said finally. "Why didn't Labrousse tell me?"

"His pride wouldn't let him," said Françoise. She squeezed Gerbert's arm. "I didn't tell you because I was afraid you'd imagine things," she said. "But don't worry. Labrousse was never angry with you, and in the end, he was even quite happy that the affair ended as it did."

Gerbert looked at her doubtfully.

"He was happy?"

"Of course," said Françoise. "She doesn't mean anything to him any more, you know."

"Really?"

He seemed incredulous. What did he believe? Françoise looked with anguish at the church tower of Saint Germain des Près standing out against a metallic sky, as pure and calm as a village belfry.

"What is her version?" she asked. "That Labrousse is still passionately in love with her?"

"Just about," Gerbert seemed puzzled.

"Well, she's mistaken." Her voice was trembling. Had Pierre been there she would have laughed disdainfully, but he was far away from her, and she could only say to herself, "He loves only me." It was intolerable that a contrary certainty should exist anywhere in the world.

"I wish you could see how he talks about her in his letters," she continued. "She'd be edified. It's out of pity that he's been keeping up this show of friendship." She looked at Gerbert challengingly. "How does she explain his giving her up?"

"She said that it was she who no longer wanted this relationship."

"Ah! I see," said Françoise. "And why?" Gerbert looked at her with embarrassment. "Does she claim she didn't love him?" Françoise asked. She squeezed her handkerchief in her moist hands.

"No," said Gerbert.

"Well then?"

"She said that it displeased you," he said hesitantly.

"She said that?" Emotion prevented her from saying more. Tears of rage rose in her eyes. "The little bitch!"

Gerbert did not answer. He seemed overwhelmed with embarrassment.

Françoise laughed derisively. "In short, Pierre loves her to distraction, and she rejects this love out of consideration for me, because I am consumed with jealousy?"

"Well, I was pretty certain she was arranging things to suit herself," Gerbert said in a conciliatory tone.

They were crossing the Seine. Françoise leaned over the railing and looked down at the polished black surface of the water which reflected the disc of the moon. *I won't stand for it*, she thought in despair. There, in the sepulchral light of her room, Xavière was sitting wrapped in her brown dressing gown, sullen and evil; Pierre's disconsolate love was humbly caressing her feet; and Françoise was wandering about the streets, scorned, content with the old remains of a jaded devotion. She wanted to hide her face.

"She lied."

Gerbert hugged her to him. "Well, I'd certainly think so," he said.

He seemed disturbed. She pressed her lips together. She could talk to him, tell him the truth; he would believe her, but it would be futile. There, the young heroine, the sweet sacrificial figure, would continue to feel in her flesh the noble and intoxicating taste of her life.

I shall speak to her, too, thought Françoise. *She shall know the truth.*

"I am going to have it out with her."

Françoise crossed the Place de Rennes. The moon was shining down on the deserted street and blind houses, it was shining over the naked plains and over the forests where helmeted men were keeping watch. In the impersonal and terrible night, nothing existed for Françoise but the overwhelming anger in her heart. The "black pearl," the precious prodigal spirit, the sorceress! A *bitch!* she thought, enraged. She climbed the stairs. Xavière was there, behind that door, ensconced in her nest of lies. Once again was she going to batten on Françoise and force her to be part of her life. *The cast-off woman, armed with a bitter patience. That,* thought Françoise, *is to be my role.* She went in and knocked at Xavière's door.

"Come in."

An insipid tarry smell permeated the room. Xavière was perched on a stepladder, daubing blue paint on a window pane. She came down from her perch.

"Look what I've found," she said. In her hand was a bottle of golden liquid. With a theatrical gesture she handed it to Françoise. The label bore the inscription, *Ambre Solaire.*

"It was in the dressing room. Sun-tan lotion is a good substitute for oil," she said. She looked dubiously at the window. "Do you think it needs another coat?"

"Oh! It'll be like a hearse. It's bad enough as it is," said Françoise.

She took off her coat. She must speak, but what should she say? She could not make use of Gerbert's revelations, and yet, she could not live in this poisonous atmosphere. Inside the smooth blue windows, in this oppressive smell of *Ambre Solaire,* was ample evidence of Pierre's frustrated passion and Françoise's base jealousy. They must be eradicated. Xavière alone could eradicate them.

"I'll make some tea," said Xavière.

There was a gas range in her room. She filled a saucepan and put it on to boil, then sat down opposite Françoise.

"Did you have fun playing your bridge?" she asked scornfully.

"I didn't go for fun," Françoise said.

There was a silence. Xavière's eyes fell on the package Françoise had made up for Pierre.

"What a marvelous package!" she said with a thin smile.

"I think Labrousse will be happy to get some books," Françoise said.

Xavière's smile spread inanely over her lips as she rolled the string between her fingers.

"Do you think that he can read?" she said.

"He works. He reads. Why not?"

"Yes, you told me that he's being very brave, that he's even doing physical exercises," Xavière raised her eyebrows. "I see him in a different light."

"Still, that's what he says in his letter," said Françoise.

"Yes, of course."

She drew up the string and let it go with a faint snap. She thought for a moment, then looked candidly at Françoise.

"Do you think that in letters people ever tell you things as they are? Even if they don't intend to lie?" she added politely. "Just because they're telling them to someone?"

Françoise felt anger closing her throat.

"I think Pierre says exactly what he means to say," she said sharply.

"Oh! I should certainly not expect him to be off in a corner crying like a baby," said Xavière. She laid her hand on the package of books. "Perhaps I'm made wrong," she said thoughtfully, "but when people are away, it seems to me to be so futile to try to keep up any relationship with them. You can think of them, but writing letters and sending packages . . ." She made a face. "I'd much prefer to have the tables turned."

Françoise looked at her with impotent rage. Was there no way of annihilating this insolent pride? In Xavière's mind, Pierre thought of them as Martha and Mary. Martha played the part of a wartime godmother, and in return, won his respectful gratitude; but it was of Mary he thought when, from the depths of his loneliness, the man at the front nostalgically lifted a grave, pale face to the autumn sky. Had Xavière passionately clasped Pierre's living body in her arms, it would have hurt Françoise less than this mysterious caress with which she enveloped his image.

"You'd have to know whether the people in question share that point of view," Françoise said.

Xavière gave a slight smile. "Yes, naturally," she said.

"You mean that other people's points of view are a matter of indifference to you?" said Françoise.

"Not everybody attaches such great importance to letter writing." She rose. "Would you like some tea?" she asked.

She filled two cups. Françoise raised the cup to her lips. Her hand was trembling. She recalled Pierre's back, bent under his two haversacks, as he disappeared along the platform at the Gare de l'Est. She recalled his face when he had looked at her a moment earlier. She wanted to keep that image intact. But it was an image that received its vitality only from the beating of her heart, and this was not sufficient in the face of this woman of flesh and blood. Reflected in these living eyes were Françoise's weary face and her stern profile. A voice whispered, "*He doesn't love her any more, he cannot love her any more.*"

"I think you have a very romantic conception of Labrousse," Françoise said suddenly. "You know he puts up with things only as long as he wants to. They're important to him only as long as he decides they're important."

Xavière pouted. "That's what you think." Her tone carried more insolence than a savage denial.

"I know," said Françoise. "I know Labrousse well."

"You can never know people."

Françoise looked at her with rage. Was it impossible to make any impression on this stubborn mind?

"But with him and me, things are different," she said. "We've always shared everything. Absolutely everything."

"Why are you telling me this?" Xavière asked arrogantly.

"You think you're the only person who understands Labrousse," Françoise said. Her face was burning. "You think I have a crude, shallow conception of him."

Xavière looked at her with stupefaction. Never had Françoise spoken to her in this tone.

"You have your conception of him and I have mine," she said curtly.

"You choose the conception that suits you," said Françoise. She had spoken with such assurance that Xavière was taken aback.

"What do you mean?" she said.

Françoise's lips were set. How she wanted to tell her to her face, *You think he loves you, but he has nothing but pity for you.* Xavière's insolent smile had already faded. Only a few more words and her eyes would fill with tears. This beautiful, proud body would be bowed. Xavière stared at her intently; she was afraid.

"I don't mean anything in particular," Françoise said wearily. "But, in general, you believe what you find it convenient to believe."

"Give me an instance," Xavière insisted.

"Well, for instance," said Françoise more calmly, "Labrousse said in his letter to you that he had no need to receive letters from people in order to think about them; that was a polite way of excusing your silence. But you've convinced yourself that he believes in communion of souls over and above words."

Xavière's lip curled back over her white teeth. "How did you know what he'd written to me?"

"He told me in a letter," Françoise said.

Xavière's eyes rested on Françoise's handbag.

"Ah! He speaks about me in his letters to you?" she said.

"Occasionally." Her hand tightened on her black leather handbag. Should she throw the letters in Xavière's lap? In disgust and rage Xavière herself would cry her defeat; there could be no possible victory without her confession. Then, Françoise would once more find herself alone, sovereign, and freed forever.

Xavière settled herself more deeply in her chair, and shuddered slightly. She was all huddled up, and her face was haggard. "I loathe to think that people are talking about me," she said.

Françoise suddenly felt very tired. The arrogant heroine she had so passionately hoped to vanquish, was there no longer; there was only a poor, hunted victim, from whom no vengeance could be exacted. She rose.

"I'm going to bed," she said. "See you tomorrow. Don't forget to turn off the gas."

"Good night," said Xavière without looking up.

Françoise went back to her room. She opened her desk, took Pierre's letters out of her bag and laid them in a drawer beside those of Gerbert. There would be no victory. There would be no deliverance. She locked her desk and put the key back in her bag.

"Waiter," called Françoise.

It was a beautiful sunny day. Lunch had taken longer than usual and, early in the afternoon, Françoise had come with a book to sit on the terrace of the Dôme. Now it was growing cooler.

"Eight francs," the waiter said.

Françoise opened her purse and took out some change. She looked with surprise at the bottom of her handbag. That was where she had put the key to her desk the night before.

Nervously, she emptied the bag of its contents—compact—lipstick—comb. The key must be somewhere. She had not set down her bag for a moment. She turned it upside down, shook it out. Her heart was beating violently. Yes, she had, for just one moment. The time it had taken to carry the breakfast tray from the kitchen to Xavière's room. And Xavière was in the kitchen.

With a sweep of her hand she jumbled pell-mell all the various articles back into her bag and rushed out. Six o'clock. If Xavière had the key, there was no hope.

"It's impossible!"

She began to run. Her whole body was throbbing. She felt her heart pounding against her ribs, behind her eyes, in her finger tips. She rushed up the stairs. The house was silent and the entrance door looked perfectly normal. In the passage the scent of *Ambre Solaire* was still noticeable. Françoise took a deep breath. She might have lost the key without noticing it. If anything had happened, there would have been some indication. She pushed open the door of her room. The desk was open. Some of Pierre's and Gerbert's letters were lying scattered over the carpet.

"Xavière knows." The walls of the room began to whirl. Searing, bitter darkness had descended on the world. Françoise dropped into a chair, crushed by a deadly weight. Her love for Gerbert was there before her, black as treason.

"She knows." She had come into the room to read Pierre's letters. She had expected to slip the key back into the bag or hide it under the bed. And then she had seen Gerbert's writing.

"Dear, dear Françoise." She had run through to the bottom of the last page: "I love you." Line after line, she had read it.

Françoise rose and went down the long passage. Her mind was not working. Before her and within her, this coal-black night. She went up to Xavière's door and knocked. There was no answer. The key was in the lock, on the inside. Xavière had not gone out. Françoise knocked again. There was the same dead silence. *She has killed herself*, she thought. She leaned against the wall. Xavière might have swallowed some sleeping tablets; she might have turned on the gas. Françoise listened. She still heard nothing. She pressed her ear to the door. A faint hope broke through her terror. There was one solution, the only solution imaginable. But no, Xavière used only harmless soporifics; any smell of gas would have been apparent. In any case, she would still only be unconscious. . . . Françoise banged on the door.

"Go away," said a muffled voice.

Françoise wiped the perspiration from her forehead. Xavière was alive. Françoise's treason lived.

"Open the door," Françoise shouted.

She did not know what she would say, but she wanted to see Xavière immediately. "Open it," she repeated, shaking the doorknob.

The door opened. Xavière was wrapped in her dressing gown. Her eyes were hard.

"What do you want of me?" she asked.

Françoise walked past her and sat down near the table. Nothing in the room had changed since lunch time. Yet, behind each familiar piece of furniture something horrible was lying in wait.

"I want to talk to you," said Françoise.

"I have nothing to say to you."

She was staring at Françoise with burning eyes, her cheeks were on fire, she was beautiful.

"Listen to me, I beg of you," said Françoise.

Xavière's lips began to tremble. "Why have you come to torture me again? Aren't you satisfied with things as they are? Haven't you done me enough harm?"

She threw herself on the bed and buried her face in her hands.

"Ah! How well you've tricked me," she said.

"Xavière," murmured Françoise.

She looked about her with anguish. Would nothing come to her rescue?

"Xavière!" she repeated in a pleading voice. "When this affair began I was not aware that you were in love with Gerbert, and he didn't suspect it either."

Xavière lowered her hands. A sneer distorted her mouth. "That little swine," she said slowly. "This doesn't surprise me in him. He's nothing but a filthy little beast."

She looked Françoise straight in the eye.

"But you!" she said. "You! How you must have laughed at me." An appalling smile bared her white teeth.

"I did not laugh at you," Françoise said. "I was simply thinking more of myself than of you. But you had left me very little reason to love you."

"I know," said Xavière. "You were jealous of me because Labrousse was in love with me. You made him loathe me, and to get better revenge, you took Gerbert from me. Keep him, he's yours. I won't deprive you of that little treasure."

The words poured from her mouth with such vehemence that they seemed to choke her. With horror Françoise saw the woman Xavière was confronting with blazing eyes, this woman who was herself.

"That's not true," she said. She took a deep breath. It was hopeless to attempt to defend herself. Now, nothing could save her.

"Gerbert loves you," she said in a steadier voice. "He did you a wrong. But at that time he had so many grievances against you! It would have been difficult to talk to you afterward; he hadn't yet had time to establish a real relationship with you." She leaned toward Xavière and said in a pressing tone, "Try to forgive him. You'll never again find me in your way."

She clasped her hands. A little silent prayer rose within her: *Let everything be wiped clean, and I will give up Gerbert! I no longer love Gerbert, I never loved him, there was no betrayal.*

Xavière's eyes flashed. "Keep your gifts," she said vehemently. "And get out of here, get out immediately."

Françoise hesitated.

"For God's sake, get out."

"I'll go," said Françoise.

She crossed the passage, staggering as though blind, and tears burned her eyes. *I was jealous of her. I took Gerbert from her.* The tears, the words, scorched like a hot iron. She sat down on the edge of the couch, dazed, and repeated, *I did that, I.* In the shadows, Gerbert's face burned with a black flame, and the letters scattered on the carpet were as black as an infernal pact. She put her handkerchief to her lips. Black, hot lava was coursing through her veins. She wanted to die.

This is what I am forever. There would be a dawn. There would be a tomorrow. Xavière would return to Rouen, and each morning wake up in a bleak provincial house with this despair in her heart. Each morning this abhorred woman, who would henceforth be Françoise, would be reborn. She recalled Xavière's face, contorted with pain. *My crime.* It would exist forever.

She closed her eyes. Her tears flowed, and the burning lava flowed and consumed her heart. A long time passed. Far away, in another world, she suddenly saw a bright, tender smile. *Well, kiss me, you silly little Gerbert.* The wind was blowing, the cows were rattling their chains in the stable, a young, trusting head was leaning on her shoulder and a voice was saying, "I'm happy, I'm so happy." He had given her a small flower. She opened her eyes. That, too, was true. Light and tender as the morning wind on the dewy plains. How had that innocent love become this sordid betrayal?

"No," she said. "No." She rose and walked to the window. The globe of the street lamp had been covered with a black metal shield scalloped like a Venetian mask. Its yellow light was like a glance. She turned away and switched on the light. Her image suddenly sprang from the depth of her mirror. She faced herself. "No," she repeated. "I am not that woman."

It was a long story. She stared at her reflection. They had been trying to rob her of it for a long time. Inexorable as a duty. Austere and pure as a block of ice. Self-sacrificing, scorned, clinging obstinately to hollow morality. She had said, "No." But she had said it under her breath, and in secret she had embraced Gerbert. "Isn't that I?" She had often hesitated, spellbound. And now, she had fallen into the trap, she was at the mercy of this voracious conscience that had been waiting in the shadow for the moment to swallow her up. Jealous, traitorous, guilty. She could not defend herself with timid words and furtive deeds. Xavière existed; the betrayal existed. *My guilty face exists in the flesh.*

It will exist no longer.

Suddenly, a great calm enveloped her. Time had stopped. She was alone in an icy firmament. It was a solitude so awful and so final that it resembled death.

Either she or I. It shall be I.

There was a sound of steps in the passage, water was running in the bathroom. Then Xavière returned to her room. Françoise walked to the kitchen and turned off the gas meter. She knocked. There might still be a chance of escaping . . .

"Why have you come back again?" said Xavière.

She was in bed, propped up against her pillows. Only her bedside lamp was switched on. A glass of water beside a bottle of barbital tablets stood on the night table.

"I'd like to have a talk with you," said Françoise. She took a step forward and stood with her back against the chest of drawers on which the gas range stood.

"What do you intend to do now?" she asked.

"Is that any of your business?" Xavière retorted.

"I have done you a great wrong," said Françoise. "I don't ask you to forgive me. But please listen; don't make it impossible for me to atone for my sin." Her voice was trembling with emotion. If only she could convince Xavière. . . . "For a long, long time I thought only of your happiness. You never thought of mine. You know that I am not altogether without justification. Make an effort in the name of our past. Give me a chance not to feel odiously guilty."

Xavière stared at her blankly.

"Stay in Paris," Françoise continued. "Resume your work at the theater. Live wherever you wish, you will never see me again. . . ."

"I—accept your money!" cried Xavière. "I'd rather drop dead. Here and now."

Her voice, her face, left Françoise no hope.

"Be generous. Accept," said Françoise. "Spare me the remorse of having ruined your future."

"I would rather drop dead," Xavière repeated vehemently.

"At least see Gerbert again," Françoise begged. "Don't condemn him without having spoken to him."

"Do you presume to give me advice?"

Françoise put her hand on the gas range and turned on the valve.

"I'm not advising you; I'm imploring you," she said.

"Imploring!" Xavière laughed. "I'm not a noble soul."

"Very well then," Françoise said. "Good-bye."

She took a step toward the door and silently looked back at that livid, childlike face which she would never again see alive.

"Good-bye," she repeated.

"And don't come back," said Xavière with fury.

Françoise heard her leap from her bed and bolt the door. The ray of light filtering beneath it went out.

And now?

Françoise stood staring at Xavière's door. Alone. Unaided. Relying now solely on herself. She waited for some time. Then she walked into the kitchen and put her hand on the lever of the gas meter. Her hand tightened—it seemed impossible. Face to face with her solitude, beyond space, beyond time, stood this alien presence that had for so long crushed her with its blind shadow: Xavière was there, existing only for herself, entirely self-centered, reducing to nothingness everything for which she had no use; she encompassed the whole world within her own triumphant solitude, boundlessly extending her influence, infinite and unique; everything that she was, she drew from within herself, she barred all dominance over her, she was absolute separateness. And yet it was only necessary to pull down this lever to annihilate her. *Annihilate a conscience! How can I?* Françoise thought. But how was it possible for a conscience not her own to exist? In that case, it was she who did not exist. She repeated, *She or I,* and pulled down the lever.

She went back to her room, gathered up the letters strewn on the floor and threw them into the fireplace. She struck a match and watched the letters burn. Xavière's door was locked on the inside. They would think it was an accident or suicide. *In any case, there will be no proof,* she thought.

She undressed and put on her pajamas. *Tomorrow morning she will be dead.* She sat down, facing the darkened passage. Xavière was sleeping. With each minute her sleep was growing deeper. On the bed there still remained a living form, but it was already no one. There was no one any longer. Françoise was alone.

Alone. She had acted alone. As alone as in death. One day Pierre would know. But even he would only know her act from the outside. No one could condemn or absolve her. Her act was her very own. *I have done it of my own free will.* It was her own will which was being fulfilled, now nothing separated her from herself. She had chosen at last. She had chosen herself.

About the Author

SIMONE de BEAUVOIR was born in Paris in 1909. After studying in a religious institution, she attended the Sorbonne where she received her agrégation in philosophy in 1929. She taught for several years in lycees in Marseilles, Rouen, and Paris, but left teaching for a writer's life in 1942. From that time on, she devoted her life to writing and lecturing, and as a novelist, dramatist, and philosopher became probably the most distinguished woman writer in contemporary France. She gained great attention in the United States upon publication of *The Second Sex*, a monumental work on what it means to be a woman. Among her many novels, *The Mandarins* won France's highest honor, the Prix Goncourt. Simone de Beauvoir died in 1986.